PHANTASIA
A Bad Day on Olympus

A PHI ATHANATOI NOVEL

EFTHALIA

ISBN 978-0-6487854-2-2
LCCN: 2020902656

DEDICATION

To my awesome readers, thank you for waiting and waiting.

Also to my Nespresso machine, without the extraction of your decadent coffee there would be no words.

ACKNOWLEDGEMENTS

I am deeply grateful to my editor Mary-Theresa Hussey. Thank you for your patience.

To Ann B. Harrison who believed in me, I could not have done it without you.

To all my friends both in the author community and outside, who have asked on my progress and given me words of encouragement, it means the world.

And to my family, for never giving up on me.

ONE

Even if you are a priest, you get in line. ~ Greek proverb

Holy Trinity Greek Orthodox Church; Charleston, SC

"*Asteievesai*—you're kidding me." Carissa Alkippes turned to face Xen Lyson, her six-foot-plus fiancé and head of the *Phi Athanatoi*, the immortals who protected humans from unearthly creatures. A few weeks ago, she had been a regular police officer.

And mortal.

Now she had a new status—daughter of Ares. But it didn't end there.

She had powers. Powers she couldn't control. Powers and perks she didn't want to think about now.

"This could be a trap." Xen's voice vibrated, adding a touch of gloom to the flash of lightning cracking across the sky and illuminating his features.

"Ridiculous. Who would attack a church?" Carissa scoffed. Sure, unusual circumstances had put her on the most-wanted list of a demigod. Hal, her once-upon-a-childhood-friend, had planned to sacrifice her for his demented, deranged, and deadly quest to gain godly power.

Hal, who'd died by her father's sword.

That didn't stop Xen bringing his *Phi Athanatoi* protection skills to the concrete jungle that resembled modern suburbia.

"Best to be prepared." He scanned the darkness, completing his full surveillance of the church perimeter before refocusing on her.

The severity of his demeanor contrasted with the ludicrous odds of attack, had her squashing into submission the laughter bubbling in her chest. "Yeah, my eighty-plus-year-old grandmother will attack us with her walking stick and a tray of baklava. That's a real trap." She rolled her eyes at her vampire. "Is it safe to go inside?" She teased, tugging the double wooden doors open.

Power surged through every nerve in her body. Instead of jerking away, she tightened her hold, becoming one with the power. Her fingertips tingled. "What on earth was that?"

"Calm yourself, *koukla.*" Xen placed a hand on her shoulder.

"My power has a life of its own." A nervous laugh left her throat.

"Well, we don't want every unearthly creature to know there's a human candle in the church, so control it."

"Okay, you have a point." Carissa had a long way to go to learn the full extent of what, exactly, she could and couldn't do and that sudden surge added to the list of uncertainties.

She closed her eyes. "*Rigos.*" She whispered the ancient Greek word that blanketed her power. A spell her father, Ares, had given her when he'd reappeared to tell her it might take longer than three days to gain an audience with the Olympian gods. It had been three weeks. Apparently, Olympus had its own administrative problems.

"Okay. I'm good to go."

"I never insinuated you weren't." Xen's wink sparkled with amusement. He handed her some coins.

She placed them into the donation box, picked up two candles, and moved over to the stand of flickering lights. *God and gods,* she thought.

An epiphany hit, and her jaw dropped. She pivoted on the balls of her feet to face Xen. "But you…you're a vampire and immortal."

He held up his hand, and a slow saucy grin spread over his face. "Now is not the time for the discussion on Greek religion. Light your candle, *koukla*."

Carissa shifted her attention away from his. Xen surprised her. Every time she thought she knew him—bang—new information to digest.

She lit her candles and pushed them into the sand tray near other burning candles. Fragrant incense hung in the air. She closed her eyes and took a deep breath and held it for fear of blowing out the candles like wishes on a birthday cake.

She straightened her shoulders and moved to venerate an icon of Mary and Jesus. Carissa completed the sign of the cross three times and placed a light kiss on the icon. Even after learning the truth about her heritage, she couldn't forget the ecclesiastical customs. Xen stood with his hip propped against the smooth surface of the pew, arms folded and watching her under heavy lashes.

"Come and meet my *yiayia*. I promise she won't hit you with her walking stick." A wicked smile tore over her face.

"Hm." The subtle doubt-filled sound vibrated in his throat.

Carissa didn't miss the devious turn of his mouth. He was up to something. They walked up the carpeted aisle toward the altar, still without a sign of her *yiayia*.

It's odd only a few lights are on. Carissa could communicate telepathically to Xen. A bonus of being bonded to him. She halted midway down the aisle.

A rock formed in her belly. Something tasted sour in her mouth. Her warrior's words from earlier repeated. Maybe it was a trap.

Xen gave her a quick nod before answering her the same way. *Let's take a look around.* He motioned for her to check the left. He took the right, walking between the long wooden pews toward the side aisle.

With stealthy steps, Carissa inspected the left side pews and arches. A loud roar cracked the air and echoed in the church. Her shoulders tightened and adrenaline rushed through her body like a mini tsunami. She spun on the balls of her feet and ran toward Xen.

She found him behind one of the arches and stopped.

He rubbed his head.

Her *yiayia* stood with her walking stick raised and her glasses halfway down her nose. She lifted her arm for another swing.

Xen held up his arm in self-defense.

"Yiayia. Stop," Carissa shouted.

"Carissa? Is that you, my child?" Yiayia squinted and put down her walking stick. "It's hard to see in here and my eyes aren't what they used to be." She pushed her glasses into place.

"The man you attacked is my fiancé, Xenocrates Lysandros." Carissa's voice softened. She should have taken Xen to meet Yiayia earlier, but life-and-death battles and training had prevented her from the introductions that should have been her priority.

"Sorry, Carissa *mou*. You shouldn't be sneaking around in the church."

Xen lowered his voice. "We were looking for you."

Yiayia lifted her shoulders. "Oh, sorry." Her feet shuffled closer and with her tiny frame she pulled Carissa in for a tight ompa-loompa-hug.

Carissa's eyes widened to saucers. Wow, Yiayia sported some skills when it came to hugging and swinging a walking stick. "Yiayia, you're cutting off my circulation." She managed to inhale enough air to speak.

Yiayia released her from the temporary vise grip. "Sorry, I don't know my own strength."

Air rushed into Carissa's lungs. "No kidding." She peered at Xen in apology.

The corners of his mouth tugged in humor. "What did you say about walking sticks?"

She punched his arm. He faked a silent *ouch*. Their bond had strengthened in the past few months. Their self-defense practice sessions often ended up in a steamy, tangled, and intimate mess. Images flashed through her mind.

"Don't project, *koukla*."

Butterflies fluttered in her belly. "I was thinking, not projecting."

Her grandmother brought the banter to an end by tackling Xen with hugs and kisses to both his cheeks. Yiayia shuffled to the side. "It's a pleasure to meet you, *paidi mou*. Please forgive me."

"There is no need to apologize." He flashed her with the smile that had its own address and zip code.

Yiayia giggled like a schoolgirl.

Carissa rolled her eyes. "This is my grandmother Vetta Atheneous."

Yiayia huffed out a short breath. "Okay, I've asked the *pater* if we could use his office to talk. I only have half an hour, so let's not waste it."

"Lead the way, Yiayia." Carissa had questions of her own. The biggest one—why her *yiayia* wanted to meet here? With Xen at her side, they entered a room off the main altar.

Yiayia pulled the door open and the aroma of *dolmades, tiropites,* and *spanakopita* wafted like sweet perfume around the small room. Her stomach growled in appreciation. "You're seriously going to feed us?"

"What?" Yiayia shrugged her small shoulders. "I make stuff for the church all the time." She smiled, and mischief danced the Zorba in her dark brown eyes. "They let me use the kitchen on occasion." She winked.

"If you want to cook up a storm, why not come home?" Carissa asked.

Yiayia took Carissa's hands in hers. "It's not safe. That is why I put myself into an assisted living home."

"Yiayia, if someone threatened you…" The words died on her lips. Never had it crossed her mind that her grandmother would be in danger for any reason.

"No, *paidi mou*. It has more to do with your *pappou's* death."

"Is there something you haven't told me?"

Yiayia's brows scrunched together, "There are things I haven't discussed with you, and I have failed to keep you from any distress." She swept an interested glance over Xen. "It appears you've found your own glorious trouble all by yourself."

Carissa caught the quick blink.

"I'm honored." Xen returned Yiayia's playful wink.

"I may be old, but I'm not oblivious to everything going on." Yiayia paused. Her warm fingers squeezed around Carissa's. "I'm sorry for the horror you endured at the hands of Poseidon's son." A tear spilled down her cheek.

Carissa's eyes misted. Her grandmother had always been remarkable in her empathy.

Realization slammed upside Carissa's head like a walking stick. "Wait a minute, how did you know?"

Yiayia clucked her tongue. "Oh, I've been keeping my own surveillance." She glowered at the wooden floor before returning her gaze to Carissa. "I should have been there so that rat couldn't get you in his clutches."

Words were coming out of Yiayia's mouth, but they made no sense. Carissa shook her head to clear the fog in her mind. Clarity. She required clarity. "No, Yiayia, how do you know about Poseidon and Xen and the whole other world stuff?"

Her *yiayia* had the nerve to cross her eyes, flare her nostrils, and pull her lips in a thin line. "I have my own spies and please… I knew your grandfather's lineage quite well." She waved a hand in the air. "And never thought I'd see a god until your father, Ares, popped in for a visit right after your mother's death." Yiayia searched Carissa's face for understanding. "He made it quite clear you were to be protected at all costs."

Her maternal *pappou*, like her father, had mythical origins? Nausea rolled and pushed its way around Carissa's stomach. She was going to retch on the polished timber floor. Here in the *pater's* office.

Xen reached over and put a palm on her shoulder. *Calm,* koukla.

He faced Yiayia and said, "With all due respect, Grandmother Atheneous, Carissa's protection lies with me, so the fault is all mine." His warm hand still hadn't left Carissa's shoulder.

Carissa took a deep breath. Images cascaded behind her eyes, pulling her into a nightmare she desperately didn't want to visit. *Hal was demented, Xen. Do not blame yourself.* She met his gaze and the look in those sea-green eyes told her he kept fighting those demons.

His jaw tightened.

Carissa cleared her throat and turned to Yiayia. "Why don't we sit and you can fill me in on what's been happening. Why did you want me to come here and not to your house?"

"That house is yours, child." Yiayia let go of her and sat. "I'm being watched and I don't want to bring any more bad things to you. You've suffered enough."

Xen arranged the other two chairs in front of Yiayia and motioned for her to sit. He dropped into the other chair. "Tell us who you suspect is tailing you and why?" Xen's tone demanded an answer.

"You're going to think I'm a crazy old woman."

Carissa placed her hands in her grandmother's. "Crazy is the new normal."

Yiayia let out a soft chuckle. "Okay, but don't say I didn't warn you." She coughed. "First, I checked myself out of the assisted living home, with a little help, to make any link with you difficult."

"And you were going to tell me this when?" Carissa asked.

"Tonight."

"What if I went there to visit you and found you missing?"

"You wouldn't have. I knew it the moment your Aunt Paula called and told me you were with Xenocrates. Besides, Paula helped me check in another one."

Carissa's Aunt Paula— Yiayia's younger cousin so it was a courtesy title--lived in Virginia. She had invited Carissa to a charity event which was the night she'd danced with Xen, but it had not been her first encounter with the vampire.

She'd have words with Aunt Paula the minute she saw her. "What exactly did she say and how many people did she tell?" By now, all of her relatives from Charleston to Greece would know. She rubbed her temple where an ache throbbed like a woodpecker going at a tree.

"Your Aunt Paula knows of your heritage," Yiayia said. "Has always known. Rest assured that on this subject, she isn't the gossip you think she is."

Carissa's heart jerked into a steady jog and spikes of rage ballooned within her chest.

Calm yourself, koukla. Xen's comforting voice filled her head and held the rage beast at bay.

"You didn't think to cue *me* in at any point?" This was rich in ways Carissa couldn't fathom. Everyone had known she was a daughter of god.

Everyone, except her.

What a fool she'd been.

"Carissa *mou*…There is so much to tell you, please don't be upset," Yiayia murmured. "Hopefully, you will understand by the time I've finished."

"Okay, Yiayia. Why don't you start."

"Last week when I was in the garden picking flowers, I saw shadows moving about. I thought maybe I'd been out in the sun too long. Then it happened for three days in a row." An anguished look settled on her features. "I thought my imagination was getting the better of me, so I asked one of my friends, Doris, if she had a shot of brandy."

Yiayia picked up a plastic plate from the table and started fanning her face. Beads of sweat started at her temple.

Carissa grabbed the carafe of iced water on the table. She filled a glass and handed it to her *yiayia* and watched as she took large gulps.

"Where was I? Oh yes, I had two shots of brandy and then went to my room, everything had been turned upside down and the bed had been ripped to shreds." Her face scrunched up in frustration. "Who would do such a thing?"

Carissa leaned forward. "Before you go on, Yiayia, were you keeping something valuable in your room?"

"No, just the usual. A bit of cash and some jewelry which were still there, surprisingly, considering the mess." Yiayia took another gulp of water. "Of course, the police did the whole fingerprinting thing, and asked questions like, did I suspect someone, or did I have any enemies."

Carissa's gaze crashed with Xen's. *Do you think it's connected to me?*

It's hard to say with so little to go on. Xen answered to her mind.

Yiayia held the now empty glass in a tight grip. "That night after we cleared some of the mess. I locked everything up tight and went to my friend Doris' room. I was worried that whoever did this might return." She licked her lips. "Doris let me have her pullout sofa and after midnight I fell into a deep sleep. A voice demanded that I wake up. Naturally, I did, and someone stood at the end of the sofa. He said he was Hypnos and he had a message."

"Hypnos?" Carissa searched Yiayia's face for confirmation.

"Yes, the god, Hypnos. The message..." Yiayia stuck out a crooked finger. "It was for you."

Carissa held both palms up. "Then why didn't he appear to me?"

"He said it was too dangerous. He couldn't go anywhere near you."

Xen cut in. "Dangerous? In what way?"

"Hypnos mentioned that something big is brewing on Olympus." Yiayia returned her attention to Carissa. "He pointed out that you should trust no one." Yiayia tossed the plastic plate on the table. "All I know is that whatever is going on up there, it has a direct link to Carissa."

"Yiayia that makes no sense," Carissa said. "I mean, I know my father's not in good graces with Poseidon, but the gods couldn't possibly want anything from me."

"Carissa is right. Hal is to blame." The pitch in Xen's voice rolled with spikes of anger.

"This isn't about Hal and Poseidon," Yiayia said.

"Then what is it about?" Carissa asked.

Her grandmother bounced between Carissa and Xen. "Hypnos said your father and the other gods are in danger."

"From who?" Xen probed.

"He didn't say," Yiayia answered.

"What's it got to do with me if the gods are in danger?"

"Since the gods are not permitted to interact with mortals, then what happens on Olympus, stays on Olympus." A lopsided grin ripped across Xen's face.

A laugh tore from Carissa. "Comedian."

"I have my moments." He did the winking thing again, with those ridiculously sexy eyelashes. Why did men always have better eyelashes? She needed new mascara.

"Now isn't the time for jokes. I'm serious." Yiayia the killjoy raised her walking stick and thumped them each on the knee.

Xen and Carissa raised their hands in surrender. You didn't mess with a grumpy *yiayia*.

"He said his brother is coming and you're the only one who can help."

Xen turned his head to look at Carissa. He lowered his voice to a whisper, "Thanatos the god of Death." He stood and pulled her into his arms. "Your training and practice will have to be stepped up. I can't afford to have you vulnerable in any shape or form."

Great, just when she thought she was out, they pulled her back in. Right now, in her mind, her godly family resembled the relentless mob that wouldn't allow Michael Corleone the peace he craved.

TWO

Syracuse is the grandest of cities, a sojourn dear to the indomitable Ares. ~ Pindar

Xen's mansion, underground gym; Charleston, SC

Xen's personal gymnasium had been designed to take the brunt of rough exercise. His *Phi Athanatoi*, a warrior group of vampires and werewolves who protected mankind, usually trained there. Tonight, though, this space belonged to Carissa and her father - Ares. She rubbed her ass for the twentieth time, the exact number of times she'd been thrown in their kung fu practice. Each time she hit the mat like a piece of tangled spaghetti.

Her father had appeared when they returned from her visit with her *yiayia*. Perfect timing or coincidence? She couldn't decide. She had yet to fill in her father on what she had discussed with Yiayia. It would have to wait until after they finished his so-called test of her ability to fight and use her power of compulsion. Yes, she had power but she had no idea how to control it.

"Focus, *kori mou*." Ares brushed a few sweaty locks from his forehead.

"It's a little tough to do that if you are in the air every minute." She pushed up to her elbows from her current starfish landing. Her energy would be depleted soon; her fuel gauge pointed to empty.

"Your mind controls the power." Ares held out his hand. Her fingers closed around his. A flow of energy danced between them. Recognition. Daughter to Father.

"I thought you said when you returned, we'd be paying Olympus a visit."

"I need to know that you can call forth your power in a crisis situation." He pulled her up to her feet. "You'll be walking into the lion's den. All they will see is a tasty morsel."

"How is tossing me around like pasta training me?"

"Now, use your power of compulsion." His hands darted to her neck, "Stop me." He commanded, his fingers tightening, tightening, tightening around her throat.

Time froze, expanded, flipped to a moment in a warehouse where a demon had his claws around her throat. Her life's essence slowly extinguishing. Death had been close. Now it was her father's hold that choked her.

She spotted Kane, Xen's trusted right-hand man and wolf, holding Xen back. A roar cracked and vibrated through the air. She had to summon her power.

Her gaze collided with her father's. In the depth of his chocolate-colored eyes, she saw flares of fire. Fire spiked and tingled through her body. Somewhere in a deep chamber of her mind, she took control. "Release me." The words a soft command.

His grip loosened, his hands falling away.

She coughed to stabilize her breathing. The air around her shifted, and Xen had her in his arms before she could swallow her next bit of air.

"Tell me why I shouldn't pierce my *xiphos* through your heart, Ares?"

"Relax, vampire. I wasn't going to harm my daughter."

"Your practice sessions leave my woman battered and bruised every time." Xen inspected Carissa's throat. "I've been patient enough with all your methods. It ends here. There will be no more."

"Xen, it's okay. I'm okay." Carissa tried to defuse the argument between god and immortal before it got messy.

"My daughter is right. If you weren't in such a fit of rage, you would have seen that she compelled me to stop with a whisper."

"Whether she stopped you or not, that was going too far." He removed his hands from around Carissa and closed the distance to Ares in two strides.

Carissa watched the nose to nose scene in slow-mo. She could see only one outcome in this - Xen hurt.

"You have no power or place to command me." Ares spat. His nostrils flared and he clenched his fists. "The *Athanatoi* belong to me. You exist because of me."

A growl ruptured from Xen, tearing through the air and vibrating in her ears. A tornado gathered and wrapped itself around her father and Xen, and now she would witness its consumption of them both.

Her mouth became Sahara-desert-dry. She had to stop them. Her body tensed, and power surged through her. She raised her hands; light glowed from her fingertips.

"*Pauó.*" The power of the ancient Greek word froze both men's mouths shut.

"*Chorá.*" Their feet began to move in opposite directions.

"Stop." She commanded when they were both a safe distance from each other. Her right foot tapped on the gym mat, and she placed herself in the pig-in-the-middle position and crossed her arms.

"Now, you will both listen to me. I love you both, but you spend too much time worrying about how I'm doing. I'm fine." She pointed to her father. "It's not me everyone should be stressing-out over. Hypnos has made it clear that you, Father, are in danger, and so are the other gods."

She shut her eyes. "*Rigos.*" The power in her fingertips and body ebbed to a flickering burn.

Ares disappeared from where he stood and appeared right beside her. She jumped backward and dropped into a martial arts stance. Xen sped to her side.

"Congratulations, *kori mou*. You can defend yourself without a weapon." Laugh lines surrounded his lips but it was short-lived. His jaw set into a hard line. "Now, tell me what you know about Hypnos." He shifted his gaze from her to Xen. "And don't leave out any details, no matter how insignificant you think they are."

She raised an eyebrow. "You want to do this here and now?"

"It would be a more comfortable discussion in my office," Xen suggested with a snarl. His anger had not ebbed. Ares did a good job pushing his buttons.

In a fractured second, she was blindsided. The air shifted, and before she could control her father's actions, they were standing in Xen's office. The sudden change crushed her balance, nausea threatened its way up her throat. She took deep breaths.

Xen wrapped his arms around her and tugged her over to the couch in his office, lowering her on the cushioned surface as though she might crack. "Let me get you a water."

She wanted to thank him, but the words were sewn shut behind her lips.

You're welcome, koukla. He spoke in her mind. She watched as he pulled a bottle from his minibar and poured liquid into a glass; she'd have drunk it straight out of the bottle.

Ares's voice broke the brief moment. "Now reveal to me what you know and how exactly am I and the other gods in danger?" He'd made quick work seating himself on the sofa opposite her, and his boots were already settled on the antique, polished coffee table.

Her eyes met Xen's as he dropped onto the cushion next to her and a mute confirmation occurred: she would lead the discussion. "We met with my human grandmother, and she delivered the news. Hypnos visited her and told her to relay a message to me. That message was that you and the other gods are in danger and that his brother is headlining the show."

"Thanatos." Ares moved his booted feet from the coffee table and sat forward. "Did she say why?"

"That's the thing, Hypnos didn't relay anything further." She flexed her hands and a chill swept over her. What if someone tried to hurt her grandmother? "My *yiayia* is none the wiser," she added.

"What do you make of this, vampire?"

"I don't trust him." Xen got to his feet and started a thinking pace on the Oriental rug. "Why would Hypnos go to all the trouble to warn a human? Also why would he not come directly to you if he had a message?"

"My thoughts precisely."

"Which leads me to one conclusion." Xen stopped pacing and faced Ares. "If you step foot on Olympus with Carissa, you'll be walking into a trap."

"You believe he's setting us up?" Carissa asked.

Xen pinned her with a stare. "*Koukla*, it reeks of ambush. It's rather odd that the gods are playing in our field." He pointed at Ares. "You, Ares, know more than anyone else how Zeus feels about the gods cavorting or interacting with humans."

"I've stirred the hornets' nest with my presence here." He rubbed the dark stubble on his chin. "Still, nothing explains why Thanatos would want to knock back an ouzo or two, with me. Yes, I'm on trial for the death of Poseidon's son, but that doesn't warrant a visit from good old death."

"Father, is there a way you could check what the gossip mills are saying on Olympus?" *He must have heard something up there,* she thought.

"My reputable sources report to me regularly on all serious matters and gossip. An uprising or trouble would have been snuffed out already…" He paused and skimmed a look between her and Xen. "…which can only mean one thing."

Carissa swallowed her last bit of air and held her breath, waiting for Ares to shed stadium lights on the situation.

"Zeus doesn't know. If the all-seeing Zeus is unaware, then someone is yanking some serious chain to pull this off. The question is who?" He jumped to his feet. "I have to be there, *tora*, which means you do too."

"*No.*" The word exploded like thunder from the depths of Xen's vocal cords and through his lips.

"Calm yourself, vampire. I would not endanger my daughter."

"There is no reason for her to be there right now. You've yet to confirm if the gods have granted her an audience."

"*Kalispera,* I'm right here." Carissa waved a hand.

Their heads snapped in her direction and toward each other again.

Great. Nobody takes me seriously. "I think I want a burger."

Xen ripped into a renewed verbal clash. "Taking her is too risky. You know it. She's magnet central for trouble."

"Taking her would help me bring to light what's really going on. You know this."

"Ares, I can't have you take that risk. Take me with you."

"You know that it isn't allowed."

"Well, make an exception. The *Athanatoi* are your creation." A vein in Xen's neck throbbed.

The wave of anger coming from him washed over Carissa. She opened her mouth to tell her father to stop, but his answers hit Xen fast.

"You are not a descendant from the gods themselves. You were mortal, you died. I resurrected you and you are a creature of the night. None of that grants you access."

"In this instance, my bond with Carissa should be considered."

"Do I have to remind you what happened when Bellerophon tried to reach Olympus and step foot on it? Zeus sent a mere gadfly to attack. Pegasus threw Bellerophon from his back."

"He died," Xen finished.

"You have no idea how much wheeling and dealing I had to do with Olympus' administrative office for Carissa to step foot where no mortal or demigod has set foot before. The gods don't agree to give a mere demigod an audience without something in return."

"I understand it is complex, but you could plead me as part of her cause."

"Impossible. They won't allow it."

"Try,"

"I. HAVE."

Carissa took in everything they were saying. If her father had truly tried to get Xen entry, then he obviously had considered there might be trouble. "Father, are you expecting things to go sour? Is that why you requested permission for Xen?"

"My reasons for requesting the presence of your vampire had nothing to do with insecurity. I have enough men guarding me on Olympus."

"Then why?" She tried to process his intention.

"Let's say my request had something to do with your emotional state at the time."

Her chest expanded, and her heart began to fill with love. The man before her, a man she didn't know up until a short time ago, was concerned for her and her well-being. That morsel of information added another layer to this complex, bad boy god. A bubble of grief threatened to rise. Gods, she had cried so much, she didn't think she had any more tears left.

"Carissa." Xen's soft voice brought her to the here and now.

"I'm fine."

He turned to Ares. "I think you should find a way,"

"I've told you, it's not possible." A vein popped in his neck.

"Then sneak me in; you shouldn't have issues with that. You're always doing something to irk the other gods. They know you don't play by the rules." Xen ran his fingers through his hair and let out a frustrated breath.

The room shook. Xen had hit a raw nerve in Ares. "I may bend the rules, but I will not break the most sacred laws. There is a difference." The minuscule tremors stopped. "Don't question me on this again."

Xen took a step closer and let his fangs elongate. "I will question you as many times as I have to. The welfare of your daughter, my fiancée, is my first order of business. It is above everything else. You, yourself, threatened me when Hal injured her, do I have to remind you?"

Carissa understood Xen's urgency to be there. She would feel more comforted having him by her side. When her grandmother told her what Hypnos had said, the niggling words that were stuck on repeat over and over danced in her mind, "Don't trust anyone." She thought that Hypnos had been trying to warn them, not set them up, but she could not forget that the gods often played with mortals by weaving complex webs of deceit. Right now, she'd had enough of the testosterone show that had been escalating. She did a quick sweep of the room. They'd smash everything if she let this go on longer.

"*Yia sas.*" Carissa stood and made for a quick exit, her strides long. Her fingers closed around the door handle, and a whoosh of air hit her in the face. Xen's strong arms were on either side of her head. "Okay, I take it that I can't leave yet?"

His right hand snaked around her tummy and tugged, her posterior connecting her with his front, his left arm stayed extended on the door. He leaned in and whispered in her ear. "The only place you will go from here is my bed."

Warmth pooled low in her belly and a quiver ran through her body. She'd been trying to stay focused; his proximity and his guttural voice undid the invisible armor she'd used to shield herself from the intense attraction that burned between them. When moments like this manifested, he won every time. She swallowed. Her mind turned to a ball of fuzz and her body grated against the evidence of his intentions at her posterior.

A low growl escaped his lips. Not the one he reserved for when he showed his anger, no, this one was only for her.

"Carissa." The sound of her father's voice splashed cold water over the fire that burned through every inch of her anatomy.

"Yes, Father." She managed to squeak out.

"We leave in the morning." Bright light filled every corner of the room.

"Now that's what I call an *exodus*," she said, smiling at the door. She had yet to move.

"There's no escape for you." Xen released his grip, and she turned around.

She took a paltry gulp of air before his mouth covered hers. The glide of his tongue against hers ignited a fierce euphoria. Her body relaxed into his, and all thoughts of Olympus dissipated.

THREE

"Not even the gods fight necessity." ~ *Simonides 556 B.C.*

Xen's mansion; Charleston, SC

"I wish you would change your mind, *koukla*." Xen had voiced his concern multiple times in the early hours of the morning. He would be in his rejuvenation sleep before sunrise, so he was working his case to keep Carissa from going.

She'd almost caved, but a lot had been riding on this, retribution for what had been done to her was the driving force, regardless of what problems Olympus had or the danger to the other gods.

Hal, her childhood friend – as well as a demigod and son of Poseidon—had kidnapped her over a month ago. Xen and his team had rescued her, but Hal had had grand delusions of becoming an Olympian god and residing on Olympus, so he kidnapped her again. This time she was pregnant with Xen's baby. An impossibility, yes, but not when divine intervention had been at play. Carissa lost her baby in her fight with Hal. After her ordeal, she decided to resign from the Charleston police force and focus on getting an audience with the Olympian gods. Once she got what she wanted—justice— she would decide on her next steps. Poseidon had to take some responsibility for his son's actions.

"I would rather be by your side. I don't trust them." Xen's words brought her out of her flashback and thoughts on her future.

Her fingers interlocked with his. "I agree. Hypnos said not to trust anyone, so I filled my bag with my version of extra precaution." She opened the duffel bag and let him peek inside. An array of guns, magazines, knives, and other weapons were packed.

The corners of his mouth tilted up. "You never cease to amaze me, but you do realize that bullets are ineffective when it comes to the gods."

"It will slow them down," she said with practicality. "Xen, I have to do this. You know that. It's for us..." she choked, unable to finish her sentence. Her aching heart pounded in her throat. She couldn't find the words to tell him it was for the child that neither of them would ever know. They didn't get that chance. Hal had made sure of it.

"*Koukla*, I understand the why of it. I just don't like the where." He paused, then severed the clasp of their hands and pulled her by the waist so that they were a kiss apart. He leaned his forehead to hers for a silent heartbeat then shifted so that his gaze pinned hers. "Ares may be strong, but you will be outnumbered. I won't even know you're in trouble."

"Trust my father, Xen. I'm sure he isn't going to leave me—or himself for that fact—without his version of a small army. Besides, I'm of no interest. This is about the gods." She'd work on that because it didn't sound convincing to her ears. A quiver in her stomach told her to expect the unexpected. "I owe Father. One, for getting me an audience with the gods and two because he is being charged with the murder of Hal. This is monumental--no god has ever been on trial for murder. I want to be there for him. They have to hear our side." Hal had hurt her, and in retaliation, Ares had unleashed his wrath. Hal had been no match for her father. Unfortunately, Poseidon wouldn't let the issue go, so a trial would be held. She wanted to share her version of the events to the godly court and hoped that Poseidon would be held accountable for his demigod son's actions against her. The gods needed to check in on their demigod children. The ruling of no gods visiting their offspring had to be changed. She searched Xen's eyes. "You know I have to go."

"I do. What I don't like is the uncertainty and length this trial might take. As you said, no god has gone through this before, so there is no precedence."

She shrugged her shoulders. "A few days, tops."

"Carissa, on Olympus, a few days can become weeks and weeks turn into months. What if it drags on indefinitely?"

"I doubt it. They'll want to get it over with fast, especially when they find out that they have bigger problems. Ares will have to bring Zeus up to speed about Thanatos' visit."

"If any harm should…" The words were gobbled up by the tendrils of thick emotion that ran through both of them. "I will find a way to climb Mt. Olympus if they so much as hurt a hair on your head. I will denounce everything the *Phi Athanatoi* stand for, I will denounce the gods, I will denounce my belief in them. They cannot exist if we refuse to believe in them, Carissa. Just remember that, that's where the real power is."

She nodded her head in understanding.

"Remember everything Ares taught you, especially your ability to use *anagke*. Don't hesitate to use it. Stick to him like glue."

"Don't worry," she whispered. Though she knew her ability to use compulsion required more fine-tuning. She wouldn't worry him more. He'd be stewing like a pot of *stifatho* till she returned. She'd have to get his mind off her somehow. Kane had told her how he'd reacted when she'd been abducted by Hal. Xen had fallen short of slaying everyone and everything just to get to her. She couldn't have that happen again. Time to change the subject and focus on someone else.

"You know I need you here. You have to get Yiayia out of those stupid arrangements she made for herself and get her home. I'm going to be living with you from here on, and there's no reason for her to sneak around like some aged ninja." Her grandmother had voluntarily put herself in an assisted living home, claiming that she needed the care. But after their secret meeting in the Greek Orthodox church, Carissa knew that had been a ruse. Yiayia had secrets, and Carissa had every intention of uncovering them when she returned from Olympus.

A laugh escaped from Xen's lips, breaking her internal musing. "You have to hand it to her—she does have a stellar style with that walking stick."

"You were playing with her. Clearly, you could have ducked if you'd wanted to." The humor in his eyes told her as much. He had let her hit him.

"You know it's not going to be easy trying to change her mind."

"I'm sure Kane and Adam can cope." Adam Pelopidas, like Kane, worked closely with Xen and the *Phi Athanatoi*. Adam reminded her of a playful pup. *Silly wolf,* she thought. "Right? They can handle my eighty-year-old grandmother and her seventy-year-old cousin." Her *yiayia* and Aunt Paula were first cousins, their mothers were sisters, and as much as Carissa hated to admit, they shared some of their quirkiness. She cocked her head to the side as scenes exploded in her mind. Mayhem, yep that's what Kane and Adam would be exposed to with her family.

Amusement danced in Xen's eyes. "I'm going to let them do this, just for the sheer entertainment."

He picked up on what she had been envisaging. "You're wicked." Her lips turned up at the corners, Xen's version of the word wicked was a euphemism for sex.

Without warning his lips met hers, hot and passionate. It promised so many things, which she knew he would not fail to deliver had she the time. With that thought, the air shimmered and crackled around them.

Ares eyed them both.

"Take your paws off my daughter, vampire."

Xen broke the kiss. "She's mine."

"Enough," Carissa shouted. The love/hate thing between these two kept blowing the Richter scale. One minute they were chummy, the next they were ready to do battle. The past few days had been immensely tiring for a whole different reason. She had been conscious of the fact that they both got off on fighting. A game to them, one she did not understand, nor did she want to.

"Yes, but she's my daughter."

"She is my wife under vampire law, so get used to it, Ares."

Her father raised one eyebrow and shot Xen an intimidating stare. Xen did the same. Unspoken words passed through their menacing competition. Time to break the tension.

"I'm ready when you are, Father. Just give me a moment to say goodbye to Xen."

Wind whipped around the room; Ares disappeared.

"*Koukla*, it's not too late to change your mind."

"You know I can't do that, Xen."

He pulled her close again and gave her another scorching kiss, his tongue dancing around hers, leaving her panting and wanting more. She stepped out of his embrace and picked up her duffel bag, rummaging through it as a last-minute check. Not knowing what to expect, she had to be as deadly as possible.

"Before you go, *koukla*, there's something I would like to give you." He moved to his desk, leaned over, and pulled out a sword.

"This is yours, *koukla*. Promise me that you will keep it on you at all times." In his outstretched hands, he held a classic Greek sword.

She moved to touch it. A tingle ran up her arms when he placed it in her grasp. A sense of familiarity eased over her.

Xen brought out a harness made of brown leather. Moving closer, he threaded it over her right shoulder and sheathed the sword into it. It felt good. She hated to admit it. Looking up into his eyes, she met his smiling face.

"Thank you. It's perfect." Stretching up on her toes, she placed a tender kiss on his lips. He seized one of her hands and kissed it. She braced herself for what was to come, and gave him one more distracting assignment. "You must help Ligi to track down Kelly. No one has seen her or heard from her in weeks." Ligi Achilles had raised the alarm that their friend Kelly Black had disappeared with a demon named Lox. Xen knew him and didn't think Kelly was in mortal danger. Ligi had insisted on working alone, but they had filed a missing person's report. Gelon Jones, her former partner on the force, now a detective and a wolf, had promised to keep them up to date.

Jones worked with Kane and Xen and managed cases that involved unearthly creatures. This minimized suspicion from humans that there were far more dangerous things walking in the night. Carissa hadn't known that Jones was a wolf or part of the *Phi Athanatoi* while he was her partner. She only found out after she met Xen.

"You're worried," Xen said.

She bit her lip and nodded. "Yes, I can't help feeling that we've missed something."

"Lox is not an easy man to find."

The thought that something awful had befallen her friend sat heavy in her stomach, "What if…" The words died on her lips.

"I know that he would not harm her or any woman."

"I'm going to trust you on this."

"It's on the top priorities list along with your *yiayia*."

She gave him a tender smile, then called, "Ares. "

Cold wind blew around them and around Xen's library, knocking small trinkets over. She rolled her eyes at her father's extravagant entrance; she knew that he did it to irritate Xen. A burst of joy bubbled in her chest, glad that her immortal warrior wasn't as childish as her father. She pulled away from Xen, his hesitant release feathered a light touch to her fingertips. Walking to her father, she took her place next to him - ready for the unknown Olympus and whatever came with it. Ares placed his arm around her shoulder. She barely had enough time to raise her hand in goodbye, when bright light enveloped her, and a familiar pull tugged at her insides. Air whipped around her and her father, and her eyes met Xen's. His fangs had lengthened, he appeared ready for battle, and then he vanished from her sight.

Xen's phone rang. He peered at the caller identification. It was Spiro from his R&D department. He swiped his finger on his smartphone to answer.

"Yes, Spiro."

"Hi, Xen. Good news, that bullet we're working on has had successful results. You can start using it."

"Have you produced enough for the weapons my men use?"

"More than enough."

"Good. I look forward to taking it for a test drive on some demons."

"Night, Xen." Spiro hung up.

That had been a new turning point. The team had developed a process to infuse bullets with poison and vitamin A. The idea had been to have a product that would disintegrate a demon. Clean-up costs had become hefty. Every time they had a skirmish with demons, it would cost them money to dispose of the bodies. This new technology would ensure they got the demons from a distance. No need for up close and personal fighting, which led to more gore and danger to his men.

His lips turned up in a smile. Taking the weapons for a test drive would distract him till his *koukla* rejoined him.

FOUR

"There are two sides to every question." ~ Protagoras

Xen's home office; Charleston, SC
Evening, mortal realm – Day 1

"I can't help you without details on your missing friend." Xen's irate tone bounced around the room.

"Listen, Xen…" Ligi paused trying to formulate the best way to tell the big scary vampire she didn't do charity. Her elbow dug in the armrest of the chair. She met his angry gaze. "…I don't need your help." Ligi didn't trust other unearthly creatures, and even though she had heard over the years that the man sitting before her, Carissa's fiancé or husband depending on which world you lived in, had a good reputation, she couldn't bring herself to accept help from those she didn't know well. Help always had a price and help sometimes burned you because unearthly creatures didn't do you favors for free.

"Carissa has a vested interest in the well-being of your friend, so in her absence and at her request, it falls to me."

"Of all the high-handed…" She gritted her teeth. "I'll say it again, in slow-mo in case you missed it." She raised her fingers to make quotation marks. "I. Don't. Want. Your. Help."

Xen stood and leaned over his desk. His fangs elongated. Ligi shivered at the sight of them. A growl escaped his lips, and he retracted his fangs. "Make no mistake that it was never a question of whether you *wanted* my intervention." She watched him watching her, taking in every minuscule movement of her body. She swallowed hard.

"Okay, keep your pants on Mr. *Nevrospasma* vampire. I'll update you on Kelly but know this…" She stood on shaky legs and cleared her throat. "I will be conducting my own search."

"Sit. I haven't finished."

She slumped into the chair.

"You know Carissa won't be happy you have not revealed your true self to her."

Heat flushed through her body. "What I do is none of your business." Her voice shook.

"Wrong. Anything that affects her affects me." His words boomed in her ears.

She dropped her head to her lap, where she wrung her fingers together. She'd thought about telling Carissa many times in their long history, and each time she weighed it up, she thought she would be doing more damage than good. Did this vampire before her not fathom the betrayal and hurt her friend would feel? Did he not envisage that she could potentially lose the best friend she ever had? Did he not know that this was bigger than her, that it included Kelly? Did he not comprehend how tormented she had been all these years holding her other self a secret?

Slowly she raised her head and met his eyes, but before she could open her mouth, he answered her. "I have evaluated every possible scenario and the outcome of each, should she find out."

Her mouth fell open, and her brain caught up. He could read her mind.

"Stay out of my head."

"Stop projecting."

"I'm thinking, not projecting."

"Well, you're thinking loudly."

She paused. "If I tell her, there's no telling how she might react. This is Carissa we are talking about. It doesn't take much to raise her hurt and anger and after what she's been through, I fear making things more difficult."

"Difficult?" Xen let out a laugh. "You do realize that she is on Olympus with the god of war." He stabbed the air. "She couldn't possibly be in a more Herculean situation. Right now, all I want is to walk in there and Arnold Schwarzenegger the place."

Ligi pushed herself out of the chair. Men were testosterone junkies who wanted to blow things up all the time. The conversation had reached its end. No one would be preaching to her on how she should conduct herself toward her friends. Least of all, a man. "Well, I guess you have a point, but I'm not marching to your tune."

Xen rose to his feet too. "Okay, then let's return to your friend. Why would Lox want to take her?"

"As I said, I have no idea what he wants with her, and just in case you missed the first memo. I. Do. Not. Want. Your. Help."

What was it with men and their refusal to accept the word no?

Males of any species couldn't take no for an answer. Well, this time, he'd have no choice.

Even though Xen was several thousands of years old, he still required his rejuvenation sleep during the daylight hours. For his species, the sun sent a lethargy that forced them into a deep slumber till dusk. They'd become, after all, a nocturnal breed. When dusk hit, he'd have a bag of blood and get to work. His age and power allowed him to push the limits of when the sun would pull him into sleep and when he would rise.

Tonight, his first appointment had sat across from him, flicked her hair, roused his anger, and managed not to run screaming. She had just gotten up to make her exit.

Xen watched with a raised eyebrow as she strutted out of his office. Her heels clacked on the hardwood floor as she closed his door. What a stubborn siren she was. He smiled at her willingness to go it alone; at the same time, he knew she would return. If his information rang true, then the flame-haired siren would require assistance from his team.

Kane swung the same door open, mere seconds after the siren left, and wolf-whistled. "Who the fuck was that hot piece of ass?"

"Carissa's siren friend, who has withheld her true identity."

Kane raised his eyebrow. "Now that's likely to get messy. Does the siren have a name?"

"Ligi," Xen answered. "Keep it in your pants, *lykos*. We don't want you acting like one of the Olympian gods."

"Hey, I can keep my luggage packed. I'm not like Zeus."

Zen rolled his eyes. "That infuriating siren won't share any info about why Lox might have taken her friend Kelly."

"Any idea where he's hiding?"

"None. And if anyone knows, they aren't telling."

Kane met Xen's stare, and the corners of his mouth lifted. "Time to use my favorite kind of method to extract information."

"I thought you might say that." Xen knew that Kane loved an occasional torture session.

A loud wolf whistle stole their attention, and they both glanced at the door. Adam strutted through with his mouth hanging half-open. "Did you see the set of tits in the foyer?"

Xen rolled his eyes. "As I recall the tits were attached to a body and therefore that body is a person with a name."

"Those tits have a name?"

"Ligi, and she's a siren." Kane answered this time, the corners of his mouth tilted up.

"Those tits sing to all the right parts of me."

"Okay, TMI," Kane threw in. "I'm getting images in my head about parts of you with tits. I don't want that kind of porn in my head."

Xen let out a bark of laughter. Then schooled his amusement to continue the discussion he had started with Kane. "Let's get back on track. Carissa has asked me to help that siren locate her friend. So far, said siren is not willing to share anything she knows. Add an AWOL demon to the mix and no willing snitches, and we have a big fat zilch."

"I have dibs harassing the siren relentlessly until she gives up what she knows."

"She's a handful," Xen said.

Adam held out his fingers and pretended to squeeze invisible tits. "She's more than a handful." He wagged his eyebrows.

This time Kane rolled his eyes. "Get your head into the here and now, *lykos*. That siren will have you for breakfast."

Adam shot a cheeky look at Kane. "That's the general idea."

The cocky wolf thought he could convince the siren to fess up what she knew. Xen rolled all the situations around in his head. The *lykos* would end up with a knee in his balls. Only one option remained. Let the wolf try to extract the information. He met Kane's stare; they were on the same page.

"Okay, *lykos*, the siren is your assignment. Follow, interrogate as you see fit, and by all means, bring us something useful."

Adam bolted from his seated position and nearly hit the desk. "Well, time's a-wastin', and I have a siren to catch." He sped out of the office.

Kane let out a slow and deep chuckle. "That *vlaka* has no idea."

"This is going to be entertaining. Glad we have front row seats. Want to start a small wager with the *Phi*?" Xen asked Kane.

Kane's expression altered from amused to serious. "When you say small, how high can we go?"

"I'm feeling rather good about this one. Let's make it unlimited."

Kane let out another whistle. "You're serious?"

"Absolutely."

"Why so much?"

"Because that siren stood up to me. I had to release my fangs to coax a shiver from her. Even then she resisted backing down. That wolf has no chance in Hades of getting anything out of her."

"Want me to get one of the guys to tail him and record everything?"

A bubble of laughter escaped from Xen's lips. "Absolutely."

FIVE

"Man is not man, but a wolf to those he does not know." ~ Plautus

Howling Cocktails, Adam's Bar; Charleston, SC
Evening, mortal realm – Day 2

Adam had only one thought. Extract information.

He'd been on the siren's tail from the moment he stepped out of Xen's office. He had hoped that he could intercept Ligi and question her. She had refused Xen's assistance to help find her missing friend. Not many people refused an offer from Xen and Adam wanted to know why. Her lack of ability to stand still in one place for too long started to grate on his nerves. His *Phi Athanatoi* business focused on obvious battles and following Ligi had proven more difficult than expected. He had decided to give it a rest tonight and retreated for a drink at his favorite spot to think about how to approach the voluptuous creature who had sashayed out of Xen's office. Her scent lingered in Xen's library and there had been something hypnotic and alluring about her. His wolf instinct had demanded he pursue her in a relentless manner. However, his human logic fought the wolf that wanted to pounce. She was still a woman and needed to be treated with care.

Adam took a deep drink from the glass and placed it on the polished timber table. When he glanced to the entrance, it hit him that the goddess Tyche must have been watching over him, because the siren he had been obsessing about had just stepped into his privately-owned bar. An inward smile raced through his body and made his lips twitch.

One thing he had noticed while shadowing her, she tended to create a unique bubble of noise and movement. She huffed as she planted her delectable derriere on a stool at the bar.

He eyed her from his position on the couch across from where she now sat. He had the perfect view. She appeared flustered as she rummaged through her bag.

He had to talk to her tonight. Stalking her for the right moment to approach had left him vexed.

Tonight he would have to use all his *lykos* charm if he were to succeed on two counts, one to get information on her friend and two to get to know the siren better.

Truth was, the longer he waited in the bar, the more he witnessed men fawning over her. He'd have to play the hero and save the damsel in distress. His cue for action would be soon because three men were planting themselves around the siren. One each to her right and left and one standing behind her. He glanced across to his security team. Not good by any means. He let out a small growl. It was time to step up and scare off these drunken humans. He kept his eyes on Ligi the whole time, his awareness noting the jerks who had started to engage in drunken conversation. He could hear them clearly from where he sat. His *lykos* hearing afforded him the gift of being able to tune in to conversations when he needed. He wanted to rip their throats out. Their language made him want to beat them to a pulp, but when the guy on the right decided to drop his hand to her chest, and the fellow on the left went for her ass, he saw red. Red anger. Red the color of blood.

No man had the right to touch a woman without consent and invitation. Adam's reaction had nothing to do with his wanting Ligi; his anger was founded on the principle that you did not treat women with disrespect. He was at Ligi's side in seconds. His fist connected with the guy on the right, as the guy on the left and behind her moved to strike Adam. However, in their state, they were easy work. By the time security came scurrying forward, the men were groaning and struggling to get to their feet.

"Do you want to press charges?" Adam asked her.

"No." She didn't look rattled at all.

He glared at the security guards. His nostrils flared. "Don't let them return to the bar."

The security guards swallowed hard. "Okay, boss, we're on it."

He turned his attention to Ligi and held out a hand so she could step over one of the men who lay at her feet. "This way."

She took it without hesitation, which startled him. He was expecting resistance. He led her to a quiet corner that consisted of oversized lounge chairs and tables. "What can I get you to drink?"

"Martini, dry."

Adam waved over a waiter and gave the order for two drinks.

"I hadn't pegged you for a martini man."

"I don't play favorites. I go with the mood."

"Thank you," she said.

Adam raised his hand. "No need for thanks. Those jerks deserved more than what I gave them." He watched as Ligi nodded.

"Haven't I seen you somewhere before?" she asked.

"That sounds a lot like a pick-up line." He wagged his eyebrows and smile broke on her luscious lips. *Keep it together, Adam.*

"It's not a line." She clicked her fingers as recognition dawned. "Xen's place."

The waiter arrived with their drinks. Perfect timing to give him time to think about how he wanted this to play out.

"So did the big bad vampire send a pup to babysit me?"

A low growl escaped his lips. "I am not a pup nor a babysitter. And I was here before you arrived."

She took a drink of her martini. "You've been hanging around that vampire too long. You sound as agitated as him. Am I your new mission?"

Adam rose his hands in surrender. "Right now, the only mission I am on is my own and that involves wine and dinner."

She raised an eyebrow at him.

The beast in him could sense the cascading emotions that were running riot inside her. Time to take advantage of those. He read his watch. "How about dinner?"

There were a million things going on in Ligi's head. The wolf before her was handsome in a cute kind of way. A quick tumble would never have been an issue before, but she was done with men and done with the emptiness that thundered within the depths of her soul after meaningless sex. Should she take his offer of dinner? Maybe it would give her a chance to relax. The Kelly fiasco was chewing up all her time. Every lead she had so far was nothing more than breadcrumbs. Maybe dinner with the wolf might not be a bad idea.

"I am rather busy, but I will take you up on the offer."

"Good. Any preference on cuisine?"

Well, this was a first. No one had ever asked if she had a preference before. Then again, it was never about the dinner with all the past dates. "I'm not fussy. I'll let you decide."

"Okay, it's settled. Do you want to freshen up before we go?"

Another thoughtful question. "Good idea. I like the way you think, wolf."

He flashed her a smile. Yes, a little time with this cutie might be the best medicine for her. She shot to her feet and made her way to the ladies' room. She smiled to herself, maybe for once she might get some intelligent conversation, and maybe it would lead to something more.

Dinner had been a wonderful affair, and she hadn't missed all the innuendo. He had offered her a ride home, and during the drive she decided to go against her better judgment.

"How about a nightcap?"

"I'd be up for that."

They climbed the stairs to her apartment in silence. She opened the door and let Adam in first.

He let out a whistle. "Nice digs."

Her block was an old one, but she had the apartment refurbished when she moved in. She liked sunshine, and this apartment had floor-to-ceiling windows. She'd fallen in love with it the moment she'd walked through the front door. She had also picked white to make it brighter.

"Glad you like it."

"I was expecting more pink." He gave a wink.

He was playing with her. "Why do men assume that women will decorate in pink?"

He shrugged his shoulders. "No offense intended; we shouldn't generalize, but I think the past couple of decades trend of pink for girls is tattooed in some of our brains."

"None taken." She waved in the direction of the couch. "Have a seat. I'll get us the nightcap." She moved away, her heels clicking on the wooden floor as she disappeared into the kitchen.

The wolf had made himself at home. When she entered the room his booted feet were on her coffee table.

She put the tray of drinks on the table. "Here." She swiped his feet off the table and put a coaster in place before setting his nightcap down.

"Thank you." He patted the seat beside him.

She indulged him by lowering herself on the lounge.

"Listen, there's something I've been mulling over all night. I want the air clear if we go further than the nightcap."

Ligi titled her head. "Okay, whatever it is out with it, wolf."

"Yes, you had seen me at Xen's office…" he bit his lip. "… and Xen did want me to follow you and talk to you."

Ligi jumped to her feet. *Stupid men.* Always thinking with mud brains.

"OUT." She pointed to the door.

He got to his feet too. "Just give me a chance to explain."

"I don't want an explanation."

She advanced, and he retreated. She closed the distance before he could take another step and stabbed him in the chest. "You all think this is a game. Women are not toys for your amusement." He retreated from her, and she reached to stab him again with her fingernail. One of her dining chairs had been facing away from the table. His legs hit the chair and landed in it.

An idea sprang to her mind, and she acted without missing a second. She pretended to fall on him.

His arms went around her.

She liked his warmth, but a better plan rolled through her head at the high-speed pace of a Ferrari on an open road. She was now nose to nose.

"You smell divine," he said.

"You're not so bad yourself." She got to her feet. "Why don't you wait here. Pull off your clothes."

She raced to her cupboard and pulled out some string. Then got a frying pan from the kitchen.

"Don't turn around; it's a surprise." Taking slow steps behind him.

"I love surprises."

He's gonna love this one, she thought. "Don't turn around yet." When she was close enough. She said, "Make sure your eyes are closed."

"Oh, they're closed."

She swung with all her might; the pan collided with the wolf's head. His head lopped forward. She dropped her weapon and checked his pulse. Yup, still alive. Ligi took out six long cable ties from her pocket and used them to tie him to the chair.

When she finished, she stood to her height and rolled her neck from side to side, admiring her handy work. She grabbed her bag and keys and headed out.

SIX

"God from the machine." ~ Aristotle

Gates of Olympus,
Realm of the gods – Day 1

Warmth cocooned Carissa, but that comfort dissipated a second later. It didn't resemble the way she reacted when Hal pulled her through those portals during his kidnapping rampage. Halirrhotius, son of Poseidon, got it in his head that he could use her as a sacrifice to gain access to Olympus and claim his right as a demigod among the Olympian gods.

No, the pulling and twisting that started in her stomach made her nauseous. Heavy pressure squeezed her chest. The words cardiac arrest danced around her mind

Her body heated, flames flickered and fire-balled through every cell. Everything slowed, stagnated then stopped.

Bang.

Time froze before someone hit the fast forward button, and it sped up. Wind whipped around them once more. Her feet landed on something slippery and hard. Head still spinning, she tried to adjust her vision. If her father's arms weren't holding her upright, she'd be flat on her ass or doubled over on her knees. A cough forced its way up her throat and helped clear her lungs. Words finally found their way through her lips. "Where are we?"

"At the gates of Olympus." Two deep, unfamiliar voices answered from behind the gates. When she blinked again, two men stood before her.

"Wow, all the fantasy pictures don't do them justice," she said to Ares.

The gates were colossal and shone.

"Sparkly. Wonder if they have unicorns too." Who would have thought that standing at the gates of Olympus would have reduced her thinking to that of a five-year-old? She stared at the rainbow lights bouncing off the columns and gates.

Ares let out a laugh. "The gates are made from adamantine, and these two lazy sods are Anicetus and Alexiares."

They bowed. "We are the gatekeepers of Olympus," Anicetus said.

Alexiares took a step forward and stuck out his hand. "Welcome."

Not sure whether to take it, she glanced at her father, who nodded his approval. Shrugging her shoulders, she closed her fingers around Alexiares' thinking of it as nothing more than a human greeting but she was wrong. Power crackled between them.

Alexiares smiled. "You've passed the test. You may enter."

The doors opened, and Ares nudged her forward.

"Anicetus, Alexiares." Her father nodded.

When they passed the threshold of the gates, they dematerialized to a house. A very large house. A house built for a god.

"Welcome to my home, daughter. There are ten rooms off this room. One of those will be your chambers."

She did a quick scan, admiring the opulence of the room they were in. *Divine,* she thought, *for divine beings.*

"I'd like you to get settled, but first, you need a bath and a change of clothes."

"I had a shower this morning." She sniffed her armpits. Nope, the scent of deodorant was all she could pick up.

"You will bathe in Olympian water. It will de-scent you from the mortal realm."

"Water is water, or is the water different here?" She raised an eyebrow.

"It is heavenly." He winked at her.

Her mouth hung open before her brain could construct words. "So general things here are unlike those in the mortal realm?"

"Exactly. Now let's get you settled."

He waved his hand, and her clothes disappeared. She glanced down, and she had been clothed in a Grecian peplos with golden sandals. She ran her fingers over the soft fabric of the dress.

"Your clothes and bag will be in your chambers."

"Delia," he called. A girl of about fifteen stood before him.

"Yes, Ares." She took a long and exaggerated bow.

"You will assist my daughter in the bathing room and then see that she has something to eat. I will return shortly."

"I thought I was to stick to your side," Carissa uttered in a hushed voice.

"You are, and you will, but first, I urgently require the services from a logographer so I can work on the details of my speech in the trial tomorrow."

"Will you be gone long?" The thought of being left on Olympus with other gods in residence sent a small quiver to her stomach.

"You are safe in my house. I will be quick."

Her brow furrowed. "Does time work differently here when you zap from one end of Olympus to the other?"

Ares laughed. "We don't zap, Carissa, we materialize." He stepped closer and pulled her into a hug then placed a soft kiss on her head before stepping away, "I won't be long." He dematerialized. She blinked at the empty space.

"Daughter of Ares, please follow me."

"Just call me Carissa." Carissa followed her through the huge house. *This place is like a palace.*

"Would you like me to help you bathe?"

"Ah, no I'm fine on my own." She had no intention of letting anyone bathe her unless it was a six-foot-three vampire with green eyes. Wicked images shuffled in her mind. An ache settled deep in her chest. What would he be doing now?

Delia led her to a huge room that had a sunken bath in it. They stood in silence for a moment.

Way to go, an indoor pool, she thought.

"Would you like me to undress you?" Okay, another weird question.

"Bless your heart. No, I'm fine, really. You can go."

Delia didn't bat an eye; she turned and left the way they had entered.

Carissa watched the receding figure. "Not the brightest crayon in the box," she voiced to the room before removing her dress.

The water appeared so blue and inviting. Her lips tilted up, and a crazy thought raced through her mind. She sprinted toward the water and did the best bomb that she could. Water splashed everywhere. Tepid water soaked her skin, and she sighed her pleasure.

Her father was right; there was something amazingly different about the water. It felt lighter, almost like a soft caress on her skin. She turned her palms down in the water and spread her fingers apart. A tingling sensation started at the tips and moved up her arms. The water started to form into a shape. She lifted her hand out of the water, and the water spiraled around her arm and hand as if it were attached to it. For some reason, she felt compelled to talk to it.

"Ball," she said, and the water obeyed. A ball began to spin in her palm. A smile spread over her lips like no other.

"Higher." The ball of water rose higher. "Higher."

"Break apart." Water splashed like large rain droplets. "Wow."

"What is wow?" Her father's deep voice came from the entrance.

She squealed and splashed. Her ears heated in embarrassment. The fact that she was naked and her father was standing there had her ducking for cover. Her arms automatically went to cover her breasts.

"Don't be shy, Carissa. There is no room for modesty here on Olympus."

"Oh."

"Now, is it the water that has you excited? Does it resemble the stroke of feathers brushing your skin? The water here is different from water in the earthly plane."

"No--actually yes, the water does feel different, lighter, but that's not it. This is."

"Ball," she called as she lifted her hand out of the water. "Higher."

"Carissa." Ares' voice boomed. His eyes were wide with shock.

The ball of water dropped.

She watched him not knowing why she'd caused him such distress. When she found her voice, confusion laced it. "What's wrong?"

"Get out and get dressed. I want to see you in my chambers and don't ever do that again or in front of anyone. Do you understand?" His brow wrinkled. "Delia, get in here and have my daughter dressed and brought to my chamber."

Carissa gasped for the second time when Delia appeared out of thin air.

"Yes, Ares, at once." She answered mechanically.

Then her father dematerialized.

That did not go well. Delia held out a bath towel for her. Carissa pulled herself out of the water with a mix of emotions running through her. Why would her father fear a simple water trick? Surely it was something all of them could do—a party trick for the gods and goddesses. She dressed without further communication. They walked in silence to Ares' chamber. Once inside, he waved, and Delia disappeared.

"Sit down, Carissa. We have to discuss your presence here."

Lowering herself on one of the couches, she couldn't shake the feeling that she'd be receiving a parental lecture about her behavior, only twenty years too late.

"I didn't…" Her voice broke.

He sat next to her and turned to face her, placing his hand on hers. "Listen. I didn't mean to upset you." He let go and pushed a wet lock of hair out of her face. "What you did with the water should not be repeated while you are here. Let's say that it's best kept under wraps until I can return you safely home."

"But why? I'm sure you can all do the same."

"No *kori mou,* we cannot. The only other person who can control water is Poseidon, and let's say we are in enough shit with him. This would anger him further."

"Isn't it a good thing that I can do this? I mean it's harmless, right?"

"No. It's not. One who knows how to wield and manipulate water can do a lot of damage. You don't want to get the other gods' attention, *kori mou,* because they will use you for their stupid amusements. Amusements that can cause death. Amusements that lead to destruction in their playing field."

A thought flickered through her head. Xen's warning went off in her head like an alarm. Maybe he was right. She would have to be extra cautious from here on in. She had one goal here – make sure the gods took responsibility for their demigod children and their actions in the mortal realm. No one should have to suffer as she had.

"Your vampire is right to warn you. Take heed and protect yourself at all costs. I'm here, but you must not attract attention to yourself. Am I clear?"

"You read my mind?"

"Yes."

"I will try to stay under the radar."

He squeezed her fingers tight.

"I have a friend I want you to meet."

"Sur..." The words died on her lips. She barely had time to prepare for the shift. They were transported to a room filled with weapons.

"I'd ask Hephaestos to make you one, but unfortunately, we're not on speaking terms. He's still angry about the affair I had with his wife. Thousands of years ago."

She raised an eyebrow. "I don't need a sword. Xen gave me one."

"My daughter will have a sword. You are the daughter of Ares." He pulled one from his collection and passed it to her. "One of my favorites."

Carissa rolled her eyes. "Men and their swords," she huffed.

SEVEN

Success is dependent on effort. ~ Sophocles

Xen's Home Office; Charleston, SC
Evening, mortal realm – Day 3

Xen sat at his large mahogany desk, shuffling around the mountains of paper that required his attention. Most were from his cover operation, the high-tech Phi Technologies. He eyed the clock on his desk. "11:15." The sound of his voice bounced around the room. Time seemed to be moving very slowly without Carissa. His thoughts of her evaporated when the air in the room shifted and crackled. His awareness spiked.

He recognized the distinct signature that came with the shift. It belonged to a specific witch. A witch who'd aided Carissa when she had been kidnapped. A witch he owed a favor to. A witch who would also help him if the occasion called for it.

She materialized and stood before him, dressed in medieval garb with long flowing red hair.

"Kirke, to what do I owe the pleasure?"

"I've come to collect." She moved to the chair in front of Xen's desk and sat.

"I take it you've narrowed a location and you require an extraction team." He dropped the pen he held and leaned forward. "Bring me up to speed."

"They're holding my man not far from here." She straightened the cuffs of her sleeves. "Myrtle Beach."

A wave of anger washed through Xen. The location had been where Hal, Poseidon's son, had held Carissa when he kidnapped her. It made sense—both abductions would have taken place at the same time. Hal had kidnapped Kirke's boyfriend and blackmailed her to do his bidding. It was only after Carissa and Kirke were thrown together that the witch switched sides. "Fitting that he'd hide your man right under our noses." He grabbed the phone on his desk and tapped the screen, and his fingers worked with speed. "I think it's time you told me the name of your man. I can't help if I don't know all about him."

Kirke folded her hands in her lap. "Odysseus."

Xen narrowed his eyes and dropped his phone to the desk. "I'm not laughing."

"And I'm not making jokes." She shifted position in her seat. "It's not 'the' Odysseus. I seem to date men with the same name."

Xen's shoulders relaxed as he studied the witch before him.

"Don't look at me like that," she said.

"Hey, who I am to judge? I do expect more than a first name."

"Fine." She blew a red lock from her face. "Ithicarus."

His lips twitched at the irony. "I don't think I want to ask where you met him."

"Everyone has their faults and weaknesses."

"That they do," he replied.

His phone beeped with quick speed he extracted it from his pocket and read the message.

Team is ready. Let's move.

"Do you want me to meet you by the cars?"

"That might be better," he said, pulling off his blazer.

The witch disappeared, and he sped into his weapons room. He collected his double-edged *xiphos* and made his way to the waiting team and SUVs. Kane sprawled behind the wheel and Kirke was in one of the rear seats.

Kane glanced at the review mirror. "Hope for your sake that he is there, Kirke."

"No more than I."

Xen turned to look at Kirke. "We will find him. Hal is sure to have left a trail of breadcrumbs somewhere."

"I wish it were that easy," she said.

Xen understood the weight of those words. Carissa had been kidnapped by the same madman. "Alive or dead, we will find him."

Xen didn't miss the grim look that flashed in Kirke's eyes. Without another word, he turned his head and focused on the dark road ahead. Maybe this night would help solve more than one question rolling around in his mind. There had to be someone else behind Hal's actions. Hal was a nobody who wanted godly power. Hal had no real power of his own. Somebody hadn't shared the truth about godhood with Hal, had told lies that he believed to go so insane. Maybe the reason Kirke's man was still a hostage was that they had other things planned for the witch. He would have to watch the witch's back just in case.

The crunch of gravel under the tires brought Xen out of his musings.

Kane pulled up three hundred meters from the location, and the other two SUVs followed. "Showtime, boss." He flashed his signature wolf grin at Xen. The *lykos* lived for a good fight.

They spilled out of the cars, and Xen opened the boot of the car and pulled out extra weapons. He slid knives into the pockets of his combat trousers. Kane went for extras too.

"Is it really necessary to have that many knives on you?" Kirke asked while she watched both men arm themselves with a bevy of weapons.

"You never know what might come in handy." Xen flashed Kirke his megawatt smile while his fingers jammed a small device into his ear. Kane followed suit.

Kirke retreated to give both men room. "There are enough of you to take out a small army with your swords alone."

"Sometimes you have to throw a few extra vitamins in the mix." Kane laughed.

"Vitamins?" she asked.

"Yes, Vitamins. The knives are laced with poison. As soon as they break demon skin, a nice cocktail of digoxin and polonium enters their bloodstream. It attacks every organ and burns them from the inside out. In ten seconds, they are nothing but ash."

"That still doesn't explain the vitamin."

Xen cut in. "The poison is pumped with a large dose of vitamin A, which causes toxicity. Deadly not only to humans but to demons. We discovered it three days ago. Since then, we've had a significant amount of weaponry manufactured with a high dose of the vitamin inside."

"I'm eager for target practice," Kane interrupted.

Xen rolled his eyes.

"Where's Adam?" Kirke asked.

"He's on a separate mission." Kane winked at her.

"Why do I get the feeling that there's something more going on?"

Flashes of the predicament the silly wolf would land himself in, cascaded in Xen's mind and humor reached his eyes. "Let's say there's money riding on this."

Kirke's eyebrows raised, and her lips turned up in amusement.

"What's the limit?" she asked.

Kane stepped closer to her. "You catch on fast for a witch."

"I need some cheering up, and since that *lykos* is always clowning around, this might be fun."

"I'll let Paris know that you want in," Xen said as he slid a final knife in his breast pocket.

Paris and his team of three had finished arming themselves and stepped closer to the group. Paris observed Kirke. "How much?"

"Five thousand. On Ligi."

Kane and Xen let out a loud whistle.

Paris shifted his stance. "You sure about that?"

"Oh, I'm quite sure, vampire." She winked at him.

"Okay, I think we should move out." Xen gave the order.

Paris and his team lead the way toward the rundown house. Kirke had pinpointed this as Odysseus's position since Carissa's kidnapping.

When they reached the hundred-meter mark, they split. Xen motioned for Kane and Kirke to follow behind him. They'd take the rear while Paris took the front.

When they were in position, Xen waited three seconds before shouting, "NOW."

The noise of splintered wood filled the space around them.

With vampiric speed, Xen raced through the house and stopped in front of Kane and Kirke when he'd cleared all areas. "Whoever was here has been moved."

"I'd kill Hal again if I could." Kirke spat.

"Agreed." Xen sneered. He had envisaged the slow torture of Hal when Carissa had been taken. He understood Kirke's rage. "Have you any idea where he might have moved him to?"

"None. This came from a very dead source."

"What do you mean by dead?" Kane asked.

Xen eyed her, knowing that her answer would involve magic. Their history stood over many years, so he was attuned to her methods in gaining information.

"As in spirit dead. Ghosts."

"Ghosts gave you this location?" The pitch in Kane's usual deep voice had spiked.

"Yes." Her flat tone confirmed she wasn't kidding.

"Okay, I'm not going to ask why or how, but it must have something to do with your mother."

"Actually, it doesn't. It has a lot to do with who I know, and let's leave it at that."

Xen watched them both. Perhaps they still had a chance. "This dead contact. When did he give you this information?"

Kirke scrunched her face in concentration. "Two days ago."

"Two days is vital when someone is missing," Kane added.

"Don't throw a hissy, wolf. I had another problem to deal with along the way."

Kane let out a frustrated groan.

"Let's focus on your contact giving the right location," Xen said, bringing Kirke's and Kane's discussion to a close.

"Paris." Xen spoke into his tactical mic piece. Paris confirmed the house and the area around it was secure. "Report."

"Something is a little off." Paris' voice bounced in Xen's earpiece. Paris was a vampire and would scent a demon.

"I'm picking something up but can't confirm what it is. It's faint. I'm following it."

It was as Xen had suspected. The demons had been trying to throw the wool over Xen's men for some time.

"Have you got backup?" Xen asked. The long pause raised the hackles on Xen's neck.

"I've got Charles."

"I'm heading your way with Kane." Xen turned to Kane. "He has a new trainee with him."

"And the trainee might be a vampire, but he is no warrior yet." Kane filled in.

"Exactly. Let's move," Xen said.

They both took off in a quick run…but Kane dropped his gear and shifted to wolf form. In seconds, they stopped just beyond where Paris and the trainee were surrounded by demons. The demons were hissing at each other.

Xen scanned the area. He spoke into his mic. "Team three. I need you here with us."

Kirke appeared at his side. "I think I can help."

"I'm never one to turn down the help of a witch."

"Tell me what you want."

"See if they are using a portal." When Carissa was kidnapped, Hal used the portals from Hades to let the demons through to the earthly plain. It was a nightmare for Xen and his men as they had to fight off large numbers. Thankfully, Kirke had been there to help.

"Not this again." Kirke breathed. "My mother will not be pleased." Hekate was the goddess who protected the crossroads everywhere, even in Hades. The use of portals was her domain, and her anger at the misuse of them had not been gentle. In fact, she had the ones responsible for giving Hal access tortured - slowly.

The other team appeared near Xen. He unsheathed his sword. "Ready, men?"

A low growl from Kane confirmed his eagerness to fight.

Xen made the first move. He sped to where two demons stood near Paris. Before they realized Xen was behind them, he communicated through his mic. "Now." Paris swung his sword through the air as Xen swung his behind the unsuspecting demon. Two heads landed on the dirt. Xen kicked and laid his boot into the body; it followed the head to the ground. When he glanced up, more demons were coming out from a thicket of trees. To the left, Kirke cast a fire illusion spell. The demons that had been advancing halted, thinking the fire real.

Kane ripped the throat out of one of the demons that Charles had been fighting. Paris sped to Charles' side, but the poor newbie had been stabbed in the heart. Paris pulled him into his arms, then sped over to the cars. A grim shadow crossed Xen's vision. The loss of the new recruit pierced his chest. They did not truly lose men often.

Charles had been recruited a month ago. New vampires had predator instincts, but they were not warriors. The training program with the *Phi* consisted of three years of study and hard training. The *Phi* fought a bevy of creatures, and teaching recruits had to be top-notch. It had been a long time since they lost one; his men would grieve.

Xen did something he hadn't done in a long time; he sheathed his swords and pulled out his gun with the designer bullets. His preference had always been swords. He took aim, and shell casings fell to his feet. The magazine emptied, and he reloaded while watching all his fallen targets writhe in pain before turning to nothing but ash on the ground.

"Witch, have you sealed the portal?"

"There is no need. They've ceased."

"Drop the fire illusion."

"As you wish." Kirke waved her arms in the air simultaneously as she spoke her spell.

Xen fired at every demon that came rushing forward. Kane must have shifted and retrieved his gear. He fired at the advancing demons.

"They don't stand a chance." Kane smirked as he fired relentlessly.

"Remind me to give the pharmaceutical and weapons team a raise for coming up with these bullets."

Around them, demons dropped and turned to nothing but ash.

But it wouldn't bring Charles back.

Xen faced Paris in his office. "You could not have predicted the outcome."

"He was mine to watch."

"They are all ours to watch. You cannot be everywhere."

"I should have left him by the vehicles."

"No, you did what I ordered. That's how it works."

"But…"

"There are no buts. You could not have predicted it. It was a skirmish. You are no stranger to losing men. You've been with me for a long time."

"With all due respect, I've never lost a newbie."

Xen placed his palms on his desk and pushed his body upright then walked around his desk. Paris brought himself to eye level. "You will take time off and recover."

"What if it's not necessary?"

"It's an order."

Paris withdrew and walked out of the office, slamming the door at his exit.

Xen pulled out his cell phone and tapped a message to Kane.

Xen: Have someone watch over Paris, but it can wait till tomorrow night.

The only thing Paris would do tonight was drown his sorrows. Xen had plucked that tidbit from this mind on his way out of the office.

Xen's phone vibrated on the wooden table and pinged its incoming message.

Kane: Done

The hackles on Xen's nape rose. Energy thick and black like smoke rose from the floor in his office. He reached out with his vampiric senses, friend or foe? He scanned the room for the incoming intrusion. He took several long strides to his desk. He would not be unprepared, his fingers closed around the sword that lay on his desk.

The darkness in the middle of his office thickened and spread. Only one god could wield the power of death. When the smoke subsided, a man dressed in black leather sat on the sofa.

Xen let his sword arm relax. "To what do I owe the pleasure, Thanatos?"

The god eyed the chair opposite him and jutted his chin for Xen to join him.

Xen sped to the chair and dropped his weight in it. He let the sword he held rest on the table in front of him.

"Speak. Why is it you are here?"

"I've come to deliver a message."

"Didn't your brother already do that'?" Xen asked.

"My brother simply gave enough for you to prepare yourselves."

"He could have been more direct, and so could you. You could have delivered it directly to Ares, who is currently on Olympus. Why waste time coming here?"

"Because it concerns not only the gods and unearthly beings but also the humans."

"This is your problem, and we do not want to be dragged into the games gods play."

Thanatos let out a loud laugh. "Cosmic order." He uncrossed his legs and leaned forward. "You take the gods and lock them up, and you'll end up slowly killing the planet and humanity with it. Nothing will survive. They control every aspect of life, yours included."

"You can't be serious."

Thanatos lips curved up in a sneer. "Oh, I never kid about death."

"What do you want from me?"

"Not you directly, but more your demigod partner."

Xen released his fangs and hissed, "The gods will not use Carissa as an instrument."

"Relax, vampire. I'm here to tell you that you have to help her, how do you say, get to the bottom of it."

"Isn't that the role of the gods?"

"It's your role, too."

"How can we possibly fight against any god? What you ask is ridiculous. Unearthly creatures do not have the power of gods." Xen gritted his teeth.

"You must find the adamantine sickle that Cronos used. You know your history, Xenocrates. I'm sure you can locate it and put it in the hands of the demigod."

"That's if it's where it's fabled to be."

"Oh, trust me, it's still lying undiscovered. Forgotten."

"Then why don't you retrieve it?"

"Because you have to put it in the hands of the demigod."

Xen gritted his teeth. "Her name is Carissa."

Xen's body tensed. He hadn't seen this coming. He would not risk Carissa in any way. He'd let Thanatos know that this would be too dangerous for his woman. He had opened his mouth but… dark smoke surrounded Thanatos, swirling around him like a mini-tornado, it rose up and up to the ceiling. "Put it in her hands, vampire." And then he disappeared.

Xen ran his fingers through his hair. The door to his library office swung open.

"Boss, why does it smell like death in here?" Kane asked.

"Because death paid me a visit."

"What?" Kane moved to where Xen was sitting.

"I'm not sure you'll want to hear this," Xen said, looking up at his friend.

"I'm a big boy. I can handle any ball you throw."

Xen raised an eyebrow. Of that, he had no doubt. "Pack your scuba gear. Death wants us to go for a deep dive."

The phone on his desk beeped with an incoming message. He swiped it from the table and read or rather stared at the photo he had been sent. He turned the phone toward Kane. Their laughter filled the room. It was a selfie of one of Xen's men with a tied-up Adam in the background.

"I want copies of that," Kane said.

Xen tapped at his phone.

"Let's say that there are going to be some very happy winners."

"You didn't send that to the *Phi* Group?"

Creases formed around Xen's lips. "I think you know the answer to that."

He typed another message.

Xen: Give the siren space for now. I'll have Kane follow up.

"I think it would be best if you tried talking to her in the next day or so."

Kane rubbed his chin and nodded his head in silent agreement. "Knowing you, something else is bugging you about this."

"We should know where Lox's loyalties lie, but let's deal with our diving expedition first."

Xen didn't say it but he welcomed any distraction right now.

EIGHT

"Whatever comes from God is impossible for a man to turn back."
~ Herodotus

Ares' Palace, Mount Olympus
Realm of the gods – Day 1

"I can do this," Carissa chanted in a continuous stream, like a thread unwinding from a spool.

Ares watched her, and she watched him watching. "*Kori mou,* stop stressing about seeing Zeus and Hera."

"But they're your parents."

"So?"

"That makes them my grandparents."

"Trust me when I tell you that they may not understand your traditional family values. Your existence, *kori mou,* is all the reason for them not to trust you. The gods are always suspicious of any offspring. It's a vicious cycle."

"In case I overthrow them?" She huffed. "But they don't know me."

She stopped and stared into her father's eyes. There the truth swirled. They would not care for or trust her. She was an outsider. A foreigner. An illegal immigrant. As far as the gods were concerned, she was standing on the wrong side. She took a long, hard swallow. A tidal wave of hurt raced through her as she blinked away tears.

"Do you feel the same?" Her voice quaked.

Ares closed the gap between them and pulled her into his arms. He placed a soft kiss on top of her head and rested his chin there. "You know that if I could have had the time with you and your mother, I would have been there to see you grow every step of the way." Ares had to leave Carissa and her mother because of some silly decree by Zeus. The gods of Olympus were forbidden to mingle with mere mortals. Silly rule since their demigod spawn were all over the planet. Her mother had remarried but died in a car crash with her stepfather not long after. Carissa had been raised by her *yiayia* and *pappou*.

His words were the truth and the tingling sensation that danced from the soft kiss he left on her head confirmed it.

"Come. Let's see what my father and mother want." Ares broke the contact.

They materialized in Zeus' chambers. His allotted space appeared much bigger than her father's. *Then again this is Zeus,* she thought. Carissa did a slow turn. Taking everything in. The details were impeccable. The marble floors were a brilliant white. The ceiling was constructed with the same substance as the Olympian gates, adamantine. The columns were Doric. The gods obviously didn't keep up with the latest trends that moved in Ancient Greece. The furniture was mega king-sized, much like the room. "How big is this guy?"

"Big. But you will see him as you see me."

"Why?"

"Because to see him in his true form would kill you."

"Is that the case with you? If I were to see the real you, would it kill me?"

"Yes, *kori mou*."

She eyed her father for a moment before turning her attention to the colossal room they were standing in. A bolt of lightning hit the marble floor a few feet away from where Carissa stood with Ares.

She gaped at Zeus. Magnificent didn't do him justice.

She raised an eyebrow. "Impressive."

"I'm glad you think so, granddaughter. Come, let me greet you properly." He held out his arms.

Her feet slowly moved toward him. *Not the greeting I expected. School your thoughts,* kori mou. Ares scolded her in her mind.

Stepping into Zeus's open arms, she pushed her father's intrusion out. When her grandfather's arms closed around her, skin tingled, her heart sped up, and warmth spread through her. A small gasp left her lips. *HOME.* The word bounced around her head, singing its discovery.

Zeus released her, and she retreated to look into the light blue pools of his eyes. "Yes, it is, granddaughter."

"But how did you…"

"When you felt happiness, you let your guard down." He winked at her.

"Okay." She'd have to work on keeping her guard up when she was happy.

"Have a seat, granddaughter." His eyes darted in Ares' direction. "Son."

"Father."

Zeus raised his hand to cut him off. "We will discuss your situation later. Right now, I want to learn more about our granddaughter."

"Our." She whispered before squinting at the ceiling where a stream of glitter rained down in a cylindrical sphere a few feet from her. A woman wearing a jeweled crown and golden Grecian gown appeared before her. *Hera.* The name came to her easily. Her arms were already open. Carissa stepped into them. Her reaction mimicked and amplified the one she'd had in Zeus's arms.

"Granddaughter. Welcome."

When Carissa stepped back, her knees buckled. This woman she knew. This woman had come to her dreams. This woman had given her the gift of life. Hera had allowed for Carissa to fall pregnant with Xen's child, an impossibility for a vampire, but gifts from gods were never questioned. When Hal had kidnapped her and hurt her, she'd lost their baby in the battle. The flashes cascading through her mind were still raw. And then her anger rose, and heat coursed through her body and flushed her face. Her nails dug into her palms.

"*Kori mou*." Her father's soft voice, a warning.

"Why didn't you help me?" She yelled to both Hera and Zeus. Tears stung her eyes.

"Come sit, granddaughter. We will explain," Hera said.

Carissa sat next to her father. Remembering Xen's advice: stick to Ares like glue. Her father must have picked up her thoughts when she hugged Hera. His posture stiffened when she edged her fingertips toward her father's leg and nudged him slightly.

Relax, kori mou. *I have your back.* He sent the words directly to her mind.

The words from her father eased the knot that had formed in shoulders. She focused her attention on Hera. "I'd like to hear your explanation."

"You know we can't meddle with humans under Zeus' decree." Hera swept a hand in Zeus' direction.

Carissa shifted her posture. "Why do I get the feeling that you are telling me what you think I want to hear?"

A deep rich laugh echoed in the room. "I admire your courage to speak freely." Zeus smiled. "Maybe, granddaughter, it might work to tell you more."

Carissa narrowed her eyes. Her intuition told her the "don't interfere,' rule didn't apply to these two. Her father closed his fingers around hers.

"As you can guess, we knew for quite some time that you were Ares' daughter and our granddaughter."

Ares shot to his feet. "You could have saved me from the extra measures I had taken to stay away from Aggie and my daughter."

"You did what the Fates would have foreseen you do, without our intervention."

"So let me get this straight: you knew the outcome and didn't warn me. Instead, you let Aggie die, and my absence caused Carissa to grow up without a father." He took several steps closer to his parents. The room started to shake. "Give me one good reason why I shouldn't tear this place apart."

In one swift motion, Hera appeared by his side. Her fingers were gentle on his left arm, trying to soothe his anger into submission. "Wait till you've heard all we have to say."

"Your mother is right. Sit down, Ares, and let us talk. Reserve your anger for when it serves a purpose."

Ares blinked from where he stood and returned to his seat near Carissa. She watched in fascination and a little fear. She squeezed his arm. "Control, as you tell me," she whispered.

Zeus and Hera moved to the couch closer to where Carissa and Ares sat. An attempt to soften the blow. She'd seen this maneuver a thousand times before. "Okay. Hit us with what you've got. We're losing time here." They'd spent a good portion talking around in circles. Time, she didn't have. She'd probably clocked up days back in her own time. Xen's face flashed in her mind's eye, and a vision of their last night glimmered through her mind.

"Ahem." Zeus cleared his throat.

Skata, she'd given them an insight of her thoughts. She schooled the random pictures running through her mind.

Zeus waved his hand, and a golden goblet appeared in her hand. Liquid sloshed on her fingers and over her gown. She moved her other palm to still the vessel and stop further spilling.

"Drink." A subtle command echoed in her head.

She lifted the goblet to her lips without question and took a deep drink.

"The wine is spelled and will confirm that Hera and I am telling the truth."

"And why am I the only one drinking it?"

"Because gods know if you are lying, an inbuilt mechanism to protect us from each other," Ares supplied before either Zeus or Hera could throw in their version of godly perks.

She took several more gulps of the wine. "Figures, you get all the bonuses."

"That should do it," Hera said and waved the cup away as well as the stain from Carissa's dress.

Carissa focused on Hera and smiled a silent thank you. Hera nodded her head once in acknowledgment.

Zeus cleared his throat. "Alpha to Omega. The beginning to the end, those were the final words of the Fates when they gave me the prophecy relating to you, granddaughter."

"I'm surprised that you told Mother." Ares' voice spiked in anger.

Carissa watched the exchange. She'd have to question her father later. "How long ago was this prophecy given to you?" she asked.

"Many millennia ago." Zeus answered.

Carissa swirled the information around in her gray matter. "Forgive me, Zeus, but I can't see how it can be relevant to me now, in this time? How could they have seen something that relates to someone so far into the future? Ares has had other children; you have other grandchildren so why me and why now?"

"A prophecy can be foretold many millennia into the future. Time does not work in the same fashion as you know it, the Fates are tied into time. Foreseeing something many years ahead is not uncommon."

It sounded a little too far-fetched for her. "What exactly does this prophecy predict? I am assuming it has yet to happen?"

"You assume wrong, granddaughter. It began the moment Xenocrates begged the gods, and Ares heeded the call. Your father's responding to Xenocrates' call did two things. It caused a ripple in your mortal timeline and in our heavenly one. Xenocrates was not supposed to make it out of that cave. The Fates foresaw a new prophecy which concerns you, granddaughter."

Xen. A chill ran over her body, and a tingling started in her chest. Could his and her fate have been etched long ago? She swallowed hard. She and Xen had not had enough time to talk about all of his ancient past. Questions cascaded in her mind. Lots of questions. Questions that could not be answered by Xen, but only by the powerful gods before her. "And what exactly does this prophecy reveal?"

"If I tell you, it may change the outcome."

Carissa scoffed and stood. She could not see its relevance. Her fists clenched. "You give me a grand entrance, and then you have the nerve to say nothing." A ripple of anger started at the base of her feet and worked its way up through her body. It flamed, burned, scorched. She wanted nothing more than to lash out at something. This was a game to them. Lure her in with false promises.

"Calm yourself, *kori mou*." The warmth of her father's palm on her shoulder soothed the rage. At some point, he must have stood to comfort her.

Ares spoke, "Father, this is ridiculous. If there's something in that prophecy that requires our attention, you should tell us."

Zeus stood and walked in Carissa's direction. His features showed no hint of anger or pleasure. She had to hand it to him; his poker face was divine. Ares' squeezed her shoulder then moved in front of her. Shielding her.

"Ares, move. I will not harm my granddaughter."

Hera popped up. "No one will cause Carissa grief. She has suffered enough."

"You're telling the truth," Carissa confirmed. "But I also know you're stalling."

I know, kori mou. Ares stepped aside.

Zeus now stood in front of her. And she'd have to say that the father of the gods was a great ball of energy. She did not fear him though, because if he'd wanted her dead, she would have been from the second he materialized in the room.

"You have no cause to fear me. What I must divulge must be only to you and in the language and vision of the Fates."

"You're kidding."

"Sadly, I wish I were."

He placed her two fingers on her temple. Pictures danced in her mind, and then a film started to play out. The Fates' prophecy uploaded to her mind, and the words stabbed a corner in her brain like sharp knives. The gibberish went on for minutes before it abruptly stopped.

Zeus broke the contact from her temple. Her knees felt weak, a shudder of spasms traveled through her, draining all her energy and taking away the ability to stand. To say that the experience of the god's touch and implanted memory left her shaken would have been mild in comparison to what she was experiencing. She closed her eyes and took a deep breath. Nausea rolled in her stomach.

Ares put his arms around her and materialized them to his chambers. She wanted to refuse help, but her lips were sealed tight. Ares placed her on the large bed. The familiar scent of the blanket told her it was his.

"Don't talk. What you are feeling is the aftereffects of Zeus' touch. His power is immense and draining for those who aren't a fully-fledged god or goddess."

Her head moved in understanding.

"I'm going to grab a rejuvenating potion. Rest, *kori mou*."

Ares dematerialized out of the room. Leaving her with an experience she never wanted to repeat. All Zeus did was implant the prophecy, but man he was potent with power. She hadn't thought she would end up like a stiff piece of wood with blinking eyes, staring up at the ceiling. *Interesting color, what is that-- duck egg blue?*

Think. She shouted to her brain. She tried to recall the whole prophecy, but it came with a string of ancient Greek. Images, so many images sifted through her mind. None were pretty. How could any of what flashed through her mind have to do with her? Famine, death, and total despair. It resembled all the dystopian movies she'd seen. She did not wield or possess power like the gods and goddesses. Yes, maybe she was able to manipulate the bathwater, but that didn't mean she had what they had. Zeus was interpreting the prophecy and images all wrong. Demigods did not have enough power to bring down the gods or cause that kind of destruction. If he thought she could save them, he was epically mistaken. None of what Zeus had imparted made any sense, but then oracles and prophecies rarely did in the Greek world.

The air shifted and Ares appeared with a small jug in one hand and a funny looking cup in the other.

"It's a *kylix*." He poured an amber liquid into the cup, then moved closer to lift her head to allow her to drink.

"Take small amounts each time. You should start to recover after the third."

When the contents were drained from the cup. Ares rested her head on the pillow. A tingling sensation fired from the soles of her feet right through her body, sparking it to life and restoring her energy.

She rose and pulled her father into a tight embrace. One thing was clear. Ares had her back. "Thank you, Father."

"No need to thank me." He pulled away. "Now, tell me what you saw."

"None of it makes sense."

"Trust me, *kori mou*, even the most ridiculous image is going to be vital. The Moirai, as you know, never lie about one's destiny."

"Wait, you mean the Fates…"

"Are still active. Yes. Even now." A grin broke across Ares' lips.

"So why not ask them again? What if it's changed, what if the prophecy no longer applies?"

"Because it doesn't work that way. Once a prophecy is given, it is, and I hate to sound cliché, set in Greek marble. What you must understand is that our Fates are not the same as the Oracle of Apollo, who are human and can misinterpret things. The Moirai personify the destiny of man."

"But how can Zeus think that it concerns me?"

"Zeus' epithet is sometimes *Moiragetes*. He commands the sisters and has the power to influence destiny. Father can see the bigger picture, but for some reason, he is letting this take its course without his usual intervention. The question that is spinning endlessly in my head is why?"

"So, if he can change it, then why not do so?"

"Because it is by his decree that we do not intervene in human affairs."

"I'm half-human, is this a game?"

"Possibly."

"Right." She sucked in a breath. Maybe the effects of Zeus' mind mumbo-jumbo had fried a circuit in her head. A loose strand of hair fell over her eye.

Ares brushed it away. "Now, tell me what you have seen and let's try to piece this together. There is more there than what we now know."

"That's what's confusing. When you told me in Xen's library about the prophecy, you said that Lachesis had said that a demigod will lead an uprising to overthrow the Olympian gods, but another demigod was destined to save the gods from a rebellion."

"Yes, go on."

"The pictures cascading through my mind are not showing me any groups that might be part of a rebellion. What I'm seeing is famine, barren land, ghost towns, storms, earthquakes, and on and on - total Armageddon. Not one drop—or scene I should say—of a group with guns, swords, or other weapons. So how on earth is that going to benefit us in finding out who the big bad demigod might be?"

"What do you remember of the ancient Greek?"

"Gibberish. I could not even understand one word." She tried hard to remember if any word resembled the modern Greek that she knew, but none were clear. She'd have to think it over and play it over in her head a few times. "It sounded distorted."

"Not what I had expected either. Maybe you need more time to see if anything further pops up."

"Maybe or maybe I just have to eat."

"Let me guess. You'd kill for a burger. Since you are in the land of the gods, maybe a gyro will do?"

"Wait, you eat gyros?"

He winked at her. "The gods cannot live on ambrosia alone. Besides, what's not to love about a gyro?"

Seriously, it sounded crazy, yet she'd gladly go with it because the growl that escaped from her stomach told her loud and clear that it required nourishment. Her lips turned up with joy. "Magic words. Coffee would be good too."

Delia appeared with their food and her requested coffee. *Talk about service*, she thought.

"Come on, let's eat, and then you need rest because the trial tomorrow is going to be long and complicated. If I know my Uncle Poseidon, and I do, he is likely to cause a stir. He's known for his elaborate antics."

"Then we best be ready." A tingling in her limbs told her that she should take the sword Xen had given her to the trial. Maybe she'd take both. She didn't possess the power the gods had, and any power she did have right now resembled baby stages. An extra layer of protection wouldn't hurt. She could hear Xen's voice, "Take the sword, *koukla*."

NINE

"The gods give nothing good or beautiful without labor."
~ Xenophon

Corfu, Greece
Evening, mortal realm – Day 4

The chopper blades sounded with a loud whup, whup.

"Let me get this straight. We're diving into pitch-black water in the middle of the night. To retrieve a knife that may or may not be sitting at the bottom of that darkness." Adam raised an eyebrow and pointed to the water below.

Xen watched him and slowly nodded.

"What about sharks?"

Kane hit him over the head. "There are no sharks in these waters, *malaka*."

"Well, I've seen plenty of swimmers getting their limbs chewed off."

"*Lykos*, that is Australia. This is Greece."

A wicked smile broke on Xen's lips. "I hear the great whites are quite brutal in their limb chewing."

"Great whites." Adams's face turned ghostly pale.

Kane let out a roar of laughter.

"He's teasing you, *lykos*. Great whites are also Australian."

"Well, that settles it," Adam shouted over the whipping of the chopper blades. "I'm never going to Australia."

"I wonder where you get your facts from." Kane shook his head in disbelief.

"Discovery Channel," Adam supplied.

"I don't know what discovery channel you were watching, but it's not the same one everyone else knows."

"Well, I might have accidentally been watching one in a foreign language."

"Seriously, Adam. I don't know what you are on, but you need to stop."

"I'm not on anything. I would have liked to have been on and over a certain redhead, but she had to be somewhere before I had the chance. My ego and emotions may be a touch delicate at the moment." Some of the Xen's men had made serious money on a bet that Adam would get more than he could chew chasing after Ligi, Carissa's friend.

Kane and Xen glanced at each other. A burst of deep laughter broke through the helicopter. When the laughing settled, Xen tapped his waterproof X5 communicator. One designed and produced by Phi Technologies. Xen's company.

"Are we in position?"

"Five minutes, boss." The voice from the pilot sounded in his earpiece. As a vampire, he didn't require an earpiece, but it was easier to communicate with all the men who were not vampires. Though the wolves had excellent hearing, the communicators ensured everyone got the message and were on the same page.

Heavily armed with knives, Kane, Xen, and Adam wore scuba gear. Everything rode on the adamantine sickle being at the bottom of this river, or in the vicinity. There was no room for error. He was growing nervous without hearing from Carissa.

It had been four days. A part of him was going a little insane, so it was good to be out. But here in Greece, he was closer to the gods and Carissa. An invisible thread tugged at him. He had to trust Ares.

"Ready in ten."

"Xen, the boat is in place," Kane said.

"Let's pray it's there. I have knowledge of one other potential site. We might have to do some research, and do it quickly."

"That's the trouble with the Greeks. There's always more than one mythical location."

Xen removed his communicator.

When they dove into the cold water, he had hoped the sickle would be resting at this location. It only took a moment to realize that they were in the wrong spot. Xen signaled the men to resurface.

When each man emerged from the river, they swam to a small boat that was already in position for them. The team climbed aboard and started to shed their diving gear.

"It's going to be a long night. There are beers and food if any of you are hungry." Xen said.

The men moved about the small boat grabbing beers.

Xen looked out at the shadowy water near Corfu. Kane brought a beer to him and held it up. Xen met Kane's raised beer and clinked it. "*Stous theous.*" They tipped a little overboard as a libation to the gods. Xen didn't care for beer, but it had become a habit around the *lykoi*. Blood was his preferred source.

"You think it's still where it fell?" Kane asked.

"It's hard to know for sure. I'm still puzzled as to why it is needed against whoever is trying to bring down the gods. The idea that we are being played for godly motives has not escaped me." Xen had his collection of artifacts from around the globe, but the topic or search for the sickle had not come up until now. Something squeezed in his gut as he thought that through. If the sickle was still where it had fallen, then the gods had wanted it hidden until now. The question of why now kept replaying in his mind.

Kane anchored his attention to Xen. "So, what's the plan?"

"I have decided that we store it somewhere safe."

"You don't mean?"

Xen nodded.

"Another artifact for your collection."

"One never ceases to be a collector as such." Xen's private collection spanned thousands of years and was something to behold. He had built a tomb under his property in Charleston that was impenetrable. There was no technology spared. He also had it warded with *mageia*, from the best of the best witches. Right now, he couldn't trust anything Thanatos or any other god told him, so it only made sense that the sickle should join his other prized possessions and sacred objects.

Diving in the Corinthian gulf and the Bolineaus river was an easier task than Corfu, Greece. There were no waves to kick up sand from the bottom and obscure things. Tyche was on his side when Xen's fingers closed around a shiny object that lay embedded in sand and rocks. The sickle itself had pierced a rock as it fell. Xen tugged to pull it free. Its luminosity from the adamantine was a sight to behold. He wrapped it under the water in a latex fabric. The fabric had inbuilt technology that neutered any energy that the sickle might give off. How had this not been discovered? Whatever left the sickle undetected, was not going to be questioned by Xen.

He signaled the men and they moved out of the water and toward a small riverbank.

Xen quickly deposited the sickle in a warded container made of the same adamantine material. He'd had seen to it personally that it was lined with tech material and then had a spell cast around it.

"That enough to keep that thing from being tracked?" Adam asked.

"Let's say that they won't see this one coming." Divine objects were tricky to handle. Even the sword that he'd given Carissa would eventually be free from its *mageia*. Once the spell had worn off, the gods would know who the sword belonged to. He grinned, wishing he were there to see it unfold. Knowing his *koukla,* Carissa would project the whole episode, once back in his arms.

The wheels of Xen's private plane hit the tarmac, and the men began to move about the plane, always eager to get to the exit.

Kane and Adam sat opposite Xen. He had been pensive for most of the flight. Not engaging in much of the banter that flew around in the cabin. His men liked to rib each other, and Xen took it all in.

"I can't say it hasn't been fun, but I really must check out what a certain redhead is doing." Adam released his belt.

"Well, she obviously isn't doing you," Kane replied.

"Not yet, but she will be." Adam wagged his eyebrows and sniffed the air. "I'd recognize her scent anywhere."

"Listen, if you know what is good for you, you won't get too close," Kane said.

"That's the trouble. I don't know what is good for me."

The plane came to a complete halt, and the men filed out. Several SUVs waited on the tarmac. Xen watched from his window, waiting for the right moment to exit.

"What's troubling you, boss?" Kane asked.

"I'm not certain what to make of it all. I am trying to put as many backup measures in place, but something is off. I can't shake the feeling that we are being played."

"And when in the past have the gods not meddled? There's only so much you can plan for," Kane said.

From behind Xen, Adam said, "Call in some favors. Some of the other wolf packs owe you."

"I have thought of it, but I don't want to do that unless we are desperate."

"Why not line things up, just in case?" Kane said.

"I may have to."

Xen watched Adam type a message on his phone.

Adam leaned toward Xen. "If you don't mind me asking, Xen, what exactly should we be looking out for?"

He had not briefed Adam properly because he had been literally tied up by the siren. The thought sent a whisper of a smile to Xen's lips. For all his playfulness, Adam managed to attract females and trouble. His work with the *Phi* was never anything but stellar, and he did trust the *lykos*. Xen eyed Kane, who nodded his approval. "Thanatos believes that trouble is going to hit Olympus."

"What does that have to do with us? The gods don't mess in our playground."

"Previously, no. Right now, they feel it is okay to visit our turf and complain of their woes."

"Still doesn't make sense." Adam ran a hand through his hair. "Why would Thanatos come to you? How could you possibly help?"

"Not necessarily me, but he thinks Carissa can. He thinks that catastrophic consequences are headed our way. Not just for us but all of humanity."

"You mean like Armageddon?" Adam asked.

"Precisely."

"Then Kane and I should talk to our home wolfpacks, so they are ready. I've already warned some. Between Kane's pack, mine, and the others, we are sure to have enough men to help." Adam folded his arms over his chest and leaned back in his seat.

"I am hoping that we won't require their assistance," Xen said.

"Have you heard from Carissa yet?" Adam asked.

"Nothing." He glanced at his feet. "It's been four days, but it's still day one on Olympus. For every day there, it is three days here."

"Glad you cleared that up," Adam said, rolling his eyes.

Xen growled at him.

Kane hit Adam over the head before addressing Xen. "I don't think Ares would let any harm come to her."

"I don't either, but some intel on what is going on with the gods would be ideal." Xen stood. "Let's move. I've only got a couple of hours before rejuvenation, and I wanted to go over the details of Grandmother Atheneous' housing arrangements. I believe you are picking up both Carissa's *yiayia* and Aunt Paula?"

"We had a minor setback, but it's a go for tomorrow, boss. There won't be any trouble on my watch." Kane followed Xen down the airplane stairs and across to the waiting SUV. "I'll drive," Kane said as he collected the keys from the waiting attendant. Two men loaded the adamantine box in the trunk. The other men were all milling around the SUVs, waiting for Xen to leave.

Xen was not going to fight over who would drive. He pulled the passenger door open. "I wouldn't be too sure about the no trouble bit."

"We can supervise them, Xen; they are just a couple of old ladies," Adam called from the back seat.

Xen had inside information that told him that Yiayia and Aunt Paula liked to get involved. His intel—research he'd done on Carissa and conversations with her—informed him that both women had spent most of their lives protecting Carissa, and that meant trouble followed them from time to time. So far, they'd managed to come out without a scratch, but Xen didn't want harm to come to those who protected Carissa.

"Xen, it's done. We are collecting them at ten sharp. Aunt Paula is meeting us at the facility and will be driving Carissa's *yiayia* home. Aunt Paula has also offered to stay with her until Carissa returns."

"We will definitely have our hands full," Xen said. "Paula likes to meddle."

"Hey, which Greek auntie doesn't like to stir the chicken filled pot?" Adam said.

Xen raised an eyebrow. He'd let Adam find out the hard way that Aunt Paula and Yiayia might cause him more trouble than Ligi.

TEN

"Anybody can become angry - that is easy, but to be angry with the right person and to the right degree and at the right time and for the right purpose, and in the right way - that is not within everybody's power and is not easy." ~ Aristotle

Areopagus, Athens, Greece, Mount Olympus
Realm of the gods – Day 1

"Where are we?"

"On the Areopagus."

"But this does not resemble the slippery rock northwest of the Acropolis. I've stood there."

"Ah, *kori mou*, that is the mortal Areopagus and this…" Ares swept his arm as if introducing the room to Carissa. "… is the gods' version of a courtroom, viewable only by godly eyes. Never to be experienced by mortals and unseen to them. They do, however, get a sense of awe from Boreas and Zephyrus as they race their winds through the slopes of the Areopagus."

"Wow, if only everyone could gaze upon what I am looking at now."

"They don't have to see it, *kori mou*, they feel it."

"But how could they possibly feel the magnitude of what I am experiencing?"

"The energy that emanates from this spot is powerful, and it is a very significant location in history. Those two things cause enough of an oscillation that when mortals stand on the Areopagus, they feel its vibrations. Even if it looks like a piece of slippery rock, it holds godly power. Never forget that."

Carissa opened her mouth to say something then closed it again, realizing that there were some things that humans and even her human half would never fully grasp or understand because there were far greater things in the cosmos and the world around them. Things that ordinary human brains could not comprehend. She brought her focus back to the room.

"Our seats," Ares motioned.

"Aren't we early?"

"Being early allows us the advantage of watching everyone arrive. Plus, as head of security, I want to ensure my men are in place."

"Good point." She wasn't going to argue with her father; he made sense. When she had finished dressing, Ares had appeared and asked her if she had taken any weapons with her. She nodded and gave him a half-smile, confirming that she was lock, stock, and maybe not two smoking barrels but definitely two shiny swords prepared. Ares then equipped her with two daggers.

"More weapons," she said as she stuck one dagger in her boot and another in the pocket of her sword harness.

"You can never have too many."

She had forgone the Grecian dress for mortal clothes. Black pants, t-shirt, jacket, and finished off with black combat boots that were worn but reliable. She resembled something out of special ops.

Ares had dressed the same, and so did his security team. They were spread around the courtroom, and they all had their weapons strapped to their bodies. They were there to keep order.

Carissa watched as the room began to fill up. "Who will be representing you? Do you have a lawyer? How does it all work?"

"So many questions, *kori mou*." He turned toward her in his seat. "It works differently to your modern court system. The gods and goddess are the jury and they decide the outcome. Zeus stands as judge but only to monitor and keep things in order."

She took in what he said. "Why does that make me uneasy?"

"It shouldn't," Ares said and placed a hand on her shoulder to comfort her.

"What if they won't listen to reason?"

"That is why we are here, to make them listen and make them understand that their demigod children should not be running around without the gods checking up on them."

"Let's hope they can see the dangers of letting their offspring wreak havoc on the earthly plane," Carissa spoke, but a deep-seated feeling had settled in her gut. She knew that the gods were set in their ways, and it would be hard to convince them that they should be a part of their offsprings' lives.

Her father had told her clearly that Zeus had decreed that the gods were not to intervene in human affairs. Having received a firsthand experience of Zeus' power, Carissa knew few would be foolish to step outside his rulings. Unless, of course, you were Ares…her father. She shook her head to disperse her inner musings. When she peered around the room, it appeared that everyone had turned up at the same time.

A man in full Greek armor materialized in front of Ares. They spoke in soft tones before her father turned.

"Carissa, this is Echion. One of my most trusted generals and also my son."

Her mouth fell open, she mimicked a fish, then closed her mouth before digging out her weakened voice. "Does that mean he's —my half-brother?" She choked out her words.

Ares glanced sideways at her and smiled. "Yes."

Echion stuck out his hand. "Glad to meet you, sis."

Carissa swallowed her words and tongue. Her fingers locked around her brother's in greeting, but her brain had taken a vacation to the Bahamas. Her mind struggled to formulate the words.

Echion winked at her and broke the contact.

"I'm sorry, Echion. It's not every day that I meet a half-sibling."

"Don't apologize, sister. You will get used to it eventually. We have many brothers and sisters."

This… she never considered. *Brothers, sisters,* she swirled it around in her head.

"I hate to break your chatter, but remember, *kori mou*. There is no judge, only jurors, and everyone you see in here is a juror. So, the task is to convince most of them that Hal died because I was defending you."

"What? But how on earth is that meant to work in your favor?"

"Each one will listen, and in the end, they vote. My job is to convince them I acted as any god would have in my position."

"But with this many jurors, anything can happen."

"*Kori mou*, even with only twelve jurors, anything can happen. Don't fear the numbers."

He had a point. She sat in a room filled with gods and goddesses; anything could occur at this trial. Carissa scanned the crowd, all types sat, stood, and lined the walls ready to be judge and jury in her father's trial. The noise level amped up when Zeus, Hera, and Poseidon finally appeared. Everyone was now seated except for Zeus.

"Ares, god of war, battle lust, and courage, please stand."

Her father shot to his feet.

"How do you plead to the charges of murder?"

"Innocent."

"Let it be known to all the jurors that stand here as witnesses that Ares has entered a plea of innocent." Zeus sat.

"Really?" she whispered under her breath. Surely there was more?

Quiet, daughter. Ares sent the words to her mind.

Sorry, Father. She held back from facepalming herself. She'd forgotten that she had to keep firm control of her thoughts. Something that would prove difficult in this lion's den. The typical American agenda as to how court proceedings ran—one she knew from her time as a police officer—appeared lacking, and her thoughts were flying around the room. *Then again, you are gods and you set your own rules.*

Ares spoke. "In my defense against the charges, I will prove that Poseidon's son Halirrhothios, known in the mortal world as Hal, acted with the intention to not only to harm my daughter but also to cause harm to the gods who had abandoned him. I will also prove that my actions were in defense of my daughter Carissa, who is seated beside me."

Collective gasps filled the air.

"You dare bring a demigod to Olympus." A minor god several rows behind them had spoken.

Carissa swiveled around to get a good look at the questioning party, and then it slapped her in the face. All the people in this room held a significant amount of power. Anything could occur, and she'd have no warning. Xen's and Ares' swords as well as the extra knives that her father had supplied to her were a good idea.

"She is here by invitation." Ares retorted.

"Who would invite a mortal to be with gods?"

"Zeus," Ares answered.

Carissa watched the lesser god shrink in his seat. A scene flashed in her mind — a tall man standing over her cot and giving her a unicorn. Her eyes darted to Zeus, to see him smiling at her. *Okay, that was weird.* Did that really happen, or was someone playing with her? She focused and willed steel doors to close around her mind. No telling if one of these gods inserted fake mumbo-jumbo in her head. She mingled in dangerous waters here. Xen had been right.

Poseidon stood. "You killed my son, and for that, you should be punished."

Whispered murmurs circulated the room like cicadas on a hot summer's day.

"Way to go, the formal procedures." She whispered to her father.

"Shh, *kori mou.*"

The corner of her eye caught movement. She evaluated the room. No one showed any sign of notice of the giant who came to his feet with his face contorted with rage. She'd seen that fixed stare a multitude of times as a police officer. That giant wanted to go for the jugular, but who was he angry with? She followed his line of vision - Zeus. He pulled out a sword.

Why on earth hadn't anyone protested his actions? Why did she seem to be the only one witnessing this? The giant started to move. *This isn't good. Time to use the mind mumbo-jumbo.* She reached out to Ares.

Father, can you hear me.

Yes, kori mou, *what is it?*

Can you see the giant?

Yes, what about him? He's sitting on our right.

No, Father, he's standing and with a sword. Ready to pounce.

Glamour, he said.

Glamour? Carissa asked.

Yes, kori mou, *we the gods and others have been glamoured not to see what he is up to. The glamour must not work on you, because you are half-mortal*

I have to stop him. She had only one thought — shield.

ELEVEN

"It is folly for a man to pray to the gods for that which he has the power to obtain by himself." ~ Epicurus

Areopagus, Athens, Greece, Mount Olympus
Realm of the gods – Day 1

The raised sword and the determination on the giant's hard and scarred face told Carissa that he would head straight to where Zeus sat, and there'd be only one outcome. Without thinking, she propelled herself forward, pushing through the gods. Using the force of *anagke*. She swept her hand and shouted *MOVE*. The crowd split and opened a clear path to the front of the room where Zeus, Hera, and Poseidon sat at the long, white marble table.

One thing spun in her head continuously - protect. She had to stop this giant at all costs. Her fingers grabbed the lapels of her jacket, and she ripped it off her body while still running. In seconds the sword strapped to her back had been unsheathed. She stepped on a stool near the table and used it to jump on to a marble bench. She had a hairline second to intercept the charging giant, who was heading straight for Zeus. The sword shivered in her grip. She slid to her knees, sword poised on her right, and came to a stop between Zeus and the slashing sword that bore down on him from the giant's momentum. When his sword connected with hers, a burst of light and a sonic boom flashed through the room.

Loud collective voices rang throughout the room as it became reanimated.

The giant's expression had been replaced by one of surprise. He narrowed his eyes at Carissa and raised his sword again. Carissa shifted to block the blow.

A sword pierced through the back of the giant and through to his chest. On the tip of the blade that poked through the flesh, an inscription read God of War - her father's. She blinked, and it disappeared.

The giant dropped to his knees and then to the marble floor.

"Good work, *kori mou*." Ares held his hand out to her and helped her off the table.

The room had built to a fever pitch with shouting and conversation.

"Silence," Zeus commanded.

Poseidon shot to his feet. "This is your doing." He pointed to Ares.

"If you know me, uncle, you would know this sort of theatrical exhibitionism is not my style. My style involves soldiers. My style would have wounded everyone in this room."

A growl left Poseidon's lips.

Zeus stood and leaned on his brother's shoulder. Whatever anger Poseidon held dispersed. He turned to Carissa. "Now, tell me what happened and why is Poseidon's son Ephialtes dead?"

"I saw the giant pull a sword and made a run toward you. Nobody could see a thing for some reason. I did what I thought was right. I intercepted his blow." She withheld the mind mumbo-jumbo she'd shared with her father and the knowledge of the glamour.

"And I ran my sword through him." Ares sneered.

"Lies." Poseidon hissed. He pointed to Carissa. "She killed him."

Ares took a step toward his uncle. "My daughter does not lie."

Zeus raised his hand to quiet any further outbursts from either of them. It surprised her that they complied without a word. "Now, granddaughter, allow me to see into your mind for the truth."

Carissa bit her lip and studied her father. He nodded for her to allow the invasion.

"Okay."

"Step forward."

Her feet moved toward Zeus.

Zeus touched her head with his fingertips.

Pinpricks stabbed under Zeus' touch. Then everything rewound. The whole encounter flashed before her eyes in a big cinema replay. When it finished, Zeus severed the connection, and her knees buckled. Strong arms held her up. "Now is not the time to get light-headed, *kori mou*."

"She wasn't lying…" Zeus spoke to the room. "…someone placed a glamour over all of us. Fortunately for me, Carissa's mortal half did not succumb to the spell."

"What broke the spell?" Hera asked.

"I'm not sure." She lied but knew Zeus could see right through.

Carissa's fingertips tingled where she held the sword. She knew exactly what broke the spell, but since the sword had been given to her by Xen, she'd keep that tiny bit of information to herself.

"Does it matter? Shouldn't we be trying to find out who cast that glamour?" Her gut told her that the responsible party loitered in the room, but with the multitude of gods and goddesses, it would be impossible to interrogate each one herself. "It's likely to take some time."

"She's right," Ares spoke.

"It is no small feat to examine each god," Zeus said.

"Why not? You could do the head replay thingy." Carissa waved her arm.

Ares turned to her, "Kori mou, *not for every single person in this room.*" The words filtered to her mind. She gaped at him and tried to focus.

"But…he's Zeus."

"Yes. Understand this. Power is not unlimited."

"You mean it can fizzle out."

"Precisely." He watched as she processed. *"It would come at a high cost for him to do that with every person in this room."*

She raised an eyebrow. "Then we investigate the old-fashioned way."

Ares pulled her into a hug.

"Seal the doors until everyone's name has been recorded," Zeus yelled.

The doors to the room slammed shut.

A scribe appeared with a wax tablet.

"You know there is such a thing as technology, Father."

"Have you ever tried to get reception up here? It's a nightmare."

From the depths of her belly, a loud laugh broke from her lips. "Guess human progress is a plus for us mere mortals."

"Oh, you have no idea, *kori mou,* and you are no mere mortal."

She rolled her eyes, then turned and watched Zeus, Hera, Poseidon, and a few other gods sit in deep deliberation. The hand movements were very animated. Poseidon did not look pleased with anything Zeus and Hera were saying. His face had turned a dark shade of red, and he stabbed at Zeus' chest.

"What do you think they are arguing about?" Carissa asked her father.

"Probably who has more to gain if they wipe out Zeus. There's no shortage of jealousy and envy here on Olympus, and this room is buzzing with it."

"Well, I can assure you it's not my doing." A deep male voice startled Carissa out of her whispered conversation she was having with her father.

"Phthonos," Ares said in greeting. "This time I have to agree that this is not yours nor Nemesis' doing."

"Did someone call?" Nemesis stood next to Carissa.

"Phthonos, Nemesis, meet my daughter Carissa." They kissed her on each cheek.

"So if you two can't take any glory for Ephialtes attack, who do you think is behind this?"

"It's not wise to talk here," Nemesis said in a low voice.

Ares nodded to both of them in understanding. "Perhaps a drink?"

"An excellent idea," Phthonos agreed.

Nemesis acknowledged Carissa and Ares. "Later then."

Carissa turned to her father. "Why do I get the feeling there's something else going on here."

"Because there is."

"ARES." Poseidon yelled. "You will pay for slaying my children." He dematerialized from the room, and a shower of water rained in the room.

Her father rolled his eyes. "Theatrics."

A scream split the air. "She's dead, she's dead."

The room erupted in loud conversation and panic.

Ares pulled Carissa behind him. "Follow me."

"Why? What's happening?" She tried to peer around him and see where he was headed.

"I think it is time we made our leave." He answered directly to her mind.

"But that will make us look suspicious. Poseidon already hates us."

Ares turned around.

She crashed into his chest.

His arms shot out to steady her. "Right now, the goddess on the ground is going to be the focus of their attention. Let's take advantage of that."

"Shouldn't we check the body?"

"You have a point, but know this, gods are meticulous when it comes to covering their tracks. Whoever did this also set Ephialtes on Zeus. Let's take a look."

He took her by the hand and led her through the tightly packed crowd that were screaming accusations against each other.

"Gee, it is getting nasty in here."

"This is mild. You don't want to see them when they start throwing their power around."

"But what if they kill each other?"

"Ah…quick lesson 101 on the gods. The Olympian gods can't kill each other. The minor gods and spirits are a different matter."

Ares glanced over his shoulder to her. She must have had confusion on her face because he continued his lesson.

"It is never simple where the gods are concerned. Gods can be crippled or dismembered, but they still live. The only way they can truly die is if they are removed from man's memory or if their domain is destroyed. In simple terms, you would have to blow up the planet. We are tied into the very air that we breathe."

"But what about Ephialtes ? Didn't your sword finish him?

"Yes, because he is from a spirit line. Put it this way; it depends where you are along the food chain."

Carissa swallowed hard. This quick lesson would take time to digest, but it didn't rule out that someone might be on a destroy the world mission. "So is the goddess dead or hurt?"

"We will have to see when we move through the crowd."

"Do you need help?"

"No, don't use your power again."

When they cleared the crushing crowd, they stood next to each other and inspected the body on the marble floor. Ares spoke to Carissa, "It's Eurynome, goddess of pastures."

Zeus appeared next to them. "Silence." Thunder followed his words, and the crowd quieted.

Carissa took in the goddess' appearance and set to work. The first thing she did was look for a wound.

"Father, help me roll her to her side."

Ares complied. Most of the gods who were arguing had finally ceased, thanks to Zeus' command. They watched as she assessed the body.

There were no entry wounds or exit wounds. What did this to the goddess? Based on what her father told her a minute ago, removal of the gods only happened when things went up in smoke. Since there were no visible wounds, she opted for the one thing every officer checks first. A pulse. She placed her fingers on the carotid artery on the goddess' neck. A light pulse throbbed under her fingers. Her eyes widened as she met her father's eyes.

"She's alive, but barely."

The voices sprung up again behind her. Three women were huddled together, crying for their mother.

"Who are they?" She asked her father.

"They are the charities. Daughters to Eurynome."

"It is as if she's in a state of immobility. Is that even possible?" She studied her father and Zeus.

Zeus bent to where Carissa and Ares where. "It is possible, but I don't like what it means."

"The fact she has a pulse should be a bonus, right?"

"Not necessarily," Zeus answered.

Her mind raced to find an answer. "What exactly do you mean?"

Ares put his hands on Eurynome and chanted *kalypto*. When his chant finished, her body disappeared.

"Where did she go?" Carissa asked her father.

"She is hidden and safe for now."

"Will she decompose?"

"No. She is frozen until we can work things out."

"What does this attack mean?"

"It means we have to get everyone out of here, and we have to talk." Ares paused and stared at her for a long second. His jaw tightened, and he ran his fingers through his dark hair. "Seriously talk."

Carissa stared at the space where Eurynome had been laying a second ago. Then cast her eyes upwards to where Zeus was standing over them, and for the first time, she noticed the light surrounding him. "I guess you are the one who can make everyone vamoose." Carissa pulled herself from her crouched position, as did Ares.

Zeus waved his arm. "Out," he said. Every god and goddess disappeared.

Ares raised his hand before Zeus spoke. "*Philaso*." He turned to Carissa. "Protection to stop the walls from listening."

"This does not bode well for mankind," Zeus said to both of them. "Eurynome is the goddess of pasturelands. Her inactivity will cause drought and, in turn, famine. Time is of the essence."

Ares' brows furrowed and his mouth cut to a grim line. "I'm going to need your help here and in the mortal realm."

"But what could I possibly do?" The gods were stubborn. Neither of them was listening to her.

"Have faith in yourself, *kori mou,* and let your godly side guide you."

"Your father is right, granddaughter."

Carissa turned and walked toward where Ephialtes had been slain. "Do you think all of what happened here is tied to someone hell-bent on destroying mankind?"

Her father answered first. "It's a possibility."

"We have a problem," Zeus spoke. "Some minor gods and goddesses are missing."

"Since when?" Ares asked.

"For a few days now."

"Are you sure they aren't busy drinking ambrosia while being pampered?" Ares asked.

"None of them have answered my call."

A rock settled in her stomach. That did not give her confidence at all.

TWELVE

"The most useful piece of learning for the uses of life is to unlearn what is untrue." ~ Antisthenes

Areopagus, Athens, Greece, Mount Olympus
Realm of the gods – Day 1

"I want you to help your father and me solve whatever has been brewing up here on Olympus."

"But, I don't…" She swallowed. How on earth could she help with something that was brewing between gods and goddesses? "…I mean, it's way above my pay grade."

"Wrong, granddaughter. It is precisely up your alley."

Carissa caught her father's eye. "You agree with this?"

"I don't want you anywhere near this. It could be dangerous."

"Zeus, I don't think I can help."

"You do realize that I can sway the vote on your father's trial?"

Ares jumped to his feet. Carissa tugged at his arm to get her father to sit. To her amazement, he did.

"You're bribing me?" A heavy feeling settled in her stomach. "I thought you couldn't decide?"

"I'm Zeus. I make the rules and I can break them. I need you on this case."

"Even if I don't have the power of these gods," she retorted.

"Granddaughter, in case you haven't realized it yet, you have abilities that exceed what half of the gods can do. For that, you are a threat to them."

She didn't think she had anything special, but her father had implied as much.

"What about you? Am I a threat to you?"

"Hardly. You are everything we fancy in a hero."

She scoffed at his mention of a hero. There was nothing remotely heroic in her bones. She did what she had been paid to do and what she chose to be, a police officer. Until she had received a tip and stepped into Jostler's warehouse, where things had turned pear-shaped. She had been cast into Xen's world. Her world now. "I think you have that wrong."

"How do you propose for Carissa to work on this?" Ares asked.

"The same way she would any other human case. Talk to the other gods and goddesses and see if you can get to the bottom of it."

"What if they are not willing to talk to me? You saw the disdain some of them held for me, for daring to come to Olympus."

"It is not their choice but mine. They will co-operate. That is why you will be working with your father."

"Why not let Father solve this?"

"Because we gods are susceptible to things that you are not. Take, for example, exactly what happened in the trial room. You were the only one who could see Ephialtes. Had you not been there, he would have hit his mark. Although it would not have killed me, it would have given someone enough time to rock the foundations of Olympus." He paused. "That is one incident. There's no knowing what I might be up against." Zeus stood. "It is why you have your father. It is why you hold in your possession the sword of Peleus.

"What?" She gulped. "What do you mean?"

"The sword you used to stop Ephialtes is the sword of Peleus. I'd know it anywhere because I had it fashioned as a wedding gift for Achilles' father. It brings the wielder victory."

Ares turned to her. "You knew this?"

"No. Xen gave me the sword." Her mouth opened then closed.

Ares raised an eyebrow. "I must remember not to underestimate that vampire."

Carissa pulled the sword from the sheath and held it in her hands, and for the first time, she saw it. Really saw it. The longer she stared, the more drawn she became to it. In her head, she heard words. Words that sent a shiver up her spine. *We are one.*

She blinked at Zeus. "It appears you are now the rightful owner." A smile spread across his face.

Her mouth did the fish thing again. Finally, some words formed, and she spat them out. "This can't be right. It must be a coincidence the sword thinks it's connected to me."

"*Kori mou*, there is no such thing as coincidence where the gods are concerned. You are either chosen, or it is fate."

She turned to Zeus. "Is this part of your plan?"

"Even I could not have planned that better, but no."

"Okay, so if you want me to help, then I want something in return."

"Name it," Zeus said.

"You have to hear my side of the story regarding Father's innocence and talk to your brother Poseidon because in his eyes, my father is already guilty, and so am I. His crazy-assed demigod son hurt me. It is Poseidon who should be facing a trial for his neglect."

"Granddaughter, I am sorry for the pain Hal caused you, and had I been alerted to what was happening." He paused and focused on Ares. "I might have intervened."

"Funny that," Ares said. "You go on about others meddling and yet, you would have interjected if it suited you."

Zeus ignored her father's words.

"I can't undo what was done, nor can you, but you could make sure that it doesn't happen again. Poseidon will be held accountable for his sons' crimes; both Hal's and Ephialtes'. You have my word. I had been talking to Hera about renewing a program where regular checks on demigods are made."

"Wait, if you had a program in place, what happened?"

"Everyone got too relaxed, and Hera spotted the flaw."

"What flaw?" She asked.

"Time moves differently here and in the mortal realm. It is easy to miss something when we have messengers moving back and forth."

"I think you should invest in technology. That way, you aren't leaving anyone vulnerable while your intel reports in."

"I'll have that put forward to Hera for the new program."

Light appeared in the room.

"Did someone call?" Hera stood in the center of the room.

"I'm filling in our granddaughter on the tracking of the demigods program."

Hera walked over to Carissa and pulled her into a hug. "We will ensure this doesn't occur again," Hera whispered close to Carissa's ear.

Deep in her soul's core, that's all she wanted to hear. That no other demigod would suffer at the hands of another demigod without the Olympians knowing what was going on. Hal thought that if he sacrificed Carissa, he would gain her power and reach Olympus, but that would never have been possible. He was deranged, and someone had influenced him to act on his madness. For millennia, the gods had abandoned their half-human offspring and left them to their own devices. Some turned out to be bad apples, causing pain and trouble for humanity, with no oversight. That had to stop. "Thank you, Grandmother."

Hera released her from the embrace. "I know all the textbooks say that we are heartless and terrible gods, but the truth is, many of us care about our children. You must understand that it is no easy task to watch everything, and there are boundaries that must be supervised. If every god or goddess came and went as they pleased as they did in the past, then your mortal realm would be nothing but chaos."

"What keeps them from doing that, other than Zeus' word?"

"Your world is spelled, granddaughter. The minute someone enters your realm, I am alerted."

"Father, the all-knowing, all-seeing eye," Ares said.

Zeus grinned.

Carissa let out a breath. "Okay. I'm good with that."

"But there is something else." Zeus took stock of both Carissa and her father.

"And?" Ares queried.

"I suspect that someone is kidnapping minor gods and goddesses."

"Then why did you not alert me sooner?" Ares went on alert.

"I thought we could take care of this with your mother."

Her father's face had darkened.

Hera walked over to where Zeus was standing. "Now, what can I do to help?"

"Not much, Mother," Ares said.

"We must have Carissa work with us." Zeus's voice boomed in the room.

Hera clapped. "Wonderful." Then winked at Carissa.

Did she miss something during the conversation? A wink usually cued the other person about inside information. Particularly in the current conversation. Then it hit her, her grandmother or Hera wanted her to work this case. *Now you understand, granddaughter.* The words filtered in her mind.

She didn't know whether she should be pleased or worried. Xen's words echoed in her head. Trust no one. She could deal with her mortal Yiayia's intervention because it resembled the ordinary kookiness of a family, but this grandmother she'd have to watch with an eagle eye. What in the gods' realm had she gotten herself into?

THIRTEEN

"You bet your baklava, I'm Greek." ~ Unknown

Assisted living, Grey Oak Manor; Spartanburg, SC
Morning, mortal realm – Day 5

When Kane and Adam walked through the Aged Care Reception area, Carissa's *yiayia* stood with her walking stick raised at the counter, and Aunt Paula was trying to climb over it.

Kane shot Adam a look, and they both broke into a quick jog toward the mayhem.

"You *booboona*," Aunt Paula yelled at the fellow.

Adam pulled Paula to the side and stepped between Paula and the counter. He raised his arms in surrender.

Kane pulled the walking stick out of Yiayia's grasp. "Do one of you lovely ladies care to explain why the staff are under attack?"

"They stole my baklava." Yiayia pointed an accusing finger.

"Baklava?" Kane's eyebrow shot up, and his lips curved up in amusement.

Yiayia made for a grab for her walking stick.

Kane lifted it above his head, while Yiayia jumped up to try to get it. He put his other hand on her shoulder to halt her attempts.

"Excuse us," he said to the nurse behind the reception desk and pulled Yiayia out of earshot. Adam did the same with Aunt Paula.

"Now, what's with the baklava?" Kane relaxed his stance and gave Yiayia her walking stick.

Yiayia gave Kane and Adam a brief once-over. "You working with the vampire?"

"Yes, we are," Adam answered.

"They do, Vetta. I've seen them before." Paula gave an appreciative look at the men.

"Okay, then I'll tell you, but you have to help me get it back. I hid something in it."

"Well, that's pretty ingenious," Adam spoke.

"I thought so too." Paula pipped in.

Kane's frustration was rising. "What exactly did you hide in it?" Kane asked.

"A key." Yiayia had a smug look on her face.

"Hate to rain on your party of master plots and ideas, but that was not a good move," Kane said. "You don't use dessert as storage."

"These places are full of spies and double agents," Paula said. "Dessert is a good place to hide stuff for a little while. Especially if they're watching you."

Kane cast his gaze up to the ceiling and rolled his eyes. This had all the makings of a long day. "What's so important about the key?"

Yiayia squared herself off with Kane and leveled a glowering look that meant business. "That key is important." She paused and righted her balance with her walking stick. "It opens my post office box."

Kane took a deep breath before asking, "What's in the box?"

"Catalogues and mail," Yiayia answered.

"Shoot me now," Kane muttered under his breath.

"What? What did you say about shooting? Is someone shooting? Quick, Paula, take cover."

Kane watched the circus unfold before his eyes.

Yiayia grabbed Paula and pulled her near the coffee table. "Take cover, boys."

"NO. ONE. IS. SHOOTING." Kane growled.

Adam observed Kane with a wide smile. "Why don't you go find the missing baklava, and I'll assist the ladies."

Kane turned in the direction of the reception desk. "Good luck with that." Kane rolled his eyes. "Xen might owe me." He'd gladly go all alpha on the douche who took the baklava and the post office box key. What on earth would he find in the mailbox? Junk mail and bills. Maybe he'd slap the guy over the head.

He prowled to the desk. "Can you tell me who might have taken Yiayia Vetta's tray of baklava? And I believe there is paperwork for Yiayia to sign as she's leaving."

"We have no idea. She came over complaining that we took her pastry, and there are spies working in here." The woman raised her index finger did a few circles to indicate that Yiayia was loopy. "Truth be told, I saw no tray of baklava."

"Mind if I do a once-over in her room?" He had reached out with his wolf senses, and he did not pick up any honey scents from behind the reception desk.

"Not at all. I can walk you over there."

Kane followed the nurse to Yiayia's room. When she opened the door, it took a second for him to realize that there'd be no baklava currently in the room. The scent of rose hung heavy in the air. He walked in and scanned the room; the material possessions had been cleared out. He reviewed one more time from the door's threshold, and that's when he saw a little flicker of something embedded into the carpet in the far corner. He strode toward the object. Crouching he picked up a small silver ball. Someone had bugged Yiayia's room. Rolling it between his thumb and index finger, he applied a little pressure. Enough to disarm the device. He walked to the door and let the nurse lock up. "Thank you." He paused. "If you don't mind, I'll get Yiayia to sign that paperwork so we can get out of your hair."

The glide of the pen on the papers gave Kane a sense of relief. Now to deal with the two women and their hair-brained idea of baklava thieves but they were right about the spies in the facility. Someone was listening in. Maybe there was more to the key and the post office box. He let out a deep breath. Getting them to the car would be a feat in itself.

"Okay, ladies and Adam. Let's move."

"But what about my baklava?" Yiayia asked.

"Well, there is no baklava here, and I wouldn't be surprised if someone ate the key along with it." He pushed them toward the car.

Yiayia and Paula got out of the big SUV and entered a huge mansion.

"Wow. Look at this place." Paula said, walking into the foyer and looking up with a small spin.

"Stop that, you're making me dizzy." Yiayia tapped Paula with the stick.

Adam walked in behind them. "Ladies, walk this way."

He led them to a lounge off the foyer.

"Have a seat. We don't want any trouble from y'all. I'll be back in a minute." He winked at them.

Yiayia pulled Paula's sleeve. She had a stupid smile on her face when the young wolf walked out. She tugged again when they were alone. "We have to get the baklava back, and I think I know where to look." Yiayia dusted the lint off Paula's jacket. "That color collects all the dust."

Paula pushed her hands away. "Stop that."

"Stop what?"

"That dusting of my jacket."

"Stay on track, Paula. We must find the baklava."

"You started it with all the dusting. Besides why didn't you do something at the Oak Manor?" Paula asked.

"I couldn't risk it."

"Risk what?"

"The book."

"What book?"

"THE book."

"Okay, you're officially losing your mind. I knew it would happen. I just didn't think it was happening this fast. I should make an appointment with the doctor." Paula fished out her phone from her brown handbag.

"Paula, you're not listening to me….we have to find the baklava."

"Baklava, book? Which is it?"

"Both."

"Okay. Now I'm really confused. Why don't you start at the beginning?"

Yiayia watched Paula cross her arms over her chest "A long, long time ago."

"Really?"

"What?" Yiayia secretly liked that line. The best stories started like that, but she wasn't going to explain that to Paula.

"You're going to start with 'a long, long time ago'? Should I take out my myth book for cross-referencing." Paula rolled her eyes.

Yiayia pointed a finger to Paula. "The myths are true, don't joke."

"Okay…just get on with it."

"The baklava has the key in it."

"Yes, and you said it's for your post office box."

Yiayia took a big swallow of air before continuing. "It is, but what's inside is what is worrying me."

"What haven't you told me?"

"There's a clue."

"Where? In the box?" Paula asked.

"Yes. We have to get to it first."

"Well, then why not go to the post office and ask them for the second key?"

"Well, that's where the problem lies. There is no second key." Yiayia Vetta shook her head to dislodge the distant memory of asking Glenice at the post office to loan her the second key because she couldn't find the duplicate key that was given to her husband.

She had searched the house from top to bottom but could not locate the key. He had stressed to her that it was imperative that she keep it safe and that the contents of the post office box led to a series of clues which lead to a book. She had to find that tray of baklava and soon. "We have to do a little investigating of our own. Away from here.

"Vetta, that's impossible, and you know it."

Yiayia covered Paula's mouth. "Keep your voice down. They've got Jaime Sommers hearing."

Paula grunted, and Yiayia dropped her hand.

"Who the hell is Jaime Sommers?"

Yiayia rolled her eyes. "The. Bionic. Woman."

"Why didn't you say that in the first place?"

"Because everyone knows Jaime," Yiayia said.

"Everyone knows the Bionic Woman. Eh eh eh eh eh." Paula pretended to do a bionic jump.

Yiayia's walking stick landed on Paula's arm. "Stop that."

"You started it with the Bionic Woman mumbo-jumbo."

"Well, how else would you have understood?"

"You could have said that these immortals have super hearing."

Yiayia scoffed. "You're impossible sometimes."

"So why are we even talking in here if they have bionic hearing? We should be in the kitchen cooking for cover." Paula shrugged her shoulders. "You know…"

"Paula, you're a genius in wolf's clothing. Let's cook."

"It's a wolf in sheep's clothing."

Yiayia blinked at Paula. "Eh? Same thing."

The delicate aroma from the kitchen tickled Kane's nose and made his stomach growl. He knew Carissa's *yiayia* and aunt were trouble, but for a split second, he marveled at the idea of having someone cooking traditional Greek food. Their cook plated up fancy dishes that did nothing for him. He shook his head and came to his senses. Why were they cooking?

He eyed his watch. Time to see what they were doing before Xen woke from his rejuvenation sleep.

Kane turned the corner for the kitchen. His eyes nearly hung out of his head. On the kitchen island, there were four large trays of what appeared to be *pastitsio*. A Greek version of lasagna. He knew there wouldn't be a single bite left in a few minutes. His mouth watered. One by one, the men spilled into the kitchen to see what was going on. He cocked a brow in surprise. The men were all salivating like him.

"Well, don't just stand there, *lykos*, come and get some," Yiayia said.

Both Yiayia and Paula were plating up big slabs of *pastchio* and handing them out to the hungry men. Every man devoured the generous helping within seconds. Kane polished his off in a few big bites.

"That's the best one I've ever tasted," Adam shouted over the lull of conversation between all the men.

Their chef Don walking in at that moment.

"Smells good," he commented.

Kane pushed a plate in his direction. "You've got competition, Don, and by the look on the men's faces. I'd say they want more meals like this than that gourmet stuff you call food."

Don huffed at Kane.

Yiayia and Paula had a satisfied look on their faces. Kane could read the mischief in their eyes. They were plotting something, and this whole feed the men *pastitsio* stank of a cover for whatever they were really up to. One thing they neither knew about Kane and his wolf abilities—he could smell trouble a mile away.

He put another forkful of *pastitsio* in his mouth and then pointed the fork in Yiayia's and Paula's direction. "What do you two want?"

Kane saw the whole cooking offering for what it was - a way of buttering them up. The saying, *never trust Greeks bearing gifts*, ran through his mind.

"One of those big black cars," Yiayia said with a smile.

"What for?"

"It was a comfortable ride and safe, and Paula and I want to shop. Knowing my granddaughter, there might not be much in the cupboards."

"Hmmm." He grunted. That excuse for the car did nothing to ease the warning his *lykos* senses were screaming at him. They'd end up in trouble, and he would regret giving them a car. However, he wasn't born yesterday; he would track them just in case.

He pulled the keys from his pocket and placed them on the bench.

"Bring it back in one piece."

FOURTEEN

Love is a cunning weaver of fantasies and fables. ~ Sappho

Ares' palace, Mount Olympus
Early morning, realm of the gods – Day 2

Carissa tossed and turned. The covers were feather-light and warm, but for some reason, they weighed a ton every time she changed position to get the comfort she craved. The trial and subsequent events had left her exhausted, and her mind raced. Raced like a sprinter in ancient Olympia. Raced to the finish line as if their life depended on it.

"Damn." She let out the curse and pulled the covers off. Soft candlelight flickered near her bed. The room that Ares prepared for her did not fall short on opulence and size. It was bigger than an average apartment in New York. She stuffed her feet into a pair of slippers and walked over to the far end of the 'room' as her father called it, to the kitchen. She opened the fridge, which had been stocked with fresh fruits of every kind and the general staples of cheese and milk. She pulled the milk out, found a drinking cup that had her father's name inscribed on it, and poured some. She placed the cup to her lips and took a small swallow of cold milk. *If only it were warm.*

The cup started to heat. Unsure, she put the cup on the kitchen bench. Her father's name was now glowing red. "How strange," she whispered.

Then the glow ebbed to a soft blue before disappearing. She lifted the warm cup and took another drink. Steaming milk hit her throat. She walked toward her bed and drank as she walked. "Guess Olympus does have its perks." She wouldn't mind a kitchen that could conjure warm cups of milk or coffee for that fact.

The milk had gone down fast. She hoped her eyes would give in to some much-needed sleep. Hopefully, tomorrow she'd be able to wrap things up and return to Xen. And that's what had been the crux of what made her toss and turn. She yearned for him. Ached to be in his arms. The more she thought about him, the more her desire to see him grew.

Her head hit the pillow with thoughts of him. She could feel him, smell him, and hear him. He was spooning her.

"*Koukla*, I have missed you." His voice a caress in her ear.

"How are you here?"

"It's your dream, and you've pulled me into it."

"I'm dreaming of you being here?"

He nodded his head, and his fingers worked their way to the juncture of her legs.

"So, we're both here?"

"Yes."

"But it's a dream." She turned her body so she could better see him.

He flashed her that devastating smile of his, the one that had its own zip code. "*Koukla*, you should know that your dream is very real right now." His lips crashed to hers, and everything inside her woke to the heated passion that his kiss burned into her. He made quick work of parting her legs and settling into her juncture. His arousal had her burning for more.

She pulled back from their frenzied kissing. "If this is really happening, then I don't want slow. You know exactly what I want, but before we get to that, I need an update from you and vice versa."

He gave her another scorching kiss, then pulled away to look at her. "Ladies first."

"I insist you go first."

He let out a sigh. "In short, your friend Ligi refused any aid. Adam volunteered to trail her."

She sat up. "Wait, you what? You let Adam stalk Ligi?"

His grin widened.

"Let me guess. You guys placed bets on that silly *lykos*?"

He nodded. Amusement sparkled in his eyes.

"Is he lying in a ditch somewhere?" She knew her friend Ligi didn't like it when men were duplicitous.

"Pretty close. She left him tied to a chair in her apartment."

She let out a laugh. "That's so Ligi. What else? Is my family behaving?"

"Let's say Kane has his paws full." Xen winked.

"Keep them in line, Xen. They are likely to drive everyone mad with their antics."

Xen smiled at her. "I like their antics; it adds flavor while you're gone."

She reached out and cupped his cheek. Neither did well without the other.

"How about you? How is the Ares case going?"

"Not good." She thought about how much to tell him and ask about the sword he had given her but decided that giving him those details would make him fret more. "Zeus has asked me to help him question some gods."

"Why does he need you to do that?"

"He thinks I can help."

"How long will you be gone?"

"A few more days at least."

He raised an eyebrow. "Another week for me here." Disappointment laced his voice.

She didn't like to see him upset. Time to change the topic. "Enough of all that." She leaned in and placed her hands on his chest. "How about you show me how much you miss me."

"Your wish is my command," he said before trailing a hot path of kisses along her neck. With a quick tug, her t-shirt tore in two, and his fiery gaze swept over her breasts.

"You have no idea how much I miss this." He squeezed her breasts before lowering his mouth to her nipple. He sucked and laved and then did the same to the other.

"I want you now," Carissa whispered.

"And I want you on fire." Xen released his fangs and bit down on her right breast. A scream tore from her lips. Her back arched as the pain and pleasure shot through her body, sending a gush of liquid between her thighs.

The rest of her clothes were removed in the same manner. He did as she bid and gave her the ecstasy she hungered for with one smooth thrust. Her eyes rolled back in her head.

"Look at me, *koukla*."

She focused her gaze on his, and the fire within his heightened her passion even more. This. This man she would die for. This man would burn the world for her. He pulled out and thrust into her wet heat. Harder. Faster.

She began to reach the delicious crescendo, her hands roaming over his chest and arms. She climbed the peak of passion just as his lips met hers. He took without hesitation. His tongue dancing with hers. His thick hard length pulled out one final time then plunged deeper, sending her into a blissful pool of ecstasy. Wave after wave of pleasure washed over her.

He slowed his movements, allowing her time to recover. It wasn't long before she could feel herself reaching the stars a second time.

"Not yet. Let's try something different." He pulled out and flipped her on her hands and knees. He slapped her bottom.

"Ouch."

The sting of his palm on her ass felt good.

"Let's see how many more orgasms I can wring out of you." His fingers dug into her hips as his hard length slid into her heat. His grunts amplified around the room. She loved the sound. The angle and depth drove her wild. She pushed her hips into him. He reached around and flicked and slowly rubbed where they were joined; her pleasure burst from inside, consuming her. He pulled out and then slammed in and came with a force. She could feel his throbbing length filling her womb. They both collapsed on the bed. Xen pulled her into the spooning position.

"Wow." Her voice was shaky.

"Wow. Indeed."

"I have to get back to you."

"You do."

She closed her eyes, only for a minute she told herself.

FIFTEEN

"Where rage seeds, repentance reaps." ~ Greek proverb

Ares' palace, Mount Olympus
Morning, realm of the gods – Day 2

Carissa sat across from her father on his opulent lounge. She cradled her hot cup of coffee. She had slept in. "Where do we start?" she asked.

"In the middle, and we work our way out."

"Sounds easier said than done."

"There is nothing easy about this, and I fear what we witnessed in the trial is only the beginning."

"The beginning of what?"

"Chaos. Destruction. Armageddon. Take your pick on which word you'd like to use."

Her father's words brought vivid images through her thoughts. A dark place, with no light and happiness. The life on the planet withering and the people nothing but scavengers. Who would win in such a world? Demons, perhaps, but which god would side with the enemy to give the world over to an infestation of demons? So far, they had little to go on. "Do you suspect anyone from your direct circle?" she asked.

"There is one possibility, but I have to be certain."

"Any of your uncles or aunts?"

"There is not even one chance that my uncles or aunts would even want to replace Zeus. We've danced to this tune many millennia ago. Trust me, Zeus' wrath is not something you want to be around for." Ares shifted. "I think it is time for us to speak to Phthonos and Nemesis." He stood and moved to where she comfortably lounged. "*Kori mou*, give me your hand." Carissa put her cup on the table and did as he asked. He smiled at her and clicked the fingers of his other hand.

Strong arms held Carissa in place when their feet touched dark marble in a noisy outdoor bar. She did a sweep of the outside setting. It reminded her of all the holiday bars in Europe.

"We've been expecting you."

Two chairs opposite Phthonos and Nemesis were vacant. Carissa took a deep breath to steady herself before breaking out of her father's hold to sit. She sat opposite Phthonos. Their eyes met, and his were like a beachgoer finishing a summer read, calm and relaxed in the sunshine.

"Spoken for," he said with a smile.

"She belongs to the vampire Xenocrates," Ares supplied.

Carissa cleared her throat. She wanted to say that she belonged to no man, she was not a possession or chattel, but instinct told her that argument had no place here and now.

Phthonos whistled, and Nemesis gasped. "A powerful union."

Father ignored Nemesis' comment. She'd probe him for answers later.

"What can either of you tell me that might confirm my suspicions or shed light as to who might be responsible for Eurynome's condition."

Phthonos' glance flickered to Nemesis, then returned to her father. "You said you had suspicions. Who?"

Father leaned in to whisper. "Eris."

"Our thoughts exactly." Nemesis said. "And she's already messing with mortals in this."

Carissa's skin started to tingle. "What makes you say that? Why would any goddess want to mingle with mortals if Zeus forbade it? And shouldn't his alarm have gone off?"

"*Kori mou*, it is complicated where Eris and her children, Strife, Forgetfulness, Starvation, Pain, Quarrel, Fighting, Murder, Manslaughter, Lies, Dispute, Lawlessness, Ruin, and Oath are concerned because they were released on mankind a long time ago. With their help, she can deceive anyone."

Carissa tapped a finger across her lips. Her father had pretty much explained the evil that lived in wicked men's hearts. The evil that she chose to fight as a police officer because she had hope. Hope that she could clean the streets up. Hope that each criminal put behind bars would cleanse the neighborhood. "Pandora's Jar," she whispered to her father.

"Yes, *kori mou*."

"But...I don't quite understand."

"When my sister's children escaped the jar."

"WAIT. YOUR. SISTER?"

"Yes."

"You think she's responsible for all of this?" She waved her arm around.

"To a degree."

Carissa mulled over his words. "This is your suspicion? Your sister?"

Ares nodded his head in agreement, and so did Phthonos and Nemesis.

She cocked her head and lifted an eyebrow. "Father, far be it for me to argue. Though if that was your suspicion, then why have you not confronted your sister?"

"Well, there's a slight problem." Ares paused. "No one knows where she is."

Carissa dropped her head into her hands and shook it in disbelief. Gods could sometimes foresee the future, and yet no one knew where to find a goddess. "We need to talk. Away from all this noise." She closed her fingers around her father's. "Do the hocus pocus thing."

"Phthonos, Nemesis. Thank you," she said.

Then they materialized in her father's chambers.

"Carissa. We must be clear on somethings." Her father motioned to the chair.

She took the same spot as before, shucked her feet out of her boots, and placed them on the table.

"*Philaso.*"

She recognized the spell that kept them and their conversation hidden. Ares sat next to her and mirrored her seating arrangement.

"That whole meeting with Phthonos and Nemesis has been deliberate on my part. I communicated to them the way I wanted the conversation to go. I had to get a rumor started, and the best way to do that is in a bar, and by laying blame to my sister, the goddess of discord."

"Wait. You don't suspect her at all?"

"No, as I said, my sister couldn't be prouder of the damage she inflicts on humans day in and day out with the help of her children. To Eris, it is a win/win."

"Won't she be upset that you are spreading rumors?"

"Not at all. I spoke to her…"

Carissa stuck her hand up to halt her father's conversation. He'd said he didn't know where she was.

He dismissed her brief pause. "…and she agreed to help. Even the goddess of discord has her limits on the complete annihilation of mankind. She'd have nothing to pass her time with, and she delights in their torment and pain."

"Great. Humans are puppets for your sister."

"Better my sister than the fate that awaits us all."

"What intel do you have, Father? Don't tell me that you don't. Who do you really suspect is behind whatever is going on up here?"

"I have a hunch that this might go back thousands of years. One thing is for certain; Greek gods don't get over their arguments as quickly as humans do. We like to hold on to things. Our curse, so to speak, is to always seek revenge."

"How far back are you talking, and what does any of this have to do with me?" Questions lined up in her head like a full magazine of bullets. A lot of whys and none the wiser. This had not been what she signed up for. Her mind raced; she had to get to the bottom of this, and the only possible success would be through total immersion. Starting with finding out who Ephialtes had been working with or for.

"I hear you," Ares said from beside her, bringing her out of her musings.

"Stop it."

"Stop projecting so loudly and mask your thoughts. All in all, I agree. How about we start with the questioning those present at the trial."

"I'm all for it, but how about lunch first."

"Your wish is my command. Any requests."

"I'd kill for a burger."

Ares moved his feet off the coffee table, and Carissa did the same. He waved his hand over it, and a burger feast appeared before them. She smiled at her father. "You know one burger would more than do."

"Eat up. You have a long afternoon ahead of you."

She didn't have to be told twice. She went straight for the fries.

"Tell me one thing," she said, moving on to her burger. "If the gods have the gift of immortality and are limitless in what they can do, why do they trouble themselves with the human condition of revenge?" She took a bite and moaned her approval.

"The Greek gods, *kori mou*, are created from humans and vice versa. We are interconnected in ways that are complex but logical. We intermingle with humans, but at the same time detest them for reminding us of our own jealousy, love, pettiness, and possessiveness, etcetera."

"Hmmm. We're going to have this conversation again, aren't we?"

"Yes, we are *kori mou*, yes we are."

The bright white marble room that Ares chose for the interviews had her wishing she'd brought along her sunglasses. Sparse furniture, fold-out chairs, and a marble table sat in the middle of the three by three area. The idea was to make those being interviewed uncomfortable. The minor god that had just dematerialized across from Carissa had had nothing of value to add. There had been no thread of substantial information. She flicked the pages of the notebook in front of her; there remained ten more gods and goddesses to interview. *Maybe Zeus had orchestrated the whole thing?* A stupid thought that she dismissed quickly.

Something smelled off. So far, the pool of gods and goddesses she had interviewed were not all sharp.

They are sharper than you think. Don't trust them. Her father's words filtered into her mind. He stood in the far-right corner, observing her interaction with all her witnesses.

Carissa tapped the desk, waiting for the next interviewee to appear in the seat opposite her. She pored over her list again. Then at her useless cell phone, which had one purpose here—to record all the witness statements. "Até." The goddess materialized before her.

"You called?"

Her blunt tone made Carissa's hackles rise. She sat up straighter. "We did."

Até took a quick look in Ares' direction. "Nothing better to do, god of war?"

Ares flashed before Até. His hands splayed on the table as he leaned over on strong forearms and put his face close to Até. "I missed your delusional escapades. Play nice and answer the questions."

Até's face contorted, and heat crept up her neck and face. "There is no need to get violent."

"Trust me, if I wanted to get violent, you wouldn't be sitting." Ares dismissed her.

"Children," Carissa yelled at both of them.

Ares stood and walked to the back of the room.

Good show on the bad cop routine, Father. Carissa projected to her father. She didn't have to look over her shoulder to know he smiled. She pressed a button on her phone to commence the recording. "Até, you know why you are here. You were present when Ephialtes attacked Zeus and also present when Eurynome was found on the floor in a state of immobility. You were there, and therefore we have to ask you if you saw anything suspicious. The questions I will ask are routine and simple. Answer them to the best of your ability."

Até nodded her head.

"Please speak. Nodding doesn't help my recording." She pointed to her phone.

"Yes. I will answer as best I can."

"Good. Let's start with Ephialtes. Did you know him well?"

Até rubbed her thumb on her dress. "As well as any other god."

The nervousness before Até's answer made the information a lie.

"Who were you next to in the court?"

"I was at the rear. I don't remember. It was crowded and there weren't enough seats."

"At the back?"

"Yes, that's what I said."

"Interesting." Carissa flicked through her notebook. "The goddess Dike says you were at the front."

"Ah…maybe I was at the front. It was all too much to remember." She rubbed her thumb over her dress again.

Carissa faced her father and smiled. His face lit up and resembled someone who had just been served their favorite meal. She turned to Até. "I understand a lot happened and fast, but give me an account of what you saw."

"Well, I remember the case starting and Poseidon going at it with him." She motioned her chin in Ares' direction.

"*Him* has a name," Carissa said.

Até huffed, then clenched her teeth.

"Let's get on track. What else do you remember?"

"Ephialtes running toward Zeus."

"Are you sure you saw him run toward Zeus? "

"Yes, that is what I said."

"That's impossible." Carissa retorted.

Até crossed her arms over her chest. "I know what I saw. I was there."

"What else did you see?"

"Lots of gods and goddesses waiting for the trial to start."

"Did you come in alone?"

"Yes. I did."

"Did you want to vote against my father? Is that the reason you came to the trial?"

"No. I wanted to support him against Zeus and his high table gods."

"So you saw Ephialtes running toward Zeus."

"I said that already."

"Did you scream."

"No. Why would I do that?" Até leaned forward and pointed a finger at Carissa. "I saw you running with your stupid sword."

"I repeat. That. Is. Impossible." Carissa's tone thundered around the room.

"And I repeat that I was there, and I know what I saw."

Silly goddess. She'd given herself away. "Father."

Gold handcuffs appeared on Até's wrists.

"What is the meaning of this?"

Ares appeared next to Carissa. "The meaning is simple. The glamour cast meant no god or goddess in the courtroom could see what Ephialtes was doing. That makes you either an accomplice or an accessory."

Até opened and closed her mouth several times. "That makes her guilty too."

"No, Até. She is a demigod, and therefore the spell did not work on my daughter." Ares leaned on the wall. "You are to be taken to the holding chambers where you will be on house arrest till Zeus decides your punishment.

"No. Not banishment again."

"You should have thought of that before you conspired against Zeus."

Ares waved a hand, and Até disappeared from the room. He held on to Carissa's shoulder. The room shifted, and they appeared in his living room again.

She pressed the button on the phone to stop the recording. She had swiped it off the table in time.

"What about the remaining gods and goddesses on our list? We have to finish questioning them."

"There will be no need to do so now."

"Father, Zeus asked for my help. I can't do this properly if we're going to cut corners. We have to interview the last nine." She ran her fingers through her hair and let out a frustrated breath.

"Okay, *kori mou,* you can interview the remaining suspects tomorrow."

"Oh no, no, no. I have to finish this now. The longer I'm here, the longer the time passes in the mortal realm."

"As you wish."

"Wait, before you zap us out of the room again. Did you suspect Até?"

"I had a hunch."

"Do you think she was acting alone?"

"I have no doubt that she is the tip of the iceberg."

"I have the same feeling, and I don't think I'll find better info from the remaining nine, but it is procedure to question everyone."

"You are right. Let's finish this."

She blinked, and they were back in the interview room. She was starting to like this zapping in and out. It reminded her of Samantha from *Bewitched*.

"It's not zapping," Ares said through gritted teeth.

It's zapping. She said it to herself.

"Pay attention. Your next suspect is about to land in that chair."

Sure enough, he did, and then he toppled over and fell.

Ares rolled his eyes. "This is going to be one long interview."

The god made quick work of righting his seat and self. Carissa tried not to laugh.

"Oh, sorry, that wasn't my fault. I was in the bar having a drink with friends when the barmaid accidentally bumped me, and as a result, I missed the mark you summoned me to."

Something about this god made her smile, and she knew exactly why. He was clumsy like her friend Ligi. Carissa held out her hand. "Hi, I'm Carissa."

"Oh…I know who you are. I'm Koalemos, but you can call me Koal."

He leaned forward and lost his balance and ended up on the floor again. Carissa swallowed her laugh.

"*Kori mou*, if you need me, I'll be at the bar." Her father's voice brought her out of her amusement.

"S…sorry, Ares." Koal croaked from his position on the floor.

"I'm sure my daughter can oversee a court jester." He snapped his fingers and vanished.

Carissa jumped to her feet. "Here, let me help you." She extended her hand to the god at her feet. He took it, and she hoisted him up.

"Thank you. Sorry about your father."

"It's okay. It has been a long day. Why don't we start?" She hit record on her phone and flipped her notebook open.

"Of course, what can I help you with?"

"I want you to try to remember what you saw or heard in the courtroom. FYI, I am recording what you say."

"Oh, right, right." His eyes rolled skyward, and he blew out a breath. "Right, right. I remember the case starting, and then it's as if we all froze. Next thing I know, you're blocking a blow from that no good Ephialtes. Then it gets a little noisy and crazy from there until Eurynome…" He choked on his words. A small tear trailed down his high cheek. "She was a good friend."

The poor thing, he had it bad for the goddess in question. Carissa knew in her heart that the clumsy god before her had nothing to do with Até and those behind the present drama.

"How can I help you find who did this to her?"

Carissa shifted in her chair. To solve this case, she would require help from more than her father. She needed some of these gods on her side. "We already suspect Até, but someone else is working with her. Right now, I don't believe that the witnesses are working with her. Whoever is behind it was not in that room. Ephialtes and Até are pawns for the god or goddess behind this.

"What do you want from me? Just ask, and it's yours."

She tapped her fingers on the table. Questioning Até would not give her the answers she required. The hatred the goddess held for Ares had been carved on her face. What if… "Is there any chance you could play Até to win her trust?"

A grin broke across his face. "Oh, I can do that and rather well too. Everyone thinks because I'm clumsy that I'm stupid, and they often say things around me that they shouldn't."

She stretched out her hand. "Deal."

He took it and shook.

Ares appeared and saw their hands clasped. He waved his toward them. "*Orkos*."

Light and heat surrounded their handshake, then fizzled. Carissa and Koal let go at the same time. "Father, what are you doing?"

"Binding your agreement as an oath, so if Koal decides to betray you, I will know."

"I have no intention of doing any such thing. I want answers, just as much as you do."

"Then the oath binding is nothing to worry about." He raised an eyebrow at Koal.

Koal turned his head toward Carissa. "Let me know if I can help with anything else."

"I will," she said.

He dematerialized.

"Allies, *kori mou*?"

"Yes, Father, and some of the best ones are the ones we least expect."

"Indeed, they are."

"Let's finish the interviews. It's dragged on long enough." She needed to plan the next steps.

Ares took a step closer, and a chair appeared next to her. "Call your next witness."

SIXTEEN

"Life must be lived as play." ~ Plato

Bill's Bakery; Charleston, SC
Early morning, mortal realm – Day 6

The old bakery had been refurbished over the years and now had a cafe attached to it. However, it didn't have high-tech security, which meant that trespassing at the early hour of one in the morning would be a piece of cake for a couple of amateur sleuths in a black SUV. Yiayia had borrowed the dark-tinted monstrosity from Kane. When she dropped the keys in Paula's hands, they both giggled. She had started to like the *lykos*, even though he seemed cranky all the time. The boys had enjoyed the *pastitsio,* and she and Paula had cleaned up and made *kourambedies*, Greek shortbread covered in icing. The clatter in the kitchen that they both made intentionally had given them enough concealment to plot their stakeout.

Fully caffeinated and behind the wheel, Paula scratched her head. "I'm not sure about this."

"What aren't you sure of?" Yiayia rummaged through a bag at her feet. "This is going to go down like good baklava." She gave a pair of gloves to Paula.

"I wish I had a slice right now," Paula said, threading her fingers into the tight leather.

"I'll buy you a tray later," Yiayia promised as she unbuckled her seat belt and prepared to do a little investigating of her own. One way or another, she would find that key. Everything pointed to that rat Basil, owner of the shop. She knew he'd come to Grey Oaks and stolen her baklava.

Xen had been nice enough to give her a Taser gun. "Just in case," he had said. She took it reluctantly since she'd told him they were going to get a few things. She knew the vampire could see through her ruse and let her carry on.

"Let's go, Paula."

"Why am I getting the feeling that I am going to regret this for the rest of my days? We probably should have packed evil eye talismans for protection."

"Relax, Paula. Nothing is going to happen. I've got everything in my bag." She held up the mammoth bag.

"Are you sure you can carry that thing? It looks bigger than you, Vetta."

"Did you know…."

Paula silenced her. "Okay. You can carry it, and I don't want to know about you being able to lift sacks of potatoes on your back or anything else."

They both got out of the car. Yiayia walked around to Paula's side. "We should be able to get through the front door."

"You couldn't be more obvious, could you? Isn't there a back entrance or something?" "Actually, you're right. There's a delivery lane."

"I'm not even going to ask how you know that."

"I know people."

Paula huffed at her. "Let's get this over with."

They walked to the rear lane.

"Maybe we should have parked here for a faster getaway," Paula said.

Yiayia huffed. Based on her knowledge and sources, there shouldn't be a need to make a quick escape because there wasn't a soul around. Her hopes were pinned on finding the key and getting out fast. She knew Basil kept all his precious stuff at the bakery. She pulled a little kit from her bag.

"Skeleton keys. You have skeleton keys?" Paula asked in her supposedly quiet voice, which echoed down the lane.

"Would you shhhh."

Vetta made quick work of opening the door.

"Wonders never cease," Paula remarked as she pushed past Vetta and inside the bakery. The delicate aroma of sugar and spices hung in the kitchen air. "Maybe we can get an extra tray of baklava since we're here."

"No, Paula, no one can know we were here."

"How will they know if a tray is missing?"

"Trust me, that bulldog Basil will know. I've seen the way he stares at the cakes he delivers at the retirement village."

"You know this because Basil stares at the cakes he delivers?" Paula scrunched up her face. "Don't you think that might be because he's hungry by the time he delivers them? You've seen the size of the guy."

"Never underestimate a baker and pastry chef. Cake is sacred."

"This conversation is getting crazy. Let's look for your baklava. Come on. There aren't that many places where it could be."

"Right. I'll check the walk-in fridge, and you check out the front of the shop. Don't mess anything up."

"Vetta, you know there's no way he'd put baklava in the fridge. It would turn to marble."

Vetta pushed Paula forward and put a finger to her lips to shush Paula. She prayed with everything in her being that the key and the baklava were here. If it wasn't, then they had big problems. *If that book ever got into the wrong hands...* A shiver ran along her spine. Maybe she should have told the wolf and the vampire the truth, but the more people who knew about the book, the more who would seek it. She had to find it before it fell into the lap of the wrong people. She'd been too relaxed in thinking no one would ever look into the post office box. Her husband, who they said died of a heart attack fifteen years ago, had left her with a dangerous task, but she had to find the key, get the clue, and then find the book.

She reached the walk-in refrigerator and pulled on the handle. The cool air stung her face. Goosebumps traveled up her arms and legs. She needed to hurry. The shelves were lined with cheesecakes and a variety of creamy concoctions that wouldn't do her cholesterol any favors.

A loud crash followed by a scream had her racing from the kitchen. Paula came running out from the front part of the shop. "We have to leave now."

"You look like you've seen a ghost."

"M… monsters," Paula stuttered.

The crashing continued, yet Vetta got the drift and turned to race out with Paula. A ghastly dark crimson creature appeared before them. Sharp teeth and yellow reptilian eyes glinted from the darkness. Fear pounded into Vetta's heart, sending it into a primitive rush. She pulled at Paula's arm and started to back into the walk-in refrigerator.

A loud snarl left the creature's lips.

Paula let out her own scream. Vetta rummaged through her bag to find the Taser. Another creature joined the one that ebbed closer. The cool air hit Vetta's back. Her fingers desperately searched her bag and closed around a solid item. She pulled it out and dropped her bag.

Paula muttered all manner of crazy things next to her. The most vivid; "We're going to die."

Vetta closed her fingers around the Taser and aimed toward the closest creature. Then she squeezed the trigger.

The beast roared louder.

Paula screamed again. "We're going to die."

Things got bloody. A wolf tore into a creature, and the head of the one that Vetta had Tasered was lopped off by a sword. Blood splattered to the floor and on the cakes. Her fingers automatically released the Taser in her hands. The creature's body hit the floor, and behind him stood Carissa's vampire with his bloody sword. Her brain hadn't decided on whether she should be scared or happy. Paula, however, had melted into a quivering mess.

The wolf turned and went through the kitchen.

Xen stepped over the body.

"What are those?" Vetta asked shaking

"Demons," Xen answered.

"Paula, are you okay?" Xen asked

"D…d…demons."

"I think we should get you both out of here."

Adam appeared at the door. Followed by Kane. "Clear, Xen."

"Were there any outside?" He did not take his gaze from Paula or Vetta.

"None," Adam answered.

"We should get these ladies home."

Kane moved to where Paula had curled into a ball and continued to sob. With easy grace, he picked her up.

Xen moved toward Vetta. "Not on your life, vampire. I'm not a baby. I can walk."

He held out his arm, and Vetta threaded hers through his. She could still feel the trembling in her body. "Where's your walking stick tonight?" he asked.

"I have a good mind to hit you over the head with it," she teased.

Xen faked a gasp.

"How did you know where to find us?"

"All our vehicles have tracking devices in them. Besides that, the late hour that you wanted to shop, and your taking the Taser told me all I needed to know."

"My Carissa has a smart fiancé."

"Adam, take the keys from Paula and drive the vehicle to Carissa's place. Kane and I will meet you there."

Vetta watched as more men scurried to and from the shop. "What will happen with all the damage in there?"

"My team will clean any trace of blood and dispose of the demon bodies. The shop itself will be staged to look like it was broken into."

"I owe you thanks," Vetta said as Xen opened the door of another SUV.

"None needed." He winked.

She climbed in, finding Paula already strapped in. She had a bottle of water and was taking small sips. The wolf sat behind the wheel. Xen jumped in the passenger seat and turned to offer her a bottle of water.

"*Efharisto*." Her thank-you sounded weak to her old ears. She put a hand on Paula's shoulder. "Forgive me, Paula. I had no idea that things like that could exist in a cake shop."

"No more snooping, Vetta. Tell Carissa's fiancé everything."

Vetta took a deep breath.

"Stop stalling, Vetta, tell them."

Yiayia studied Paula and saw fear. She shook. They'd come close to death tonight. "Okay…here goes. Listen up, years ago, my husband told me a story about a book that he had been charged to protect. He had gone to many lengths over time to change its location. Each of these locations and the trail leading to the book was a challenge in itself. There were times he'd come back so battered and bruised that I thought he'd somehow gotten into trouble with a mob. Every time he assured me that his injuries were because of where and how he had hidden the book."

"Pardon me for interrupting you, Yiayia, but did he ever tell you what the book was about?"

"The book is a codex of monumental power."

Xen carefully probed Vetta's and Paula's minds. He had enough information, but it was always best to get it from the source, that way they would not be afraid of him. The trepidation bouncing off both women vibrated in the SUV. As a predator, he would exploit that fear and use it to his advantage. Though these women were Carissa's family and human, and he would never harm an innocent. He expected Paula to go into shock, she was barely holding it together. Yiayia seemed to be doing much better than Paula.

When they reached Carissa's home, the men helped them out of the car.

"Xen." Kane's voice was low. "What are you going to do with them?"

"I think the best course is to sedate Paula, then get more details from Vetta and offer her something to help her sleep. I don't want to compel them if I don't have to. It will mess with their minds."

"Want me to get it organized?"

"Yes."

Yiayia broke in. "You know we can hear you. We might have peed our pants a bit, but we're not deaf."

"This way, ladies," Xen said. Trying to steer them to the front door and away from that argument.

SEVENTEEN

The beginning is half of the whole. ~ Hesiod

Xen's Mansion, Library; Charleston, SC
Evening, mortal realm – Day 7

Xen puzzled over why demons would turn up at one of Vetta's and Paula's ridiculous missions. It could not have been a coincidence. Someone had led them there. But who?

"Why them?" Kane's question echoed his thoughts.

"I don't know. The only plausible explanation is Vetta's and Paula's connection to Carissa and Carissa's connection to me."

"You think someone has sent a message to the underworld that Carissa is yours, and now they are trying to get to you via her family?"

"They tried to do that to Carissa when I met her. I wouldn't dismiss the idea." Xen toyed with the pen on his desk.

"I've asked Adam to scan any street footage. He notified me earlier that there appeared to be a figure in the shadows."

Xen peered over from where he fiddled with random items on his desk. They had been down this path before. Many times over. They'd have a demon skirmish they'd eliminate the problem, and then they popped up again. Somewhere along the line, though, Xen became a direct target, and it appeared that they were determined to get to him through those around him.

"I think we did the right thing by taking Yiayia and Aunt Paula to their own home. I'm surprised they kept it together. I had expected worse."

"You would have had to wipe their minds."

Never Xen's preference, but when humans came face to face with the evil of the night, their brains didn't cope with it too well. "I'm glad it didn't come to that. Carissa would never forgive me if I tried to do to her family what I had tried to do to her in the warehouse when she stepped into our world."

"I remember that well."

"Get Adam to send me that footage. I'd like to have a look at who our new nemesis might be."

Kane lifted his muscled frame from the chair. "Roger that, boss." He made his way out of Xen's library, closing the door with a soft click.

Alone with his thoughts, Xen replayed the events of earlier. If someone had made the codex their mission, then the demon episode at the bakery signified the beginning of many attacks. He had posted men at Carissa's *yiayia's* place in case the occasion called for it.

His computer pinged. Adam had sent the footage.

Xen opened the file and pressed play. A darkly clad figure in a long coat and hat pointed toward the bakery. The demons had been acting under instruction. Oh, how he would pay when Xen caught up with him.

Xen tried to zoom in on the image except he couldn't get a clear view of the man. His fingers flew over the keyboard, punching out a new message to Adam.

Get all the footage from the surrounding streets. There has to be a better picture. I want to know who this man is.

His jaw tightened and his fangs elongated. He had to let off steam. Time to spar with his *Phi Athanatoi.*

EIGHTEEN

Beneath every stone, a scorpion sleeps. ~ Anonymous

Abandoned naval base, Charleston, SC
Evening, mortal realm – Day 8

Xen's desire for vengeance fueled the rage humming through every fiber in his body. His muscles tightened, and the *xiphos* in his right hand sliced through the air severing the demon's head. The body followed the head to the floor. He glanced at the body, which now lay at his feet. *Vlaka.*

They had been notified by their connections within the police force that there had been activity in one part of the abandoned Navy base. It had been idle for twenty-five years, but new businesses, government agencies, and non-profit organizations were finally making use of the space. Except for the hospital district, where Xen stood. Upon their arrival, the *Phi* found five demons feasting on dead humans. Xen eliminated each demon with swift speed. He had ditched the newly developed bullets for his *xiphos.*

"Clean what you can and leave the human bodies." The police would have to be alerted. It would be another unsolved psychotic killer case. Or maybe rival gangs. There were plenty of potential excuses.

He turned to Kane and Adam. "Let's check the rest of the base."

They did a quick sweep. Xen's vampire speed allowed him to cover more ground faster.

"It's clear," Xen reported to Kane and Adam. "Let's get out of here."

The remainder of the team had cleared what was left of the demon bodies. Once they removed all evidence, they piled into their respective SUVs.

Xen sat in silence, always thinking, and always trying to plan two steps ahead. Once at his mansion, he sped out of the car to his library without a word to anyone. His frustration had been building for days. The only contact with his bonded he'd had, had been through a dream. As much as he tried to reach out to Carissa again, that connection appeared to have been one-way. It grated on his nerves that he had no control or vision of what was happening on Olympus.

NINETEEN

"The energy of the mind is the essence of life." Aristotle

Carissa's chambers, Mount Olympus
Evening, realm of the gods – Day 2

After they wrapped the interviews up, Ares materialized them to Carissa's room. She sat listening to her recordings, yet they held nothing further. She pressed pause.

"Any other news from my brother Echion?" she asked her father.

"I'm waiting to hear from him."

"This is frustrating. I feel like we are getting nowhere."

"*Kori mou*, you are not dealing with a human case here."

"I'm aware of that."

Light flashed before them.

Koal dropped on the floor. Carissa rushed forward, checking for signs of injuries. The only visible one, blood on his cheek, looked like a knife slash. She helped him up.

"Thank you." His voice seemed weak.

Light flashed again, and Echion stood before them.

"Father, sister," he said with a bow. He pointed over to Koal. "That fool is lucky that I happened to be walking past Até's holding room. The damn idiot should count his blessing that Até didn't slit his throat." Echion folded his arms across his wide chest.

"It's just a scratch."

"And if I hadn't pulled you out of her room, your guts would be all over the floor now."

Ares silenced them. He snapped his fingers, and a goblet appeared. He gave it to Koal. "Drink."

Koal took the goblet. After two drinks, the cut on his face disappeared.

"Now that could come in handy. Can you give me a bottle?" Carissa asked her father.

Ares raised an eyebrow. "No."

"Well, you can't blame a girl for trying."

Echion let out a laugh. "I like her."

"Enough." Ares roared.

Carissa took the hint. "Koal, why don't you tell us what happened?" She motioned for him to sit. He took the seat nearest her. Her father and Echion decided to stand and practice that menacing look they did so well.

"I thought I'd try to get Até talking and I was doing well until she realized that she'd accidentally divulged too much information." He sighed. "Then she took a small dagger out and pretty much made me the target."

Carissa couldn't help the smile that tugged at her lips. She had been right in taking a chance on Koal. He might come across as not being the brightest, but he knew exactly which buttons to press at the right moment. A valuable ally, but he needed protection.

"You should have warned us that you were going in."

"I knew you were busy with more interviews."

"Still, you need to keep us in the loop," she said.

Ares moved forward and sat in the chair in front of Koal. "What exactly did Até have to say?"

"I made out that I was fed up with Olympus, and that got her to loosen her tongue. She started to rant and rave about how Zeus and Olympus are outdated, and there should be changes. Too long has he held power and that he overlooks the lesser gods as if they serve no purpose. Someone had to do something."

"Which someone?" Ares asked.

"That bit she didn't say, even though I probed her. What she did say is that they'll all rot in the damp labyrinth. Let Zeus feel what we feel."

"A cave…obviously, that's where they're holding the missing gods and goddesses. The question now is, which one?" Ares said.

"No easy feat, considering there are over ten thousand caves," Echion said.

"Ten thousand on the godly plane or mortal realm? What exactly are we talking about?" Carissa asked.

"*Kori mou*, there are no caves where the gods dwell."

"Roger that, so the mortal realm for caves." So far, the godly realm appeared enormous and so vast that she had no idea what she was dealing with here. It wasn't like you could get in a car and go for a drive. They all popped in and out to their locations. It really did resemble an episode of *Bewitched* with all the zapping in and out.

"We don't zap." Ares chided her.

"Okay, you materialize." *Same thing.* "And stop reading my mind."

"You're projecting again."

She concentrated. *Philaso*. Her mind sent up concrete walls. No one would be reading her thoughts now.

"You're learning, *kori mou*."

"What do we do now?" Koal asked, interrupting the banter between Carissa and her father.

"I have another question, Koal." Something about Zeus tugged at her insides. "Do you think Zeus might be the next target?"

"I don't think anyone is stupid enough to do that after the last attempt in the courtroom. I mean, you wouldn't want to piss off the big kahuna." Koal gaped.

Echion decided to join the discussion. "It would be foolish."

Carissa digested the information before her. Até would not give information freely. Protocol dictated that they should speak to her, but goddesses behaved differently because they had power. This negotiation wasn't a run-of-the-mill human procedure. The fact that Até had a weapon and had injured Koal meant that she would do the same to Carissa if she caught her. "Father, why did Até have a weapon if she is under watch?"

"Até causes delusions and possibly obtained the weapon from one of the guards while being confined to the room."

"We must speak to her again. I know it's pointless and dangerous, but it must be done," Carissa said.

"I agree but you will not see her on your own."

"I had no intention of seeing her on my own."

"Good, then you and Echion will interview her. I want to have a word with Koal."

When she glanced at her brother, he stood ready, his hand outstretched to her. She got to her feet and placed her fingers around Echion's.

Her eyes flashed over to Koal, he had his thumb in his mouth, and his body shook.

"Father, be gentle."

He smiled. "Always."

She hadn't heard his reply because they materialized in front of Até's holding room. Hers wasn't the only one in the long corridor. There were two guards stationed at the door. *Olympus' jail,* she thought.

"Remove the spell so that we may enter," Echion said to the guard on the right. He nodded his head and did what had been asked.

They entered the room to find Até lying on a single bed at the far end. Again, everything about this room screamed spartan - bed, table, chairs. The goddess didn't shift her gaze from the ceiling when they entered. Only when the door slid shut did she turn her head to look, then return to her previous position.

"We'd like to ask you a few questions," Carissa said.

"I have nothing to answer."

Echion walked over to the bed. "You will rise and assist in our line of questioning."

"I'll get up when I feel like it."

"Rise, or I will resort to painful methods."

The goddess got up and swung her feet to the floor. "There, happy now?"

Echion said nothing more to Até but raised himself to his full height and folded his arms neatly across his wide chest.

Carissa moved to the chair and table and sat. Took out her notebook and phone to record the conversation.

"I would prefer it if you could sit near me." She motioned to the chair. To her surprise, Até moved to sit across from her.

"I'm not going to try to trick you into naming who you are working with. I'd rather I ask, and you tell me."

Até let out a laugh. "My business is not yours, and you should not concern yourself."

"Actually, you are quite wrong. It does concern me, especially if you are using my realm to hold hostages."

"And who do you think built your realm? Who do you think gave you pathetic humans the realm you have?"

Anger flashed through Carissa's body, but she held it together. She did not require a lesson on creation. She wanted answers. "I'm fully aware that the gods created everything around us, but that's not what I asked. I asked you, who are you working with?"

"No one."

"Answer the question, Até , or I will use force," Echion said from where he stood behind the goddess.

"Why don't you get me some ambrosia? Then I'll answer any question you want."

"You will answer the question, and then, when I think you've given us a satisfactory answer, I will consider giving you ambrosia."

She dropped to her knees. "Please, Echion, give me some ambrosia first, and I'll give you the answers that you seek." She crawled slowly toward him. Then seized him around the legs. "I'm hungry."

"Let go, Até."

"I have to have ambrosia. I've been stuck in here, and no one has bothered to ask me if I might need something."

"You do realize that you are under house arrest? This isn't a party." Carissa said.

Até hissed at Carissa. The hair on her neck stood to attention. Até was up to something, and it had nothing to do with helping them by offering up any names. No. Her over the top behavior spelled diversion.

"Give us the name, Até, and we will give you the ambrosia and maybe some to take with you," Carissa said.

She had hit the mark because Até released Echion's legs and made her way back to the chair.

"Why don't you start at the beginning?" Carissa asked her.

"In the beginning, there was darkness." She said sarcastically.

Echion walked up to Até and pulled her to her feet. "Enough with the foolish and childish behavior." He dropped her in her seat then moved around the table. "What other gods are working with you?"

"Go to hell, Echion," Até said and moved to the far end of the room.

The room started to vibrate and shake. A portal opened up near Até and in seconds, she stepped through.

Echion raced forward only to be met by two demons stepping out of the portal before it vanished. Echion drew his sword. They had a tiny problem. She hadn't taken her sword. *Stupid move, Carissa.* "Father," she called. She hoped the spell placed on the room would not slow him down. Echion fought the demon closest while the other stepped around and made its way to Carissa. The demon did not reach its destination. Her father appeared with his sword drawn, shielding her from danger. The demon's head dropped to the hard marble floor.

She peeked in Echion's direction. His sword swooshed through the air and hit its target. The head joined the other on the ground.

"Well, that brings new meaning to heads will roll," she said, stepping from behind her father.

"*Kori mou*, now is not the time for bad jokes."

She bit the inside of her cheek. "Sorry, it's a reflcx."

The doors to the room were thrown open, and soldiers filled the room. The men were all dressed like Echion.

"I want this mess cleaned up. Then I want you, Echion, to find Hekate. Someone is using her portals on Olympus. I. WANT. ANSWERS." When Ares unleashed his anger, everyone cowed at his booming voice.

"I will get the information you are looking for." Echion dropped his head and dematerialized.

When Ares had finished issuing a ton of orders to different men, and the room emptied, he turned to Carissa.

"Are you okay, *kori mou*?"

"Never better. Thank you for getting here on time."

He winked.

"I guess Até's actions have given us the answer of who she is working with - demons."

"Yes, but behind the demons, there will surely be someone else."

"I guess this has more to do with my territory than I first thought."

"I may have to send you back sooner than I had planned," he said.

Music to her ears. The problem on Olympus was becoming bigger than the classical Clash of the Titans. She wasn't going to lie to herself, she'd rather be on her own territory surrounded by her own brand of madness. She wanted time to process everything. One thing she had to take into consideration was time. Maybe someone in the mortal realm was using the time difference to plan and string out their purpose.

Até disappearing just now meant that she would have a few days on her side in the mortal realm by the time her father zapped her to Xen. And having the demons show up here on Olympus confirmed Koal's information of a cave. She yearned to be home. Her father was right; he had to return her soon.

She titled her head to her father. "I guess we can get out of here now. Since we no longer have our prime suspect."

Ares took her hand, and they dematerialized.

TWENTY

"Open your mouth and shut your eyes and see what Zeus will send you." ~ Aristophanes

Ares' office, Mount Olympus
Early morning, realm of the gods – Day 3

Carissa stood near her father and peeked over his shoulder at the map he'd been staring at for a good ten minutes. "Give me a map." She stifled a yawn and poured another cup of black coffee.

"Here." He passed her a few rolled-up maps. But when her hand touched her father's, a shared knowing sprang to her mind - someone would appear in the room any second.

"Good. Tap into your power. You'll be better prepared if you learn to recognize an intrusion before it appears."

Bright light engulfed the room. She squinted to stop the glare.

Hera stood in Ares' room.

"Mother," Ares greeted.

"We have a problem, son." She appeared ashen.

Ares dropped the map he had been scouring for cave locations. "What's the problem?"

"Your father has been taken."

"From where?"

"His office."

Ares grabbed Carissa's hand. She didn't have to read minds to know exactly where they would materialize - Zeus' chambers. They appeared first, followed by Hera.

Ares broke contact and moved toward the blood that had been used to inscribe a message. "The mouth of the giant is wide."

Carissa moved closer and watched as her father put his finger to the blood and tasted it.

"It's Father's," Ares said.

"Why the bloody message?" Carissa asked her father. "And why leave this now? It makes no sense."

"They are toying with us, *kori mou*. It's a game. It's always a game with the gods."

"A sick way of saying you can't catch me," Carissa said.

"There's that too."

"Honestly, I'm starting to think that the *Diagnostic and Statistical Manual of Mental Disorders* is based on all the actions of gods."

"You wouldn't be wrong," he replied.

She swallowed. What kind of crazy was this? She'd have to pull out her old psychology textbooks.

Ares repeated the phrase under his breath. "It's a description of the cave..." He let out a breath. "...and most caves have a wide mouth. This doesn't make singling out the cave any easier."

"What do you suggest?"

"It's a goose chase. They want to keep us distracted. I have to send you to Charleston. You will use Xen and his men to find the cave. The faster we narrow it down, the better. I hate to sound cliché, *kori mou*, but there's a storm coming, and it will be nothing like anything you've ever seen before."

"What can I do to help?" Hera said from behind them.

"I'll need you here, Olympus has to be protected and you, Mother, must ensure you can cast enough spells to keep anyone or anything from entering or leaving. With Zeus gone, his law about gods intermingling with humans won't stand. You must ensure that this place is impenetrable."

"And what of you?"

"I'm going to visit Uncle Hades. I think some of the answers we seek might become more transparent once I know what is going on in his domain, and I have reason to believe that he might require help. You might want to alert Uncle Poseidon. You'll require his power too."

Hera walked over to Carissa and pulled her in for a quick hug. "Be careful, granddaughter." Then she popped out of Zeus' office.

"I'm ready for you to zap me home."

Ares smiled. "Okay, I'll let you have the zap reference this once, but remember it's not zapping."

She got a kick out of him trying to correct her each time, and she knew he didn't really mind what she called it. The evidence showed in the humor that lined his lips.

"Let's get you to your chambers." He put his hand on her shoulder.

She was starting to like this quick mode of travel. "You think I'll ever be able to do this?"

"No, *kori mou*. Only the gods and goddesses can materialize. Consider yourself lucky for not having this power. You'd be a bigger threat to them."

She thought about his words, and in all truth, she did not want multiple targets on her back.

"Collect your things. I'll return in five minutes. There's something I must take care of first."

The silence of her room encased her. She sat alone with her thoughts. She welcomed them. The most pressing issue now was to find the cave and Zeus. Time was against them. They would demand all the help they could get. Somebody had a grudge and a big one at that. She would have to do her research. Yeah, sure she knew the basic mythical stories, but she had no idea who would have enough of a grudge to want the destruction of the gods and of earth. One thing stood clear; whoever pulled the strings in this caper was no ninny.

First things first, they'd had to find the location of the cave. Then they would plan from there. This had not been what Carissa had expected when she'd stepped foot on Olympus. Yes, some resistance because of the trial and her wanting protection and acknowledgment of demigods, but not this.

She moved around her chambers with her thoughts racing at a hundred miles per hour. In minutes she had everything thrown in her bag, and her sword sheathed and strapped. The only thing that remained was her father's presence.

A familiar recognition danced on her skin; someone would be appearing in the room any second now. No doubt her father.

A breeze whipped around the room, and before her stood Athena. Something stuck in Carissa's throat. It took her a moment to find her voice. "Goddess, what do I owe the pleasure to?" She gave a small bow.

"Niece, there is no reason to bow to me."

Carissa straightened her spine.

"My brother has filled me in, and we have been working together. I understand that you realize the urgency we now face."

"I do."

"When my mother and uncle spell Olympus, I will be with Ares and his men and my warriors. If you need me, I want you to know that you can call me."

"But…"

"Your secret is safe with me. The other gods won't like to know that a demigod can reach them or possibly compel them. I also know that you don't have full control of your powers. I will help you when all of this is over."

Carissa took stock of what the goddess said, but her mind could not comprehend the offer. "Why? Why would you help me?"

"The *Phi* don't belong solely to Ares. They are also mine to command if I ever see fit. When your father saved Xenocrates, it was at my request that he do so. Man has always desired help from the gods, even if Zeus forbade us to intervene. Without us, there is no you. Do you follow?"

"I'm keeping up, but will have to mull it over."

"Good. There is more, but we have not the time now. Remember, I'm on your side."

The goddess stepped closer to Carissa and placed a small round disk on a chain around her neck. "To activate it, you say, *phaino.*"

"What is it?"

"It's a shield as strong and protective as my father's aegis. It will defend you when you have need."

"Thank you, Athena." She held her aunt's hands in hers. Familiar power danced between the two of them. "*Egeiro,*" Athena said.

"Now, your power is awake, and you will know and recognize the different signatures of each visitor." She winked.

"Before I thought you were Father."

"Exactly, because we are both children of Zeus."

It makes sense now. "I had a feeling when we were interviewing Até, but that power resembled dread. I hadn't expected a portal to open in the room."

"Trust your instincts; they serve you well." The goddess stepped back. "Niece." She made a slight nod and dematerialized.

One goddess gone and another god on the way. The power recognition hit her harder this time. She swayed as it began in the pit of her stomach and raced through her body. This time she recognized her father.

She straightened her spine, ready to receive him.

"Daughter." Ares said when he appeared.

"Ready when you are, Father."

He did not hold on to her. She was thrown into the darkness on her own. She had this. She could do it. *Remember to focus.*

The words danced around in her head. If she stayed focused, she would not feel nausea.

Lightning crackled around her. She landed in a crouch in the middle of Xen's office. The sword strapped to her back pulsed with power. The force with which her father had sent her home proved the gods wielded more power than they showed in the mortal realm.

How easy it would be for any god to use that limitlessness to their advantage.

Familiar scents hit her senses and glad to be home would have been a mild statement. Joy punched her heart at one familiar scent.

Her body thrummed with power. Newly awakened power pulsed through her and became part of her. "*Rigos*." She spoke to mask the power.

She stood, and her gaze locked with a pair of green eyes that belonged to a face that her mind and body could no longer do without - Xen.

TWENTY-ONE

"So immense the clash as the war of gods erupted."
~ Homer, The Iliad

Xen's office; Charleston, SC
Evening, mortal realm - Day 9

"Carissa." Xen's smooth voice skittered across her skin.

Within seconds the vampire had her in his arms. There was no time for words. His mouth crashed to hers. How she had missed him.

"Ahem. Get a room." Adam's voice registered in her mushy brain.

They were not alone. She broke the searing kiss to find she did indeed have an audience. Adam wagged his eyebrows. "Now that's what I call an entrance."

"For once, I have to agree with him. Good to have you back." Kane said from where he sat. He got to his feet as she made her way in his direction.

She hugged Adam then Kane. "Glad to finally be home." It occurred to her that there had been no nausea rolling around in her stomach this time. An effortless trip.

She turned to Xen. "We must talk."

Kane and Adam moved toward the door.

"No. Stay. You both have to hear this too. We need all the *Phi.*"

Xen put his hands on her arms. "Are you sure you don't want to rest first?"

She shook her head. "Talk first, rest later."

"Okay, why don't you start." Xen steered her to a sofa facing Adam and Kane. "Water?" Xen asked.

"Yes."

She took a breath, and Xen sped to his minibar to get her water. By the time she blinked it had appeared in her hands. In one long drink, she emptied half the cool and refreshing liquid.

"When I left here. I left for other reasons…" She turned to look at Xen. Understanding passed between them. "…but when I got to Olympus, more was going on than what we thought."

"How so?" Kane asked.

"Ephialtes tried to kill Zeus during my father's trial. A spell had been cast over all the gods, and my mortal side was immune to it. I acted and sure enough blocked the blow with the sword Xen had given me." She turned to him. "Really, you could have told me it was Peleus' sword." She removed the sword with its sheath and set it on the coffee table in front of her,

The corners of his mouth turned up. "And you, *koukla,* would not have taken it if I had told you."

"He gave you what?" Adam asked.

"Where the hell did you get that?" Kane threw in behind Adam's question.

Xen shrugged a shoulder. "I've been around for a while."

Carissa watched as Kane eyed Xen. "You're not getting off that easy, this is to be continued," Kane said to Xen.

"Noted," Xen said. "Continue, *koukla.*"

"Okay…so I saved Zeus with the help of my father, but it seemed that it had been a smokescreen, or rather there was more than one target for that day. The goddess Eurynome is in a suspended state."

"So, what does that have to do with us?" Adam questioned.

Carissa knew that would be the question because she thought the same. "Without her, the pasturelands will deplete."

"And inevitably that will cause famine and death," Xen finished.

"Now you're following."

Distant thunder sounded.

She shuddered.

"In the midst of all this, minor gods and goddesses have been snatched. Father sent me back when Zeus was taken. Whoever is behind it all made a play for the big guy and got him. It's open season. I have to request the help of the *Phi* to find Zeus and the other gods and goddesses before it is too late."

Xen, Kane and Adam all let out a whistle.

"Exactly." She said with a sigh. "Without Zeus, storms will rage, but rain won't fall, and lightning will set the earth on fire."

"Are there any leads as to who is behind the kidnapping?" Xen asked.

"In Zeus' chambers we found a message written in blood. *The mouth of the giant is wide.*

"A riddle?" Adam said.

"It's a cave," Carissa replied, saving him the trouble of trying to work it out. Ares knew as much before Zeus disappeared. "The message has only confirmed what we had learned from a suspect who had been kept under lock and key."

"If the gods are being taken from Olympus, then it adds up that whoever is doing this is hiding them here, in the mortal realm. Right under our noses and where Zeus has forbidden the gods to play," Xen said.

Carissa reached over and squeezed Xen's hand. "I know why my father thinks that without you and the *Phi,* this is not achievable."

Adam coughed. "I've been trying to tell you all that our brand is all shades of awesome."

Kane growled at him.

Carissa picked up a cushion and sent it flying like a torpedo, straight to Adam's head.

He caught it before it could connect. "Awww, you missed me."

"And you know it." She winked at him then turned her head to Xen, who didn't look too pleased with Adam.

"Relax, vampire, we know she's your woman." The silly wolf teased his boss.

"Okay, guys, let's get on track here. If it's a cave, then where do we start?" Kane said.

"Let's pull out the maps after we've all rested and review what we think the message means," Xen said.

The images of the blood flashed in her memory. Ares had tasted the blood, and it had been the blood of Zeus. If his kidnappers were draining him, then it wouldn't be long before rain ceased to fall, and the earth dried and cracked. On cue, thunder and lightning tore across the sky outside. Another shiver ran through her.

"Then we should hurry, *koukla*."

Xen had been reading her mind. "You know the whole mind-reading is a thing on Olympus. Everyone can do it."

"Really?" he asked with a smile.

"You already knew."

He shrugged his shoulders. "Maybe."

"I'm calling it a night and will pick things up in the a.m." Kane said as he stood.

"It is a.m." Xen retorted.

"It's two a.m., and I need some sleep to function," Kane said. "Glad to have you home, Carissa."

"Glad to be back."

"What he said." Adam pointed at Kane.

"Good to see that some things stay the same." She grinned at Adam.

"Is that an insult?" He questioned her.

"Not at all." She stood.

The silly wolf bowed to her and made his way out of the office with Kane.

Turning to face Xen, she asked, "So how have things been around here?"

"Is that a conversation you want to have now?"

"I figure I might as well get a question in before I lose all ability to think and speak."

A growl escaped Xen. Before she could utter another word, his lips claimed hers, silencing her with a dizzying kiss.

TWENTY-TWO

"Learning is not child's play: we cannot learn without pain."
~ Aristotle

Xen's office; Charleston, SC
Evening, mortal realm - Day 9

"Carissa?" Ligi did not expect to see Carissa standing in Xen's office with a bunch of unearthlies. Neither had she thought that she would be asking the vampire for any favors, especially after their last meeting nine days ago. Hindsight proved she should have taken his help when he offered. She watched as surprise and recognition showed on her friend's face. Then in seconds, they were both hugging and squeezing with a whole bunch of "I missed you" being tossed about.

"What are you doing here?" Carissa asked when she pulled away from the tight embrace she had given Ligi.

"I came to see Xen."

Ligi watched Carissa blow out her cheeks. Her eyebrow raised in question. "I'd like his help." Before she could say anything else, Carissa bombarded her with questions.

"Were you able to locate Kelly? What happened? Do you know where she …"

Ligi put a hand up to Carissa's mouth to stop the litany of questions. "We should have a one on one." There were things she had to say, and she didn't want to say anything with an audience.

Carissa nodded in understanding.

"*Koukla*, we have a few things to go over, so we will give you some space to reconnect with Ligi."

"I'd rather stay and watch." Adam threw in. He had a grin on his face.

A growl escaped Xen's lips. "No."

That silly wolf never gave up, and as much as Ligi thought a quick fling with him would be fun, she was just not that into him. He should have gotten the message when she left him tied up in her apartment. The wolf standing next to Adam gave him a slap upside his head.

"Okay, okay. We'll let the ladies be," Adam said as he followed the other men out of the office.

"So, where do I start?" Ligi said under her breath when she heard the quiet click of the door.

"How about we start with when you last saw Kelly. Did she act weird or troubled?"

"Ha. This is Kelly. She's always acting weird with that family of hers."

"What was the last conversation you had?"

"She said she had the inside scoop for a new story in Romania."

"Well, if she was traveling, then there'd be a booking of a hotel, flights, etc."

"Logically, yes, and I checked it all, but she never made her flight."

"So, she's still here."

"That's what I assumed, but every lead I had is cold. No one in her family has seen or heard from her."

"Have you been to her apartment again in case she's turned up and is wallowing?" Kelly had a bad habit of disappearing to do family stuff, and then when she did resurface, she always wanted a few days to herself. This time it was different because they knew that some guy name Lox had taken her. Still, that did not stop Ligi from having hope that she could outwit him and return home.

"Last week, but I plan to go again. That's the next item on the list."

"Okay. Check that out and let's go from there. Did you want me to come with you?"

"No. I would like you to check another lead. One of her coworkers said they were on the phone with her when the line went dead."

"Give me the details, and I'll follow up. Is that why you are here?"

"Yeah, I was hoping Xen could spare someone. I didn't know you were back from your vacation." Carissa didn't know that Ligi knew the whole story about Hal, the psycho demigod. They had yet to have that discussion. When Carissa gave Ligi Xen's contact number and told her to let Xen help in finding Kelly, she hadn't mentioned Xen was a powerful immortal. Alarm bells had gone off in Ligi's head when she'd walked into his office. She recognized his kind and vice versa. And, of course, there was the fact that everyone knew who Xenocrates Lyson was.

"Listen." Ligi stepped closer to her friend and motioned for her to sit. "Xen told me what happened."

When they were both seated, Carissa met Ligi's eyes. "I know it sounds crazy, but it is true."

Ligi interrupted. "I have a confession of my own to make." She cast her eyes downward and took a deep breath. Xen was right that she had to speak up. She owed it to her friend to divulge the truth about her past. She could taste the bittersweetness already.

"Ligi. There is nothing that you could say that would change things between us. If anything, I should have kept you in the loop no matter how crazy I might have sounded. I think it is I who hasn't been a good friend."

Ligi grabbed Carissa's hands in hers. She wanted to hug her friend for keeping the blame to herself. "Okay, maybe we both could have told each other shit, even if it was cray, cray, right?"

"Yes, we should have trusted each other."

"I don't think it was trust that held either of us back from disclosing everything. Let me start at the beginning." She nodded to Carissa, who returned the nod to continue. "Okay, back in college when we met, well, I knew you were different."

"Yeah, I couldn't date if my life depended on it." Carissa let out a pained laugh.

"Well, yes, you were fussy, but that's not what I was getting at." Ligi waited a moment to recollect her memory. "My meeting you was no accident."

"That's funny, because as I recall…."

"Okay, okay, okay, that was my clumsy self, but you see, I knew your name and that you were a demigod." Ligi waited and watched her friend's face go from surprise, shock, anger, and finally hurt.

"Wait a minute." Carissa pointed her index finger. "So, you're saying that you were planted. Why?"

"It's a long story, but I owe you this."

"Hell, yeah. You do."

This wasn't going the way Ligi planned. Avoiding it further wasn't an option. "There is more to the story, but I'll start somewhere. Three days before my epic fall into the quarterback who shall not be named, I was approached in a dream by a goddess. She said that I had to find her granddaughter."

"Hera," Carissa whispered.

"Correct. At the time, I brushed the first dream off, but for three nights, she stalked me in my dreams - actually told me that if I failed to keep an eye on you, she'd blast me and my kind into oblivion."

"You and your kind." Carissa let out a laugh. "You mean clumsy has a species?"

Ligi twisted her fingers together. Heat colored her cheeks. There were no scenarios where what she was about to say would resemble smooth sailing.

"No, Carissa. I'm a siren."

"You got that right. Men fall all over you."

Ligi took her friend's hands in hers and squeezed her eyes shut before blurting, "Girlfriend. I. Am. A. Siren." She waited for the gears in Carissa's brain to click into place.

"You mean the luring sailors to their death kind?"

Ligi nodded.

Carissa's eyes widened.

Okay, this news had Carissa's head spinning. Between being kidnapped and fighting off murdering gods on Olympus, she wondered whether her father had returned her to an alternate universe. One thing was certain; moments she'd shared with Ligi that she couldn't explain clicked into place. She now understood her friend's bizarre behavior and her actions in the past, but as things became clearer, she couldn't help but feel a pang of betrayal. Why hadn't Ligi trusted her enough to tell her?

Other questions bombarded her front cortex, ones she wanted answers to.

"Does Kelly know?"

"Yes."

"How did she react when you told her, and why didn't you tell me too?"

"I didn't have to tell Kelly."

Ligi's words dug around in Carissa's head. How stupid. Of course, "Because Kelly is an other, so you didn't need to tell her and vice versa."

Ligi clucked her tongue.

"What is Kelly?"

"Kelly is a harpy."

"That fits Kelly's profile, since Harpies are known for disappearing and causing things to disappear."

Ligi nodded in agreement.

"So, keeping me in the dark about this was for my protection?"

"Entirely," Ligi said.

"So why tell me now?"

"Well, things have changed. You aren't necessarily all human and have bonded with a big bad assed vampire, and since Kelly has been abducted by a demon… Well, it made sense to talk about it without you thinking I'm crazy."

"You have a point, Ligi, but I can't help but feel a little shocked that you didn't try to show me or convince me. All this time I've thought I was going crazy. That night at the hospital. You should have told me I wasn't crazy and that creatures like Xen and wolves existed. I would have believed you."

"Would you? You say that now, with the knowledge of what you have seen but girlfriend, you know it's not easy to believe in things like vampires, wolves, or anything other unless you've witnessed it firsthand."

Carissa's gaze settled on Xen's desk. Ligi had a point, but she could have tried to tell her.

"I have some more questions, and then I will leave you."

Ligi's shoulders dropped, and she nodded her head slowly.

"Was our friendship phony from the word go, and did you only stick around because you feared Hera?" Carissa paused and fought a tear. "Does this mean that you are done and no longer required to watch over me?"

Carissa watched as Ligi's nostrils flared. "You didn't just ask me that…" Ligi stood. "…of all the hare-brained things I've heard from you…" Ligi turned and pointed a finger at her. "…that is one of the stupidest things, in like the whole cosmos. How can you question our friendship?"

"How can I not? You were ordered to watch over me by Hera, queen of the gods, or witness the death of family and friends. You must hate me."

Ligi took a step to where Carissa was sitting and pulled her into a tight squeeze. "My friendship with you has nothing to do with what Hera demanded of me. I liked you the minute I met you, and all this doubt you have swirling around in the big cranium of yours has no business being there. We're in this for the long haul, and I never want to hear idiotic stuff like this again."

Carissa sniffed.

"And don't you dare cry soppy tears on my shoulder and ruin my silk blouse."

A laugh rumbled up from Carissa's chest, and Ligi joined her.

They were both being stupid. Regardless of what Hera wanted, Ligi spoke the truth. They'd bonded from the first moment they met and got on like a house on fire. It had been a BBF moment. A Big Baklava Feast at the local Greek patisserie.

The door to Xen's office burst open. Carissa pushed Ligi behind her. Preparing for whoever would come through. There was shouting, and a smile broke on Carissa's lips. Yiayia and Aunt Paula came charging in. Followed by a very unimpressed Kane. Xen strolled in with a smile on his face. Obviously enjoying the whole drama.

"Carissa, *paidi mou*," Yiayia screamed as she came barreling toward her with her walking stick. Carissa braced for the impact.

Yiayia gave her an award-winning, squeeze-the-stuffing-out-of-you hugs. Then she stepped aside to let Paula do the same. "Carissa *mou. Kalos irthes.*"

"Yes, welcome home, *paidi mou*. Now there is so much to tell."

"Yes, Yes, Vetta and I have much to discuss with you."

Carissa's glance flicked over at Xen. They hadn't done enough talking last night.

Sorry, koukla. There were other matters that were more important. She heard his response in her mind.

They look serious. Should I be scared?

This time he voiced his answer. "Yes."

"Thanks, you could have warned me."

"And miss all the drama? Never." He flashed her that smile with its own zip code. It devastated her, and her heart did a small gallop.

Ligi stepped aside, and the shrieking started again. "Ligi, where have you been? I've missed you," Yiayia said.

"You get sexier every time I see you." Paula threw in with a wink.

Carissa studied her friend. Okay, she had the siren effect on women too. She smiled and wondered how many girls were secretly crushing on her at college.

Kane had stepped over to Yiayia and Paula. "Ladies, please sit and stop terrorizing this house."

Paula raised her bag to whack Kane, and Xen intercepted it.

"Paula. Please. Have a seat, and I'll get everyone a drink."

"Oh, okay."

Carissa witnessed the exchange with clamped lips. Her laughter threatened to break free. Her mind raced at how much she'd missed while on Olympus. There were things going on here, in the mortal realm, that appeared to be as important.

"Carissa. I should get going. You have to spend time with your *yiayia* and aunt."

"But I thought you wanted to talk to Xen?"

Ligi checked her watch. "I can pop in tomorrow evening."

"How about I call you when we finish here?" Xen said.

Carissa watched as Ligi fiddled with her car keys. Then glanced over to Xen. "That sounds good. I could use a few extra hands."

Xen didn't answer. He just watched Ligi hug everyone and leave the room. Again, something was going on there, and Carissa wanted answers. Did something happen between them?

A loud growl sounded in her ear and arms wrapped around her from behind. "There is only you, *koukla*."

Their brief interlude was disrupted by the clearing of throats.

TWENTY-THREE

"We know nothing for sure: truth is hidden at the bottom of well."
Diogenes Laertius

Xen's office; Charleston, SC
Evening, mortal realm – Day 9

"But…"

"Your friend is stubborn to a fault. She has refused all help from the *Phi,* but let's give the stage to your family now. There are things you ought to know."

Xen released her and went over to his bar to get cold water for Yiayia and Aunt Paula.

Kane stood with his arms firmly placed across his chest. He watched as Yiayia and Paula whispered things to each other.

"*Lykos,* what's the problem?" Carissa asked.

"Where do I start?"

"Don't tell me they drove you nuts?"

He raised an eyebrow. "That's putting it mildly."

Xen gave a glass to both women, and Carissa didn't miss that they were both enraptured. Then they giggled, and Carissa put her face in her palm.

Kane cleared his throat. "Want me to stay, Xen?"

"No. I think we should be fine. Besides, you should rest. I'll see that everyone gets home safely."

Kane gave a slight nod to Xen and wink to Carissa and then left.

Carissa started. "Yiayia, Aunt Paula, what did you want to tell me?"

The color drained from Yiayia's face. She swallowed hard. "There's no easy way about this. Do you remember when you were a child, and your grandfather used to play that key game with you?"

Joy bubbled and danced in her chest. She remembered those fun games with her *pappou*. "Yes."

"Well, the games were a test for you to find the key and move on…"

Carissa answered. "…the magical book. The codex"

"The codex which has magic linked through it," Yiayia said.

Carissa's eyebrows rose. "You mean to say that the book exists? I believed it to be a game."

"No, with that game he was preparing you. Your grandfather had been tasked with protecting it."

"From who?"

"Well, that bit would be revealed to the next protector in due course. That would be you, Carissa *mou*."

She took a moment to gather her thoughts. "Where's the book?"

Paula broke her silence. "That's the problem. We don't know because the key was stolen along with the baklava."

"Wait a minute, the key to the post office box? What does baklava have to do with it?"

"Those rascals at the home took it," Paula said.

"It was that Basil from the cake shop."

"Okay, time out, forget about the baklava. How can the key be missing when I have it hidden in my treehouse?"

A gasp left Yiayia's and Aunt Paula's lips. "And all this time, I thought that key had been lost. I asked for the second key from the post office, and now that key has been stolen."

"And lucky for us, your fiancé turned up and saved us from demons."

Carissa shot Xen a look.

We will talk later.

I want the novel-length version of what's been going on. Carissa was firm.

You have my word.

Of that, she had no doubt. What had she come back to?

"Carissa." Yiayia's voice broke her wondering thoughts.

"We have to find the book before whoever stole the key does."

Yiayia's color hadn't improved, and what on earth was she going to deal with first? Zeus and the other gods? Kelly? The book? What else demanded her attention? Everything seemed to be an impossibility from where she was sitting, but she had to give her *yiayia* and *thitsa* hope that she could find this book before anyone else.

"Yiayia, let's you get you and Aunt Paula home, and I promise I will start first thing in the morning." She paused. "Zeus has been kidnapped. It's why Father sent me home."

Yiayia and Paula gasped again.

Yiayia licked her lips then turned bug-eyed to Xen and Carissa. "Then you have to find this book now. If Zeus is in trouble, you may need it."

"Why would the book matter?" Carissa asked her *yiayia*.

"Allow me to answer that, *koukla*. The book has the power to remove every institution of religion. From the most primitive of worship to the most modern constructions. Without any belief, humanity will be cast into chaos. A chasm of hate and violence."

Yiayia pointed at Xen. "What he said…but…" He flashed her a wicked smile. "Oh," Yiayia said, piecing it together.

Carissa took in everything Xen had just revealed. The book and her Olympian-sized case were the priority. As was Kelly, but what to do there?

"Xen, could you assist Ligi by allowing the *Phi* to help her zero in on a location for Kelly."

"I've had my men working on it in the background. I'm afraid at this stage, no one has been able to get a scent of either Lox or Kelly. I have one source I think might be able to help."

"Then let's try your source. In the meantime, I'm going to take Yiayia and Aunt Paula home. Then I will attend to the key."

"*Koukla*, I think it's best if I stay with you, but I have a few things to wrap up first."

"Something tells me that we need a head start anyway." She looked over to her yiayia and Aunt Paula, they would put up a fight before she got them off to bed. She reached over to the coffee table and grabbed her sword.

"That's some sword, isn't it, Vetta?" Paula said.

A big cheeky grin broke on Yiayia's face. "It sure is. You sure you're my granddaughter?"

Carissa let out a laugh. Her mortal family ebbed on crazy, but she loved them because she knew them. Her divine family, a definite problem. Certifiable madness there.

"Okay, Yiayia and *thitsa*, get to bed." Both women stood in their pajamas in the living room. Carissa had retrieved the key from an old biscuit box she had stashed in her tree house. She turned the key in her hand. Trying to remember the drills she did with her grandfather.

"We want to help," Paula said.

"Trust me, auntie. I need peace and quiet to remember the routine Pappou taught me."

"We can be as silent as a mouse," Yiayia threw in.

"It's quiet as a mouse," Paula said.

"That's what I said."

Carissa rolled her eyes. These two quiet? Not possible. They were anything but. Noise followed them around. "I'm not having any of that, up to bed with both of you."

"You can't keep us out of the loop, Carissa *mou*. We must help," Yiayia said.

"I'll let you help in the daylight hours. There is no way I would risk either of you. You've already experienced demons, and they are not something you want to come up against again."

Carissa caught the shiver that ran through Aunt Paula.

Yiayia's face paled. "Okay, we get it, but tomorrow we help where we can," Yiayia said.

"Deal, but tomorrow you will tell me everything that happened." Carissa focused on both women. "Promise?"

"We promise," Aunt Paula said. They turned and slowly made their way up the stairs. Carissa stood at the bottom watching till they'd taken the last step up. The soft sound of doors closing was music to her ears.

"Now, time to rehash some old puzzles." She clutched the key. "First place, the liquor cabinet." If only Yiayia knew half the stuff Pappou stashed in the liquor cabinet. There was a hidden compartment behind the bottles. He used to stash cigarettes in there and have one when Yiayia was out for the day. Her mouth turned up at the memory. Trouble was, Yiayia knew he was smoking when she wasn't around. He thought he had her fooled. She'd catch and throw out the packet. After that, he wasn't as game to smoke the others he had stashed away.

Carissa focused. A hidden memory tickled her consciousness. "If this key ends up in your hands, you have to follow its trail. The key will take you to a post office box. Inside will be the first clue. There are twelve clues, and only you will be able to decipher which one is the right one. But that won't stop the gods, demons, witches, and others from trying to get ahead of you."

"Why twelve, Pappou?"

"That's the perfect question, Carissa *mou*. Twelve Greek gods, twelve labors of Herakles, twelve Apostles, twelve sons of Jacob, twelve tribes of Israel, twelve stars on the Virgin Mary's crown, twelve days of Christmas, twelve calendar months, twelve is a composite number. I will repeat this over and over again until you remember each one. Remembering them will help you sift out which clue leads you to the book."

Carissa's breath caught, and her fingers tightened around the key. How would she sort through those twelve areas and find which one held the most relevance? Her grandfather had left her with a difficult task, but given the importance, she understood the need for complexity. Now, if she could only remember what her grandfather had meant.

A knock at her back door startled her.

"It's only me, *koukla*."

She hurried to open it.

Xen stepped in and pulled her into a kiss. It left her with jelly legs.

"How are they?" His arms were still wrapped around her.

"I sent them to bed."

"Any progress?"

She held up the key. "Well, I have the key."

The corners of his mouth turned up. "I guess I'll let Kane and Adam know that they don't have to chase down the missing tray of baklava."

She let out a laugh. "What do you think…. should we head to the post office and see what clue is waiting for us?"

"A perfect start."

"Xen, my grandfather had been training me to solve his puzzles. What if I can't do this, what if everything he told me to look for is lost inside my head?" She tapped her index finger to her temple.

"We will find a way. You forget that I have an extraordinary pool of contacts."

She smiled. "Let's do this." She grabbed her keys.

"You don't need those. I'm driving."

"Okay, but I get to choose the music."

"Deal."

Carissa double checked all the windows and locks. Satisfied, she locked up and headed to Xen's car. "Were you trying to impress me by bringing your Porsche?"

"Are you impressed, *koukla*?"

"Totally."

His lips creased at the corners. "Shall we?"

"Yes." She pulled the door open, scanned the street. Nothing stirred, but from experience she knew that didn't mean someone wasn't watching.

"Relax, *koukla*. My men are in place."

"Right. I forgot that you can pick up heartbeats and other things."

She got in, and Xen started the car.

"Which post office?" he asked.

"Broad Street."

"I guess we're doing a little breaking and entering."

"Wait, won't we set off an alarm or something?"

"Leave it to me, *koukla.* "

Xen sped to their location. Thunder boomed in the distance. The roads appeared empty tonight. It seemed ominous, and she didn't like it.

It is rather still. Xen projected to her mind.

"And there is something eerie every night. I suppose."

"From a *Phi* perspective, yes. You never know when something will go bump."

She whacked him on the arm, though he had brought her out of her dark musing.

With Xen's driving, they were at the post office in a short time. When he pulled to a stop, she released her seat belt and got out of the car. She checked the street again. "I'm being paranoid, aren't I?"

"I would have said cautious." He flashed her a smile before grabbing her hand to walk to the post office.

A small ache started in her belly. *What if it's empty?*

"Calm yourself, *koukla*. We will deal with it one step at a time."

"You need to get out of my head."

"And you need to get a wrap on your emotions."

"There are a thousand things running through my mind at the moment. How can I catch a god who has kidnapped Zeus? How can I protect my *pappou's* legacy? How can I get justice for other demigods? How am I supposed to figure out who is behind these attacks on the gods?"

"There is a mastermind engineering all this and his been planning this for a while. These are not spur of the moment attacks. Someone had to have intel from inside. I have seen the pattern for thousands of years."

Carissa felt the truth in Xen's words.

Xen pulled out his phone and opened an app. She heard a beep. "Alarms and cameras disarmed." He pulled out a small kit and inserted something into the locked door. With a small twist, the lock popped. "Ladies first," he said as he pushed the door open.

They headed to the boxes, and she fished the key out of her pocket. Her grandfather had scratched a number on it: 212.

Xen had already moved further down the boxes, and Carissa followed. "Here's 212."

"How did you know?"

"Your grandmother told me."

Carissa put her hand to the box, and it popped open. A gasp escaped her lips. Her skin tingled, and a rock dropped in her belly. Someone had gotten here first. The scratch marks around the box were evidence that someone desperately wanted what resided in the box. "Guess we don't need the key anymore." Her humor fell flat. She opened the box all the way. The inside was empty. No trace of whatever had been waiting.

Xen raised an eyebrow, "If what you say is true and your grandfather began teaching you how to break his clues, do you think that you could lead us to the second clue without the first?"

She stared at the empty box, willing her grandfather's voice to guide her. What would he have instructed her to do if this had happened? Because her grandfather would have known that someone might have cleared out the contents. He expected it.

Her glance flicked sideways at Xen and then to the box. An epiphany punched her in the head. "That's it." Excitement worked its way through her body. "The first clue was always a dud. Left on purpose." She stuck her hand in the box, letting her fingers look for a separate compartment. She pulled away when her index finger ran across something small and sharp. She sucked the blood.

"I could do that for you." Xen's nostrils flared, and his eyes dilated. At least her vampire had some control.

"You have no idea how hard it is for me not to pull your finger into my mouth."

She rolled her eyes and gently ran her fingers over the top of the box, then pushed her fingers upward. A click sounded. A part of the top opened and a small scroll dropped into her hand. She closed her fingers around it and quickly put the wrapped scroll in her pocket, then checked the box once more. When she was done, she closed the top chamber and locked the box.

"I have it in my pocket. Let's not take anything for granted. Someone could be watching."

"That much is true, but if they were close enough, I would have already picked it up."

"I thought my grandfather was paranoid, but I know one thing now. He knew it would come to this. That someone would try to follow the trail to the codex. We need to find out who was here before. Any chance your guys can hack into the cameras here and across the road? Hopefully, they caught something."

"I have already asked the *Phi* to look into it. I had a suspicion when Yiayia's key went missing."

"I should have realized that you would be one step ahead."

He pulled her in for a soft kiss. "Always." He smirked, then released her before they walked out of the grand building. Xen locked the doors before activating the alarm system. Carissa watched as he paused over the button to start the cameras. Their eyes connected, and the hair on her neck stood to attention. She didn't have time to react.

Xen pushed Carissa behind him at the sound of screeching tires, but she side-stepped.

"You're not going to have all the fun."

He unsheathed his sword, and so did she.

Xen turned and winked at her before the rogue vampires were out of the car.

"Not these guys again," she whispered and pierced her sword in the first guy who sped to her. She had enough of them from when Hal had kidnapped her.

Xen moved forward to block another two vampires. He moved with his vampiric speed, fast and graceful. He decapitated one of the rogue vampires that he'd fought. The other turned toward Carissa. "Come and get me, you goon."

He sneered at her. His sword sliced the air, and she blocked the strike. She lifted her leg and kicked him hard in the abs. He staggered a bit, but not before he'd raised his sword to take another swing. The motion never came because his head dropped to the pavement. Xen stood behind the headless body.

One vampire remained behind the wheel of the SUV; he didn't wait around.

Xen pulled out his phone and gave quick orders. He asked for a clean team and trace on the license plate that sped away.

The vampire Carissa had stabbed moaned on the floor.

Xen locked eyes with the vampire. "Who sent you?" He sheathed his sword. There were two classes of vampires in their political structure. One was the *Lamia Corinthia,* which included all of Xen's *Phi Athanatoi,* and the others were the *Lamia,* one of whom lay at Xen's feet. The *Lamia* were rogue vampires who didn't value structure and could be bought for the right price. They also enjoyed killing humans and taking all the blood they wished. They were, in most cases, feral animals.

Carissa placed the tip of her sword near the vampire's throat. She channeled her power of compulsion. "You will answer him." Her voice was soft.

"I do…don't know."

"That is a lie." Xen's fangs elongated, and he crouched beside the bleeding vampire. "You know what awaits you."

"Answer him," Carissa spoke again.

"There are many players in this game. I don't know who is who. I'm just following orders."

Xen peered up at Carissa. "We will take him to headquarters and use my method of extracting information. I'm sure he knows names that will prove useful."

Doors opened and closed on a pair of black SUVs that Carissa recognized.

Adam was beside her in seconds. He let out a loud whistle. "I do like that blade. Any chance we can trade?"

"No trade happening here, wolf. It's a present from Xen."

"He sure knows how to romance a girl." Adam wagged his eyebrows.

Carissa let out a laugh. She moved her sword away from the vampire and sheathed it. Kane assessed the bodies before coming over. "I take it we're going to have fun with this one."

"Indeed," Xen said, pulling the vampire up before Kane strapped on a pair of *Phi* branded cuffs and moved him to the SUV.

"I take it they're not your generic type cuffs," she asked.

"No, *koukla*. These send small pulses to the wearer, causing them much discomfort. In a couple of hours, he will be pleading for me to take his head." Xen watched as the car pulled away.

"Come on, *koukla*, let's get out of here."

Back in her room, Carissa pulled the scroll from her pocket. Xen lay on her bed in his boxers. He had made quick work of getting himself comfortable.

"You don't waste time, do you?"

"Not where you're concerned, koukla."

"Well, I don't have your speed."

"Would you like help?" he said, grinning.

"No." Her clothes would end up torn. That's what his version of help consisted of.

"I think we should look at this first."

"Good idea." He patted the space beside him.

She made her way to him. Taking a deep breath, she pulled the string from around the scroll. Then she broke the wax seal underneath to unroll the paper.

The scroll was addressed to her.

"Read it, *koukla*."

She did, with a steady voice.

Carissa, if you are reading this, then things are critical. I will assume that the first clue is gone from the box, and you were clever enough to realize I installed a secret compartment. The next clue lies with your yiayia. *Once you have that, you will be able to find the codex. The twelve clues were to throw off anyone looking for it other than you. This should buy you some time, though I expect you don't have much.*

You can do this. You were born to do this.

Love, your grandfather.

"Well, that was not what I was expecting." She let out the breath she had been holding.

"Your grandfather thought this through."

"I had assumed he'd always want me to solve his puzzle of twelve, but there you go, he designed it as a decoy to throw others off. Why teach me?"

"Because it's not a puzzle if someone knows the secret already. He knew you'd work it out."

"I don't know if I believe that I can succeed."

"You will, *koukla*. Have faith. Now enough of all that."

He pulled her to him. His lips crushed hers, and before she could catch her breath, she was under him moaning her approval. He broke their fevered kissing. "I'm going to take it slow, but first." He rose on his knees, put his hands on her t-shirt, and tore it from her body. The rest of her clothes received the same treatment.

She watched his hungry gaze dance all over her body. He dropped soft kisses all over her breasts before elongating his fangs. He started to lick and suck around her nipples; the scratching from his fangs had her lose all thought of the outside world. She gave in to the pleasure of his tongue on her body.

Xen brushed his fingers over Carissa's sleeping form. He had work to do, but first, he would put in a call to Kane. He walked over to her window and lifted his finger to move the heavy drapes. His men were positioned around the house.

He dialed Kane.

"Sup, boss? Was just about to turn in."

"I would be indebted if you could swing by here in the morning."

"You need something?"

"Not directly, no. Just keep an eye out here."

"You mean watch over Carissa."

"Something like that."

He ended the call and walked over to where he had a bag with his laptop in it. He sat in a wingback chair and started firing out e-mails pertaining to both his Phi Technologies Company and matters related to the *Phi Athanatoi*. Then he read all the headlines and signs of bad crops and extreme weather that were being reported around the globe. He hoped that the goddess Tyche stayed safe, because they required lots of luck and maybe a miracle.

TWENTY-FOUR

"What you leave behind is not what is engraved in stone monuments, but what is woven into the lives of others." Pericles

Carissa's yiayia's house; Charleston, SC
Morning, mortal realm - Day 11

Carissa's eyes flicked open. The sight of Xen's profile in his rejuvenation sleep sent her heart into a fast gallop. She took the opportunity to skim her fingers over his strong jaw and face and plant a kiss to his lips. Euphoria sped through her whole body. She loved her vampire, and the joy racing through her at being here with him was not something she ever wanted to end.

She stretched, and the events of the prior evening cascaded through her thoughts. She could do with a bit more sleep, but that would mean leaving Yiayia and Aunt Paula alone. Given their ability to attract mischief, they couldn't be trusted together without supervision. *Funny thing, they are fine when on their own,* she thought.

Right on cue, a knock sounded on her door. "Carissa, breakfast is ready." Aunt Paula's voice sang from the other side of the door.

She bounced out of bed and threw a dressing gown around her, then opened the door just enough. "I'll be down in a minute."

Aunt Paula tried to sneak a peek over Carissa's head by going on her tippy-toes.

"Really, *thitsa?*"

Aunt Paula shrugged, "What? You can't blame a girl for trying." Aunt Paula winked at her, turned, and walked away.

Carissa rolled her eyes, then poked her tongue at her receding aunt. *He's mine.* Where did that come from? She knew Xen had that whole irresistible thing going on, and her aunt meant no harm. Hmmm. She'd have to re-think the possessive streak. She didn't want to start acting like her rejuvenating vampire.

She raced around the room, pulling drawers open and clothes out of them. The faster she got downstairs, the less time her *yiayia* and aunt had for trouble. After she showered and dressed, she walked over to her vampire and placed a kiss on his lips. *See you later, handsome.* She sent that to his mind.

She headed downstairs. Something told her the day ahead would be long, and she needed caffeine. Caffeine appealed to her human side more than her demigod side. Caffeine equated to ambrosia for humanity, and she wanted a good strong cup of the brew.

The minute she rounded the corner to the kitchen, she backpedaled on "this was going to be a long day" and updated it to, "this had all the makings of a year-long day." Yiayia was up on a ladder, and Aunt Paula halfway up. It tilted, and that little movement sent Carissa's heart to her throat. She ran over.

"What do you two think you are doing? *Thitsa*, Yiayia, both of you get down now." She steadied the ladder.

"Oh, don't get your feathers ruffled. We're both fine," Paula said.

"Fine, my…"

"Don't you dare say it." Yiayia scolded her from her position on the ladder.

Her aunt had begun to descend the stairs.

Carissa maneuvered around the ladder to give them both room.

"What on earth were you both doing up on the ladder?"

"I have a secret box hidden on top of that kitchen cabinet."

"A secret box? Yiayia, there's nothing on top of the cabinet. I would know because I've cleaned the dust from up there, more than once."

"Just because you can't see it, doesn't mean it's not there."

"Okay, this is madness." Carissa let out a frustrated sound. She knew she was playing into Yiayia's and Aunt Paula's delusional games. "Move over." The women moved out of her way, and she climbed up to prove that there was nothing but dust. She ran her fingers over the dust, then turned slightly and showed them to the women below. "See nothing up here." Point made, or so she thought.

"Run your hand over the wall panel," Yiayia shouted at her.

Carissa did, and a familiar click sounded.

"You've got to be kidding me." She huffed under her breath.

"I heard that," Yiayia fired back. "Just bring the box down, and we can have coffee."

"Magic words," Carissa said, pushing the slightly opened panel. Inside sat a pristine gold metal box, the size of a shoebox. "And the surprises keep coming." One thing Carissa knew well was her family, and knowing them well meant that whatever was inside the box, it was going to add another level of complexity to an already muddled-out-of-the-stratosphere situation. "Dare I ask what's inside?"

"Well, that depends," Yiayia said.

"On what?" Carissa asked.

"On whether you believe in magic."

"Yiayia, you are seriously not asking me that." She shook her head as she descended to the floor. So much had happened since Hal kidnapped her, and her family didn't know about her powers that had amplified on Mount Olympus. "Okay, how about I show you something, but it has to stay between us. Father would be very angry. He thinks that I could become a threat to the gods." Carissa poured water in a glass. "Keep your eyes on the glass."

"Maybe you shouldn't show us, *paidi mou*," Yiayia said.

"Just this once." She needed them to know that she could do this. She couldn't justify her reason, only that they had to witness this.

Aunt Paula placed the steaming cups of coffee on the table, as she watched.

Carissa raised her hands over the glass and tried to focus. "Ball." The water started to spin in the glass, then rose to a spherical shape between Carissa's hands. When her aunt and *yiayia* gasped, she let it fall, spilling water everywhere.

"Magic." She wagged her eyebrows.

"I think I should sit," Aunt Paula said.

"You have things to tell us, too, don't you, Carissa?" Yiayia asked.

"Yes, but I'd like to hear everything from you two first. Then we can talk about what's in the box and finally me."

Yiayia and Paula exchanged a look and nodded in approval. "It started when Basil from the bakery stole my key."

Carissa's eyebrows rose to her head. *Ridiculous*, she thought. She'd known Basil since she was a child. She had a sinking feeling that this was more to do with date Yiayia went on with Basil a year ago. He'd tried to make a move on her, and it didn't go down well with Yiayia. The poor fellow found himself the victim of her umbrella, right over his head. "Yiayia, that doesn't make sense. We've known Basil for years."

"Well, we were attacked by demons in his shop and if…" Aunt Paula swallowed hard, "…your vampire hadn't turned up we'd both be…" A tremor ran through her.

Carissa sat and steadied Aunt Paula's shaking hands. "What on earth were you two doing snooping around late at night?"

"It was Vetta's idea," Aunt Paula answered. She got up and finished making the coffee.

"Like you didn't like driving that big SUV the *lykos* Kane loaned us."

"Let me get this straight. You two borrowed a car from Kane to go sleuthing, and were attacked by demons at Basil's bakery?" Aunt Paula put a steaming cup of coffee in front of Carissa.

"Yes." They answered in unison.

"And Xen gave your grandmother a Taser," Aunt Paula said.

Carissa's mouth opened and closed. She raised her coffee to her lips and swirled the information around in her brain while savoring the flavor. If they were attacked by demons at the bakery, then someone was following them. Her grandmother and aunt might be in more trouble than they knew. She'd have to make sure that Xen had men in place around the clock.

"What exactly do you know and aren't telling me? For the demons to come after you, it means someone led them to you."

"The key, Carissa," Yiayia answered.

"No, *yiayia*, I think there is more to it. If it had been just about the key, the demons could have turned up earlier. Why wait for you and *thitsa* in the bakery? Someone is trying to send a message to me." Carissa drew in air and exhaled slowly. "I know it's all connected. I just don't know how."

"We will help you work it out," her aunt spoke confidently.

"No, let's get one thing straight. You two are not to go anywhere without telling me first. Agreed?" She pointed at each woman in turn.

"*Entaxi*," they both said.

"If you must know, Pappou had set a dud trail, so whoever has the key and whoever cleaned out the box is on a bogus adventure." She grimaced. "Stop stressing about the key in the baklava."

They both gaped, registering what she had said.

Paula's mouth tightened before she could speak. "You and that stupid key and baklava! We almost got killed."

Yiayia's chin started to quiver. "I'm sorry, Paula, I didn't know. I always believed that the contents were important."

"I know you both did what you thought was right, but no more sleuthing without one of Xen's men."

"*Entaxi*," they said again.

"Now, tell me about this box."

Yiayia wiped away a tear. "Your grandfather was very good when it came to keeping things hidden but also good at improvising and coming up with other means if the book should have ever fallen in the wrong hands. I don't know all the details as we have just proven." She sighed. "He put in the box a piece of magical Greek papyri. That I do know."

Carissa reached for her coffee cup. "Where did he manage to get that?" The warm brew gave her comfort.

"Egypt, through some dodgy art seller, many years ago."

"You said Pappou was not all mortal, when we were at the church."

"Time to tell her…" Aunt Paula took a sip of coffee, "…everything, Vetta."

Yiayia let out a labored breath. "Your grandfather, up until his death, lived a long time, much like your vampire."

Carissa digested that for a moment. "How old was he when you met him?"

"I'd rather not talk about that now, let's just say old in years but not appearance."

"So, what happened to Pappou?"

"Believe it or not, my child, he had a good old-fashioned heart attack."

"I remember that, but if he was immortal, surely…" A chill raced up her spine. A small part of her became convinced that her grandfather hadn't died from what they said he did. She had been a preteen then, and there had been no cause to investigate when she became a cop.

Yiayia's fingers feathered across Carissa's "It is up to the Fates to decide when and where that will be."

"So how does this help what is going on? I already knew Pappou had passed from a heart attack."

"Yes, but the conditions that surrounded his death always plagued my mind. I found your grandfather near his favorite cigarette stashing spot."

"The liquor cabinet," Carissa supplied.

Yiayia nodded. "The house had been turned upside down. Nothing was left unturned except for the liquor cabinet. It was the strangest thing. The police went through the whole house trying to get prints, but there were none."

"You think his heart attack was induced by a robbery."

She nodded as did Aunt Paula. "It's what we suspected when we found him."

"It was a frightful sight, seeing him on the floor like that," Paula added.

"What exactly do you mean by like that?" Carissa asked.

"He was found in a fetal position in front of the liquor cabinet." Yiayia shook with the recollection of the old scene.

Carissa pondered the information. What could have possibly caused her *pappou* to curl up like that? To be in such a position, he must have been repeatedly attacked. "Did the autopsy show any signs of a struggle?"

"None," Yiayia said.

"Anything missing."

"Nothing."

"Any fibers found on the body?"

"None."

"Signs of forced entry?"

"None."

She let her gaze travel to the ceiling, allowing her thoughts to bubble. Something definitely stank. There was more to his death than a simple heart attack. "Whoever turned the place upside down had been someone Pappou let in."

"Oh, I never put much thought to it, but yes, that is very possible."

Aunt Paula shifted in her seat. "You should have told her ages ago, Vetta. She might have shed light on it."

Her grandmother raised a finger to her lips. "Shhhh, Paula."

"Don't get upset, Yiayia. Aunt Paula has a point, but at the same time, I understand why you've been keeping it to yourself."

"Thank you, Carissa *mou*."

"But Pappou's position and the cabinet don't make sense. Something bigger is at play. Everything about the scene indicates he was trying to protect himself. And that untouched cabinet has me perplexed. Why leave the cabinet? Had the police searched it or asked about it?"

"Come to think of it, they never mentioned it at all."

Carissa would have to call in a favor from Gelon Jones, her police officer friend who was also part of Xen's *Phi Athanatoi*. If he could pull the file, they might get a clue. She was no longer on the police force, so there was no way they'd give her access. Maybe the box on the table held a clue. "Let's have a look at the magical papyrus."

Yiayia's shaking hands reached over to the golden box. When the lock clicked, all three released a gasp. Yiayia opened the box and pulled out an old rolled-up piece of papyrus. It had been tied with a piece of string that had a key entwined with it. The whole thing appeared delicate, ready to splinter, to disintegrate with a touch.

"Hang on, Yiayia. Maybe we need the food gloves that are in the pantry. I don't want the papyrus disappearing on us."

Aunt Paula stood. "Good idea. I'll get them."

Carissa watched her aunt pull them from the topmost shelf in the pantry cupboard. Then passed them around so they could slide them on their hands. When protected, Yiayia lifted the scroll from the table. "I think that maybe you should open it."

Carissa reached over and took it from her grandmother. "Did Pappou leave any instructions?"

"He only said that things would become clearer once the words from the magical papyrus were read."

Carissa pulled the string and unrolled it. A gush of air blew out from the document and hit all three of them in the face. A loud thud came from the living room. Carissa sprung to her feet with the papyrus in one hand. She rushed to the drawer and grabbed a knife.

"Quiet," she whispered to her grandmother and her aunt, who had both grabbed other kitchen utensils and were ready to do battle. Yiayia with a rolling pin and Aunt Paula with a spatula. Carissa swallowed a laugh. They seemed ridiculous, but still she let them carry on. With slow steps and the shuffling of her grandmother's and aunt's feet. Carissa led her SWAT team to the living room. She rounded the corner with her knife raised and poised to strike, but her eyes widened at the figure standing close to the liquor cabinet. "Kirke," she shouted, then lowered the knife and dashed over to her friend, pulling her into a tight hug.

"Who is this, *paidi mou*?" Yiayia asked.

"Oh, sorry," Carissa said to her grandmother and aunt, who were watching with great curiosity in their eyes.

"This is my friend Kirke."

"She looks like someone out of Camelot. Should we be expecting King Arthur?" Paula asked, stepping close with Yiayia in tow to greet Kirke.

Kirke let out a laugh. "Trust me when I tell you that Arthur had anger issues."

The women gasped as they greeted Kirke with kisses on both cheeks and self-introductions.

Carissa waited till they were done. "Why are you here?"

"Someone released a strong illusion spell, and it brought me here."

Carissa eyed the papyrus and key and then glanced over to her grandmother and aunt. All of them wore the same expression, one of realization. Kirke's special talent was casting powerful illusion spells. "The magical papyrus," she said.

"Were you the one who released the illusion spell?" Kirke asked her.

"I have a feeling that unintentionally we have, through this papyrus."

Kirke examined the delicate parchment in Carissa's hand. "Where did you get this?"

"From my grandfather, and it's a long story. I think I have to have more coffee or something stronger."

"Great, let's have ouzo," Aunt Paula said with a smile.

"*Thitsa*, it's way too early for ouzo. Besides, we need to think, not numb our brains."

"Why don't Paula and I get fresh coffee?"

"That would be great, Yiayia."

Carissa motioned for Kirke to sit. Her friend's movements were swift, elegant, and regal.

"I'm glad you are here." Carissa lowered herself on the seat next to Kirke and placed her knife on the coffee table.

"So am I. Now tell me about that magical papyrus."

"My grandfather entrusted my grandmother with it and said that things would become clearer once the spell was read out aloud. All I did was pull the string off and unroll it."

"Carissa, a warning? The power that brought me here when you opened that scroll? It ripped right through me."

She gulped at Kirke's words. "Okay, then this spell and whatever it is hiding will be a big revelation. I think it has to do with that liquor cabinet." She pointed to the cabinet. "Maybe I missed something, and maybe my grandfather has something hidden in it."

Kirke blinked her eyes then narrowed them in the direction Carissa had just pointed. "Ah, Carissa. There is no liquor cabinet where you're pointing."

Yiayia and Aunt Paula walked in and heard the last bit of conversation.

"What do you mean there's no cabinet. It's right there." Aunt Paula said, putting the tray she held on the coffee table and waving her arm in the direction of the cabinet.

"Kirke, are you telling me that you can't see it?" Carissa asked.

"There is a wall."

Then everything fell into place. Her grandfather, his position on the floor in front of the cabinet, and the lack of damage to the liquor cabinet. "He cast an illusion spell to protect it, and only we can see it. That's why it was the one thing left standing when the house was turned upside down, and why it wasn't questioned by the police."

"So that spell in your hand, does what exactly?" Yiayia asked.

"I have a feeling it reveals the cabinet to others."

"But it holds nothing but liquor bottles and maybe an old packet of your grandfather's cigarettes," Yiayia said with a huff. "I hope he didn't die trying to save those darn smokes."

"You did give him grief about it, Vetta."

Carissa watched the exchange. Knowing her *pappou*, there was something else going on with the liquor cabinet.

"Ladies, why don't we find out what the spell reveals?" Kirke said.

Carissa surveyed Kirke, her grandmother, and her aunt. "Let's do this." She fidgeted with the papyrus in her hands. "Do we just read it?"

"Yes, but we must do this together. A spell is nothing if you don't have a witch to assist with the incantation. Let us see if we need anything before we perform the spell."

Kirke stepped closer to Carissa and they considered the papyrus and the ancient Greek writing. It said nothing was required before the spell was invoked. "All we have to do is read it."

"Okay. Tell me when."

"Now."

"Oh, great wide-shinning goddess Aleithea, daughter of Zeus, reveal to me all that has been hidden by words of illusion, so that I may finally see and know the truth."

The air in the room thickened, and the house shook. Yiayia and Aunt Paula wrapped their arms around each other for support.

The liquor cabinet moved to the side, and in its place, a blue door appeared.

Collective gasps filled the room.

"I can see the cabinet and the door," Kirke whispered.

"Not what I was expecting," Carissa said.

"What on earth?" Yiayia questioned.

"Bet you hadn't banked on that old goat being this inventive," Paula said.

"Trust me, Paula, that old goat invented being inventive." Yiayia gave a laugh.

"This is what Pappou died trying to protect." Carissa stared at the door then turned her gaze to Kirke. "You think there might have been more to my grandfather than meets the eye."

"Hard to say. I'm not sensing any magic coming from the door. Though the cabinet that only you three could see was sending out magical vibrations. I couldn't see it, but I knew something was there."

Carissa took a deep breath and walked toward the door. One thing she knew for certain; whatever her grandfather kept hidden behind that door wouldn't contain the codex. Still, she hoped that it would give her a clue. She slid the key in the lock and turned. The door creaked open and a lit stairway manifested. The women were all right behind her, looking down the stairwell. She turned her head. "Anyone care to join me, or will I take a look on my own?"

"I'm in," Kirke said.

"I'd like to join you, but I don't think I could handle those narrow stairs," Yiayia said.

"Well, if Vetta is staying here, then I best keep her company. Besides, I don't like basements. I have an allergic reaction to small and dark places."

"Okay, Kirke, let's do this."

"I'm right behind you."

Carissa descended with quick brisk steps. Every step she took, she wondered when her grandfather might have completed this project. Neither she nor her grandmother had any knowledge that there might have been a basement dug deep under their home. No light shone ahead; she had no torch. She took the last step, and the lights came on. "Scrap needing a torch," she whispered to herself. She scanned the deep expanse of the basement. Huge didn't cover it. The footprint resembled the living space of the whole house above.

It contained multiple rooms. Her feet shuffled further in. Bookcases lined walls. Display cases with objects filled most of the space. Whatever her grandfather had going on here, it appeared he had been guarding and collecting for a long, long time.

"Carissa, this is..."

"...remarkable." She finished Kirke's sentence.

They walked around from room to room, taking in the collection of written texts and artifacts that were in display cases. The room right beneath the kitchen upstairs held an office. From the way papers and assorted documents lay about the desk, her grandfather must have spent a great deal of time in here, but how did Yiayia not know? Then she remembered. Those trips to the bowling club were probably just a cover. She sat at his desk and looked at the paperwork. They were letters from various organizations. She read over some, which revealed that her grandfather had been inquiring about artifacts. She saw he wanted a libation bowl from the temple of Athena. Her grandfather was either a collector, or there'd been a need for him to have it.

Kirke stuck her head in. "I don't know what to say. Just the collection of magical spells is cause enough to keep all this away from prying eyes. Maybe your vampire might be able to tell us something more?"

"I dare say that Xen will have a field day in here."

"I think you're right, but we should cover that door again."

"But if you recast the spell that my grandfather had in place, I will not be able to lift it on my own."

"That is true. Maybe there is another way of hiding the door?"

"Yeah, pushing a huge piece of furniture in front of it."

Kirke let out a laugh. "Somehow, I can't see you pushing a cupboard out of the way each time. Let me think. Maybe I could teach you a smaller version of an illusion spell to keep the door hidden."

"Let's get to Yiayia and Aunt Paula. They might think we were gobbled up by a monster."

"I could use a cup of coffee."

"Me too." She stood from behind the desk and followed Kirke out. They started their ascent.

Closer to the top of the stairs, Carissa could hear Yiayia and Aunt Paula arguing about taking one of her grandfather's shotguns and heading down the stairs.

"It's okay, we're fine," She shouted out, coming into sight.

"Thank goodness, *paidi mou*," Yiayia said. "We thought there were booby traps or something else."

"Quite the opposite. No traps. Just lots of stuff," Carissa said.

"More like a museum under the house," Kirke added.

"I knew he was up to something," Aunt Paula said to Yiayia. "Remember, he'd disappear for hours."

"Paula, it's no news to me that he worked on secret projects. He made me promise never to investigate, and I stuck to my word because I trusted him. He believed the more I knew, the more danger it would bring to me."

Carissa heard Yiayia's words and knew that she would have done everything to protect her mother and stepfather from a drunk driver and danger too. She herself had seen enough when she was a police officer. "Okay, ladies. Let's break it up. I need something to eat and some coffee."

"I'll second that," Kirke said.

"You two go ahead," Carissa said to her aunt and grandmother. When they were out of earshot, she turned to Kirke.

"Now tell me what is happening with you? Any leads?"

"We had one, and it led us to where Hal had been keeping you when Xen rescued you the first time."

"Myrtle Beach," Carissa whispered. The memories cascaded through her mind. She shook her head to dislodge the thoughts. "Why there?"

"I suspect he kidnapped Odysseus at the same time as you."

"Wait. You said Odysseus."

"Yes."

Carissa raised an eyebrow. "You mean the Odysseus." *Could things get any weirder around here?*

"Oh…no, no, no."

Carissa stifled her laughter. "Okay, so he is mortal."

"Yes, but a very handsome mortal." Kirke winked at Carissa. "With a little extra in the pants."

"Whoa. We are seriously not going to talk about your man's junk." Why on earth did her friends feel the urgency to impart this knowledge? There were some pictures she didn't want in her head.

Kirke opened her mouth to say something, and Carissa held up a hand. "Keep it PG."

The witch let out a laugh. "I was going to ask if you think I have a chance of finding him."

Carissa contemplated the problem. "Has anyone made contact with you?"

"Like who?"

"Another witch or someone?"

"No."

"How do you know he is still alive?"

"I placed a spell on him. I do it for all the men I am involved in. Comes in handy if I have reason to doubt their devotion."

"That's a bit much, girlfriend."

Kirke let out a laugh. "I know, but I'm a witch. It's what we do."

"So, this spell acts like GPS?" Kirke nodded in agreement. "Then why haven't you been able to locate him?"

"Because something or someone is blocking it."

"That means Hal had more than one witch under his clutches. Maybe Hal's plot was larger than we thought. It just doesn't add up." She took a deep breath. "Do you have a witch network?"

Kirke raised an eyebrow in question. "You mean online?"

"Well, yes and no. A way that you know where all your people are?"

"Witches are very private and do not share their location. I can't begin to tell you how much energy we expend in protection spells to keep people from finding us."

"Okay, I get that, but someone has to know where all witches are at all times."

"Not possible," Kirke said.

"I reckon I can help with that." Kane walked into the room with a plate of food.

"What do you mean, wolf?" Kirke's tone choked with displeasure.

"I mean Xen has one of the largest databases on where most otherworldly beings reside. We leave them alone but need to know where they are." Kane shrugged.

"Even me?" Kirke asked.

"Yes. Witches are harder to find."

"That information would be valuable. What about hackers?" Kirke asked.

Carissa answered that one. "Knowing Xen, he probably has the best hackers and multi-layered encryption and state-of-the-art systems in place."

"That he does," Kane said with a wink.

Carissa smiled. The path and possibility had been right in front of them the whole time. "Kane, do you think you could run something to see if any witches have gone off the grid?"

"I could, but I'd tell you that Xen has already done that. In fact, he runs it every day looking for the slightest anomaly. Still, with witches, it's tricky because of all their layered spells."

Kirke let out a sigh. "It's hopeless then."

"No, not hopeless. It means that whoever placed the blocking spell on Odysseus is probably not one of the witches on Xen's database. As Kane said, they would have registered strange movements, and that would have given the *Phi* a reason to investigate. It's someone else."

"Who else can place a spell?" Kane asked Kirke.

"Gods and demigods."

"Kane, I think you should relook at the demigods in your database. How many of them can cast magic?"

Kane finished chewing. "From memory, only one."

"We must find that one," Carissa said as she jumped to her feet. "Come on, Kirke. We have work to do but first help me push this cupboard in front of the door."

Kirke waved her hand and the cupboard moved in place.

"Do I want to ask what that is about?" Kane queried.

Carissa would show him when she showed Xen. "No, that's for later."

"The coffee and food are ready," Aunt Paula yelled from the kitchen.

Carissa flicked her gaze at a waiting Kirke and Kane before answering her aunt. "Can we get it to go?"

TWENTY-FIVE

"Character is in destiny." - Heraclitus

Phi Technologies; Charleston, SC
Midday, mortal realm - Day 10

Kirke and Kane made their way to Phi Technologies, Xen's multi-million-dollar tech company. Carissa would brief him when he woke from his rejuvenation sleep in the evening.

The SUV came to a slow stop when they approached the gates of Phi Tech. "You sure about this?" Carissa pointed over to the security booth. "That guy looks scary."

Kane let out a laugh. "Relax. He's a gentle giant."

"Not from where I'm sitting. What's it with you *Phi* lot? Every time I think I've seen the biggest dude, I see one bigger than the last. You sure you guys aren't taking stuff to look like that?"

Another laugh left Kane. "Nope. One hundred percent pure muscle via rigorous training."

The boom gate lifted, and Kane drove them through and to an underground car park. Guards were stationed everywhere.

A gasp left Kirke's lips. "Sheesh, this is like Fort Knox."

"I totally agree, sister," Carissa said. "This place is huge."

Kane smiled. "And this is just the carpark."

They parked at a reserved spot and headed toward a guarded elevator.

Kane nodded, and one of the men pressed a button to call the elevator. A second later, it pinged that it had arrived. They moved inside, and Kane pressed a few buttons. It began to move, and to Carissa's surprise, it headed down, not up. She inspected Kirke, who shared the same look as she watched the numbers on the elevator panel. The car jolted when it reached the 7th floor. Curiosity hummed in her veins.

The doors slid open.

Her mouth dropped open.

Kane put a finger under her chin and closed it. "Come on," he said with a grin.

"I didn't expect this." She thought what she'd seen from the top was big. Under here, it resembled a city. Xen had offered her a tour, but she had turned it down to spend time with him. Priorities. *Wow.*

Kirke elbowed Carissa. "I know." She spoke because they were thinking along the same lines. "Words fail me," she said.

"And me too," Kirke added.

"Well, now you know that your vampire takes his business seriously." They followed Kane. He led them to a little golf cart, and they jumped on.

"I've always wanted one of these," Carissa joked.

Kane gave her a side glance. "Don't say that around Xen unless you mean it, because you know there will be one sitting in your driveway."

Now that she thought of that, he'd do it.

Kane zipped through a large space and brought them to a section that had a sign that read UDMR and underneath in small writing - Unearthly Database Mortal Realm.

They left the golf cart, and Kane presented a security card that unlocked the door to the area. Inside was no different from what you'd see in any corporate office building: workstations, computers, and people doing all matter of administrative work.

"Are all these people…" She hadn't finished her sentence.

"Yes and no."

"You mean some are unearthly and some human."

"Yes."

"How…" she paused, "…is it safe?"

"We run checks, and we only take humans who have experienced unearthly contact."

"So, you're saying that these people have come across wolves, vampires, etc."

"Yes."

"And they are okay with working alongside unearthly beings?"

Kane shrugged his shoulders. "Xen pays well, and there are great benefits."

She let out a laugh. "We're working for the wrong people, Kirke."

"I could do with some extra benefits. Working solo has no perks." She sounded just a bit thoughtful.

"Please come this way." He led them to a vacant office. The style reminded her of Xen.

Kane glanced over at her with a half-smile. "Yes, it's Xen's, when he comes in."

"How did you know I was thinking that?"

"It's written all over your face. Your eyes have the same sparkle you get looking at Xen."

Heat crept up her face. She hadn't realized she'd been that transparent.

"It's that obvious, huh?"

"Very," the wolf answered. "Let's fire up his computer and see if we can find you a demigod with magic." He dropped his weight into the black executive chair.

Carissa and Kirke leaned in behind him. He punched away at the keyboard, bringing up screen after screen of security passes. Once through, he opened the database and punched in a search for magic and demigod. The computer scanned through its records. "This will take a few minutes. Do you ladies want a cup of coffee?"

They both nodded.

He picked up the phone and ordered. They had barely enough time to move to the chairs when there was a knock on the door.

A bubbly young girl with short, cropped, dark red hair who appeared to be no more than twenty brought in a tray with coffee.

"Thank you," Kane said.

"Anything else?" She was beaming at him.

Carissa didn't miss how besotted with Kane this girl was.

"No, that will be all." He didn't turn from the screen.

Carissa opened her mouth, but Kirke silenced her.

When the girl got to the door, Kane glanced up. "Thanks again."

At this point Carissa decided it was time to say something. "Kane, are you aware that you guys have a certain allure and that most females across the species seem to be drawn to that magnetism?"

"I'm well aware. Why?"

"Honestly, that girl was drooling."

Kane took a long sip of his coffee and put his cup on the table. "Carissa, we're mindful that it is the animalistic mesmerism. There is nothing we can do to control it. Some find it frustrating, others love it, but it's not an excuse to manipulate and use every woman who looks our way."

"That is understandable, but all that young lass wants is recognition for her effort, and that is different to something more."

"Noted. I'll try to be friendlier."

The computer pinged, and Carissa and Kirke raced to see the results."

"Bingo," Kane said.

"Who do we have?" Kirke asked.

Carissa read the name out. "One name. Cali Nereus."

Kane scribbled the details on a small notebook. The plus side was that this demigod's address meant that they didn't have to travel far.

"Let's pay her a visit." Carissa was eager to get going.

Kane exited out of the database and shut down the computer.

Then they retraced their steps out Phi Tech's secret underground city and made their way toward Cali's house.

"I've called Adam, for standby."

"Are you expecting trouble?"

"Not really, but you never know. We don't know the details of her magic."

"Not to worry, wolf, you have me. I will bind her powers while we are there," Kirke said.

"We should be fine then."

Something told Carissa this meeting would reveal a few things. Who was Cali, and what was her story? She just hoped that when they knocked on the door, Cali didn't do a run. When a police officer, Carissa had hated the whole chase them and tackle them scenario. Really a waste of good energy.

"You ladies take the front, and I'll take the back. Just in case."

"Roger that, on the same wavelength," Carissa said to Kane.

"You think she's our girl?" Kirke asked.

Carissa glanced at her friend before pressing the doorbell. "I hope she is. We need answers."

Soft footfalls sounded from behind the door.

"Hello," The young blonde said.

"Hi, I'm Carissa, and this is Kirke. I know this is going to sound super crazy, but we were wondering if you can cast a spell."

The door slammed in their faces. "Go. Away." The voice boomed.

Carissa rolled her eyes. Ah, the chase. How she hated the chase. This was how it always started. She rang the bell again.

"Want me to do some hocus pocus?"

"Not yet. We don't want to threaten her before we have to."

"Good point." Kirke nodded in acceptance.

Carissa rang the bell again.

"I. Said. Go. Away."

"We just want to talk," Carissa said to the white wood in front of her.

"I have nothing to say."

"I don't want to force you, but I will if you keep acting like a child."

Silence.

A minute later, the door opened, and Cali did a sweep of her hand.

They entered and were led to a living room.

A knock sounded at the back door.

"That would be Kane the wolf, and I'd answer that."

Cali gulped and went to open the door. A second later, he appeared in the living room.

"What can I do for y'all?" Cali asked.

Her tune had changed, but it didn't fool Carissa. Cali was eyeing every exit.

"Cali, sit down, please. It will be easier if you let me do the talking first." Carissa pointed to the seat opposite hers.

They all sat except for Kane, who stood with his arms folded across his chest and his feet apart.

"We need your help. I cannot divulge everything to you, but I want you to know the most important thing here is that we share something similar."

Cali nodded her head in understanding.

"I'm a demigod too, Kirke is a witch and Kane a wolf. I take it you're familiar with unearthly beings."

"Yes, I am."

"Good. There is no need to fear us. All we require is basic information."

"Okay."

"Have you cast a concealing spell recently?"

"I did for some guy a few months ago, and he gave me quite a bit of money."

"Let me guess. Bald and in a white suit?"

"Yes. How did you know?"

"Let's just say he's been a thorn in a lot of people's sides."

"Seemed real nice to me."

"Because you weren't his target," Kane said from where he stood.

Cali swallowed hard again.

"Cali, Hal was not a nice man. He would not have blinked if there had been cause to kill you. Can you remember details about the spell?"

"Sure, it was for some dude named Ody."

"Where is he?" Kirke asked. Her hands were visibly shaking.

"Calm yourself, witch." Kane threw in her direction.

"Cali, Ody is Odysseus, and he is Kirke's partner. The man who gave you the money is now dead. We want you to remove that concealing spell."

Cali jumped to her feet, and so did Kirke.

Kirke stepped around the coffee table and into Cali's space.

The shit hitting the fan episode started to unravel. Either she did something, or Kirke would throw something at the demigod. Time to use her compulsion.

"*Pauó*," she said to the women. Their hands dropped to their sides.

"*Chora*." The women separated.

"You will both stop, and we will try to solve this like adults. Cali, my father is the god Ares. Now, unless you want a war god on your doorstep, I suggest you lift whatever spell you have on Odysseus."

Carissa shot a look at Kane. The grin on his face told her that he had enjoyed the show.

"There is only one problem," Cali said. "I'll need something of his."

"Well, that's not a problem." Kirke waved, and a watch appeared. She gave it to Cali.

Cali commenced her incantation, and the watch disappeared from her hand. "The watch found its way to him. The spell has been lifted."

"Thank you, Cali," Kirke said.

Kane moved over to Carissa. "Time to wrap this up."

She jumped to her feet and held out a hand to Cali. "Thank y…" She didn't finish her sentence.

Cali disappeared, and the house began to shake.

"Let's get out of here." They made a run for the front door and out to the front lawn.

"Typical," Kirke said.

Kane shook his head. "What's the matter with the youth today?"

"She's young and angry. I assume she probably had to learn things on her own. Is there a way you can keep an eye on her from a distance?" Carissa asked Kane. "I'm sure she'll pop in."

"Trust me. Once I let Xen know, he will be keeping a close eye. Especially since she helped Hal. There's no telling if she dipped her spells in other areas."

"Good point. I'm glad she complied before taking off. Kirke should be able to locate Ody now." Carissa's limbs were light. Happiness boomed in her chest. At least her friend would get her partner back and have some closure.

"If you no longer need me, Carissa, I'd like to find Odysseus."

"Go already, will ya?" She pulled her in for a hug. "Let Xen know if you require more men for extraction."

"Thank you, but first, I must see him with my own eyes. If you need me, call."

"That's a definite, because I know I'm going to need magic somewhere."

They broke their hug, and Kirke nodded in Kane's direction. "Wolf."

"Witch."

Then the wind picked up, and she was gone.

"Damn, I wish I had that ability."

"Would come in handy," Kane agreed.

"Let's get back to Yiayia and Aunt Paula. No knowing what those two have been up too." She fingered her watch. "Besides, I think Xen might be nearly up."

"Yeah, we need to bring him up to speed."

Once in the car, she spent a few minutes going over the day's events. With Kirke's problem solved, she could focus on finding the codex and the location of the cave where Zeus and the other gods were being held. Right on cue, thunder cracked across the sky and the heavy dark clouds rolled in.

TWENTY-SIX

"Old things become new with the passage of time" ~ Nicostratus

*Carissa's yiayia's house and Phi Technologies; Charleston, SC
Evening, mortal realm - Day 10*

Xen sat at the kitchen table with Yiayia and Aunt Paula. He had been laughing at something Paula had said.

"I see you are all behaving," Carissa said, stepping in through the kitchen door with Kane.

Xen got to his feet and pulled Carissa in for a kiss. "Relax." She whispered to him when he broke the kiss. Her face heated.

"Get a room," Paula said.

Yiayia raised her walking stick and thumped Paula.

"Ouch."

"They are in love. It's normal."

"Well, not in our day. We had to be modest."

"Is that what they called it? More like a bunch of prudes. Nothing wrong with a couple expressing affection for each other. Besides, Paula, you are only seventy."

"Go, Yiayia. Didn't know you were such a romantic." Carissa said.

Yiayia blushed. Carissa didn't mean to embarrass her grandmother.

Xen cleared his throat. "I hear you've been busy."

"Yes, we have, and there's something I want to show you and Kane."

"There's a massive underground room," Paula said.

"Come on." Carissa tugged at Xen's hand.

"Ah…not to be party poopers or anything but Paula and I are going to go to pop out and see one of our friends."

"We are?" Paula asked.

Those two were up to something again.

"I will have one of my men drive you," Xen said.

Thank you. Carissa sent to his mind.

No need, koukla. Those two and trouble are interwoven.

She led Kane and Xen to the living room. "Help me push this cupboard aside."

"*Koukla* let me."

She stepped aside.

Xen gave it a push and it slid out of the way, exposing the entrance.

"Okay, you both have to see this." They followed without a word. At the bottom, when their feet had taken the last step, the lights came on.

Kane let out a whistle.

Xen's reaction showed pure control. As she had expected. Vampires didn't expose their thoughts. "Well, I think your grandfather and I have a shared interest."

"You can say that again, boss."

"Xen, look around. My grandfather was looking for something new. I'd like you to check the papers on the desk."

"It would be my pleasure." A whoosh of air hit her. Xen had gone into vampire speed.

Kane, however, took his time looking at the display cases and books.

Xen called from the office. "Join me, *koukla*."

She headed in, and Kane followed. "What do you make of all of it? Do you think it can help us in any way?"

"Oh, it more than helps," Xen answered. "The artifacts in this room are relevant to the codex too. There are many items here that contain religious power. Power that ties humans to the gods."

"The modern Greeks are monotheistic in belief."

"Not all, *koukla*. Just because the old religions are not around more does not mean that they hold no power. You are living proof of one old religion."

"Are you saying the Egyptian, Roman, etcetera, and their gods are very much alive?"

"Absolutely."

"Then what of the Christian God?"

"This is where it gets complicated. Let's say for argument's sake that there was only one god and he was all-seeing and all-knowing. Now let us apply that same concept to the ancient Greek pantheon. One god reigns supreme over all others."

"Zeus," she said.

"Exactly."

"But this means there is more than one god."

"We can't bunch all religions into monotheistic thinking. Christianity was born as a result from the religions that existed around its time, and monotheism appeared early in Egypt. You have to understand that religions of any kind, whether we are talking about monotheism or polytheism, are very powerful because of human belief. If people did not believe, their gods or religion would not exist. Are you following me?"

"Yes. If I was to turn into an atheist tomorrow morning, then the gods would be dead to me," she said.

"Take that one step further, when you lose a worshipper then yes, a piece of religion dies. Lose many, and well, you get the drift. The gods die, and everyone and everything falls into chaos and the dark chasm of nothingness where it all began."

"Like a big bang."

"Science, religion, and everything in-between are all related. As much as we like to sever one from the other, we truly can't. There will always be beliefs that intervene in science and vice versa."

"So how does the codex fit into all of this?"

"The codex, as I have heard, has power on a cosmic level. I don't know the extent of its power. It has never surfaced before, and the rumors are inconclusive."

"My family must have been good at hiding it."

His lips turned up. "I say you're correct, *koukla*."

"Okay, so we need to find the codex before it falls into the wrong hands."

"We do, and it has to be protected. If I am not mistaken, that task is now yours."

"She's going to be forever fighting off people for it," Kane said from where he leaned on the doorjamb.

"She is."

"Great. Now I have a permanent target on my back."

Kane straightened to his full height. "I hate to say it, Carissa, but yes, you do."

"Not the news I wanted to hear, but I'm getting a lot of that lately. I think I should take a vacation."

Xen's lips twitched. "I agree."

"No time now. We need the codex, and if the key led to a wild goose chase, then how do I work out where it is?"

"You and your family knew your grandfather best."

Down here, something led to the codex as his message to her had stipulated. "What do you make of what he was working on?"

"He was trying to buy a libation bowl from the black market. I know these people. I can reach out and see if they had any discussions in private."

"You think that's what might have led to his murder."

"Murder?"

"We believe he might not have died from a heart attack. He was found in front of the glamored liquor cabinet."

Xen and Kane shared the same look. "He died protecting that door, Carissa," Xen said.

She pondered what they had said, all the bits of information started to click into place.

"All this has been woven into time from long ago," Xen said.

She knew that for a fact. Zeus had revealed that both her and Xen's lives were interlaced long ago. Everything in this room had to be protected. She'd have to pick up the baton of her grandfather's work.

"How do we protect this room and my grandfather's work?"

"That is the least of your worries, *koukla*."

"I think you got a good idea of Xen's version of security today," Kane said.

"Indeed, I did."

Xen raised an eyebrow.

"There is something else we have to discuss. We helped Kirke."

"You found a lead?"

"We did more than that boss. We found the demigod who cast the spell to stop anyone locating him." Kane lifted his fingers and made a gun gesture. "All thanks to Carissa."

"It was nothing. I'm just sorry we didn't ask the right questions earlier. I hope she found him."

"Kane, can you get this place secured? I want the walls and ceilings redone, so they are bulletproof. Nothing gets in or out."

"Sure, boss." He tipped his head in Carissa's direction. "Later, Carissa." He was moving before she could shout her gratitude.

"Thanks for everything, Kane."

"Pleasure." His footsteps sounded on the stairs.

When they were finally alone, Xen walked around the table and pulled her close to him.

"One thing puzzles me?"

"What's that?"

"Why did Kirke come today? Did you call her?"

"Why is that puzzling?"

"Because witches are hard to find at the best of times and usually only appear on their own terms."

"I didn't call her, she just appeared. I found the magic papyri that my *pappou* had hidden, and when I took it out of its box, it sent a magical pulse that brought Kirke here. It was a strong illusion spell that hid the door to this basement. I could not have revealed the door without Kirke."

She saw the gears turning in Xen's head.

"If the pulse reached Kirke, then I fear that it may have also alerted others. This basement is like the holy grail. We will require extra spells all around the house for protection."

"I can't cast them. We need Kirke."

"For magic, yes, but for basic totems and protections, we need only to look at those books out there." Xen pointed to the filled bookcases.

"Why can't any of this be straightforward? You know, teen walks into the service station and steals a candy bar. Gets caught. Police called; we let them off with a warning."

"Ah, *koukla, koukla*." He tsked. "This isn't candy."

"Well, I know that. Okay, maybe that was a bad way to get my point across."

"I knew what you meant. Life is bigger and can't be measured with simple analogies." He had yet to release Carissa. Xen gave her a kiss on the nose. "Tell me about this demigod you found."

"Kirke mentioned that she had placed a locator spell on her lover and that something was blocking her from finding him. I asked Kane whether you had a demigod in your database who could cast spells. Sure enough, there was one, so we visited her. She removed the spell."

"That simple, huh?" he asked.

She nodded her reply.

"And her motivation?"

"Hal."

Xen's arms tightened around her. "Tell me everything."

She gave him the detailed version, and Xen agreed that they would up the surveillance for Cali and for Carissa's family.

A loud noise brought them out of their discussion and up the stairs. Her legs moved fast, but they were no match for Xen's speed.

Wind whipped around the room. Carissa recognized the visitor.

Athena. She communicated the thought to Xen as the goddess materialized.

Carissa bowed as did Xen.

"Goddess."

"Auntie," Athena replied.

Carissa walked over to the open arms of the magnificent goddess and greeted her properly. "What do I owe the pleasure?"

A grim look crossed the goddess's face. "My news is not good."

Carissa took a step away. Bile rose in her throat.

"Your father has been taken."

Yep, nausea was a bitch.

Strong arms wrapped around her. She regained her composure enough to croak out, "How?"

"As we planned, when your father sent you back, we visited Uncle Hades. He believes that this was set into motion long ago. When you told your father that Thanatos appeared with a message, we paid him an unofficial visit. He had been trying to warn you that whatever was brewing on Olympus had links here. Hekate has also made her displeasure known upon finding her portals have been breached again."

Xen relaxed his hold on Carissa. "So, who do you suspect?"

"At first, we were not certain, but the whispers in the underworld are that there are lesser gods, demons, and possibly some humans working with Kronos."

"But surely he could not have breached Tartarus?" Xen said.

"He has," Athena answered.

Carissa swallowed hard. She wanted to double over from the sheer magnitude. This had to be the punch of all punches. "How do we defeat a god who is time itself?"

"It's not about defeat but more about tactics and capture."

Xen had a smile on his face. Obviously, he thought this to be a fun challenge.

"Still not going to be easy," Carissa said. Something passed between her vampire and the goddess. She would have to ask Xen later.

"No, but you will have my support when the time comes." The air whipped around them, and the goddess dematerialized.

"This is all getting crazier by the minute."

"No doubt it is, *koukla*, but first we must seal your grandfather's room."

She did as she was told. Xen moved the large liquor cabinet in place.

A thud at the front door had Xen pulling Carissa behind him, but he relaxed his stance a moment later. "Looks like your *yiayia* and *thitsa* are home."

Carissa made her way to the front door, followed by Xen. Her fingers closed around the door handle, and she opened it, Aunt Paula fell through the door. "Ouch."

Xen rushed to her side and checked to see if anything was broken before helping her up.

"What is going on?" Carissa asked her family.

Yiayia's eyebrows were lowered and pinched together. "Paula had too much ouzo."

Aunt Paula held up two fingers. "I only had three shots."

Xen let out a chuckle, and Carissa held hers back for fear of the look on Yiayia's face.

"Come on, Yiayia. Let's get you upstairs and ready for bed." Thunder cracked outside.

"You need to find the codex."

"I know, Yiayia. It's my number one priority."

Xen helped Aunt Paula up the stairs, and Carissa helped her *yiayia*. They climbed in silence.

"I am capable of putting on my own pajamas," Yiayia said, when they got to her room.

"I never doubted you. I think Aunt Paula might need help, though."

Yiayia nodded in agreement. "She sure will. That woman doesn't know how to say stop."

"How many did she really have?"

"Seven."

Carissa let out a gasp.

"She embarrassed me, in front of my friends. She was loud and obnoxious. Laughing like a loon."

"Yiayia, there is nothing wrong with Aunt Paula having a drink. Look at it this way; you've both been exposed to demons, been on the run, been spied upon, and discovered Pappou's secret. This is Aunt Paula's way of dealing with it, and there's nothing wrong with that, so long as it doesn't become a crutch. Pappou liked to throw a few back, and that never bothered you."

Yiayia opened her arms. Carissa stepped closer and leaned in for a hug. "Thank you, *paidi mou*. I overreacted. It's the stress of the situation."

"Totally understandable." She walked to the door. "*Kalinychta, Yiayia.*"

"Good night, my child."

She closed her grandmother's door and headed to Paula's room. Xen was exiting. He put his finger to his lips. "She's out."

"She'll be sorry tomorrow."

"Most certainly. She threw a few punches."

She let out a laugh. "I'm sorry I missed that."

"How did you manage before?"

"It wasn't that bad. It's when they are together that trouble really starts." She let out a long exhale of frustration. She still had to find the missing gods and goddesses and that the codex. To top it off, her father had now been snatched. A rock formed in her stomach. Everything seemed wrong but she had no idea how to explain the multitude of emotions running riot on the inside. "I'm beat, do you mind if I have an early night?"

Xen grabbed her hand. "Come on. I'll help you relax and stay till you've fallen asleep."

"Will you stay the night here?"

"Indeed, but you might want to consider moving Yiayia, Paula, and yourself to my place for a short while. I want to secure that room properly."

"Why not move everything to one of your locations?"

"It would draw too much attention. Artifacts that hold power send out signals. If we bring those items up all at once, we'd be sending an invitation to every unearthly creature across the globe. It's one party I don't want to have."

"Point made." She laced her fingers with his. She gave him a slight tug and led him up the stairs. *You, me, naked.* She projected to his mind what she wanted. He picked her up and threw her over his shoulder and sped them both to her room. When he put her down, their hands were a frenzy of activity, peeling away their clothes. Xen's speed made things easier.

"You know that's a bonus."

He wagged his eyebrows at her and stopped whatever else she had been about to say with a hot and heady kiss. He lifted her up, and she wrapped her legs around him, his hard arousal probed at her entrance.

I need you now. She sent the thought to his mind.

He didn't require more of an invitation.

TWENTY-SEVEN

"Force has no place where there is a need for cleverness."
~ Herodotus 420 B.C.

Charleston, SC
Early morning, mortal realm - Day 11

Xen had finished talking to all the illegal dealers in artifacts. It never ceased to amaze him that for the right price, not only did people speak up, they'd be willing to give him a private viewing of what they held.

He managed to track the libation bowl that Carissa's grandfather had tried to obtain sixteen years ago. It had been bought and sold a few times. Its current owner thought he paid way too much for mere pottery and had been trying to sell it for over two years to no avail. Xen threw a price at the owner.

"You must have rocks in your head."

"That is a possibility." Xen smiled into the receiver of his phone then waited while the owner digested his offer.

"You have a deal."

"I will make the necessary arrangements." The man on the other end of the phone wouldn't understand the value of an artifact even if it slapped him in the face. The upside, the collector lived in Charleston. The Fates must have been smiling on Xen for a change.

"Pleasure doing business with you, Mr. Lyson."

"The pleasure was all mine."

The thought that this might have been just an artifact for Carissa's grandfather's collection had crossed his mind. Another look through her grandfather's journals and research would be warranted. Xen knew that libation was supplication for the gods; therefore, the significance of the vessel made sense. What he didn't know was why Carissa's grandfather wanted it.

There were still things that didn't make sense to him. If Kronos was behind all this, what would he gain by destroying belief in the divine in every culture and religion? It made no sense. In any case, they required to speed up their search in locating the gods, including Ares, because if he ceased to exist, then so would Xen and his *Phi Athanatoi*. The lightning outside had become constant.

The other matter he wanted to look into was the death of Carissa's grandfather. It didn't sit well. Someone knew what he was protecting. The question remained; who?

He punched Gelon Jones's number.

"What do I owe the pleasure?"

"I need a favor, and it concerns Carissa's grandfather."

"Is she home?"

"Yes, she is." A snarl rose to his throat. Mine.

"Relax. I know she's yours."

That calmed him. "Her grandfather's death looks like there may have been some unearthly connection. Can you go over the report of what happened?"

"Sure. I'll see what I can do. Where are you?"

"At my bonded's place. Thank you, wolf."

"It's for Carissa."

The phone went dead in his ear.

Xen had been pretty sure that Gelon's feelings for Carissa were more than just friends. In fact, his actions proved it. Xen would not let anyone near his bonded. He craved to make things more official from a human perspective. He smiled, thinking about Vetta and Paula trying to organize a wedding.

"Time to shift my thinking. If I were Kronos, where would I hide the gods?" He spoke softly, pacing the floor in the living room.

A cave, but which cave?

Words swirled around his mind.

Hidden.

Unreachable.

Invisible.

He stopped mid-pace. "Of course." The conundrum he thought it would be. His fingers closed around the phone in his pocket. Kane could confirm his suspicion.

"Kane, what was the name of the demigod that placed the spell on Kirke's man?"

"Yeah, thanks for waking me up."

"The name."

"Testy, aren't you?"

"Kane."

"Cali Nereus."

"Does she have any other name?"

"Yeah, Calypso."

"Bingo," Xen said.

"What's this about?"

"I think I know where the gods are being held. We need to talk."

"I've had a few hours of sleep, let me get dressed and I'll be right over."

Xen continued his pacing after the call had ended. He made his way downstairs and waited. They would scout out the area first. No telling who Kronos had working for him. A plan began to form. He would hit the cave from every angle. He required five teams.

A soft knock sounded at the door. Xen made his way there. Kane had brought Adam along. He let them in and lead them to the living room.

"Let's keep it as low as possible," Xen said.

"Not a problem," Adam said.

Kane headed for the living room. "Spill, Xen."

"We said we had a hunch that all of what is happening right now with the gods disappearing, started long ago, but I did not expect it to have ties with Hal."

Kane raised his hand. "Wait. You think what happened with Carissa is related to what's happening now."

"One hundred percent."

"How can you be so sure?" Adam asked.

"There are things that are co-related, and they have puzzled me. It all became clear when you confirmed that the demigod that placed the spell on Kirke's man shared the same name as the nymph Cal-y-pso." Xen put emphasis on her name.

"In ancient Greek it means hidden," Kane translated.

"Exactly."

The air in the room thickened then blew out like a wind blast. Xen stood ready for who might appear, but his acute senses recognized the magic.

A familiar face caught his before dropping to the floor with a thud.

Footsteps sounded from above and down the stairs, his bonded stood with her sword ready.

"*Kirke*." Carissa called out and ran to her side. Xen gave a hand to get Kirke to her feet then helped settle her in a chair.

"Let me get some water," Carissa said, as she darted toward the kitchen then raced to Kirke's side. "Here, drink this. You look like hell."

"I feel it. I've used a lot of power." Kirke scanned the room then settled her gaze on Xen. "You know."

"I do."

Carissa shifted her gaze at him then to Kirke. "What are you talking about?"

"He's worked out the location. He knows all."

"I wouldn't say all. I know it's all tied to Hal and the events that commenced with him."

Carissa dropped to the floor and kneeled near Kirke.

Xen sped to Carissa's side, then lifted her and put her in the armchair. "I will explain."

"Well, yes, please do because I have no idea what anyone is talking about," Adam said.

"As I was saying to Kane and Adam. Everything began with Hal. Odysseus, Kirke's partner, was not taken as a means of leverage to get her to do Hal's bidding. Odysseus, or rather his name and his connection to Kirke, plays a role in this whole disappearing gods debacle."

"What role might that be?" Carissa asked.

"How many of you remember the events in the *Odyssey*?"

They all mumbled a collective familiarity.

"Let's recap. Calypso kept Odysseus on her island for seven years. Until Athena intervened." They all nodded.

"I still don't see how it's all related."

"Hal took Odysseus and had Calypso, who is a demigod, put a spell on him."

Adam held up a finger. "Wait, there's a Calypso demigod?"

"Yes, and I'll fill you in later." Kane said. "Just keep up."

"The spell wasn't just to keep Kirke from finding him. It was to have the nymph Calypso keep the kidnapped gods and goddesses presence invisible to all."

"So, Odysseus is on Calypso's island?" Carissa asked.

"Yes," Kirke answered.

Adam raised his hand to ask a question like a schoolkid.

"You're not in kindergarten," Kane said.

"Well, I didn't want to interrupt. When you say Odysseus and Calypso, are we talking *the* Odysseus?"

Xen had the words ready to answer. "No. He has long passed to where the shades reside."

He watched as Carissa reached for Kirke's hand. "So, what you are saying is that Calypso's island is where Odysseus and the gods and goddesses are."

"Exactly, *koukla*."

"You know we've got no chance in locating Calypso's island under a glamour." Kane supplied.

"Wrong, wolf." Kirke's voice was raspy. "I managed to do it, but as soon as my foot hit the soil, I had to fight off demons. I barely had time to spell myself here."

Xen mulled over Kirke's words. "Then we have less time than I thought. Someone would have already notified Kronos."

"Kronos?" Adam, Kane, and Kirke asked at the same time.

"Yes. Athena appeared and advised us as to who she and Ares suspects," Xen said.

"And Father is missing too."

Kane's brows knitted together. "Well, that's not good."

"No, it's not. Without Ares, we will lose the will to fight. Without that, the *Phi* become nothing more than a bunch of supernatural guys hanging out with beers."

"How fast can we assemble a team?" Carissa asked.

"It is already in motion." He smiled at her

"Kirke, we will need you to reveal that island."

"My power is your power."

A knock sounded at the door. Xen knew who it was, and so did Adam and Kane. This one he would leave for Carissa. She rose to her feet. "I'll get that."

"Joooones." Carissa squealed his name and made a beeline to tackle him with a hug.

"Good to see you too." He squeezed her tightly before letting her go.

"Come in, come in." She waved her arm to get inside from the thunder.

"Awful storm coming."

"You have no idea." She led him to the living room, where all the others were assembled.

He let out a whistle when he saw familiar faces. "Wow, having a late-night party." He winked at Carissa.

She bumped his shoulder. "More like a save the gods and goddesses mission party."

His mouth dropped open. "What have I not been told?"

"Lots, pup," Kane said from where he sat.

"Then fill me in, old man."

Kane grinned at the banter. Riling up Jones was something he and Xen enjoyed doing but the pup enjoyed giving it back.

"In short. Gods and goddesses have disappeared. Kronos is behind it, and if we don't return them soon...."

"No more planet as we know it," Jones added.

"Spot on," Adam said. "Kill Zeus, and you weaken Ra and Jupiter. All one thread."

"What's that in your hands?" Carissa asked, noticing the large envelope that Jones held.

"That would be the information Xen requested on your grandfather."

Carissa shot a look over to Xen. *Thank you.*

"Any new light on the circumstances?"

"Everything appears to be as reported. Break-in, senior citizen suffered a heart attack, but there was no proof of whether it happened while the break-in was in progress. One thing bothers me, though. The coroner's report. Given he had a heart attack, there were no blockages in the aorta to cause the heart to seize."

"Magic," Kirke added.

"I wouldn't rule it out," Jones said.

Her grandfather had died trying to protect everything under the house. "I knew it the moment we found the room."

"What room?" Jones and Adam asked.

She didn't get to answer because her family had the best timing. Not. "Carissa, what is all the noise about." Yiayia and Aunt Paula were standing at the living room entrance. They both gasped. Then had a fit of joy at seeing Jones.

"Gelon." Yiayia pulled him in for a squeeze.

"Move over, Vetta, let me get a hug in." Paula said. "Are you married yet, Gelon? We have to set you up with a nice girl. I have a…"

"*Thitsa*, stop it," Carissa chided.

"I want a nice girl. Why does he get the nice girls?" Adam mumbled from where he was sitting.

Kane reached over and gave him one upside the head. "*Malaka.* Stick to the program."

"Okay, enough, everyone," Xen bellowed. "Kane, Adam, meet me at my place and Kirke, we'll see you at the tarmac tomorrow."

Carissa watched as everyone cleared out. Kirke blew her a kiss from where she sat. She gestured goodbye. Kirke zapped out of the room. Carissa turned to face Xen.

"I take it we overdid it?" she asked him.

"Every moment we spend clowning around is another moment that Kronos will succeed. We will have time for jokes later."

Yiayia and Aunt Paula were whispering to Jones. "Okay. Let me get my grandmother and aunt back to bed."

"A wise idea. I need a further word with Jones."

"Be nice."

"Always."

She stepped closer and put her arms around him. "Don't think I haven't noticed all your alpha growling when he's in the room."

He leaned in and gave her a small kiss on her nose. "You're mine."

"Well, we have established that, Mr. Neanderthal." She gave him a quick peck on the lips, then stepped away to get her family to bed. "Yiayia, auntie."

"Is it true?" Yiayia said to Carissa and Xen. "About your grandfather?"

"Yes, it appears so," Xen said. "We will keep looking until we know exactly what unfolded that night."

Carissa could see the conflict on her grandmother's face. She stepped in and ushered the women toward the stairs. Rest would help them.

She heard Xen say, "Gelon. A word before you go."

The wolf gave him the large envelope he'd been holding. Jones was an undercover detective on the police force for the Phi. Any unusual cases that involved unearthly beings were managed by him. Those cases were then passed to Xen and his men for further investigation. "If this was handled by your predecessor in the police force, do you think he left any note or indication of who he might have suspected?"

"I have gone through everything. The detective left a note with a question mark on it. Your guess is as good as mine."

Xen let out a sigh. "Could mean anything, but I can't shake the feeling that it is all connected."

"I'll keep looking." Jones made his way to the door.

Even though Xen felt protective of Carissa, he knew that Jones would be a great asset to the mission. "I'd like you on the team."

"You know I can't take time off. Different story if it was on home turf."

"I understand, and thanks for the information." He lifted the envelope.

Carissa came down the stairs.

"Thanks, Jones. I owe you a burger."

"You'd better believe it." He grinned and gave her a tight hug then turned to leave.

Xen tried to keep his beast under the wraps. He didn't like other men too close to his woman. Logic told him it was okay, but his predator side didn't listen to reason. An unfortunate vampire reflex action.

"Night." He waved as he walked to his parked car.

Xen watched the lightning flash across the sky. With a bit of luck, they'd put Kronos back where he belonged – the dark chasm of Tartarus.

"What's on your mind? You look miles away." She shut the front door and locked it.

"There's one more thing I want to talk about before it's time for rejuvenation. You know I don't want to leave, but I will have to as there is much to prepare before we set off on our mission."

"I know. What was it you wanted to say?"

"Let's go up to your room." They made their way up the stairs in silence. He'd tell her what he needed, and then he would have her. His desire for her was always at the forefront of his thinking. She was his biggest preoccupation and his biggest weakness. There were small details to his plans that he had to go over, but he'd rather spend time with her. They entered her room, and Carissa closed the door behind them with a soft click.

"What I have to say, must stay with you."

She held up a hand. "*Philaso.*" She whispered the spell to conceal the room. The proverbial cone of silence.

He smiled at her.

"Impressive, eh?"

"Very, but let's get on track. When you were on Olympus, Thanatos paid me a visit. He said that I had to find the adamantine sickle that belonged to Kronos and put it in your hand. That it would be the only way to defeat the god behind all the disappearances."

"I'm going to go out on a limb here and say that you found that sickle."

He nodded. "I did."

"Why me? I'm a nobody."

"Wrong, *koukla*. You are the daughter of a god."

"There are other children from the gods. Even others by Ares in the past."

"You were chosen, and there is nothing more to be said on the matter."

"I keep hearing that, and I have a hard time trying to figure out why anyone would pick me for such a quest."

"None of us can truly know. The Fates have decided things long ago. All we can do is follow the road and see where it leads."

"What if I don't like where it leads me?"

"Then we will assess the situation together."

He pulled her into his arms and sought out her lips. He pried them open and gave her the kind of kiss that showed his hunger for more.

He broke the kiss. "I need you."

Everything would have to wait for a few hours. Their journey ahead would be bumpy. He wanted something to ground him, and his delectable female was in his arms. That was enough for now.

TWENTY-EIGHT

Stand a little out of my sun. ~ Diogenes to Alexander the Great

Charleston, SC
Early morning, mortal realm - Day 12

The early morning rays tickled Carissa's face. She popped an eyelid open and scanned her surroundings. If Xen had slept here, the blinds and curtains would have been drawn. He must have pulled one open before he headed out. A white envelope blinked in brightness on the lamp table. She stretched out and took it. Who even did this in this day and age? Everyone just sent text messages. She sat up with a little excitement fluttering around in her chest. *Romantic,* she thought.

Good morning to the woman who is the ray of sunshine in my darkened world.

We have a dangerous mission ahead, I have made the necessary arrangement, and will see you on the plane.

With all my love,
Xen

She glanced at the clock, 7:00 am. "Time to get the day in motion," She mumbled to herself. Then pulled back her covers and pushed out of bed. Her feet landed on the plush carpet, and a tingling raced through her body. "*Rigos.*" She spoke the spell to control her power.

Her head turned toward the roof when she heard soft tapping. *An animal?* She shrugged her shoulders and thought nothing more of the noise. She headed for the shower.

When she stepped into the kitchen, the coffee had been poured, and breakfast lay on the table: an assortment of fresh fruit and Greek yogurt, plus fresh bread.

"Yiayia, what time did you get up?"

"Not long after your fiancé left."

She prayed they weren't too loud. Heat crept up her face.

"Why are you all red? It's fine. I was young and in love once."

Great, just what she wanted to hear from her grandmother.

"Where's auntie?" Carissa tried to divert the conversation.

"Still sleeping."

Carissa spooned some yogurt into a small bowl and added fresh berries. She took a mouthful while watching the small television. The news reported storms and bad crops. The fearsome weather was escalating, and they needed to stop it. Actually, she had to stop it.

"Yiayia, did Pappou ever show you the codex?"

"No, my child."

"I can't recall him ever showing me."

She finished her yogurt, but something in her mind said she had to go upstairs and investigate that tapping sound. She had a flicker of recollection about the room in the attic. In the dark recess of her memory, something probed her to investigate.

"Excuse me, Yiayia."

She made her way up the stairs. With each step, she could hear a light sound. She stopped to listen. Again, a tap, tap, tap sounded. *Mice,* she thought. No matter what, she'd have to find the source.

Aside from it being annoying, it was as if the tapping was calling her. Carissa dashed into her room and opened her bedside table drawer. Her fingers closed around a set of keys. She headed out of her bedroom and to the end of the corridor. Carissa felt herself trembling as she slid the key in the door and turned. She could see light filtering from the attic window. She had forgotten that the attic had been converted to a bedroom with an office.

She took the stairs two at a time. Her feet hit soft carpet, so where was the tapping? She scanned the room. *Nothing out of place.* The room itself was the size of her own, and it also had an en-suite. She stared out the window. The view had its advantages.

There were cupboards along one side with bay window seating and small cupboards underneath. Maybe there was a mouse or other critter in a cupboard. She opened the doors and peered through each carefully. The first few were filled with clear tubs of linen and bath towels, the last three filled with books. Her fingers ran along the spines. Everything had been put in alphabetical order. She dropped to the floor and sat cross-legged beneath the bay window. She opened those cupboards. "Hmm. More books." These were not in any order. One of the cupboards held a collection of romance novels. She smiled. These were her mother's. An image streamed in her mind, her mother sitting in the reading chair with her nose stuck in a novel. Her mother really did like her happily-ever-after stories.

Carissa pulled a few out and read the blurbs on the back. Maybe she'd grab some for nighttime reading. Her brain, as if on cue, flashed her images of Xen. There'd be no reading with him around. He'd show her happily ever after. Smiling at her silliness, she pulled a few more books out. Her fingers brushed against something hard and cold. She squirmed to get a better look. A hidden compartment, just like the one in the kitchen. She pushed, and it revealed a safe. What clue would Pappou have left in here?

She sat and thought about the combination her grandfather might have used. Then she remembered, and the whole situation came to life. Carissa put her fingers on the round dial. She'd done this before, but not here. Her grandfather used to get her to practice on a toy safe. Twelve to the right, twelve to the left, twelve right and then break twelve to six on the left and six again on the right, pull lever. A click sounded and the door opened.

"Okay, not what I was expecting."

She pulled out something covered in linen. She wondered if she should get gloves, but the linen didn't look old. She repositioned herself on the floor. Her fingers made quick work of unwrapping what appeared to be a book.

She gasped as her fingers ran around the codex.

This was what her grandfather had been protecting, and it had been hidden under everyone's noses the whole time.

She heard a clink in the safe box. A letter sat waiting. "Where did you come from?"

The envelope was addressed to her. She could hear her pulse pound in her ears.

She opened the letter. It had been written by her grandfather.

Carissa mou,

I can't express the importance of keeping this codex from falling into the wrong hands. I'm afraid that if you are reading this then I am no longer here to explain our duty and why our family has the responsibility of keeping this codex safe.

Protecting the codex is now your duty. This codex has the ability to erase all belief, but it can also be a weapon to stop those wishing to harm humanity. Many will try to obtain it, but you cannot allow them to succeed. Only you can wield it.

Every few years, I went to great efforts to move the book to ensure its safety. You must also do the same. Remember to set up wild goose chases to help buy you time but also to alert you that someone is coming. Only you must know its location. This fact makes you highly vulnerable.

One more thing. This codex is only to be used in an extreme emergency, where the fabric of creation and belief are threatened. Once the balance is restored, the codex must once again disappear.

Keep it safe.

With all my love,
Your Pappou.

P.S. Do not despair. The codex will guide you.

"Great," she said to the room. "I'll never not be a walking target."

She re-wrapped the codex and put it aside. She locked the safe and hid it again with the books.

"Right, dear old codex. You and I are going to have a long relationship as well as be cozy travel companions, so you better get used to me."

Warmth and light radiated out from the linen around the codex. It had heard her.

"Wonderful. So not only do you have all this power, you can hear me." Warmth glowed again.

Time to figure out how to travel with the codex. She put the attic room in order then made her way down the stairs. Now that she had found the book, she would have preferred to have never known about it. It came with a heavy burden. One she would have to carry on her own as much as Xen and his *Phi* would support her, this was her responsibility. She could not risk its discovery.

With slow steps, she made her way to her bedroom. The sunny rays that had roused her were now gone.

Time to pack what she needed.

As the letter said, only in an emergency. "Definitely one now." Who knew what they would face?

Lightning hit somewhere close. A shiver ran up her spine. She walked over to her small closet and retrieved a duffel bag. In its wide space, she layered dark clothes at the bottom then put the book on top, adding another layer of clothes. She held her hand over the bag. "*Philaso*." She breathed. Hopefully, that would keep the book protected until she required its help.

"Carissa." Aunt Paula's voice sounded from behind the door.

"Yes, *thitsa*."

Her aunt pushed the door open. "Are you okay? Yiayia sent me up. Said you disappeared."

"I'm on my way down."

Receding footsteps sounded in the hallway.

She placed her sword on top of the bag and remembered the necklace Athena had given her. She wore it still. Athena had said it was a shield. "Let's hope it works when called for."

Content with her packing, she folded her grandfather's letter and put it in her jeans. Though it weighed nothing, the sensation of it in her pocket resembled a piece of lead.

She took the stairs two at a time. She wanted to talk to her grandmother and aunt, in case she didn't make it back.

They were sitting at the table arguing about the color of some socialite's dress on the TV. She cleared her throat and dropped into one of the chairs.

"Would you like something, dear?"

"No, Yiayia, I'm fine. Besides, I can make something myself."

"I never said you couldn't." Her grandmother eyed her with suspicion. "Why the somber mood?" Yiayia filled a glass of water for her from the carafe on the table.

She thought about how to answer her grandmother and aunt. She didn't want to lie or keep anything from them, but this burden would be hers to carry. The more she stayed here, the more she put them in danger. She wanted to live with Xen—she was bonded to him and married by vampire law. Xen had men and equipment to deal with a variety of unearthly problems. Here her aunt and grandmother only had pots and pans to fight with. Although the image did make her smile.

"That's better," Aunt Paula said. "Thinking about your vampire."

She spluttered. "I wasn't thinking about Xen." She choked back a smile. "Well, not in any way you might think I'd be thinking."

Aunt Paula reached over and stroked her hand. "Sure, dear."

Okay, enough silliness. She needed to talk things through with them. "I was thinking about the danger I brought to you and Yiayia. I'm not happy about that, and we need to work something out."

"We'll be fine," Yiayia said.

"Not if a bunch of demons or unearthly creatures turn up on your doorstep."

"We've got Xen's men watching."

"One day someone will be late, or something will happen. It only takes a second. Neither of you can defend yourselves against a real threat."

She could not let anything befall her family. There had been enough death. "Xen mentioned that we should move in with him so they can secure Pappou's room. I think it might be wise if I move in with him on a permanent basis."

Paula gasped and Yiayia protested. "I won't stop you from the choices you decide for yourself, but I want you to understand that your *pappou's* wards have held for years. He might have gotten sloppy toward the end, but this house has been warded. And I believe it will continue to be safe because your vampire won't let any harm come to you or anyone he cares about."

"She has a point." Aunt Paula spoke wisely.

"How do you explain Pappou and the break-in? They found him. Magic was used."

"I'm not going to guess what might have happened that night. I'd drive myself crazy," Yiayia said. "But that duty was his well before Ares met your mother, and this thing started."

"Vetta is right, Carissa."

Her grandmother leaned over the table and took Carissa's hands in hers. "Let's take it one step at a time. I'm sure the right path will reveal itself."

Carissa placed her other hand over her *yiayia's*. Then Paula put her hands over theirs.

Tears flowed. "Thank you, Yiayia and *thitsa*."

"Just doing our job," Paula said with a wink.

These women, for all their craziness, were her family. No matter what lay ahead, these women would always be in her heart. Wherever they were, that's where home resided.

"One last thing. I leave tonight with Xen. We have a location. If anything happens to me…" She held her breath.

"…nothing will happen to you." Aunt Paula finished.

Yiayia pierced her with a penetrating gaze. "It is your destiny. You. Have. This."

"It's, You've. Got. This." Paula corrected.

"Same thing."

"Doesn't have the same ring."

"My ears are ringing from listening to you." Yiayia tossed a glare at her cousin, who stuck out her lip in a pout.

Carissa let out a laugh.

"You know people pay good money to see women banter like this."

"What, you mean that *My Big Fat Greek Wedding*?" Yiayia tossed her head.

"They've got nothing on us," Aunt Paula agreed.

No, they didn't. These two were on a planet all of their own, and Carissa wouldn't have it any other way. Even though there were times she herself could throttle them.

"I sent one of the wolves to pick up a baklava."

"I'm not having it if it's Basil's." Her *yiayia* said.

Carissa took a drink of water.

"Really, Vetta, you should as the British say, just bonk him and get it out of your system."

Carissa sprayed the water in her mouth all over yiayia and Aunt Paula. Forget demons, these women would be the death of her.

TWENTY-NINE

In all things of nature there is something of the marvelous
~ Aristotle

Charleston Executive Airport; Charleston, SC
Mid-morning, mortal realm - Day 13

Kane and Adam had collected Carissa from her grandmother's house. When she had boarded the plane, she found a gift-wrapped package on her seat. They'd been in the air for ten hours and had another six to go. They had stopped over in New York and collected more of the *Phi* team, both vampires and *lykoi*.

Carissa glanced down and admired her newly booted feet, a smile tugged at her lips. She turned her head over to her right and caught the sea-green gaze of Xen.

"Thank you."

"You've already said that, *koukla*."

"I really love them."

"I know." He leaned in and gave her a quick peck on the lips.

"Why don't you get some rest? It's a long flight."

"I will, but first tell me about Calypso's island. Is there anything I have to know? Does it have any monsters or animals unique to it?"

"Good question. No, it does not, but don't forget there may be demons working with Kronos."

"What about the terrain?"

"Now that's where it's interesting. What you see may be different to what you will experience. The land is not all dry rocks. There are vines and plants growing all over it."

"How do you know?"

"It has been talked about for many millennia and somewhat of a quest to heroes."

Adam, who sat behind Xen and Carissa, joined the conversation. "I thought that Calypso's cave was at Gozo in Malta."

"No, it's not." Xen took a breath and continued. "Calypso's cave is not visible to anyone because it has always been cloaked by a spell. It's basically as invisible as the fictionalized version of Paradise Island in *Wonder Woman*." That line got a laugh out of the men sitting around them.

"So, the tourist attraction on Gozo?" Adam questioned.

"Is just that, a place named to wow the tourists," Kane threw in.

Carissa shifted in her seat and put her head on Xen's shoulder. Maybe she'd close her eyes for a few minutes.

Light fingers stroked her face and hair. "*Koukla*, time to wake up."

A dream, she thought. Xen's voice coaxed her again. "I'll have to leave you on the plane."

Her eyes snapped open. Her vampire had a silly lopsided grin on his face. "Really, you'd leave me on the plane?"

"You know the only place you will be is by my side." He dropped a light kiss on her nose. They stood to address the teams on the plane.

"Okay, listen up. From Malta, we are taking three boats and one helicopter. The chopper is going to fly over Calypso's island once the spell has been removed. That team will parachute to the island from the northeast and await my command. Make sure you have your night vision goggles and all tech communication." He focused on Kirke. "Your job is to extract Odysseus and leave. Do not wait around."

She nodded her approval.

He turned to address his men. "The boat teams will hit the island from the northwest, southwest, and southeast. Are we clear?"

"Roger that."

"Clear."

"Clear."

All the men acknowledged the directions.

The wheels of the plane hit the tarmac. The hive of activity from Xen's team made it all more real. This was the moment they saved not only her father, Zeus, and the other gods and goddess but humanity as well. Carissa waited with Xen as the men cleared out. She pulled her duffel bag from the overhead compartment and retrieved her sword.

"Here, let me help you with that."

She turned and gave Xen access to the harness straps. She hated to admit that he tightened it better than she did, but then again, the gear was new. Sheathing the sword Xen had given when she left for Olympus, and having it in on her back gave her a sense of confidence.

All the men and Kirke had exited the plane.

"Xen, listen." She had to say what had plagued her. "A lot can go wrong. I need to know that you will care for Yiayia and Aunt Paula."

Xen pulled her close. "I don't want to hear you talking like this. We will succeed and you can make all the arrangements yourself. With my assistance, of course."

She smiled. "This is bigger than me. I don't know what the Fates think I'm capable of, but I don't share their opinion on the matter. Let's face it. I know myself better."

He let out a laugh. "You know, *koukla,* that you have to accept who you are. You have power, yet you still don't believe in yourself."

"I can't control any of it, Xen."

"When learning to ride a bike, we don't have that skill. But we have the courage to try. Sure, we fall a few times, but we don't give up."

"That's the problem. I keep falling."

He pulled her in. "No, you don't, *koukla*. I've seen changes in you that you fail to recognize in yourself."

"I want to be the heroine everyone wants me to be, but I don't know if I can."

"Believe."

She dropped her gaze.

His fingers touched her chin and lifted it so that her eyes meet his. "I trust and believe in you. You should, too."

She wanted to. Oh, how she wanted. She stepped out from his embrace.

"There's something I want to share with only you." She fumbled with her pocket and pulled out the letter that weighed more than the paper it had been written on. She gave it to him, but when he touched the letter, it burned his fingertips. He shook his hand.

Her eyes went wide. "I'm so sorry. Are you okay?"

"I've had worse," he said with a hint of humor. "Hold it up, and I'll read it."

"Yeah, yeah, sure." She did as he asked.

"It's blank."

"What?"

"There is no text on that sheet of parchment." She flipped it over, and text danced before her eyes. The spell would not reveal what her grandfather had written.

"I believe what is written is for your eyes only."

She glanced at the letter. Then after debating internally whether to read it out aloud, she decided to put it back in her pocket.

"You know I can lift it from your mind if you let me in."

"No. This one is mine to carry."

"Spoken like a true warrior, *koukla*."

She admired his confidence and strength. She wondered whether the Fates had it all wrong. Xen knew there was a prophecy, but she had yet to describe the images she'd seen when Zeus gave her the potion. "I have one more thing I want to tell you."

"Go ahead, *koukla*."

"When I was on Olympus, Zeus gave me a memory about a prophecy that involves you, and me, and a champion who will help defeat an uprising. But the images I saw in my mind made no sense, and I saw no champion or bad guys, just famine and destruction."

"What does it have to do with me?" he asked.

"Zeus said that the minute you called on Father, and he heeded the call, it caused a ripple between the realm of the gods and the mortal realm. You were never supposed to make it out of the cave. You altered your future."

She watched as he mulled that over. He looked at her intently. "One thing I know for sure. You are mine, and whatever lies ahead, whether good or bad, we will work through it together."

He pulled her in and gave her a kiss that left her legs weak and trembling.

"Xen, we're ready." Kane's voice echoed.

"Be right there."

She puffed out her chest. "Let's do this."

"Now, that's the girl I want to see."

They exited the plane, and got into the last black van. Lightning boomed louder and closer as they drove to the docks. The storm had picked up. Soon it would be out of control. They needed to hurry or they'd never find the island.

Her thoughts strayed to her father. What had befallen him?

"The team riding in the helicopter is unsettled. They didn't want to complete the mission." Adam's voice brought her out of her musing.

Father. "Then it has begun. What if the men bail?" she asked.

Xen seized her hand. "That is a risk that we have to take."

"You guys aren't getting that feeling." She questioned Kane, Adam, and the others in the van.

"Not on your life, sister," Adam said with a wink.

Kirke had been too silent for her liking. She turned to look at her friend. Kirke's gaze remained glued out the window. "You will save him. Save them all. I will never be able to repay you for this."

"Is that why you are quiet? It's what we do for each other, and it's not about repayment. You have done plenty for me."

"I could have done more," Kirke said.

"Forget the past. Let's look forward with new hope." She squeezed Xen's hand.

The rest of the trip passed with everyone lost in their own thoughts. Her own contemplation spiraled in different directions. This mission should have been hers and hers alone. Like the codex.

Her burden.

Her albatross.

Her dilemma.

Why bring Xen and the *Phi* to their doom?

Xen's voice in her head answered. *That's where you are wrong. Our stories are long and complicated. We were created to fight. It's what we do.*

It should be no one but me going in there. She answered.

Wrong again. We are a team. Your quests are mine. We are bound in more ways than one.

"I won't argue with you. I hope we can pull it off."

The low hum of an engine turned off made the hackles on her neck rise.

Xen tapped his communicator. "We are ready to transfer to the boat."

Ten minutes later, he turned to Kirke. "It's your show now."

Kirke removed the cloak she had drawn tighter around her as they sped on the water. She raised her arms and chanted an incantation. "*Apokalypto to nisi.*"

The cloak that had masked the island disappeared. Even in the darkness, one would be drawn to the beauty of its beach. Xen nodded to Kirke.

Carissa stepped close and hugged her. "Go find him."

"That I will," she said and disappeared.

They dropped anchor and Xen tapped his earpiece. "Teams, check in. Have you a visual?"

They must have confirmed, because the whole team's faces filled with joy. That elation turned sour in a blink.

"What's happened?" she asked.

"The helicopter crashed," Xen said. He touched his communicator again. "Team on northwest location. You are to travel northeast and check the crash site. Bring me up to speed as soon as you are there."

"Xen, this was what I was talking about."

"Carissa, listen. This stuff happens. We are not always in control. The men on that helicopter are immortal, and they will recover. We are here to fight because we don't want some crazy-assed god who has a grudge against our gods to rise and succeed," Kane said. "Now, let's get off this boat and set up camp."

"Everything he said is true," Xen said.

"Then why did you all look like they were fried for good?"

"Because it is always a disappointment to have a team left inactive and injured until they can heal. The *lykoi* heal a little slower than the vampires so long as neither are pierced in the heart, they will recover.

"Xen, I'm sorry about your men."

He pulled her in and gave her a panty-melting kiss. He broke the spell he had put her under. "There is nothing for you to be sorry about. I'll be in rejuvenation in two hours. We have to unload our equipment." He turned her and pointed in the water where one of a few small dinghies had been dropped, so they could row to the island. "You'll go first with me." He grabbed her to help lower her. Adam and Kane had jumped in ahead and helped her stabilize. The boat rocked, and she found a small space to sit.

The trip to shore was brief. They made quick work of setting up camp in a small cave. "I take it there is more than one cave on Calypso's island?"

"Total of seven," Xen answered.

"Where will you take your rejuvenation sleep?"

"We're setting that up now."

"But how?"

She scanned the equipment and watched as Kane and Adam unloaded the rest. Nothing appeared big enough to fit Xen."

Adam placed a large steel box with a lid on it on the rough surface of the cave. He took out a remote and pressed a few buttons. It started to open up by lengthening. Her mouth hung open. Xen put a finger under her chin and closed her mouth. "In that," he answered.

"I should have known." She rolled her eyes. "Another Phi Technologies invention."

He smiled. "I can't take credit for that one. That beauty is the brainchild of Paris."

"Speaking of which, where is he? I have not seen him at all."

"We've placed him on leave. He lost one of his cadets in a skirmish with demons."

"How did he die?"

"Sword through the heart."

She swallowed hard. "Poor Paris. I can't imagine what he is going through."

"He will push through it with time."

As more men came to shore, they brought more of the same steel boxes. One by one, they opened them up. A total of eight. She moved over to inspect them. "Will we have to stand guard?"

"Only one, the rest of you will be doing reconnaissance."

She examined the cave. A chill went up her spine. "Don't worry, *koukla*. These portable sleeping tubs are safe from outside attack."

"But--"

"Shh." He placed a finger to her lips. "Let's get a spot ready for you and the others. You should sleep. You cannot keep my hours."

The men used their vampire speed to set up inflatable mattresses. The *lykoi* dispersed and found a spot for their sleeping bags. The vampires got busy with their rejuvenation boxes and equipment. Xen led Carissa to a spot near his. "I'll cuddle with you till you fall asleep."

She nodded and dropped the bag she had still been holding and pulled off her sword and harness, and placed them on top of the bag.

The bag would have to be protected. "Is there room in your sleeping box for my bag?"

"Why would you want to put it in there?"

She dropped the shield in her mind. *Let's just say it has something to do with the letter you couldn't read.*

His eyes widened for a split second. *Say no more.*

She put her mind shield in place and held out her bag. He placed it in his box.

A sense of relief tingled over her body.

"Come on, *koukla*. Rest with me and sleep."

She knew it wasn't time yet for his and the other vampires rejuvenations, but she had to have sleep, and so did the *lykoi*. The comfort of being in his arms helped her drift off.

THIRTY

In critical moments even the very powerful have need of the weakest. ~ Aesop

Ionian Sea, between Greece and Sicily, Calypso's Island revealed, Morning, mortal realm – Day 15

A loud thud brought Carissa out of her sleep. She blinked her eyes and shot straight up, almost head butting the face that had been staring at her. Koal fell on his ass.

In a flash, Kane and Adam were on either side of him with swords drawn.

Koal put his hands up in surrender. "I mean her no harm."

"He's an ally," Carissa said.

Kane and Adam moved their swords.

Carissa got to her feet and held her hand out to help him up. "What are you doing here?"

"Who is this guy?" Kane asked.

"Oh, sorry. Kane, Adam, this is Koal."

Koal bowed. "God of clumsiness and stooges."

"Great," Kane said. "More clowns."

Carissa watched as Kane scrutinized him. "Why are you here?"

"Get in line, Kane. I already asked that," Carissa said.

Koal cleared his throat. "Your father asked me to follow you and only reveal myself once you arrived safely. Ares told me to remind you to keep your powers masked, because gods can sense power. It will bring their attention to you, and I don't think you want that." He waved his arm around the cave.

"Thank you, Koal. I will ensure I have my guard up and power masked."

"So, you've been following Carissa all this time?" Kane asked.

"Yes."

"Xen needs to come up with a god detector," Adam said.

"He's working on it," Kane fired back.

Carissa's train of thought turned in a different direction as realization at his words got her gray matter working faster. "You… you." Heat crept up her throat. "You haven't been watching while I've been with Xen."

Koal held up his hands. "No, no. What do you take me for? I'm no perv."

"Perving could have advantages." Adam wagged his eyebrows.

Kane hit him over the head. "*Skasi malaka*, keep the weird shit to yourself, *lykos*."

"Eewww," Carissa said.

Koal cleared his throat. "I have been watching only when you're on the move."

She let out a sigh of relief. Coffee. She craved caffeine now. "How about some coffee before we set out for the day?"

Kane and Adam headed to the food supplies.

"Will you join us?" she asked Koal.

"It is much faster for me to pop in and pop out around the island."

"But won't that alert the other gods to your power?"

"No. Your father lent me his uncle's cap, which keeps my presence and power pretty much invisible."

"Oh great, a Harry Potter cloak of invisibility," Adam said.

"Hey, the gods invented it first," Koal retorted.

Carissa rolled her eyes. "Koal, be careful." She pointed outside to the sky, lightning still flashed and thunder boomed. "…we haven't much time."

"I understand." He bowed and vanished.

Adam held out a cup of coffee. "Here."

"Thanks." She took a sip. "Mmm. Good."

"You think he's going to be a problem?" Kane asked.

"No, he can be trusted. He helped me on Olympus."

"Then, I will give him the benefit of the doubt."

"He's clumsy but trustworthy. I'm surprised Father has given him a task. Not many gods want to be around him, but he is genuine where other gods are cunning."

She watched as Kane and Adam processed what she said. "He might be of use in more ways than one." Kane toyed with an idea.

It had been on her mind too. "I was thinking the same."

"I, on the other hand, was thinking how useful that cap might be. Think of all the girls I could sneak up on."

Kane hit Adam on the head. "Get your head out of the gutter."

"Can't blame a guy for dreaming a little." He downed the rest of his coffee.

"That's the problem. You dream too much." Kane retorted.

"You love me anyway." Adam walked over to his equipment and started to buckle and strap knives to his body.

These guys didn't do weapons by halves. "You sure you going to need all that?"

A lopsided grin appeared on his face. "Best be prepared."

Carissa took that as her cue to get moving. "I guess then I should prepare too."

"You do that, Rissa," Adam said with a wink.

"Rissa?"

"Well, you can't expect me to call you Carissa all the time. You should have a nickname."

Kane leveled a glowering look over at Adam and crossed his arms over his chest. "Move it, wolf."

"Aye, aye, captain."

Carissa stifled a laugh. The day ahead would be filled with unique Adam moments, and she did not mind one bit. It made the Herculean task somewhat lighter. The news online and on TV had been grim. Fires were breaking out, crops were dying, and farmers were struggling. The missing gods and goddesses had caused climate changes throughout the world. The *Phi* had to locate them and put a stop to it.

She finished her coffee and walked over to her gear. Some of the other men had woken and raced about the cave, putting on gear and grabbing coffee and snacks. "Ready, Rissa." Adam threw a protein bar in her direction.

Rissa, she thought. Something told her that her jealous vampire would throttle Adam when he heard him. "Time for reconnaissance." She moved out of the cave."

Kane tapped his headset. "Head out."

The island had not been what she expected. It was the opposite of the dry rockery she had experienced on the Greek mainland and other islands. Why she envisaged it like that, she hadn't a clue. There were cypress trees and cedar trees as far as her eye could see. She took in as much as she could.

After an hour, they came to a clearing. "Let's stop for a drink and ten-minute break." She had just crouched to look at a small violet when sandaled feet entered her vision. She recognized them immediately and shot to her full height. "What news do you bring, Koal?"

Kane and Adam rushed over to where she stood.

"The cave is to the east. About a forty-minute walk from here. The entrance is heavily armed with demons. Inside, Iapetos has all the gods and goddesses in adamantine cages. Only Zeus and Ares are chained between two stalagmites.

"Wait, did you say Iapetos?" Carissa asked.

"The piercer," Kane said.

"The what? I thought this was Kronos' doing."

"Kronos is part of it, but it is Iapetos who wants revenge for having been thrown into Tartarus."

"Great, now we have two targets," Adam said.

Carissa took a hard swallow. "How on earth are we going to distract both of them? Each wields more power than I can summon."

Koal turned to her. "Trust in yourself."

"We are going to need to separate them." She let out a frustrated sound. It seemed that this task had been multiplying in complexity. She turned to Kane.

"Do you want to continue?"

"I think we should at least set our eyes on the location to have a better understanding of how we are going to attack. If there's only one way in and out, it makes our job difficult."

She pondered what Kane had said. He made valid points. She turned to Koal. "Is there any way of knowing for certain if there is another way in?"

"I will check and report back." He disappeared in a cloud of mist.

"Let's press on," Kane ordered the team with the motion of his hand.

At the end of their walk, they came across a cave opening that had a trailing vine over the hollow; it had a sweet aroma and drooped heavy with blooms.

Kane signaled his men to scout. They moved with speed and precision. They watched from their positions for a few minutes. Koal had been right. Demons were posted at the cave's entrance.

Kane gave the signal to move out. Their reconnaissance complete. Once they were thirty minutes away, the conversation started. Kane pulled Carissa back to walk with her.

"What's wrong, Carissa? You haven't said much."

"Just thinking."

"About?"

"So much, Kane, so much."

"We all have stuff going on. None of us is without issues."

"I know that, but it always feels as if my worries are bigger than anyone else's. Trying to defeat two gods will be difficult. Our only hope lies in separating them long enough to free Zeus and Father. I have no idea how to win this, Kane. None."

"We will work it out together, and we will fight it together."

"If only it were just a simple demon skirmish."

"Where the gods are concerned, it is never simple."

"You can say that again."

They retraced their path and stopped in a clearing. The vegetation, which had some flowers and greenery hours before, had turned brown. "Guys, look." Turning in a circle, she pointed to the trees and what had been leafy green foliage.

"Eurynome is dying." At the mention of her name Koal reappeared. He surveyed the surrounding greenery, and a tear escaped.

"*Skata*," Adam said.

"Koal. I'm…" She choked.

"Don't apologize, it's not your doing."

She'd never felt more useless than what she did looking into Koal's eyes and seeing the dead vegetation that surrounded them.

"You need to speed your ambush up. I'm going to see what I can do. Call your brother. Oh, and there's only one way in and one way out."

"Wait, Koal." He had already disappeared.

"Why do I get the feeling that he will do something stupid?" Kane queried.

"Because that's what he does," Adam answered.

"True. We should move. We have to get men into position."

"Have you heard from the others?"

"We have. I have given the SW team the coordinates. They will be in place by the time we get there tonight with Xen and the rest of the team. The others have been accounted for and are healing. They will take a few of the vamps from that team and leave the others to recover. We're bringing the boat around the northeast position. We will leave the island from there once we've made the rescue."

"Let's hurry, Kane. It won't be long before that sky darkens, and all we get is thunder and lightning." On cue, thunder sounded.

They moved faster now, and each of her steps was heavier. The weight of the situation began to push her further into the earth. Its effects crushing her both physically and mentally.

Once at the cave, the men passed around pre-made sandwiches and water. She ate quietly as she watched the sun outside slowly subside. Once the sun went down, Xen and the others would be up. She thought about what Koal said about calling her brother. She might have to.

They needed all the help they could muster. She had Athena, too, but she would be her last card. No sense revealing one's hand to Kronos and Iapetos.

Xen's sleeping chamber clicked, and the lid started to slide open. "Miss me, *koukla*."

She jumped to her feet. "You have no idea."

He was out of his portable bed before her slow limbs could move. He stepped in and seized her lips.

"Get a room," Adam shouted.

He pulled back and must have noticed her embarrassment because he yelled out, "Quiet, wolf, or I'll have your head." Turning to Carissa, he gave her a tender smile. "Now, bring me up to speed."

She commenced and gave Xen all the details of the day. From Koal's appearance to his new intel on who was holding the gods.

"We have a colossal-sized problem. Kronos isn't acting alone-- he's working with his brother Iapetos." She finally added.

"That's not good. You know that his children are the ancestors of mankind."

"I didn't know," she said. So, the god of mortality wanted everyone and everything dead. "I guess this is the blame game."

"Blame everyone except himself for his past actions," Kane said.

"There will be no reasoning with him. We need to hit him where it hurts and hope that by freeing the other gods, they'll help us detain him." Xen said.

"Okay, travel light and make sure you have enough weapons. No telling what they will throw at us once they know we are there."

The air shimmered around them. "Relax," Carissa directed to Xen, Kane, and Adam, who had all pulled out weapons. She recognized the signature.

Kirke appeared and stepped close to Carissa for a hug.

"Why are you still here?"

"Well, I almost got to Odysseus, but you have no idea how many demons are stationed around him. I couldn't get him out." Her shoulders slumped in defeat.

Carissa pulled her in for another hug. "Then it looks like you are coming with us. You are going to find the perfect opportunity to spring him when all mayhem breaks loose."

"I will meet you all at the entrance, better to have me there." Kirke turned to Xen. "Your men have arrived and have set up a perimeter."

"Thank you, Kirke. I was just about to contact them."

In true Endora from *Bewitched* style, she waved her arm and disappeared.

"I'd really like that superpower," Adam said.

"So, would I. Very practical." She grinned at him.

"Lucky for us, neither of you can do that," Kane said flatly.

"Oh, lighten up, wolf," Carissa said.

"I'll lighten up when this mission is over." He walked over to pick up the rest of his equipment.

Carissa made a hand motion with her thumb. "What's gotten into him?"

Adam shrugged his shoulders. "Not really sure."

"The tension of the situation has stripped some men of their enthusiasm. A few are holding on to the last threads of fight left in them. The sooner we get Ares out, the better," Xen supplied.

Carissa let Xen's words sink in. Her fingers closed around her duffel bag on the top of Xen's resting box. With a swift tug, she threaded it over her arm. "I'm good to go."

"I can see that."

She gave the cave a once-over. "What about the rest of the stuff in here?"

"We will stack them and leave them. We had no intention of bringing them back with us. Once we leave the shore, this island will be cloaked again."

She nodded in understanding. They had one shot. One shot to defeat two very angry gods.

A shiver ran up her spine. Why did she have a bad vibe about it all?

Xen strapped all his gear on with the speed of a vampire. "Let's move out."

They started the walk to what would be an epic fight. Thunder boomed and lightning flashed. A few of Xen's men lost the drive to fight.

"If we don't get this over with soon there will be no more men left to fight." Xen didn't answer her.

When they reached the cave, Xen's teams gave him a quick update. The problem they had was there was one way in, which meant they would be easy pickings. She had to do her thing.

She closed her eyes and focused. "Echion," she whispered.

The air shifted around her.

"You called me, sister?"

She placed her hands on his arms. "*Rigos*," she said. "I did, and I have a plan. I need your help."

"I am at your disposal, sister."

She quickly updated him. "Whatever I ask you to do, you must remember one important thing."

"And this is?"

"To cloak your power; otherwise, Kronos and Iapetos will sense it."

"Consider that part done. Now, what did you want."

"Assemble what attackers you can over there at the west side of the cave."

"But it's just rock with no entrance."

"Exactly. We're going to blast it and pull the wool over their eyes."

"You really want to make an entrance, sis."

"We have to divert their attention. Then we'll send in Xen and his team to free the gods from the cells. But you and I must get to our father first. We want his battle lust and anger to drive this."

"Something tells me that his anger is going to be epic."

She smiled, thinking of the devastation that their father would cause. "And that's what we're banking on, to win this."

Echion bowed and dematerialized.

She turned to Xen, who sported a grin. "Notify the men and let them know that once that big bang goes off, we hit with everything we've got."

Kane and Adam had heard the exchange between Carissa and Echion. "I'm glad you have him on your side, Rissa," Adam said.

"Rissa?" Xen growled.

"I think that's my cue to ensure the men are ready." Adam slipped away

"Rissa?" Xen said again. "Wolf…" But Adam had gone. Leaving Carissa and Kane laughing.

"I should have made a bet," Kane said.

"Me too." She winked at Kane.

"If he calls you that again. I'll rip him to shreds. It sounds like he is calling a pet."

"Calm down, vampire. He wanted to give her a nickname."

"She is not his buddy, so there is no need for a nickname."

"Ah, hello, I'm here and she can decide if her friends want to call her something other than Carissa."

"I will not have him reducing your name to a pet's name."

Carissa's anger rose. "Xen, stop."

"You are okay with being called a pet's name?"

Carissa let out a huffed breath. "It's just a nickname. Kids do it all the time, it's harmless."

"Yes, *koukla*, kids."

She couldn't fathom why Adam's silliness could get Xen so riled up. The wolf was her friend and nothing more.

Xen dropped what he had in his hands and sped to her, picking her up and heading to a thick tree. He put her down, then pushed her against the tree. Her sword and bag made things a little uncomfortable. His fangs elongated. "That's right, he's your friend, and you are mine. I want him to respect the name you were given." He retracted his fangs and lifted her in his arms. Her legs wrapped around his waist. His mouth found hers and they both battled who would dominate the kiss. She was angry, and she pushed back, but his anger overpowered hers with his possessive kiss. She surrendered after the third attempt. After a few moments, he released her. "Did I make myself clear?"

"Jealousy does not become you. As I said, he means no harm. It's just for fun. We will talk about this more when we get home."

"I can't help what I am, but I can try to be better." He picked her up again and sped back to where all the men were assembled.

Her heart had melted a little. She knew his jealousy came with his vampire possessiveness.

"You stay with me at all times," Xen ordered.

"Likewise."

The lightning had intensified, and big droplets of rain had started. "This isn't good." Xen inspected the night sky. "It is growing more and more out of control. It won't be long before it becomes wild and unpredictable."

"We have to get to Zeus." Her power tingled in her fingers and through her body. "We've run out of time."

Remember to mask your power, kori mou. She heard her father's voice in her head.

Yes, Father.

Oh, *skata*. She'd had gotten emotional and dropped her guard. Way to announce I'm here. "*Rigos*."

THIRTY-ONE

"The air is Zeus, Zeus earth, and Zeus the heaven, Zeus all that is, and what transcends them all." ~ Aeschylus

Cave of Calypso, Greece
Evening, mortal realm - Day 15

The chains of adamantine rubbed against Ares' wrists. He sensed his daughter's power. *Remember to mask your power, kori mou.* He spoke the words to her mind.

Yes, Father. She spoke back to him.

He reached out searching to see if he could sense her.

Nothing.

Good.

She had done what he had asked.

His eyes burned with rage when he caught another glimpse of Zeus. Iapetos would pay for this dearly. He had been draining Zeus's power and trying to absorb it. So far, it had proved difficult. Which made Iapetos lash out at the minor gods, whose powers were easier to drain.

Rage he understood well, even blind rage, but everyone had a limit. At some point, even he, Ares, would listen to reason. He might have had a bad name when it came to battle lust and violence, but there was a place for it on the battlefield. He did not carry that anger everywhere he went, contrary to the rumors. Iapetos was in his estimation beyond redemption.

Around him, the minor gods and goddesses were almost lost, some hanging on by a thread. This only fueled his anger. He hoped that Carissa had her vampire and his men with her. He would not call to her, because he didn't want to risk exposing her.

An explosion sounded on the west side of the cave. Kronos disappeared to investigate.

At the same moment, the eastern front of the cave became a flurry of activity. Demons were dropping. Much to Iapetos' dismay. Serves him right for siding with that vermin. Ares pulled against the chains and they chafed his skin.

When the first team cleared the east entrance enough for the second team to slide in, Carissa wanted to marvel at the beauty inside the cave. Never had she seen anything like it. In the middle sat an elaborate hearth. Cypress trees encased the cave walls. There were four fountains and a meadow with blooms growing over it. *Phantasia*, the word repeated in her mind. She shook her head to dislodge the strange feeling that had come over her.

"Athena," she called.

The goddess appeared in full battle gear. A gold helmet on her head. Her shield one to behold or fear and the gleam of her spear ready to strike.

"I think you know what you have to do."

"Indeed, I do, niece. You tackle your father, and I will get mine." Her eyes blazed as she made her way for Iapetos.

"You should have told me you had that kind of backup," Xen said.

"I didn't know whether she would heed the call."

"Good point."

"Apart from Father, it is hard to know what their motives are and whether they are genuine."

Echion appeared next to her. She had to do this with her brother. "Xen, start freeing the gods and goddesses so they can rejuvenate. We may require the collective power to fight off both Kronos and Iapetos."

"Do not do anything till I return," Xen said to her.

"I won't, now go."

"Echion. What of your men?"

"They are fighting Kronos at the western side. Call if things get dire."

"You have to capture Kronos."

"We are doing what we can, but he has an endless supply of demons."

"Why is it always those guys?"

"Because bad guys breed more."

"That's an awful thought."

Echion winked at her and dematerialized.

Around the cave, Xen's men fought. She scanned the area for Xen and watched him release gods and goddesses from one cage, but there were still many more. Adam and Kane had joined him.

The goddess Athena fought Iapetos. The clash of shields and spears echoed above the rest of the confusion. Each deflected the other's blow, and each strike harder than the previous.

"I have to get to Zeus and Ares. Looks like Athena can more than manage Iapetos."

Unsheathing her sword, she made her way to her father. Xen would not be happy, but she couldn't hang around and watch.

"Father."

"Carissa. Why do you not have your vampire with you?" His eyes flashed.

"He's freeing the gods and goddesses."

"His men can do that."

"Hush, Father. Now let me help."

She tried to dislodge part of the adamantine chain, but it was no use.

"Use your sword." Her father said.

She braced herself and raised the sword of Peleus. Its power acknowledged her and became one with her. Carissa smashed it on the adamantine chain. The blade sliced the hard surface like ax to wood, shattering the binding. A surge of power danced up her father's arm.

She moved over to break the next one. "Carissa, to your side," her father warned. A demon came rushing. She prepared to fight off whatever blow he threw at her. A blur of activity appeared before her.

Xen.

In one graceful movement, his sword sliced through the air, and he took the demon's head.

"What part of stay, don't you understand?"

"I had to do something."

"Not without me. We discussed that."

"Let's not fight now, Mr. Alpha Vampire."

"We will continue this later." He said as a demon rushed his side. He stuck out his sword, and it pierced the demon in the heart. The look Xen held on his features resembled that of boredom, all that was missing was the yawn.

"*Kori mou*, get moving." Her father's voice brought her out of her little tete-a-tete.

She raised her sword and struck the remaining adamantine chain. Once free, he grabbed her and gave her a hug. "Thank you, but we need to get across to Zeus and free him." He stepped back, and Carissa sheathed her sword as did Xen.

"I haven't enough strength yet to dematerialize near him, but I do have the strength to fight."

Xen didn't wait for an answer. He grabbed Carissa's hand and tipped his head to Ares. "Follow me." He led them around the path to where Zeus had been chained.

"We have to get him out of the adamantine chains."

"Allow me." Unsheathing her sword, she pulled back and brought the sword down. Power raced through Zeus's arm, but he was weak. Her father slipped in next to him to hold his weight up, but as Carissa readied to take the next strike a swarm of demons descended.

Carissa stabbed the demon next to her and angered him. He took a step closer but didn't make it. The demon's head dropped to ground. Xen's sword dripped with blood.

"Vampire, toss me a sword," Ares shouted from where he held Zeus.

Xen unsheathed his other sword and threw in Ares' direction. Ares joined the action, and they eliminated the demons that had tried to lay waste to them. The skirmish, however, got Iapetos' attention, and he did not appear pleased. Iapetos raised his hand and blasted Athena with a surge of power that sent her crashing into the cave wall.

A gasp left Carissa's mouth.

"She's okay, *koukla*," Xen supplied from beside her. "We must free Zeus."

Carissa raised her sword but failed to deliver the blow. Kronos appeared and threw a surge of power at her, and it knocked her away from Zeus.

Xen sped to her side. Leaving Ares facing Kronos.

"Ouch, that feels like one of Father's spaghetti training flips."

"My *koukla*, even in pain, you find humor."

Xen helped her to her feet. Her sword and the duffel bag she had threaded on her back weighed a ton. She shook off the pain and spotted Zeus, Ares, and Kronos in a heated shouting match. Iapetos appeared and joined in.

"How do we beat them?"

"One at a time and with this." Xen pulled a long metal box from his black utility vest. "Inside is the adamantine sickle. The very same weapon that Kronos defeated his father with. You only have to pierce him with it to render his power mute long enough for us to bind him."

"When did you pack that box?"

"I'm afraid that now is not the time for this discussion."

"You know that's becoming the standard line with you."

His eyes took her in and zeroed in on her lips. "There is nothing standard about me."

"Now is not the time for that discussion." She decided to throw his line back at him.

He gave her a brief smile. "Let's return to this box and the sickle."

"Why can't you do it?"

"Because Thanatos said it has to be by your hand."

Her chest tightened. "I don't even know if I can get close enough to him."

"I will get you close, but it is you who must strike. Remember, anywhere on his body."

"Won't he realize what we are up too?"

"Let's hope when the Fates decided this, they were in our favor."

Hmmm. "I'm starting to think I must have pissed off someone in another life."

He grinned at her. "Well, let's go piss off some gods."

Together, they moved through the cave. The sound from the gods above had only amplified. Carissa could hear her father's booming voice. Athena had joined the altercation.

In the other corners of the cave, Xen's men fought demons, some with swords and some with guns, while others of the team protected the weaker gods.

They were joined by Kane and Adam. From behind them, Kane spoke, "If they keep arguing it might just give us enough of a gap to get Zeus free."

"Carissa and I will try to take out Kronos. The rest of you will have to deal with Iapetos until we can free Zeus."

Adam's face soured. "Why do we get the difficult one?"

"I don't think there's anything easy about trying to take a swipe at Kronos," Carissa shot back.

"I guess you are right, Rissa."

Xen eyes narrowed. "Do. Not. Call. Her. Rissa."

Carissa tugged his hand. "Everything is crumbling around us, and you're worried about some stupid nickname." *Men really had their priorities wrong sometimes.*

Xen stopped them before they reached the landing where the gods bickered.

Carissa turned to Xen. "I need to clue my father in."

"If you bring your shield down, they will all be able to read what you say to him. You have to hope that he understands what we mean to do."

She let out a breath. "Okay, let's hope this works."

Another blast sounded from the west end of the cave. The vibration sent pieces of rocks toward them.

Xen grabbed Carissa's hand. "Looks like Echion decided to take out some demons with a different method." He waited. "It's stopped their arguing. Move now," Xen ordered.

With brisk movements, her booted feet moved along the path in the cave. When they were in position, Xen gave Kane the signal.

He pulled out the metal box. Her shaking fingers closed around it and opened it. A burst of power hit her in the face. Oh, there would be no keeping this quiet now. She took that moment to rush Kronos from behind.

Kronos turned, and in his tight grip he held another sickle. One of his eyebrows rose in disbelief when he caught the gleam from the one she held in her hand.

Carissa's brain went into overdrive. There were two possibilities, one, he would wound her, or two she would have to make this a home base slide and take a jab at him on her way to being safe. She saw it all in slow motion. Kane and Adam were in position but

Adam had maneuvered to try to free Zeus. Iapetos blasted him with such a force he flew up in the air and landed below on the rocks. *Nooooo*. Her mind screamed in anger.

Kane had transformed to his wolf and made a charge for Iapetos. He held out his spear, but Athena deflected it. The wolf took a bite out of Iapetos' arm before being thrown. Athena now fought Iapetos.

She had a split second to execute her blow. *Make this one count, Carissa. This one is for all the years you sucked at baseball.* She threw her body into a slide. Kronos swung with the sickle, taking aim at her. Xen's sword deflected the blow. Her arm shot up and sliced Kronos right across the thigh. Xen used his vampire speed to pick her up and move them both a safe distance.

Kronos staggered. "YOU. WILL. PAY," he roared.

Small bursts of light escaped from the wound she had given him.

The commotion got Iapetos' attention.

Athena, wise goddess that she was, raised her shield and broke the bindings that were holding Zeus. The force of it sent adamantine shards everywhere.

Xen grabbed Carissa and pulled her into him. Giving her protection against the sharp shards that battered down on him.

"No, Xen."

"*Koukla*, I can recover from this a lot faster than you."

Iapetos flashed to Kronos and grabbed him but Ares had already regained some of his power. He sent out a blast and hit Kronos in the stomach. Making him double over before the two Titans dematerialized from the cave.

Athena helped Zeus to where a part of the cave had opened to the thundering sky outside. He sat and raised his hand to the opening and pulled a lightning bolt directly to him. His power surged.

Xen released Carissa.

"Are you okay?" she asked, checking his arms and back. The small nicks from the adamantine shards were healing. "I'm okay. Go."

She raced to her father and gave him a hug. "I'm so glad you are okay."

"We will recover, but I have a score to settle."

"Not on your own."

"She has a point," Xen said.

"Where did you get Kronos' adamantine sickle?" Ares wanted to know.

"I can't take credit for that. It's Xen's doing." He took out the metal box and had her place it inside. Then slid it into his utility vest.

"You make quite the team."

Carissa's lungs expanded with pride at his words.

Xen beamed with satisfaction. "Glad you're starting to see things my way."

"XEN!" Kane's voice sounded from below.

They rushed to the edge and peered downwards. Kane held Adam.

"No, no, no, no. Take me down there now." Her throat seized, and tears burned in her eyes.

Ares grabbed her and materialized next to them.

She checked for a heartbeat. A light pulse throbbed under her fingertips. Adam bled from his head. A bone stuck out from his right leg and another from his left arm.

"Broken leg and arm," Kane informed her.

Anger rose in her. Consumed her. Selfish gods they were. Toying with their own creations like puppets. From her peripheral vision, many demons still fought.

Fury bled into her veins.

She stood on shaky feet. Blind with rage. A storm built from her feet up. She held out her hands to the portal and demons. *"Pauó,"* she screamed. An explosion released from her hands in a ball of light and burned the demons in its path. The power hit the portal and expanded then imploded and disappeared, leaving nothing but smoke behind.

She dropped to the dirt on the cave floor, tears blurred her vision. Xen pulled her up and hugged her to him.

"How can I help Adam?" she cried.

Ares kneeled next to the *lykos*. "His wounds are not fatal."

"Perhaps I can help." A soft voice floated to her ears. The goddess wore a white peplos.

"Panacea," Ares greeted his great-niece.

She leaned over and placed three purple drops from a vial she held in her hand over Adam. The wound on his head started to close, and his broken limbs were pushed into place. "You will need to treat them and plaster them. I cannot heal him completely as my power does not regenerate as fast as your father's."

"Thank you, goddess." Carissa gave her a once-over and saw a familiar face. It reminded her of someone.

The goddess smiled. "Yes, I am Dr. Aci's sister."

The doctor who had given her the news of her pregnancy before Hal had kidnapped Carissa, injured her, and killed her unborn child. Another tear escaped.

"Thank you," Kane said.

"It is the least I could do. You risked your lives to save ours."

Ares lifted his chin in the goddess's direction. A shimmer of gold replaced her presence.

Echion now stood where the goddess had been a second ago. "I confirm that the west end of the cave is clear." He gave a half-smile to Xen. "I may have to invest in some of those weapons you have."

Xen nodded.

Echion turned to Carissa. "Sorry about your friend, sister."

"Not as sorry as those who caused this will be."

"I wouldn't get her angry." Xen beamed.

Ares puffed out his chest. "Nor would I." He agreed, emulating Xen's cheerfulness.

"What did I miss?" Echion asked. "I knew you'd have the better end of the show."

"The show needs to end now." A stern and booming voice sounded from behind them.

Zeus.

Followed by Athena.

He did a quick examination in all directions. Gods and goddesses were still slumped in parts of the cave, trying to regain their power, others had used the power they had left to dematerialize and flee, while the remaining *Phi* still fought demons.

Zeus raised his hand. Lightning balled in it, and with one sweep, the remainder of demons were disintegrated.

"Any chance we can bottle some of that?" Carissa said.

"No granddaughter, you don't need it. Come to terms with it and embrace your demigod status. You have enough power of your own. As we have all witnessed."

"Why do you resist it?" Athena asked.

"I am not resisting anything."

"There is a part of you that doesn't want to accept who you are. It is why you don't have control of your powers." Zeus spoke sternly.

"That has nothing to do with it. I simply don't know how to use the powers."

Zeus pinned her with a knowing stare. "Accept them, and you will become one with the powers."

Adam started to murmur.

Kane's posture tensed. "Xen, we should clear the men out."

"Do you have an exit plan?" Athena asked him.

"We do. We have boats waiting on the northeast of the island."

Ares stepped forward. "Echion, why don't you help most of the *Phi* to the boats?" He turned to Carissa, Xen, and Kane. "I will move Adam to your desired medical facility first and come back to assist with the remaining gods and goddesses."

A buzzing noise came from Xen's earpiece. He tapped it and then relayed the message. "I have a team of injured men at the northeast location."

"Good, they managed to get the northwest team to safety." Relief coursed through her.

Echion nodded at her father's orders.

Zeus cleared his throat. "I will make sure they are all accounted for. Do you have decent communication with them?"

"I do but will only work when we are in range. That message that came through had been patchy."

"I will ask them to contact you before your communication cuts off."

"Why would it?" Xen asked.

"Because you will not be sailing with them. I will be moving us to my granddaughter's house after I have given the gods and goddesses ambrosia." Zeus flicked a glance in Carissa's direction.

The silliest thought ran her through her head: *I hope the house is clean.* While she pondered her ridiculous musings, Ares disappeared with Kane and Adam.

Echion went to gather up all the men, and she watched as people moved about. Her huge adrenaline rush had subsided, and the enormity had hit her. They'd managed to free the gods and goddesses, but the two madmen responsible for causing all this were MIA.

"We will find them, granddaughter, but first, let us help our family."

Zeus dematerialized. Carissa watched as the immortals tested their remaining powers.

"You have both fought well." Athena smiled at the *Phi* and Carissa.

Xen took a bow. "Thank you, goddess."

"Please, if you're going to marry my niece, it's Athena."

"Thank you for the honor, Athena."

Carissa watched the exchange. The truth, however, rattled around in her brain. "Athena."

"Yes, niece?"

"This isn't over, is it?"

"No, it isn't. What you experienced here was mild. They were lucky Zeus' power had been low."

She thought about that for a moment, and it didn't take her long to conclude that she would not want to be anywhere near Zeus when he went full throttle.

You can say that again, koukla.

I'm projecting, aren't I?

Yes, you are, koukla, *and have been for most of the battle.*

Athena stifled a laugh. "You two are cute. I can't wait for the wedding."

"Wedding?" She choked out.

"Yes, I'm sure we're all invited."

Oh…this had not been something to cross her mind.

"I haven't been to a wedding in an age. In fact, the last one was for Thetis and Peleus."

Carissa's eyes widened. "That's over two thousand years ago."

Athena had crossed one arm under her chest, and with the other she tapped her index finger to her head. "Let's hope there isn't any drama this time."

Carissa gulped. Oh, my gods and goddesses she was going to have the biggest fattest Greek wedding in history or mythology.

Indeed, we are.

I'm still projecting.

Yes, koukla.

"Well I'll make sure there are no apples." Carissa threw in.

Athena laughed, winked, and dematerialized.

After a minute with her mouth open, she did the only thing she hadn't done for some time. She pulled Xen in for a hard kiss. She put all her happiness, anger, frustration, and sorrow in it. They'd survived two Titans and rescued much of their family. Still, they had a lot to do, but they'd gained allies. It had been intense and she wanted something to anchor her. Xen was her bedrock. She broke the kiss to come up for air.

"If I could zap us home I would."

He grabbed her and moved closer to the entrance. "Let me check in with the teams." He tapped the receiver at his ear. "Report progress."

The corners of his mouth lifted in delight. "See you at headquarters."

He wrapped his arms around her and gave her a kiss on the nose. She couldn't help but smile at him. At least they would be heading off the island, may it forever remain hidden. She wouldn't be considering this place for a honeymoon. Nope, no mai tais here.

The air around them became charged; she recognized the power and stepped out from the embrace she had shared with Xen.

"How is Adam?" she asked when her father appeared.

"He has regained consciousness."

A sigh of relief bubbled up her chest. "What now?"

"We wait for Zeus and Athena to finish, and we vamoose off this island. Speaking of which." He searched the cave before shouting, "CALYPSO."

A woman appeared before him.

"What is it, Ares?"

"You will release everyone from this island, or my wrath and Zeus' will be upon you for as long as you live."

The woman bowed. "Yes. Ares." She muttered under her breath, taking a bow in acknowledgment and vanishing.

"Will she obey?" Carissa asked.

"She would not risk my wrath."

She hoped Kirke had made it off the island. She reviewed her surroundings, and the cave appeared close to empty except for the last few receiving ambrosia from Zeus and Athena.

She spied her father, who had folded his arms across his chest, and then glanced to Xen, who mirrored her father. If body language was anything to go by, they were back to not liking each other.

She shook her head. "I take it we are back to normal."

Xen's eyes sparkled. "For the time being."

Ares growled.

Carissa stuck her hands up in the air. "Even the gods are Neanderthals." Her feet started moving in the direction of Zeus and Athena, a few steps before she reached them a tremor hit the island.

Stalactites started to fall from the cave ceiling. Strong arms wrapped around her. "I have you, *koukla*."

Zeus and Athena had finished with the administration of ambrosia. They both stood, and Ares materialized next to them. "Time to go."

"Perfect timing," Zeus commented.

Ares put his hand on her, she stayed in Xen's arms.

They dematerialized, leaving the battle behind.

THIRTY-TWO

"Always envious the eye of the neighbor."
~ Ancient Greek proverb

Carissa's grandmother's house; Charleston, SC
Evening, mortal realm – Day 15

They all landed in the living room with a loud thud. Wind whipped around the room then subsided. Carissa unhooked the duffel bag she had fastened to her back and dumped it near her grandfather's liquor cabinet. Thank the Fates she did not have to pull the book out. She would have to think of a safe hiding place for it.

Commotion from the staircase could be heard in the living room, right before Aunt Paula shouted. "What's all the noise about?" Her footsteps got louder on the staircase. She rounded the corner to the living room. Carissa watched her aunt's face mimic a goldfish. Yiayia collided with Aunt Paula and then pushed her out of the way. She adjusted the haphazard glasses that were thrown on her nose.

"Is there something wrong with my eyewear?" she asked.

"No, Vetta."

"Are they?"

"Yes, Vetta, they are."

"Should we bow or something?"

"Good idea. We should."

Both women bowed. "Are we supposed to say something?" Aunt Paula asked.

Zeus turned toward the women. "There's no need to bow, Vetta and Paula."

"What can we get you. A drink, something to eat?" Yiayia offered.

Her grandmother wasn't silly—she knew the god who had laid down the law to guest hospitality or *xenia*, stood in her home. It would be offensive not to receive him properly.

"I would be delighted to receive anything you wish to offer."

"We'll be right back." The two women shuffled out of the living room.

"Please sit." Carissa waved an arm for everyone to take a seat. They all did. Her father stretched out and put his booted feet on the coffee table.

"Let's begin," Zeus said. "The strike from the sickle slowed Kronos, but it will not take long for him to regain his strength and power. Good work on that to both of you." Zeus turned his head toward Xen. "I take it that was you're doing.

"My doing on the instructions of Thanatos."

"That's puzzling."

"How so?" Xen asked.

"I had foreseen most of what transpired, but I had not seen Thanatos' involvement anywhere."

Carissa rubbed her neck. "Do you think he too is behind all this?"

"I doubt it, *koukla*. He had given me a heads up."

They all sat in silence until her *yiayia* and aunt reappeared with tea and sweets.

Yiayia smacked Ares' feet from the coffee table. "You might be my granddaughter's father, but I treat you the same as any son-in-law. Keep your feet off my table."

Ares let out a deep laugh, and everyone joined in.

"Thank you, Vetta and Paula," Athena said.

"You're welcome, goddess."

"Oh please…just call me Athena."

Yiayia and Aunt Paula gave each other a knowing look. Carissa knew her family so well it wasn't difficult to read the sheer excitement. Faces beaming and bumping their shoulders together like young schoolgirls. They would not be going back to bed because they were both in the throes of hysteria. "We won't linger. Just shout out if you want anything else." They left without anything further, but Carissa could hear their giggling.

"What's the plan, Father?" Ares asked Zeus. "You know that both Titans are on the loose, and we have to locate where they disappeared to?"

"We have to get them back to Tartarus where they belong."

"And how do we do that if we don't know where they are?"

"I think it's time I talked to my brother Hades. Athena and Ares, you will assist me, but first." He waved a hand, and the cakes and tea disappeared from the plate and cups.

Carissa blinked and understood that he'd accepted the guest offering of food and drink her grandmother and courtesy aunt had given.

A gentle breeze blew on her face, and they were gone.

"Not what I was expecting."

"Nor I."

He got up and walked over to her. He held out his hand. She placed hers in his, and he pulled her into his embrace. "How about I take you up to bed?"

"Sounds like the best plan."

He picked her up and sped them upstairs, placing her on the bed. "Let me find out if everyone is accounted for first. Don't move a muscle."

He grabbed his phone and punched the numbers. "Kane." The conversation between them was low. "Let me know if there is any change."

The next call went to teams on the plane, and then he hung up the phone. "Everyone has been accounted for. No men MIA. The vamps and *lykoi* that were on the helicopter had only minor injuries and have recovered."

"Well, that's good to hear. How is Adam?"

"He will pull through. They have him drugged at the moment, so he is resting." He walked over to her.

"How about we forget about everyone else? We need a shower." He tugged at her hand and led her to the bathroom. Once inside, he started the shower.

She had already unlaced her new boots. They'd survived the island without a blister or tear—though she'd have to clean the now caked dirt off them.

"Here, let me help you." He pulled them off with a simple tug. Then took one look at her and tore everything from her body with vampire speed. She stood naked, and he admired his handy work with the clothes. "You know you can't keep doing that to my clothes."

"You know that I can, and I will." He gave a lopsided smirk as he undressed.

Her eyes roamed over his body, admiring his muscles. It made her dizzy with desire just looking at him.

She met his gaze.

Xen's smile spoke of the best wickedness. It sent a shock of excitement coursing through her body and to her center. She could feel the wetness, and the only thing would fill that ache stood hard and ready. She licked her lips, and let one hand fall in-between her legs. Her fingers found a rhythm. Her other hand moved to palm her heavy breasts, one then the other. She pinched her nipples.

"You have no idea how incredibly sexy you are right now."

He stepped closer, and his own hand went to his manhood as he continued to watch her.

Small gasps left her lips.

"I'm going to touch and kiss you everywhere, and then I'm going to have you hard and fast."

His words sent a flow of liquid fire coursing through her. Her skin warmed, and her fingers became wet with desire.

Having him watch her fueled her passion. She started to pant, and the steam in the bathroom made her dizzy with lust.

He moved closer to her and bent his head, taking one breast in his mouth, sucking and then biting. His fangs elongated. He bit down and her breast and the tension that had coiled inside her from her own ministrations shattered. She splintered, and her knees buckled.

"I've got you." He pulled her into the shower and allowed her to recover as he washed her hair, then his own. When he had finished, he faced her toward the glass, pulled her arms behind her back so that her breasts were up against the glass. Then with one hard thrust, he made her eyes pop with pleasure. She groaned at the feel of him. He set a tempo that drove her wild. The more he gave, the more she wanted. Stroke after stroke of pleasure.

"More," she said.

Those words undid him. He pulled out, turned her around, lifted her with ease, and pinned her to the wall. Xen's mouth crashed to waiting lips, and his tongue danced deep with hers. He pulled away from his kiss and nipped her lips with his fangs, then licked the spots of blood. His nostrils flared, and he thrust in her. Her panting and moaning had become louder and more prominent. He pumped until pleasure consumed her, and white light burst from her eyelids. She could feel his own climax close. "May I draw from you?"

"Yes."

He kissed the spot where her neck met her shoulder then sank his fangs in her. Her pleasure renewed and reawakened and sheer euphoria coursed through her, building to a new crescendo. He withdrew his fangs and licked the puncture. She shattered with a loud moan and her body convulsed. His release was right behind hers.

"Wow." She let out a satisfied laugh, and he did too.

He gave her another scorching kiss before putting her on shaky feet. He gave her a bar of soap and took one for himself.

She started to soap him up. By the time she finished, he had turned rock hard again. She smiled.

"Another round?" She raised an eyebrow.

"You better believe it."

When they'd finished washing each other, he led her out of the shower. He used a soft towel to dry her off, and she did the same for him. Every time her hand hit his cock, it bobbed up and down. She loved knowing that she aroused this man.

He took her to bed and showed her another round of wow.

THIRTY-THREE

"No human thing is of serious importance." ~ Plato

Xen's mansion; Charleston, SC
Late afternoon, mortal realm – Day 16

"Well, does this mean I get a promotion or a medal for bravery?" Adam took a bite out of his Greek cookie, and icing sugar fell all over his t-shirt. They were at Xen's place, and an around the clock medical team was monitoring Adam. It did beat hospitals. The *lykos* had regained consciousness and had started with his usual maddening conversation. Kane's lips twitched. He wouldn't have it any other way.

Yiayia and Paula had popped in to visit, and for once, they weren't causing a ruckus.

"We'll make you *kotosoupa* and bring it tomorrow."

Adam beamed at both women. "When I'm better, I'm going to take you both out to dinner." The silly wolf liked trouble, and things kept getting crazier.

Both women started giggling. Paula patted her hair to make sure it was in place.

Kane rolled his eyes. His mood had been getting darker, and he had to get it under control before it started to interfere with everything else.

What he wanted right now was a drink.

"I might head out for a bit." He announced to Adam and company.

"Stay." Adam drunkenly waved his non-broken arm. The wolf needed to sleep off the painkillers.

"You should rest."

"I'm already resting, as you can see."

"Yes, but you have to have more shut-eye."

"You're such a party pooper, Kane."

He had been ready to rip a few not so pleasant words toward the wolf but Vetta cut in.

"Adam. Kane is right, *paidi mou*. You need to sleep off those happy drugs." A giggle left her lips, and Paula joined in.

"Aw. Don't go yet."

"We will be back tomorrow with soup." Paula gave him a wink.

The two women shuffled to their feet and said their goodbyes.

"Thanks for the cookies," Adam shouted as they opened the door to leave.

They gave Kane a kiss goodbye too. He told them, "There's a car waiting to take you both home."

"Thank you, wolf," Yiayia said with a small smile.

He had to admit, as much as they drove him nuts, they were growing on him. When the door closed behind the two women, Kane walked over to Adam.

"How are you really feeling?"

"I should be up and about in another day or so. I hate this cast."

"You need it."

"Can you imagine having this on for months?"

No, he couldn't. "Just as well that you're a *lykos*."

"Amen. The only plus side of having the plaster is having the nurse give me a bath." He wagged his eyebrows.

Kane let out a laugh. "I bet it is." He walked over to the door. "Get some rest."

Adam lifted his unbroken hand in a salute. "Roger that and give me a full report on things tomorrow. My brain should be back to normal."

"I thought it was."

Adam flicked him the bird.

Kane's lips twitched in amusement.

He made his way out of the room. He hesitated a moment, then his feet changed direction. He'd have that drink. The Vrykos pub had been calling his name all afternoon. He took the stairs down to the underground parking, his head filled with his own musings. When his booted feet hit the last stair, his phone chimed.

Certain redhead is at Vrykos pub.

He smiled as he made his way to his car. The drive didn't take long. He found his reserved parking spot around the back and made his way up the stairs. Pulling the door open, he was hit by a wave of sound. He hadn't expected the pub to be so full, but you could never predict when you would find it quiet or when it would be bursting at the seams. Kane stepped over the threshold.

His eyes scanned the crowd. Familiar scents hit his nose, but a distinct fragrance danced in the air. Carissa's friend Ligi was here.

His gaze darted in the direction of the intoxicating scent, and sure enough, the siren sat in a booth on her own, nursing a drink. Her body language was easy to read. He knew it intimately - the posture of someone who had hit a brick wall and had to re-assess the situation.

His feet moved in her direction. It would be a good opportunity to see if she had any decent leads on the demon Lox who'd taken Kelly.

Maybe the evening wouldn't be so bad after all.

THIRTY-FOUR

"Fire, women and sea, the mighty three." ~ Aesop

Vrykos Pub; Charleston, SC
Early evening, mortal realm – Day 16

Ligi had just hung up from another dead lead. Trying to find Kelly had become near impossible. No one knew where this demon Lox had disappeared to with Kelly. Tired and worn from coming up empty she did the only thing she could think of, she steered her car in the direction of the Vrykos pub to have a drink and maybe a bump and grind with some other unearthly creatures. If luck decided to offer something muscular and male, she wouldn't turn the gift down.

The music in the pub pulsed in the background. Ligi had chosen a table in a dark corner. She needed alone time and she preferred it somewhere where she could people watch, without it looking like staring or stalking.

A waitress sashayed over to her table.

"What can I get you?"

"I'll have a martini. Dry. Please."

The waitress took the order and disappeared.

As she stared out into the crowd, she wondered why this Lox guy would have taken Kelly. She hadn't at any time given the indication that she had been in trouble or that she was seeing someone. Everything about the situation seemed sinister. The fact they kept coming up dry only meant one thing. The guy was dangerous and crazy, and her friend might be in a ditch somewhere.

As a siren, she could sometimes see into the future and, at times, into people's pasts. With Kelly, she got nothing, and that made her stomach rock hard. A shiver ran up her spine. Some siren she was, couldn't even see her friend's whereabouts.

She had been so consumed in her thoughts that she didn't even notice when the waitress put her drink on the table.

She picked it up and placed the glass to her lips, the burn of the gin tickled her esophagus. She wanted a few of these. Unfortunately, she'd driven, so that meant only three drinks at the most if she wanted to drive home. She lifted her drink and took a deep sip this time.

"Looks like you need more than one of those." She knew the face. One of Xen's men. Hopefully, not like the last one. "Mind if I join you?"

"Not at all."

He held out his hand to her. "We've never been properly introduced. I'm Kane."

She took his in hers and marveled at the warmth. "Ligi," she said, giving it a good shake.

He slid into the booth, taking up most of the space. Xen's men were all huge. She'd taken a good look at them the rare visits to his office. A woman could dream up all sorts of fantasies. He had his sleeves rolled up, and he linked his hands together and rested his forearms on the table. He shifted his body weight forward.

"Can I get you another drink?"

"Sure, but your drink will be my limit. I'm driving."

"No problem." He waved down the same waitress who took her order and placed their drink order.

"Sure, sugar. Is there anything else I can get for you?" The waitress pushed her tits out.

Ligi rolled her eyes. Why were some women so obvious? A turn off for sure. Take it from a siren who knew exactly how to charm men. No tit wiggling necessary. Men liked to take their time looking, it built up the anticipation.

"No that will be all." He dismissed the waitress and her over the top antics.

Ligi had to give him a tick of approval for looking annoyed and not ogling.

"So, what brings you here tonight, Kane?"

"I don't know when you last spoke to Carissa, but the skirmish with the gods got ugly. Adam ended up badly injured."

Goosebumps traveled over her body. "Is he all right?"

"We were fortunate to have a healer goddess on site. He is mending."

"How bad were his injuries?"

"Broken bones and a head injury. I don't think he would have fared well if we didn't have Panacea there to heal him."

"Is he in a hospital? Can I visit?"

"Sure you can visit, though he's at Xen's."

The waitress appeared with their drinks. She set them down and didn't linger. She must have read into Kane's tone.

Ligi watched as he eyed her carefully.

"What's happening with Kelly? Any new leads?"

"Nothing. I fear the worst."

"Based on what Xen has told me, Lox isn't a bad guy."

"Then why keep her isolated? She's probably sick with worry. Kelly wouldn't stay away for nearly a month." She lifted the fresh drink to her lips.

"Maybe she's fallen in love."

She choked on his words.

"That's your answer to all this?"

His lips curved in a devastating grin. "It's possible."

"No. I refuse to believe that she's falling madly in love and has not given two hoots about everyone back here who is worried sick about her."

"You can't discount that maybe something is going on between them."

"Oh, ridiculous. It doesn't happen that quickly. Wouldn't she have surfaced? No one can have that much sex. Not even me."

Kane pinned her with a hot molten stare, and something told her that he'd give a woman orgasms for months on end.

"Then you haven't met the right man." His magnetic gaze never left hers.

She shook her head. No, she would not cross that boundary with one of Xen's men. Adam had been tempting until he'd divulged there was a bet riding on him adding a line to the bedpost. It infuriated her that men thought they could charm her into having sex with them. Yes, she liked it, but she didn't drop to her knees for every man at the click of their fingers.

"Your heartbeat has risen. I am not Adam, nor do I wish to take you to bed tonight. I admit, you're a powerful and sensual woman, but I saw you and thought to see how you were progressing with your leads. You are Carissa's friend, and she's been concerned."

Ligi took a deep breath to calm herself for the nonsensical thoughts. "How did you know what I was thinking?"

"Body language and it's not rocket science. It's the way our discussion went and your interaction with Adam."

"Thank you, Kane."

"No thanks necessary. Now back to your friend. Anything at her house that may give you an indication of why she might have caught Lox's eye?"

"Kelly sometimes takes private jobs."

"As in investigating?"

"You could call it that."

"That's evasion and you know it."

Her lips turned up. The man in front of her was as knowing as Xen.

"You're not just a pretty face," she said.

"Nor are you." He winked.

"She takes some special jobs trying to retrieve stolen artifacts."

"I'd be surprised if Xen didn't know her."

"She steers clear of that vampire."

"Why is that?"

"Because Kelly thinks everything belongs in a museum and Xen has other ideas."

"Xen's smart. You wouldn't want to cross him."

"I know, right?" She let out a giggle.

Kane laughed.

"He's a kitten, just don't get on his wrong side."

Somehow, Ligi didn't believe that, but then again, her friend Carissa had fallen head over heels for him so maybe he didn't show his true self to everyone. "Anyway, I didn't find anything amiss at Kelly's place when I went through her apartment."

"Maybe you missed something?"

"It's possible. I've been there twice, but I might have another look tomorrow."

"Good idea, and shout out if you want a hand." He downed the rest of his beer.

"Would you like another?" she asked.

"No. I've got to return to Adam. It will be better for all of us once he's more mobile."

"How long do you think that would be?"

"We heal fast, so I think another week before he is back to normal."

"And driving you mad?" she said with a laugh.

Kane's lips turned up. "You don't know the half of it."

She thought about the bet and asking for details. How had they picked her for a joke? "How did the betting start?"

"No disrespect to you, Ligi. It's just something we do to pass the time. I'm not going to apologize for liking women and sex and acting like a typical male when it comes to them."

"I'm not fishing for an apology. I want to understand how I became a joke."

His nostrils flared then. "Let's get one thing straight. You were not nor will you ever be a joke. It was a bet to see who could turn your head. You are a sexy woman. Any man would have to be blind not to notice." He leaned forward and positioned his face close to hers. "We noticed."

Okay, a hundred points to Kane. The more questions she asked about the bet, the deeper she seemed to get.

"Best to put it down as males being males and move on."

"Exactly. No harm would have befallen you. Nor did it."

"I'm going to let this go as the song says."

"Good idea."

She finished her drink and grabbed the check to pay. Kane's hand gently landed on hers.

"This one is mine," he said.

She wasn't going to argue with this alpha wolf. Power exuded from him. It enticed her, but also sent waves of nervousness through her body. A bittersweet feeling. Kane wasn't a man you crossed, and she had no intention to do so, not now, not ever.

"Does this mean we're friends?"

"Any friend of Carissa's is a friend of mine."

"Looks like she's won you guys over."

"Carissa is by vampire law bonded to Xen. That makes her family. Her interests are now our interests."

"Okay, so we're all one big family."

"You got it."

He stood to pay and leave. "Let me walk you to your car."

Her mouth fell open, and she recovered quickly. That she hadn't been expecting. "Thank you. It's really not necessary."

"I insist, and Carissa would have my head if she finds out I bumped into you and didn't take care of you."

"Okay, just this once and for Carissa." She'd have words with her friend. She didn't like to be smothered and somehow, she got the feeling that's what would be happening in this big family.

Tithonius Sabas watched Xen's right-hand man talking to the one woman who might lead him to his new bounty. He'd been observing her from the moment the redhaired vixen sat. *Delectable.* Though he stayed out of sight across the crowded bar.

He flicked the pages of the dossier in front of him. He'd been trying to track Kelly Black down since he'd been given the file two weeks ago. Every turn he took, he came up empty. He'd never had a case like this. Usually, he found his fugitive quickly. Kelly Black had failed to appear in court for charges of theft, and now it fell to him to retrieve her. For a hefty price.

He focused on their conversation.

The redheaded beauty and Kelly were both friends with Carissa. What a coincidence.

His ears perked up.

Because Kelly thinks everything belongs in a museum, and Xen has other ideas.

Interesting, it's likely why she landed herself in trouble in the first place.

Anyway, I didn't find anything amiss at Kelly's place when I went through her apartment.

Maybe you overlooked something.

It's possible. I might have another look tomorrow.

From the rest of the conversation, it appeared that she didn't know where her friend was hiding. He'd have to make sure he swept her apartment himself.

He had enough for tonight. This case had no traction. He collected his file and his keys and made his way out of the pub.

In the parking lot, he sat pondering on whether he should continue to follow the redhaired beauty. He switched the engine on when he noticed Kane walking her to her car. He bid her good night when she had started up the car and left. She drove off like a woman on an obstacle course.

He smiled. She was clumsy. He witnessed some of her mishaps from the shadows. He'd followed her for two days. Tonight he realized that he wasn't the only one who couldn't find Kelly Black. Other unearthly creatures were looking for her and so far, everyone was empty-handed.

The thought that Kelly might be buried somewhere did cross his mind, but something told him she ran because she did the wrong thing. Maybe even something worse than missing her court appearance.

His fingers found the claymore sitting on his passenger seat. Maybe a little demon hunting might lift his spirits. As he sped through Charleston, his pulse began a rhythmic beat. A little action would give him a better view on the whole situation.

THIRTY-FIVE

"Summer, autumn, war." Ancient Greek proverb

Francis Marion National Forest, Charleston, SC
Evening, mortal realm – Day 15

Wind swirled around Lox. His feet were firmly planted on the wet soil beneath. Two demon factions stood ready for battle.

The kakodaimones stood on the opposite of Lox and the Eudemonia. The air shifted around him.

"Are you ready?" The voice, familiar.

"Why are you here, Hades?"

"I wanted front row seats."

"Leave. You don't belong here, and you are not part of this fight."

"What? And miss the best show?

"This isn't a show." He gritted his teeth. He was tired of the same endless battles. The eudemonia and the kakodaimones were once one entity. One spirit who walked the earth and spread good fortune on those who deserved it and gave misfortune to those who did not. But their age ended, and the entities were sucked into the underworld. There, they became two separate species. The kakodaimones were bloodthirsty and reckless and did everything in their power to destroy the eudemonia. Fortunately for Lox, he'd saved the last five hundred eudemonia—the good fortune side—and had managed to break the curse that bound them to the underworld and to Hades himself. The man standing beside him.

"Oh, you are wrong there, Lox, my boy. This is definitely a show. You're outnumbered."

"Numbers don't always matter."

"When you are fighting bloodthirsty creatures then numbers tend to come into the equation."

"Have you come here to laugh?"

"Now, why would I do that?"

"Why are you really here? You've never taken an interest in what goes on with the eudemonia and kakodaimones. Why start now?

"As always, you lesser creatures fail to see the grander picture."

"And what might that grander picture be?" Lox raised his fingers and mocked some air quotations.

"Mount Olympus has been compromised, two Titans are on the loose, and I need to find out who is giving these morons access to the Hekate's portals."

"I thought that problem was solved."

"Ongoing," Hades replied in a dry tone.

Lox watched as Hades' face contorted, his gaze on the men assembled to do battle.

"What happens on Olympus should stay on Olympus, and what does it have to do with me?"

"Everything and nothing."

"That is not even an answer." Lox barked. Fury colored his vision. One thing, he didn't like was riddles and cryptic answers. "Give it to me straight."

"What happens on Olympus and between the gods, mortals, and unearthlies matters to us all. We are connected. How would you feel if your band of five hundred soldiers were wiped from this mortal realm?"

Lox considered what Hades said. For thousands of years, he and his men worked to break the curse that bound them. He had recently found love and would not give up this chance without a fight. His men would not either. Life in the mortal world had been far better in the short time that they'd been here. He'd kill anyone or anything that stood in the way of his happiness and that of his men. "You have my ears. What do you want from me?"

His scalp prickled as soon as he said the words. Agitation twitched in his gut. He'd become a cynic, thousands of years in underworld did that to you. He'd either regret asking or lose men in the request made.

Hades turned toward Lox, eyes blazing like torches. One would never cross this god. Sure, they had a banter going on, but he'd never deliberately anger the god. Hades' wrath would leave nothing but devastation.

Lox knew what came next. Hades would demand an *orkos*. An oath that would bind Lox to whatever Hades had in mind. If he broke the *orkos,* he'd be subjected to Hades' punishment and the censure of the other gods. Everything about it stank and any sane demon would not indebt himself to a god. However, there had been something in Hades' body, language, and aura. Lox knew it. *Monumental.* The word filtered through his mind.

"Swear me the oath first."

"How about for once you tell me first, and then I'll swear."

"What's to stop you from backtracking?"

"You know I keep my word."

Hades watched him under narrowed eyes before relaxing. "Zeus has a granddaughter, Carissa, who is the daughter of Ares, and is bonded to the vampire Xen Lyson. There is unrest coming in the future, and I want to ensure that you and your five hundred will be an ally when they come for help."

"I respect Xen, but why would I meddle with his organization's affairs? He has enough men to face many circumstances."

"For what is coming, he will need an army."

"How do you know this? You have never meddled or taken interest in what happens in the mortal realm or Olympus. Why now?"

"Because the oaths and curses of men have reached the Eyrines and therefore it falls to me to forewarn you that if you choose to do nothing, you will be consumed by darkness."

Lox blinked. "What about them?" He pointed across to the kakodiamons. "What's their role? Will they too join?"

"They can never join, and you know it. Nor will they be as lucky as you and your five hundred. They will never see the light."

"Well, they are seeing it now."

"Not for long."

"Does that mean you are cheering for my team?"

"Don't push your luck, Lox."

Yes, he should quit since he was ahead. "Why do you care?"

"As I said before. We are all connected."

If what lay on the horizon was more than what he and his men alone could handle. Maybe he should consider allying himself to others in the mortal realm. He knew his men were competent, but they were all who had survived. With no women to match with, they would eventually have no one left. Lox had to do something, and he did. He wasn't going to destroy any chances he or his men had to procreate and bring more fortune and good to the realm they now stood in. It was what they were designed to do, it was what they did, and they fought hard to ensure that they survived so they could once again walk in the mortal realm. "Will you keep me updated as you know more?"

"You have my word," Hades said.

"Then I will swear the oath and make the necessary sacrifice with prayers. First, I have more pressing problems." He pointed to the assembled kakodaimones. "How did they even get here?"

"Hekate's portals are many. We are working on the problem."

"Could you work on it faster? I've had enough of those violent imbeciles."

"You know they are like ants. You must destroy the queen."

"Then lift the glamour that makes them all look the same. I want to see who I am laying waste to." He raised an eyebrow at Hades. A dare.

"I grant you this only once and never again. See that you make your oath and sacrifice." The god waved his arm over to the kakodaimones and dematerialized.

Without the glamour that was part of their curse, the kakodaimones appeared to be ordinary men. "Now that's what I call visibility."

Terillos came to join him at his side. "I think I will enjoy this."

"At least we can identify their bastard of a leader now." Lox clenched his fists at his sides. "On my command, be ready to unleash hell."

Terillos' lips drew back in a snarl. "It would be my pleasure."

"Before I do. Is Kelly safe?"

"I have men guarding her from every angle."

It comforted him to hear that. When he had crossed paths with the woman, something deep inside of him had awoken. She called to him in ways he couldn't at the time understand, but one thing he did recognize was that she belonged with him. He'd wasted no time in taking the female. Yes, she was initially reluctant to even speak with him. She had been terrified of him but slowly she began to trust him, and now she was his. He pulled out his sword.

"Leave none standing!"

Terillos shouted, "Now."

A sea of swords clashed on shields. The advantage the eudemonia had over the kakodaimones was that they held shields when they fought. The kakodaimones used the advantage of their ghastly faces to scare their opponents but right now that glamour had been removed and Lox's men had nothing to fear, not that they ever did. They had become accustomed to fighting them.

Bodies fell under Lox's feet as he slashed his way through, carving a path as he went. Some men followed him and fought anyone coming from behind.

Three other groups of men were sent to ambush the *kakodaimones* from right, left, and back.

Lox saw as demons began to fall from all the raided angles. Victory would be theirs once he got to their leader. A man he could see in the center of the attack. That was their current leader. Other demons surrounded him to protect him. "Kill the queen." Hades had said. If he killed the leader, the rest of the *kakodaimones* would fall apart, just like ants and bees.

A few more before he could break through the demons surrounding the leader. Lox's sword flew through the air, weightless and hitting its mark with each swing of his arm.

"Circle." He shouted to the men fighting beside him. He did not have to give more instructions. They understood his plan and his motivation. Steel met steel. His sword arm continued to slice its opponents. Only one more demon stood before him and the prize.

Terillos stepped in line with him and removed the demon Lox had been eyeing as his next target.

Lox stepped over the body and into the circle. The demon leader did not waste time. He made a dive for him. He stepped out of the way with a grunt. If this moron embodied true leadership, then he'd be doing all the demons a favor by removing him. The demon took another swing but missed. Lox took that opportunity to strike. His sword met flesh, deep enough to cause damage. The demon dropped to his knees, his sword clattered to the ground. Lox struck, and his blade hit hard vertebrae before coming clean. The demons that were trying hard to keep the circle broke away, trying to put distance between themselves and Lox.

Victory belonged to the eudaimonia.

"Some battle, eh?" Terillos said. "Let's face it. They didn't present a challenge."

"True, but we've been fighting them for thousands of years and in large numbers."

He thought about what Terillos said. This was all his men ever knew. The time for fighting them ended now. "Keep a few alive. I need to deliver a message." Hoping this would be the last battle for a long time.

"Get a team to start cleaning up the bodies," Lox instructed Terillos as he walked from the battle site. The glamour that Hades had lifted returned, showing their foes resembled reptilian creatures once more.

The men around him worked to remove all the demons. They dug pits to throw them in before burning them.

Lox had enlisted the help of a few men to prepare a sacrifice. They prepared a makeshift altar and brought a lamb they had been keeping in their camp. Shame that it would be slaughtered and discarded. It was not a festival, so they could not partake in the roasting and eating of the meat. This animal was only for swearing an oath.

He watched as Terillos gave orders and then made his way over to him. "Are we preparing to sacrifice in celebration of our victory?"

"No."

"Then what is this for? Don't tell me you swore an oath to the unseen one."

"It is not as drastic as you think."

"What have you bound us to this time?"

Lox's fists clenched at his sides. Everything he ever did was for his men. He always put himself last and to have his friend insinuate that he might have been reckless, and put the men in a position of danger made him see red. "You know the men come first."

"Then what is this about?"

"Hades wanted me to swear an oath that if Xen and his bonded turned up and asked for help that we would be their ally."

Terillos cocked his head. "And why does what happens here concern us?"

His friend loved movies, and there would be only one way he'd get the message loud and clear. "Because it's going to be a big ba-da boom." He crossed his arms over his chest.

Terillos swallowed, and his eyes went wide. "Then swear your oath already."

"Thought so." Lox walked off to finish the preparations.

The sheep bleated. Lox had always wondered if the sheep knew of its impending demise.

He stepped closer to the sheep with a knife in his hand. "I swear to Zeus, Athena, Apollo, Demeter, and the Styx that I will ally myself and my men to the *Phi Athanatoi* and Carissa, a daughter of Ares, and that I have sworn this to Hades." He slit the throat of the sheep and caught the blood in a vessel. "Whoever is to do wrong by this oath, let their blood flow to the ground like this wine." He poured wine to the ground.

The necessary libations were poured, and prayers were said.

Lox slaughtered another animal in honor of their victory. Hopefully, all of what had transpired today would be for the good of his men and himself.

THIRTY-SIX

Basil's Bakery; Charleston, SC
Mortal realm – Day 16

"Why are we even here, Paula?"

"Because you two should talk."

"I have nothing to say to him."

"You have lots to say to him. You're stubborn and pig-headed."

"Okay, fine. But if I'm not out of that shop in thirty minutes, you have to come and get me."

"Deal." Paula left Vetta standing in front of Basil's cafe.

"Great, this is going to wake some memories." The very same shop that both of the women had first encountered demons. She sighed and pushed the door open. A little bell rang above the door. Basil's shop had always been a place for comfort and friends in the past. But that was pre any demon episodes.

The fragrant aroma of cinnamon, vanilla, and other exotic and delicious spices hit her nose. She closed her eyes and inhaled deeply.

"What can I get you?"

The voice sounded in her ear, and she knew it well. She turned to face her nemesis.

"Nothing, Basil, I don't want your cakes. I can make my own."

"I never said you couldn't. You're in my shop, so I thought you wanted sweets."

"What if I don't want cake, and I just want to watch people buying it and eating it?"

Basil shook his head. "You know that's demented."

"Oh great, so now I'm demented." She stomped her walking stick, showing her displeasure.

"Are you causing a commotion again?" Kane's voice said from behind her.

"Wolf. What are you doing here?"

"I could ask you the same."

"Wait a minute. Why is he a wolf?"

"Because he's devilishly handsome and is as sly as one."

Kane's lips turned up and he gave Basil a megawatt smile.

Bless him. She'd have to be nicer to him.

Basil eyed Kane from his head to his feet and grunted in disapproval. Vetta didn't miss it, and she wasn't going to pass up the opportunity to get under Basil's skin.

"He's my new toy boy."

"It's boy toy, and you've lost your mind. He wants your money. That's why he's hanging around."

Kane let out a growl and held up his hands. "I'm no one's boy toy."

"She just said you were. Are you going to deny it now?"

Kane grabbed Vetta's walking stick. "Here, feel free to thump him over the head for me too."

Basil stepped aside. "Okay, maybe I overreacted. Can I get you a coffee and cake?"

"That might help calm my nerves," Vetta said.

"Nothing for me. I've had enough drama for one day." Kane stepped closer to Basil. "If you harm her, I'll break your legs."

Basil's face turned white. "I wouldn't harm a hair on her head," he replied.

"Make sure you don't." Kane gave him a loud and hard slap on the back, which threw off Basil's balance. For an almost seventy-five-year-old he'd been reasonably healthy, but not strong enough to withstand the warning pat from Kane. Vetta had quite a few years on him.

Vetta watched as he opened the door and stepped out to the sidewalk.

"Nice guy," Basil said through clenched teeth.

The corner of her lips lifted. "He's one of Carissa's friends."

"You know you could have said that from the beginning.

"What and miss all the fun?"

"Take a seat. I'll bring out your favorite." Basil walked away, looking annoyed.

Vetta made her way to the tables. Inside she did a little victory dance. She loved getting on Basil's nerves. She'd know him for so many years. They were good friends but after her husband died, their friendship became uneasy. He'd started to act weird around her. It was worse now--Basil was up to something, and she had to find out what.

"Here you go. One Greek coffee and a *bougatsa*. The custard is fresh."

She eyed the warm pastry that had icing sugar and cinnamon sprinkled over it. She salivated at the thought of cutting into it and tasting that vanilla custard on the inside.

She caught Basil's examination and batted her eyes. "Will you join me?" She felt silly, but she wanted answers.

"How can I refuse you, Vetta? Just give me a moment."

When he returned to the table, he had coffee and a slice of baklava in his hand. She waited for him to sit before bombarding him with questions.

"You know, Basil, on the day you turned up at the retirement home with a tray of baklava, my baklava went missing."

"Vetta, I've told you. I wouldn't take your baklava." He waved his arm toward the cake displays. "Lots of baklava here."

Maybe he had been at the wrong place at the wrong time, and someone wanted her to think he took it. She pondered that and took a sip of her coffee and a bite of her custard pie.

"Best *bougatsa*."

Basil's chest puffed out. "Thanks." He winked at her. The old goat flirted with her regularly when they were on friendlier terms.

"Who do you think might have taken it? I mean, you know all the people in the home just as well as me."

"Are you kidding, Vetta? If you leave a tray of baklava laying around what do you think is going to happen?"

"They're gonna circle like vultures."

"Exactly. It could have been anyone."

He had a point. Maybe she had jumped to conclusions. She watched him take a bite out of his own baklava. She realized then that she had indeed judged without having the evidence.

"Why do you care so much? It's just cake. You would have made a whole bunch of them happy. You know we shouldn't be eating this stuff. All I hear is you can't have this, and you can't have that. If cholesterol doesn't kill you, diabetes will."

"You are right." She thought about it. She knew there were a few people there who had a sweet tooth. That tray of baklava didn't stand a chance. It would have been polished off in seconds. She had to face it. She wouldn't find out who took it nor what fate the key had met with. Probably in a bin.

None of this had anything to do with wanting that key back, Carissa had found the original. No, it had plagued Vetta's mind as to who would know Carissa's identity and what her grandfather had hidden. She took another bite of the pie.

"You're quiet."

"Just thinking."

"What happened to you? You've lost the smile that beamed like a ray of sunshine?"

Her lips turned up a fraction at the corners. "I lost my other half."

"Vetta, it's hard but he would have wanted you to live."

Basil reached over and put his hand over hers.

"I know. I need time."

"Something we don't have a lot of," he said. "I've gotta go, they need me in the kitchen but stay as long as you like. I'll have a tray of baklava ready for you to take out to Paula."

"Hey, how did you know?"

"I have eyes in the back of my head."

"What? Are we five?"

"Not five but predictable." Basil cleared the table and walked into the kitchen.

Vetta scanned the inside of the shop then glanced out the window. Paula stood across the road. "Some spy," she whispered under her breath. "Time to move."

She made her way to the counter to collect the baklava. The hackles on her neck rose. A man with beady eyes watched her. She'd have to do the evil eye mumbo-jumbo when she got home, no point in risking headaches and vomiting from it. She whispered something her aunties in Greece had taught her to ward off the evil eye. "Oregano to your bum and garlic to your eyes." That should do it. She flagged Paula by waving her arms with the walking stick.

Lucky they weren't parked far from the shop. "Here, Basil sent this," She said when she reached the car. They both got in, buckled up, and the car started moving.

"Baklava." Paula squealed in joy. "And what happened?"

"Nothing, really. I had coffee and a *bougatsa*." She'd keep the business about the missing baklava and key to herself. Paula would have her head. She insisted that talking to Basil would be of benefit.

"And?" Paula asked.

"And nothing. The wolf happened to be there."

"Yes, I saw him come out of the shop. He didn't look too impressed. What happened?"

"Oh, we had words. I called Kane my toy boy." The memory brought a smile to her lips.

Paula slammed the brakes hard. "Vetta, you didn't." Paula let out a laugh.

The car started moving again. "You know, Vetta, one of these days, you're going to get yourself in a lot of trouble, and none of us are going to be there to help you out."

"I wasn't in any trouble."

Paula gave her a sideways glance. "I don't believe you."

"Believe what you like. Oh, before we go home, I'd like to stop in at the Greek Shop. I want a new *mati*."

"Why do you need a new evil eye? You have plenty of them."

"I want a new one."

"Is this where our conversation goes around, and around till you get your way?"

"You better believe it." She shifted in her seat. Everything troubled her, and the frequency had doubled. She had delayed seeing her doctor.

"So, what did you talk about over coffee?"

"Not much."

"Didn't look like not much from across the road."

"We talked about losing partners."

Paula's look turned solemn. "That's the hard part of life." She pulled into the parking spots in front of the shop. "Nothing like Greek retail therapy to help lighten the mood,"

They got out of the car and made their way into the Greek Shop. It stocked every Greek trinket you could think of, all imported from Greece.

Vetta made her way to the evil eye collection, and Paula joined her.

"Ooo, they have some nice ones." Paula picked up a sample.

"What do you think of this one?" Vetta held out a large blue eye, the size of her palm.

"I like it. It's a good one for by the door."

They took their time looking through homewares before paying for their purchases.

The hair on Vetta's neck decided to stand to attention again. She dismissed it as being from the overexcitement of having toyed with

Basil. She really did get a kick out of stirring him up. He'd always been an easy target.

"Thank you, ladies," the assistant behind the counter said. They made their way to the exit but as they passed the table with all the eye amulets, Vetta spied the same man from Basil's cake shop. At first, she thought she made a mistake but she couldn't mistake those beady eyes.

She got behind Paula and pushed her to walk faster out of the shop. Outside, Paula stepped aside.

"What has gotten into you?"

"*Skasi,* Paula, we are being followed."

"Who? Where?"

"Great, just stand on a box and shout out where you are."

"Oh, calm down. Just tell me where?"

"He's in the shop and about to exit. Let's get to the car."

They moved fast. Once tucked inside the car, Vetta got Paula to wait. "Don't make it obvious, but he's just stepped out of the shop." Vetta pretended to be looking for something in her bag.

Paula reached out and adjusted her mirror. "Okay. I've got him. Short and round with a cream color suit."

"That's him. He was at Basil's."

"You'd think if you're going to follow someone, you'd wear a dark suit not cream. That's like a flag. You-hoo, here I am."

"Paula, start the engine and head to Xen's mansion. I'll ring Carissa and let her know." Vetta reached in her bag and pulled out her phone. She pressed Carissa's number.

"Yiayia. What's up?"

"Paula and I are heading over to Xen's place."

"Oh, okay. Any reason?"

"Yes, *paidi* mou, we're being followed."

"I will alert Kane and his men and meet you there. Do not stop anywhere, come straight here."

"Okay."

"And Yiayia…"

"Yes."

"Tell Aunt Paula to drive normal. You don't want them knowing that you know."

"It's just one guy but I'll tell her." Vetta hung up.

"What did she say?"

"Act like you don't know you're being followed."

Her lips turned up in a wicked grin. "Piece of cake."

Carissa's gaze lingered over Xen's body. She hated to leave him but would make the necessary calls to have a few of Xen's men stay in the house while he was in rejuvenation. As much as she loved this house, they would require something safer. He stayed here for her, to keep her happy. Safety would be an issue at some point. She couldn't risk him being attacked when he was the most vulnerable.

She picked up her cell phone.

"Kane."

"Yeah."

"We have a problem." She paused. "Yiayia and Aunt Paula are being followed. They are heading to Xen's place."

"I saw your grandmother earlier. I probably should have tailed them."

"It's not your fault. Trouble seems to find them."

"You're not wrong there."

"I'll meet you at Xen's place. Can you get men over here to guard Xen?"

"I've already got men watching the house. I'll get them closer."

"Why would anyone want to follow them? They are harmless."

"Harmless…when's the last time you saw them in action? They get people riled up."

She let out a little giggle. "Yeah, real ninja warriors." She went quiet. Kane must have picked up her discomfort.

"If it's any consolation, I'm already on the road. We had a tracker placed on your aunt's car. We'll get there fast."

"Thanks, Kane."

"No need for it."

She hung up and raced around her bedroom throwing jeans on and t-shirt, then slipped on a pair of flat shoes. She rushed over to Xen and placed a kiss on his lips. Then raced downstairs to grab her car keys. If anything happened to her family, she'd never forgive herself.

The drive to Xen's house resembled a blurred painting. She passed houses and buildings, and nothing registered. She gained access to Xen's underground garage and drove her car in, then raced up the stairs and out to the main foyer and collided with a brick wall.

"Phil." She recognized the wolf she'd crashed into.

"Carissa, what are you doing here?"

"My grandmother and aunt are being tailed by someone. They're headed here. Kane should be behind them."

"Okay. Let me make a few calls. We'll get the shadow." Phil walked toward Xen's office.

"Oh, and Phil."

"Yeah."

"It's good to see you again."

He gave her a wink. They had both been kidnapped by Hal. Xen and his men had come to their aid.

She paced, thinking about how her life had changed from that moment she came face to face with Xen.

"No need to fret." Phil had come out of the office. "We've got every angle covered. The guy tailing them is as good as ours." He sneered.

Her shoulders sagged, and she let out a deep breath.

"Smile, Carissa. We've got this."

Phil tapped his ear communicator and motioned for her to move out the front door. They watched the gates at the front of the property open. Her aunt's car drove up the long drive and to the front steps. Carissa raced to get them both out of the car and into the house.

"We're okay," Yiayia said to her.

"I know, but I want you inside." She ushered them up the stairs.

She glanced at the long drive and saw the flurry of activity. The guy tailing her grandmother and aunt had been boxed in by Kane and the other men. Phil had been correct, they had him.

Carissa stepped through the door and to the foyer. "Let's have a seat in Xen's office."

They hadn't had too much time in their seats when a loud scuffling sounded.

Kane had a short guy in a cream suit by the collar.

"Tell me why I shouldn't throttle you, Benny."

Carissa raised an eyebrow.

"You know him."

Kane growled. "You could say that."

Carissa moved toward the man; her fists balled. "Who is he, and why is he following my grandmother and aunt?"

Kane gave the short man a slap over the head. "Answer the question, Benny."

"I… I wasn't going to harm them."

"Why are you watching them."

"Listen, lady." He held up his hands in surrender.

Kane slapped him over the head again. "Her name is Carissa Alkippes, and she's Xen's fiancée. The women you were following are her family."

Benny gulped, and his complexion turned white. "X…Xen's…" He stuttered.

"Yes, and by going after her family, it's like going after her."

He turned to face Kane. "I get it. I get it."

"Now explain yourself before I make good on my threat."

He took another hard swallow. "I was at the Vrykos pub drinking when some guy said he had a job for me. Look, the money he threw on the table would set me up for life. All I had to do…" Benny reached in his pocket.

Carissa readied herself to pounce as did Kane.

He pulled out a key.

And the room erupted like a bunch of brawling fans at a football stadium.

Gasps filled the room. Yiayia and Paula jumped to their feet. Yiayia barreled toward him swinging her walking stick. Paula swinging her bag.

Phil happened to be walking into the library. His eyes darted from Carissa and around the room. It took him a second to act. He jumped in front of Benny and Kane stepped in to block both Yiayia and Paula.

Carissa sat there with her mouth open and energy pulsing inside her, she had to make them stop. "*Chora*," she screamed. An invisible hand came down and separated everyone.

"This is ridiculous. Yiayia and Aunt Paula, if you can't sit quietly until we get some answers, I'll send you to the kitchen."

The two women studied their feet with flushed faces.

Aunt Paula lifted her gaze. "Sorry, Carissa."

Yiayia let out a long breath. "Sorry, *paidi mou,* but that's my key."

"I recognize the key, Yiayia. But we have to establish how he came to have it before you go hitting him on the head."

Carissa's eyebrow rose in Benny's direction. She could throttle him for scaring her *yiayia* and *thitsa* but she needed answers first. "Benny, how did you get the key?"

He cleared his throat. "As I was saying. About two weeks ago, I was in the pub having a drink when some dude threw a lot of money at me. He put the key in my hand and asked me to retrieve what was in a post office box. The only problem was that the box held nothing but a note. I took the note back to the pub and gave it to the guy."

"Did you read the note?" Kane asked.

Benny rolled his eyes. "Of course, I did."

"And?" Carissa asked.

"I don't know why he spent that much money for a note that tells him nothing. I opened the note and it contained only one sentence. *'The end is the beginning.'* That's it."

"You found nothing else in the box."

"No. Nothing."

She smiled on the inside. Only she and Xen knew that there had been a secret compartment. "Did the man you gave the note to question you?"

"No, he just took it and gave me the rest of the money."

"Then why were you following my grandmother and aunt?"

"A guy doesn't pay you that much money for nothing. I figured I should look into it and report back to these guys if I found something. I didn't think a couple of old ladies warranted the attention of Xen."

Kane had been standing with one arm crossed over his chest and the other hand under his chin. He pulled it away. "Did you get this guy's name?"

"You know I never ask these things upfront."

"Was he human?" Kane asked.

"No. He had an energy about him that I couldn't place."

Carissa walked over to him and held out her hand. He placed the key in it.

"Do you think he'll be back?"

"Depends if he wants more work done."

"Benny, I want to know the minute this guy approaches you."

"Got it."

"Get your ass out of here and stop harassing older women."

Regret lined Benny's face, and he turned his attention to Carissa. "My apologies." Then he glanced over to where her *yiayia* and her aunt sat. "I didn't mean you any harm, but honestly, you're both nuts."

"I'll show him out," Phil said.

Kane and Phil exchanged a glance. Carissa knew that they'd be tracking Benny's movements.

"I'd like to show him out," Paula muttered from where she sat.

"You and me both, Paula." Yiayia pipped in.

Kane stepped closer to Carissa. "You see what I mean."

"Oh, I know what you mean."

"Admit it. They make life crazy." Kane smiled.

"Hey, I'm a product of that crazy."

He let out a laugh. "Yeah, I guess you are."

Carissa turned to both women. "Time to get you two home."

The women walked past Kane. "Thanks, wolf," Yiayia said with a wink.

"I'm not your boy toy," he said as they reached the door.

Carissa raised an eyebrow. "Do I even want to ask?"

His lips turned up in a grin. "Nope. Somethings are better left unsaid."

THIRTY-SEVEN

"The gods know all things." ~ Homer

Carissa's yiayia's house, Charleston, SC
Evening, mortal realm – Day 16

Carissa had volunteered to cook an early dinner for everyone, but her *thitsa* and her *yiayia* were having none of that; they got involved. She hadn't realized how much she'd missed having time with both these women.

Even though the day's events turned out to be nothing sinister, she couldn't shake the emotions that had bombarded her when she thought their lives were in real danger. They had to establish ground rules and one of those involved calling her and letting her know their every move.

"I've been thinking, would it be a good idea to get Yiayia to visit you, Aunt Paula?"

"Vetta is welcome to stay anytime she likes; she doesn't even have to ask. And I think it is time I headed back to Virginia. I've been here for almost a month."

"Thank you, *thitsa*." Carissa kissed her on the cheek.

"Vetta can decide on her own vacation." Yiayia jested about herself in the third person.

"Vetta is likely to stir up trouble if she stays here," Paula interjected.

"Have you ladies been misbehaving again?" A gravelly voice sounded from the kitchen entrance.

Carissa's lashes swept up, and everything in her ignited when she met Xen's mesmerizing green eyes. *School your thoughts,* koukla.

He dragged a hawkish gaze over her and gave her a panty-melting smile.

Yiayia and Aunt Paula coughed.

"Yes, they have."

Xen took the seat opposite Carissa. "What colorful activity did you get up to?" He asked both Yiayia and Aunt Paula.

"We kind of got followed," Her aunt croaked out.

"Well, you either were or weren't." His eyes crinkled at the corners.

"They were and by Benny," Carissa added.

Xen's amusement faded. His eyes flashed with anger. "What did he do?"

"It's a long story but in short, he had the missing key from the post office."

She brought him up to date with the day's adventures.

"I take it Kane has taken the necessary steps."

"He asked Benny to let you know if the mysterious man turns up again."

Something bigger is at play. Xen spoke to her mind.

I know.

"So, that's why you were trying to twist Vetta's arm into staying with Paula."

"Yes."

"I'm fine here," Yiayia said.

"I have spoken to Carissa about having modifications added to the house. This means the house will be uninhabitable during the renovations."

"Renovations could be costly." Yiayia contemplated

Xen saw the concern on her face and raised his hand. "Carissa is by vampire law my wife. You are her grandmother."

"Wait a minute. There was a wedding, and we missed it?" Aunt Paula spoke up.

"No *thitsa*." Her face burned, she didn't want to have to explain this, but they had to understand how it all worked.

"Would you like me to explain, *koukla*?"

"Well, somebody better. I'm not happy that I've been robbed of the opportunity to eat cake."

"No one robbed you of anything, Aunt Paula."

"Then how are you his wife?"

"When I agreed for Xen to take blood from me and vice versa …" She stumbled to find the right words, "…during you know…" She opened her eyes wide, willing them both to get it. They didn't. "During sex…yes when I took his blood, and he took mine we became bonded. That's married by vampire law."

Yiayia looked at Aunt Paula and Aunt Paula looked at Yiayia.

Xen had a cocky grin on his face. This entertained him.

She rolled her eyes. *Happy?* She threw at him.

Oh, you have no idea.

"So, when do we have a proper wedding?" Aunt Paula asked.

"Yes, when?" Yiayia added.

Xen's grin got wider. "That's up to Carissa."

Oh, she was going to kill him.

I look forward to it. Mischief danced on his face.

Awareness prickled in her scalp. She sensed it before she heard the loud thud in the living room. Carissa's gaze collided with Xen's.

Her father was back, and so were the other gods.

Ares had appeared in the living room with Zeus and Athena right behind him. They were in a heated discussion about which god had been pulling whose chain. The air shifted, and everyone froze.

Bright light shone through the room. Hera manifested, accompanied by Poseidon.

Xen sped to Carissa's side.

"Relax, vampire. I am not a threat," Poseidon said.

"Poseidon?" Zeus questioned.

"Olympus is besieged, demons have surrounded the base, and the muses are fighting with the aid of Artemis, Aphrodite, Hephaestos, Echion, and a group of his men," Hera said. "And Kronos and Iapetos have taken prisoner more than half the gods and goddesses again."

"How did they manage that?" Ares asked.

"Kronos froze time on Olympus and with the help from Até and some others. They've had inside help all along." Hera answered.

"Do you know who the others are?" Zeus questioned.

"No, and that's what makes it worse. They've been very clever in deceiving us all. Traitors among us, free to roam."

"How is it that you escaped with Poseidon?" Carissa asked.

"My chambers are spelled from numerous things. Being Queen of the Olympian gods does come with a danger package."

"Grandmother, I was not accusing you or implying…" Carissa didn't finish, and she hoped that Hera did not take it the wrong way.

Hera raised a hand to her. "No offense taken, granddaughter."

Ares stepped closer to Hera. "We will find them, Mother, but first things first. Have they breached the hearth?"

"Yes."

A muscle twitched in Ares' jaw. "And Hestia?"

Experience told Carissa that her father knew the answer but wanted the confirmation.

"Captive," Hera replied.

Zeus took small slow steps around the room. Stopping to look outside the window. His silence sent a quiver to her stomach. The hearth consisted of all things family, religion, and political in ancient Greek belief, but Carissa could not fathom how it could complicate matters more than having both Titans on Olympus wreaking havoc.

Zeus turned toward her. "If the fire goes out, all those images that ran through your head when you drank the potion on Olympus would come to pass. If we lose the hearth, Olympus can no longer exist, nor can the gods. That hearth and the retrieval of Hestia is vital."

A full-blown shiver ran through her body at Zeus' words.

"What is your game plan?" Xen asked from beside Carissa.

"This can only end two ways. They cast us all into darkness and oblivion, or we do them the favor and throw both Kronos and Iapetos back where they belong."

Poseidon, who had been quiet during their discussion, stepped to where Zeus had been staring out the window. He whispered something.

"We leave now," Zeus announced.

"But we would be walking into a trap," Ares stressed.

"I agree with my brother," Athena said from the entrance to the living room where she'd been listening.

"I beg to differ," Zeus assured. He waved his hand around the room.

Oh, no, you don't. Carissa realized the nature of his action and raced to the liquor cabinet where she had dropped her duffel bag and sword. Xen's arms closed around her body as her fingers tightened around her bag and sword.

They materialized on Olympus in the chambers Ares had given her as her own. Xen's arms were still clasped around her.

Poseidon pointed in their direction. "He should not be here." He pointed his trident toward Xen.

"He is here by my invitation," Zeus said with a wink in Carissa's direction.

Thank you, grandfather. She sent to his mind.

He gave her a quick half-smile.

Xen's arms relaxed around her at Zeus' approval.

"His presence will cause a disturbance."

"Please, uncle, look around. You can't get any more disturbed than what Olympus currently is." Athena threw in Poseidon's direction.

"She has a point," Hera said.

Carissa's lips moved before she had time to structure her reply to Poseidon. "The time is not for fighting among ourselves about who should and shouldn't be here. We have a fraction of time to save the hearth and Hestia. I suggest we all focus on the big fish." This wasn't about Xen. In truth, he would not only protect her but would fight to keep the balance among mortals, gods, and unearthly creatures.

Zeus caught Ares' attention and raised his thumb in approval. They nodded to each other. Something passed between them, but none of that was relevant right now. They had two Titans to fry, and neither would be easy to snare.

"We need to lure them to the same place," Ares said. "Somewhere that gives us leverage."

Everyone in the room put their out of the box thinking to the test, except for Xen, who was busy taking in her chambers. Though he didn't know these were her rooms. *I do now,* he spoke to her mind.

She grinned at him, and then she had an idea. "In the courtroom. The Areopagus."

Surprised flashed in all the gods' eyes.

"That's it, *kori mou.*" Ares walked toward her and gave her a hug.

Xen growled.

Her father returned it in kind.

"If you two are done with the alpha pissing contest, then I suggest we put my granddaughter's idea into action." Zeus fired the words in both Xen's and Ares' direction.

"Will we be enough to defeat them?" Carissa asked.

Athena stepped closer to her. "It's all about tactic and strategy."

Zeus waved his arm around the room, and they dematerialized.

They appeared in the courtroom and were spread out. Zeus and Poseidon had commenced a discussion in their corner, and Hera,

Ares, and Athena contemplated the best way to lure both Kronos and Iapetos to the room.

Xen leaned close to Carissa's ear. "I don't like this. It feels staged."

"Same here. I can't help but feel the Titans are one step ahead of us."

The air shifted, and Koal appeared beside her.

She didn't have time to open her mouth, her balance had been thrown, and she tried not to wobble. She had a good view of Xen's back. She stabilized herself and peeked around Xen.

Koal's hands were up in surrender.

"Xen, it's okay." She stepped out from behind him. Xen's vampire fangs had extended, and a small growl vibrated in his chest.

She whacked him on the arm, and his composure returned. "This is Koal." She introduced.

"Ni... nice to meet you." He stuck out his hand for Xen to take.

With the introduction out of the way, Koal stepped forward. "I think I might be able to help get Hestia back."

The other gods had stopped talking.

"Speak, Koal." Zeus' voice boomed from across the room.

He visibly shook from Zeus' command.

"I know where they are keeping Hestia and the other gods."

"Which other gods are with Hestia?" Athena asked.

"Ap…Apollo, Demeter, and Aphrodite."

"What about Artemis?" Athena questioned again.

"As far as I know, she's doing what she can to get in and save her brother and the other goddesses."

"Where?" Zeus' voice thundered again.

Koal swallowed. "The throne room. They didn't even bother to remove her from the hearth. They want her to watch as the embers slowly die, and they hope your powers will fizzle out."

Carissa understood they wanted the demise of all of the Olympian gods. For that, they had to drain them of power, so they became weak and their domains on the mortal plain suffered. If human and unearthly life in the mortal realm suffered, then they would lose their worshippers. *Vicious cycle,* she thought.

"What of Bia, Kratos, Nike, and Zelos, the daemons who protect my throne?"

"They gave Kronos and Iapetos a good fight, but the Titans had a human weapon that subdued the daemon's long enough for Kronos and Iapetos to bind them."

"What human weapon?" Xen interjected to query.

Carissa had opened her mouth to ask the same question.

"It is a gun that shoots out wires."

"Stun guns." Carissa supplied. "Koal, how did you get in and out?"

Carissa trusted Koal, and he had sworn an oath not to betray her. Ares would know the minute he did.

"Zeus has a sealed room with an observation mirror. I was in there talking to Dionysus when the whole thing broke out."

"And where is Dionysus?"

"He's gone for reinforcements. He told me to find Ares."

"Dionysus' reinforcements might be more than a little inebriated," Athena mocked.

"Any help is good help," Koal defended his friend, his chest puffing out.

"So, what's the plan?" Carissa asked.

Ares moved to where Carissa and Xen were standing. "We need a massive diversion to get Hestia, Apollo, Demeter, and the throne guards out of there."

Xen shifted from his position. "If we go in guns blazing, so to speak, then we achieve nothing, and will risk being added as hostages." Xen proclaimed.

A collective agreement went around the room.

"What do you suggest, vampire?" Zeus queried.

"Bait."

"None would be a better carrot than myself," Zeus said. "Olympus is my domain and my responsibility. I will materialize to where they are and try to get them to follow me to this courtroom."

"You work on that. Carissa, Xen, Koal and, I will materialize to the observation room to look for weaknesses in the Titans hostage situation." Ares was planning his battles.

A thought ran through Carissa's mind. "Koal, do you still have the cap of Hades?"

"Yes, I do."

"Good. Then getting in while Kronos and Iapetos are busy with Zeus will be easy. Release the guards first. That should give the three of us enough time to materialize near Apollo, Demeter, and Hestia."

Smart, koukla. Xen sent to her mind. She lapped up the compliment, but the fact that the Titans were equipped with stun guns bothered Carissa.

I agree, koukla.

"Zeus, you are forgetting one thing," Xen spoke. "They have human weapons, stun guns and from what Koal said, you might not be immune to them."

"Good point."

"I suggest you use your aegis. It will be your bulletproof vest."

"Good thinking, Xen." Carissa beamed at him.

When she turned to Zeus, his aegis sat secured to his shoulders and over his chest.

"Before I offer myself up. Everyone here will have to play a small part in this courtroom. Starting from you, Xen." Zeus snapped his fingers, and a pair of adamantine cuffs dangled from Xen's hand. "I'll be relying on your speed for those to work, plus Kronos and Iapetos won't expect you to be here."

Xen nodded in understanding.

"When I rematerialize, Athena, you will be at my side, as well as Hera and Poseidon. We will need to keep them busy, and you three," he pointed over to Xen, Koal, and Ares, "must be quick in releasing the hostages."

Zeus walked over to Carissa. "And for you, granddaughter…" He snapped his fingers, and a net appeared in his hands. "… your job will be to watch for the right moment, then toss the net over the

Titans. Again, your presence here will not be expected." He passed the shimmering net to her.

She fingered the fine work, its weight nearly insubstantial. "It is a difficult task to sit and watch and wait for the right moment."

"Your role is important, *kori mou*." Ares added.

"I hear what you are saying, grandfather, but what if I can't cast the net?" She let out a frustrated groan.

"Worst case scenario, we fight till we've won," her father said.

Something didn't sit well with her. She had the book in her duffel bag, but what good would it do if she had no clue on how to use it?

"The best-laid plans are the ones that are simple," Athena said, bringing Carissa out of her musings.

"Let's put this plan into action. Athena, Hera, and Poseidon, prepare this room." Zeus disappeared.

Carissa turned to Xen. "Do you think we can pull this off with minimal damage? I mean those two can give us a good fight."

"That's what we're hoping for, *kori mou*," Ares answered her.

"Let's hope that Zeus can bring them here. Then it's up to Tyche," Xen concluded.

"Ready?" Ares asked.

Carissa braced herself.

They materialized in a large room that appeared like the watching end of an interrogation room. Ares silenced them so they wouldn't make a noise. They peeked through the glass, and saw Zeus throwing bursts of power toward both Titans. The goddesses and gods were bound near Zeus' throne, and his guards were doing everything they could to remove the adamantine bonds secured around their wrists.

Carissa whispered, *"Philaso."* To protect any conversation leaking to the Titans and given that she projected loudly, she wanted to make sure anything she said stayed in the room.

I'm opening up the mind mumbo-jumbo, she sent to the other three. *Koal, have you something to break the adamantine?*

He lifted his hand, and gold bolt cutters appeared. *This should do the job.*

She gave him a megawatt smile. *Okay, your turn. Be fast.*

He nodded, then disappeared from view. They watched the release of the first guard.

Our turn, she said to Xen and her father.

Ares stepped between them and dematerialized them to where the gods and goddesses were near the throne. Ares lifted his hand, and additional sets of gold bolt cutters appeared in Carissa's and Xen's possession.

Carissa set to work and required all her strength to get the adamantine to snap. Xen had speed and completed the task faster.

Bursts of power shook the room when both Titans realized that their hostages were now free.

Zeus took that opportunity to blast both of them with small thunderbolts. The Titans staggered. Anger flashed in their eyes.

"Come and get me," Zeus yelled at them and blinked out from the room.

"Apollo, get Hestia and Demeter to safety." The god nodded and they all vanished. "Bia, Nike, Kratos, Zelos, are you okay?"

"Yes, and what in Hades did they hit us with?"

"Human weapon, but we will talk later. Arm yourselves and be ready in case they re-appear."

They acknowledged Ares' command. "Koal," he shouted.

He appeared. "Yes, Ares."

"Help guard this room and use any means necessary to make sure my father's throne, the hearth, and the flame are secure."

He confirmed the order with a slight nod of his head.

"Father," Carissa said, as he grabbed her and Xen and zapped to where all the action was going down.

Their feet hit the marbled courtroom floor, and the scene before them could only be described in one word. Chaos. Large cracks had split parts of the walls.

The Titans were now fighting with weapons. Something crashed in the pit of her stomach, telling her that something was terribly wrong. She brought her musings and emotions under control and prepared for the task she had been given. Her sword hung at her back, and she wouldn't hesitate to use it.

Thunder, wind, and lightning bombarded the room, and then a portal opened and out stepped Até with Hestia. Who propelled her in Kronos' direction.

Carissa's jaw dropped. "How the…" She didn't finish her words. Her feet propelled her into action. She jumped onto one of the tables to give herself extra height to fling the net.

To say the scene before her represented something out of every movie she'd seen would be an understatement. What she saw represented anger of the worst possible kind. Kronos now held Hestia to him and had a sickle to her throat. Iapetos had somehow managed to capture Hera. She, too, had a sickle to her throat.

Everyone froze.

Carissa watched Xen and her father. Even with Xen's speed, they would not be quick enough to get to both goddesses. She held her breath.

"What's it going to be Zeus? We'll give you these lovely ladies if you give over Olympus."

"You must both take me for a fool," Zeus boomed.

"Don't dare me to slit their throats," Kronos shouted.

"You'd do that to your own daughters?"

Kronos tightened his hold on Hestia. "Why not? I've seen nothing good from either."

"You were the one who swallowed them up, and you want to see good?" Zeus reminded his father of his actions.

"Enough talking. Give up your throne."

"You cannot take my throne. Olympus is my domain. It only functions with me on the throne. You must have missed that memo."

"Then we will have to make some minor adjustments." Iapetos sneered.

Carissa watched as Xen and Athena attacked from behind, and Zeus, Poseidon, and Ares charged them from the front. Hera and

Hestia were both blasted away from Kronos and Iapetos. They landed hard against the courtroom wall.

Xen charged with his sword drawn. He slashed them in swift motion to weaken them. One thing the Titans didn't have was Xen's speed.

Athena took the opportunity to further sap their strength with stabs from her spear, but the weakness didn't last long. The Titans threw out blasts of power that flung all the gods and Xen flat on their backs. Carissa took the opportunity to toss the net when they were both distracted. The net did not connect. Iapetos clapped, and it turned to tiny shimmering diamonds on the floor.

Zeus took a fraction of a second to throw out his thunder to both Kronos and Iapetos.

They both deflected, and the bolts of lightning shook the room.

"Is that the best you've got, son," Kronos sneered at Zeus.

"My best is yet to come, and it won't be from me."

"Enough with your insufferable supposed wisdom." Iapetos spat.

Ares, Athena, Poseidon, and Xen had taken advantage and lunged forward again. Hera and Hestia joined the fray. Carissa's power picked up a surge. Someone was about to make an entrance. The wind picked up, and Apollo and Demeter appeared fully armed.

Kronos and Iapetos threw another blast of power, but the gods together deflected it and sent it back toward them. Swords, spears, tridents, sickles, and godly power thundered and shook the room. It resembled a small earthquake, and then Carissa had a realization.

This fighting up here would have consequences in the mortal realm. The revelation struck like the thunderbolts Zeus had been dishing out, straight into her solar plexus.

Olympus was embedded in the mortal realm.

Together.

One part.

Of a whole.

The room began to shake harder. Pieces of marble started to fall. She jumped over the table to grab her duffel. With shaky hands, she dug into the bag; she didn't have much time.

She pulled the book out and unwrapped it. A burst of power hit the room. Everyone stopped. Multiple sets of eyes fixed in her direction.

Xen's lips curved and sported his zip code smile.

She opened the book while still shaking. "Tell me," she whispered as her fingers stroked the cover of the codex. The book flipped its pages and stopped where it wanted her to read from.

Kronos and Iapetos roared, and the fighting continued on. Zeus and Poseidon hit with their power at the same time. The Titans were winded and staggered backward. Ares pierced them with his spear to further weaken them. They dropped to their knees.

Now, koukla! Xen shouted into her mind. He sped to Kronos and Iapetos, and sealed the adamantine cuffs on both.

Até took that opportunity to duck through the open portal, but not before Ares threw a blast of power in her direction. The portal she'd escaped into shrunk and closed in on itself.

Carissa scanned the page before her. She would have to read and put the names in where there were blanks. She swallowed hard. *Okay, Carissa, this is up to you now.* She began to read. "I call upon the very first creators to spread their wings and cover the earth with protection from the two Titans standing before me. Banish them. Banish these Titans to whence they came. Firstborn founders of our universe, golden-winged who light the darkness and bring forth peace. I call on you to banish Kronos and Iapetos to Tartarus."

The book slammed shut. Power and light burst from the book. She closed her eyes. *It's safe, koukla.* When she heard Xen speak to her mind, she cracked open an eyelid.

Kronos and Iapetos were gone.

"Well done, *koukla*," Xen called out. He came to her side. He tried to pull her in for a hug, but the codex burned him. "Ah, now I understand the letter on the plane. This is what you were trying to tell me."

She nodded her head.

The book pulsed with power. She took the codex and wrapped it, then put it in her duffel bag which she threw on her shoulder.

The other gods and goddesses gathered around her.

"Thank you, granddaughter," Zeus said.

They had put up a good fight. If she hadn't found the book they might not be standing here.

"Let's not think that now, *kori mou*. You found it. You brought it with you, which was a smart move."

"That codex is yours to protect, Carissa, a duty passed along your family line." Hestia spoke for the first time. "It was created from the hearth itself."

Carissa filed that nugget of information for when she didn't feel like her legs were going to give out on her. Xen squeezed her tight but spoke to the room of gods. "You realize that everyone will want this, and it will be near impossible to protect in the mortal realm."

"We shall have to ensure that it can't be found," Athena said. "Give me your necklace Carissa."

She put her fingers around her neck and removed the necklace Athena had given her. She had completely forgotten that it was there. She placed the miniature shield necklace in the goddess's hand.

"Bring the codex."

She hesitated, but Xen nodded. She pulled out the codex again, and its power pulsed in the room.

Zeus stepped forward. "I think this one is mine to bind."

Athena dropped the necklace in Zeus's hand. "Granddaughter, place the book in my hand."

She did as he asked.

"*To kleio.*"

The book shot a beam of light to the roof of the room then shrunk into the necklace.

Zeus held out the necklace to her. Carissa's fingers closed around the chain.

"Let me help," Xen said. He fastened it around her neck.

"Guard it well, granddaughter," Hera added.

"Not yet," Ares said to the room. "All hands on mine." They formed a circle, and each god and goddess placed a hand on Ares' hand in the middle. "Now you, vampire." Xen didn't hesitate. "And you, *kori mou*." She did as he bid. "*Orkos*." Her father said. Light and heat radiated from their joined hands.

She understood that these gods were now sworn never to betray her or the codex. When their hands fell away, she surveyed the damage to the room and pondered the depth of having these gods on her side. She cast her attention to Zeus. "You might want to redecorate."

They let out a laugh.

Her father stepped in for a hug then released her.

The air shifted and gods, goddesses and a bevy of minor deities started to appear.

"I'd say order is restored, *koukla*."

The adrenaline that had been riding high began to dwindle. She'd come to Olympus with her father to get retribution for what had been done to her, but her path had altered. Good or bad she would settle for it now. Even Poseidon and his reluctance and disdain in having Xen on Olympus had fought alongside them. She still had a bone to pick with him about his son Hal, but she would let it rest for now.

"We will handle it together." Xen's voice appeared faint from all the chatter around the room.

You will have your say, granddaughter, when your father's case resumes. Carissa turned her head toward Zeus. He had heard her inner rambling and answered to her mind. It gave her hope, but right now she wanted her own realm and her own bed. "How about you flash us home?"

Zeus stepped closer. "It would be my pleasure."

Lightning thundered around the room. Xen pulled her close. Then they were gone.

They landed in the living room of Carissa's home. Air zipped around them for a few seconds then it ceased.

Yiayia, Aunt Paula, Kane, and Adam all ran into the room. Yiayia and Aunt Paula beelined for her, and she braced herself. They smothered her in hugs.

"Care to tell us what happened?" Kane questioned.

"That, my friend, requires a few drinks." Xen and Kane locked arms in a shake.

"What did I miss?" Adam queried.

When Yiayia and Aunt Paula had released Carissa she flew into Adam's arms for a hug.

"I'm so glad you are back to normal."

"Hey, Rissa."

Xen let out a growl.

"Relax, vampire." She tossed over her shoulder. She turned to face them all. "I guess we could ask, what did we miss?"

"Well, it's been horrible and catastrophic," Aunt Paula said. "The news is just filled with horrible stories."

"How about we make some tea, and you can tell us all about it." Carissa took her aunt and *yiayia* in interlocking arms and walked toward the kitchen.

"Oh, and about your wedding, Yiayia and I have made plans."

"I've been gone for half a day, and you're already making calls?" She heard Xen's laugher from the kitchen.

Trust me, you'll be the one wanting to elope from this big fat Greek wedding. She whispered to his mind.

THIRTY-EIGHT

"One cannot evade destiny." Ancient Greek proverb

Carissa's yiayia's house, Charleston, SC
Evening, mortal realm – Day 16

Xen, Kane, and Adam threw back another shot of ouzo and slammed their glasses on the table. They'd alternated between that and scotch.

Carissa had sent her grandmother and aunt to bed an hour ago.

Kane stood. "Xen. I think it's time to call it a night."

"He's not wrong. A few more of those, and I won't be able to move." Adam groaned getting to his feet.

"Have one of the men outside drive you. I'll see you both out."

"Night, Ris…sa." Adam hiccupped.

Carissa gave him a kiss on the cheek and one to Kane. "Night, guys."

Kane grabbed Adam by the arm to lead him out. He waved from the kitchen door.

She stifled a laugh. They were funny in their tipsy state. They had talked into the wee hours of the morning, and they were at the point where no one could keep their eyelids up. Except for Xen, because these early hours were his daytime. The wolves had great staying power but required some sleep.

The only thing that remained…the mess. She moved about the kitchen, clearing and tidying. Carissa had told this small group of trusted friends and family what had transpired but not before she uttered a spell to protect the room from anyone listening in. The necklace was her secret and Xen's, and it would remain so. If you didn't want people knowing, then best not tell anyone.

"Let me help you, *koukla*." He sped about the kitchen and did most of the work in minutes. He stopped and pulled her into a tight embrace and placed a gentle kiss on her lips.

"I know you're tired, but there's one thing I'd like to discuss with you before I take you upstairs." He paused, his lips turning up in that wicked grin.

"You are insatiable."

"You can't blame me."

"You're turning me into a wanton woman."

"Good."

"What did you want to talk about?"

"I'd like nothing more than to officially give you the Lysandros name." His tone was low and husky. He rubbed his nose with hers.

Butterflies fluttered in her belly. She wanted that more than anything and over the past few days, she realized how much she desired to take that step. Desired it fiercely. "So we should make it official."

He speared her with a look that made her heart beat faster. That expression belonged to a boy whose Christmas wishes had come true.

"You have no idea how right you are with that analogy." He wagged his eyebrows and rocked her into his groin. She'd ignore that growing surprise until later. Otherwise, they wouldn't finish their conversation. "We should discuss dates." She bit her lip. "That's if my aunt hasn't already booked everything."

"I might have to have a word with her."

"You think?" She slapped him on the arm. "I know you are enjoying this."

"I enjoy you a lot more." He lowered his lips to hers. He parted her lips, and his tongue danced with hers in slow lazy strokes, then he deepened the kiss and claimed her mouth.

The air around them shifted. They broke the kiss. Carissa recognized the power.

Kirke stood in the kitchen.

"Carissa, Xen, you're going to want to see this."

Kirke stepped forward and placed a hand on both of them, uttering a spell. They dematerialized and appeared at the edge of a large, open field. It was still dark. Torches, hundreds of them, lit up the area.

"What do you think happened here?"

"Whatever happened, someone did us a favor. Can you imagine the damage this army of demons could unleash on humanity?" Xen asked from beside them. He stepped a few feet away to look at the carnage and Carissa did too.

"No." Kirke answered, "I don't want to think about what they would do."

"We have someone to thank," Carissa added.

"We do," Xen confirmed.

"How did you come upon this?" Xen questioned.

"My house is under glamour in this forest. Please keep that to yourselves. I don't need busloads of unearthly creatures turning up at my door and asking me for love potions and the like."

Carissa raised an eyebrow. "They ask you for love potions? This is a thing?"

"Biggest seller," Kirke said with a wink.

"I don't know what to say to that."

"There's nothing to say. It's an old remedy and well... people want love."

Xen's lips tugged up with humor. "You have my word that your location will stay off the radar. I don't have a desire to be fighting off love potion mad unearthlies."

"Now what do we do about all this? I don't want it stinking up the place."

"I imagine you don't. I can get a clean team out here, but it will take some time to organize something of this magnitude."

They were all standing next to each other, and Carissa tapped Xen's chest. "Look over there." She pointed in the distance. It appeared men were carrying bodies to a ditch. "I don't think you'll have to do anything. Someone is already cleaning up."

Xen scanned the area. "And I know who is responsible for it."

He stepped behind Carissa and pointed her head in the direction of the leader. "Can you see that big man with the long hair?"

"Probably not as well as you, but I can make his shape out."

"Lox," Xen mouthed close to her ear.

Carissa's mouth opened. Then closed. "Kelly," she whispered.

"I think our witch here has stumbled across your friend."

"You think one of your friends is here, in this carnage?" Kirke asked, brows furrowed together.

"I think there's a good chance she might be." She pointed in the distance. "That buffoon over there kidnapped her."

Kirke's lips thinned in a straight line, and she squinted her eyes. "I hate kidnappers."

"I know you do."

"Want me to blast their asses?"

Carissa and Xen let out a laugh.

"Easy witch. Questions first."

"What's there to ask? He took her friend."

"Yes, but we should establish if it's mutual." He spoke from behind Carissa. We don't know if Carissa's friend Kelly has something going on with the demon.

"What, like Stockholm syndrome?"

"That's what I'm thinking."

She turned around her brows snapped together, "*Asteievesai?*"

GLOSSARY OF GREEK TERMINOLOGY

Anagke	Force.
Apokalypto	To reveal.
Asteievesai	You're kidding.
Booboona	Idiot.
Bougatsa	Custard Pie.
Chora	Separate.
Efharisto	Thank you.
Egeiro	Awaken.
Entaxi	Okay.
Gamoto	Swear word for fuck.

Gyros	Grilled meat on pita bread with salad and yogurt sauce.
Horkos	Oath.
Kakodaimones	Demons.
Kalimera	Good morning.
Kalinychta	Goodnight.
Kalispera	Good evening.
Kalos irthes	Welcome back.
Kleio	Shut, close, confine.
Kori	Daughter.
Kori mou	Daughter mine, my daughter.
Koukla	Greek endearment, meaning doll.
Kourambedies	Greek shortbread with almonds, covered in icing sugar.
Kotosoupa	Chicken soup.
Logographer	Professional authors of judicial discourse in Ancient Greece.
Lykoi	Wolves.
Lykos	Term used for wolf.
Mageia	Magic.

Malaka	Wanker.
Mati	Evil eye.
Mou	Mine.
Nevrospasma	Used to show when someone is angry.
Nisi	Island.
Paidi mou	My child.
Pappou	Grandfather.
Pastitsio	Greek version of lasagna.
Pauo	Cease, stop, bring to an end.
Phaino	To make visible, bring to light, appear.
Phantasia	Fantasy.
Phi	Immortals protecting mankind. Also known as Athanatoi.
Philaso	Hide.
Rigos	Cover.
Skasi	Shut up.
Skata	Shit.
Stifatho	Beef stew.
Stous theous	To the gods.

Thitsa	Auntie.
Tora	Now.
Vlaka	Idiot.
Xenia	Hospitality.
Xiphos	Sword.
Yiasas	Good bye but also hello.
Yiayia	Grandmother.